Mal and Chad

Stephen McCranie

The BIGGEST, BESTEST TIME EVER!

Philomel Books 🐾 An Imprint of Penguin Group (USA) Inc.

For my dad.

PHILOMEL BOOKS
A division of Penguin Young Readers Group.
Published by The Penguin Group. Penguin Group (USA) Inc., 375 Hudson Street, New York, NY 10014, U.S.A. Penguin Group (Canada), 90 Eglinton Avenue East, Suite 700, Toronto, Ontario M4P 2Y3, Canada (a division of Pearson Penguin Canada Inc.). Penguin Books Ltd, 80 Strand, London WC2R 0RL, England. Penguin Ireland, 25 St. Stephen's Green, Dublin 2, Ireland (a division of Penguin Books Ltd). Penguin Group (Australia), 250 Camberwell Road, Camberwell, Victoria 3124, Australia (a division of Pearson Australia Group Pty Ltd). Penguin Books India Pvt Ltd, 11 Community Centre, Panchsheel Park, New Delhi—110 017, India. Penguin Group (NZ), 67 Apollo Drive, Rosedale, North Shore 0632, New Zealand (a division of Pearson New Zealand Ltd). Penguin Books (South Africa) (Pty) Ltd, 24 Sturdee Avenue, Rosebank, Johannesburg 2196, South Africa. Penguin Books Ltd, Registered Offices: 80 Strand, London WC2R 0RL, England.

Published simultaneously in Canada.
Printed in the United States of America.
Edited by Michael Green.
Designed by Richard Amari.
Library of Congress Cataloging-in-Publication Data
McCranie, Stephen, 1987– The adventures of Mal and Chad: the biggest, bestest time ever / Stephen McCranie. p. cm. Summary: Fourth-grade genius Mal and his talking dog Chad shrink themselves to microscopic size and travel through time, but girls and the school bully present bigger challenges. 1. Graphic novels. [1. Graphic novels. 2. Genius—Fiction. 3. Dogs—Fiction. 4. Time travel—Fiction. 5. School—Fiction. 6. Interpersonal relations—Fiction. 7. Adventure and adventurers—Fiction.] I. Title. PZ7.7.M42Ad 2011 [Fic]—dc22 2010036904
ISBN 978-0-399-25221-1
7 9 10 8

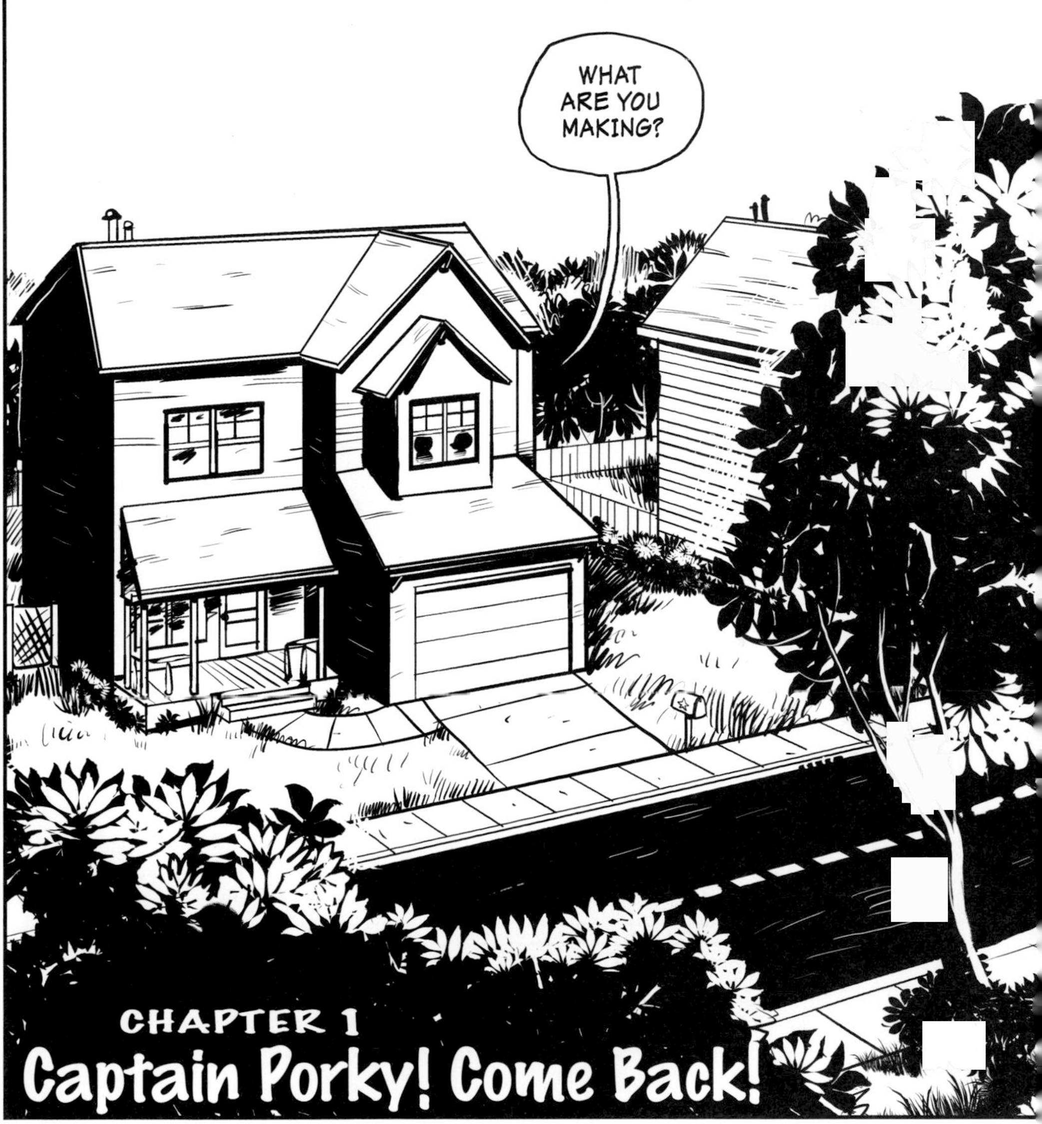
WHAT ARE YOU MAKING?
CHAPTER 1
Captain Porky! Come Back!

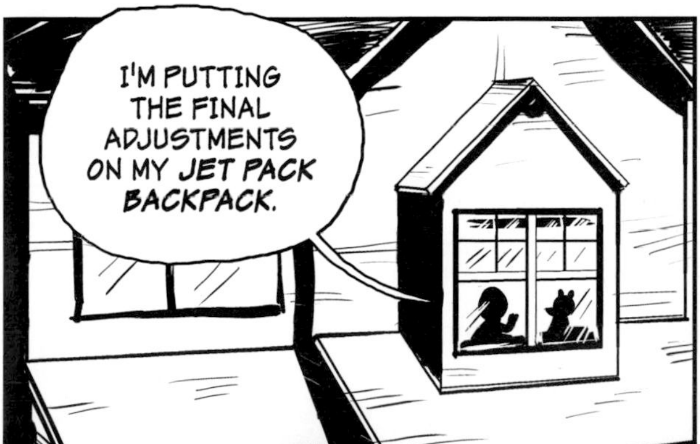
I'M PUTTING THE FINAL ADJUSTMENTS ON MY JET PACK BACKPACK.

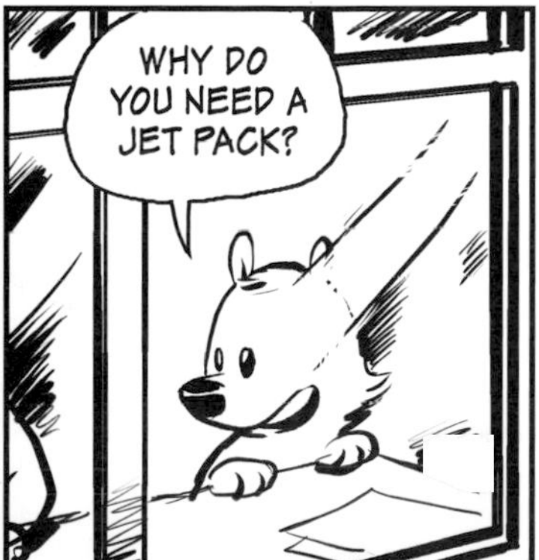
WHY DO YOU NEED A JET PACK?

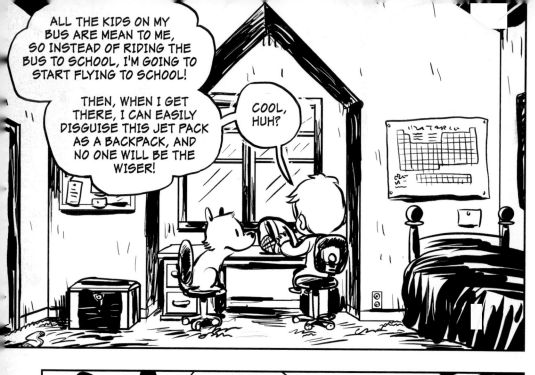

ALL THE KIDS ON MY BUS ARE MEAN TO ME, SO INSTEAD OF RIDING THE BUS TO SCHOOL, I'M GOING TO START FLYING TO SCHOOL!

THEN, WHEN I GET THERE, I CAN EASILY DISGUISE THIS JET PACK AS A BACKPACK, AND NO ONE WILL BE THE WISER!

COOL, HUH?

UM, MAL, ISN'T TAKING THE BUS A LITTLE MORE...

...SAFE?

I'LL BE FINE.

THERE... ALL FINISHED!

YOU SHOULD TEST IT OUT FIRST...

I MEAN, BEFORE YOU ACTUALLY FLY IT YOURSELF.

WHAT, DO YOU WANT TO TEST IT OUT FOR ME?

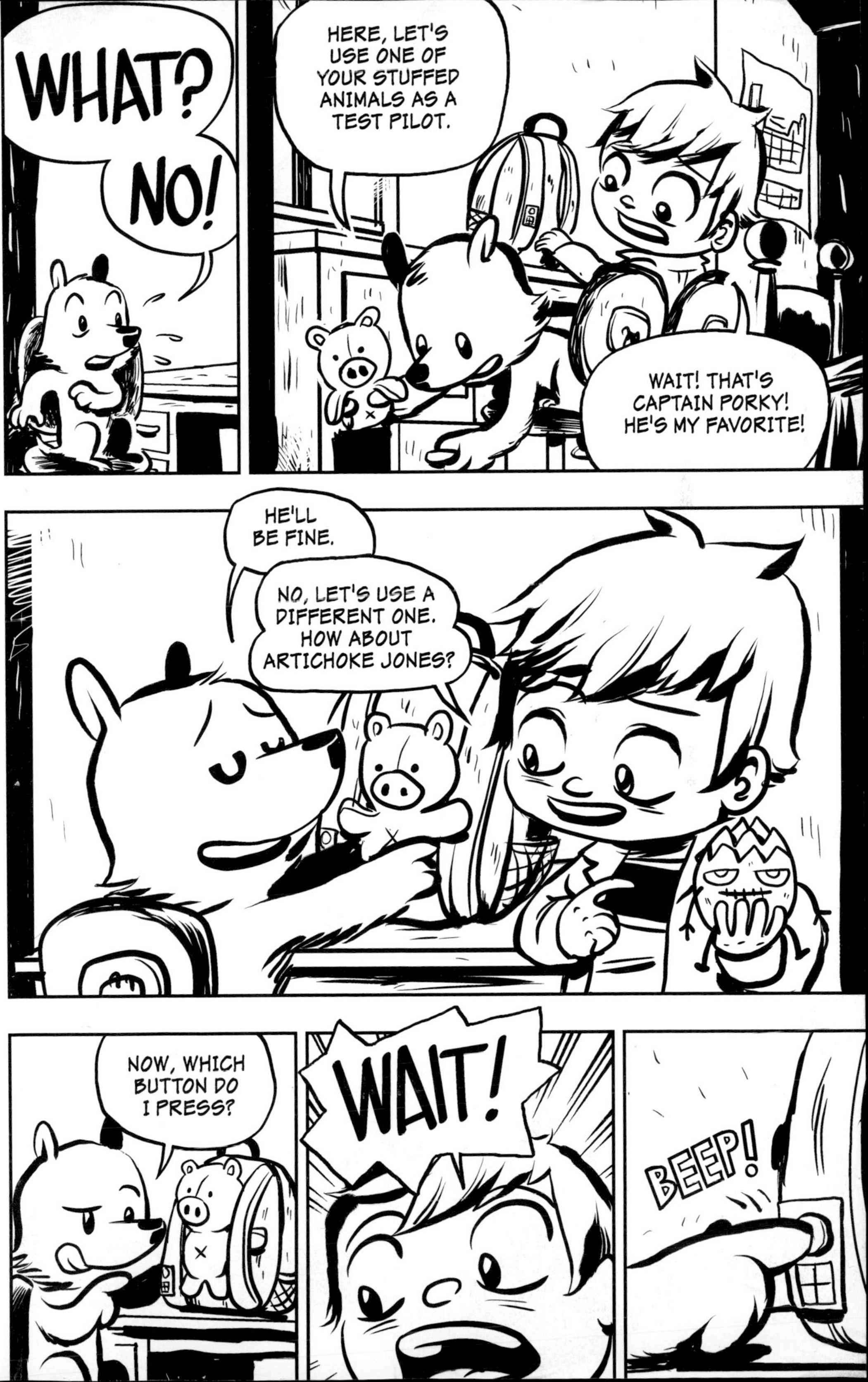
WHAT?
NO!
HERE, LET'S USE ONE OF YOUR STUFFED ANIMALS AS A TEST PILOT.
WAIT! THAT'S CAPTAIN PORKY! HE'S MY FAVORITE!
HE'LL BE FINE.
NO, LET'S USE A DIFFERENT ONE. HOW ABOUT ARTICHOKE JONES?
NOW, WHICH BUTTON DO I PRESS?
WAIT!
BEEP!

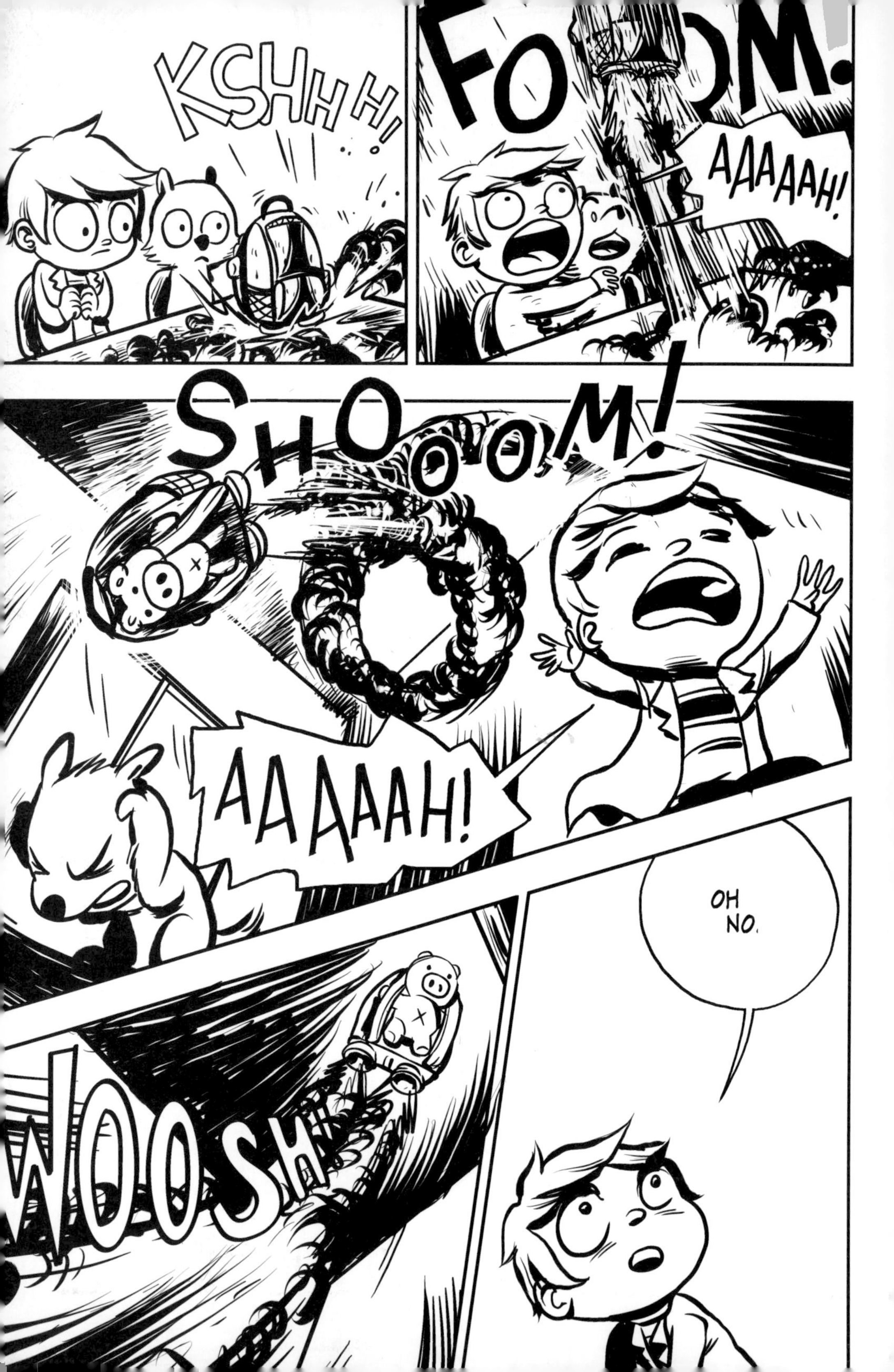
KSHHHH!
FOOOM!
AAAAAH!
SHOOOOM!
AAAAAH!
OH NO.
WOOSH!

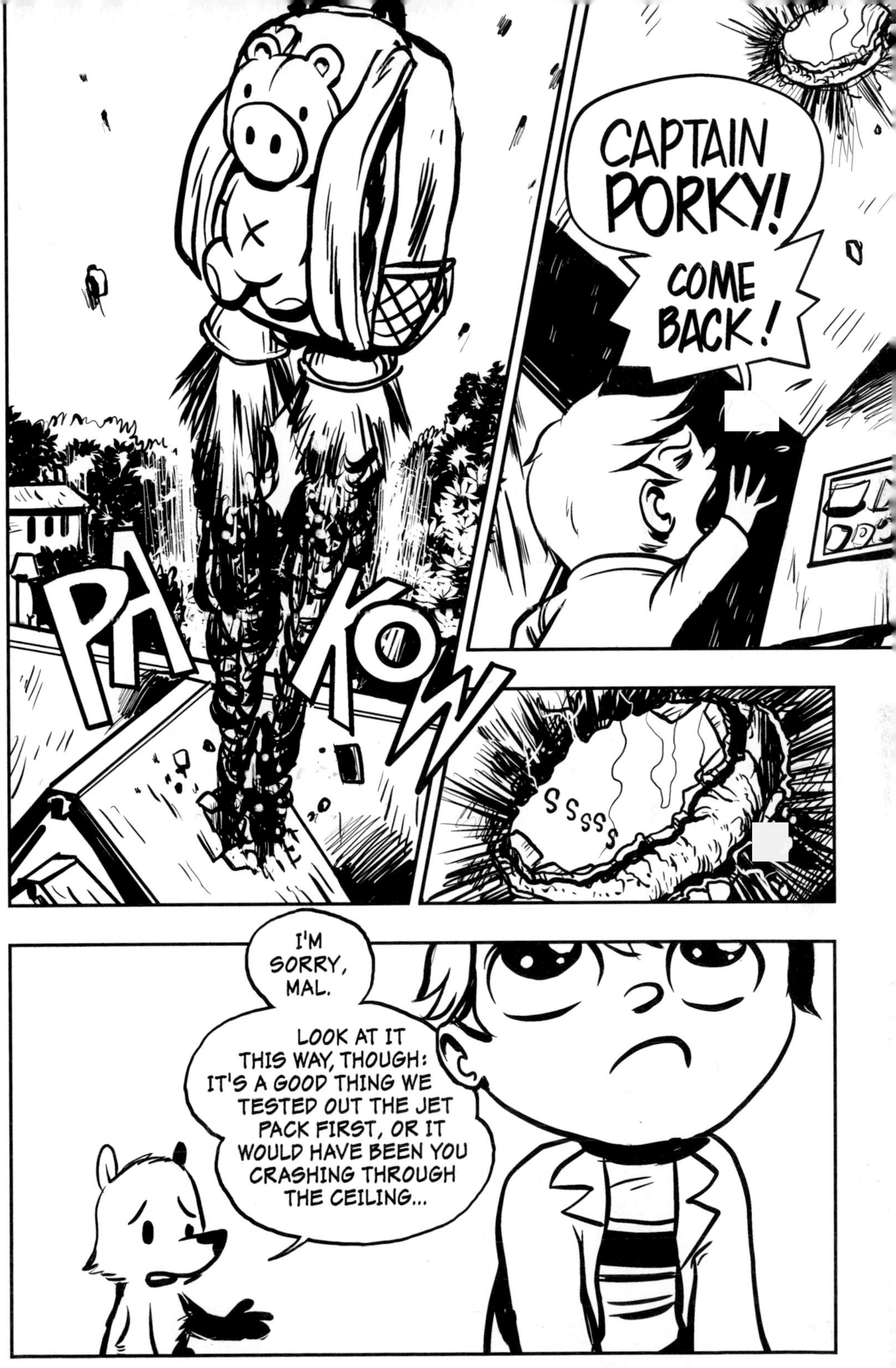
PAKOW
CAPTAIN PORKY!
COME BACK!
SSSSS
I'M SORRY, MAL.
LOOK AT IT THIS WAY, THOUGH: IT'S A GOOD THING WE TESTED OUT THE JET PACK FIRST, OR IT WOULD HAVE BEEN YOU CRASHING THROUGH THE CEILING...

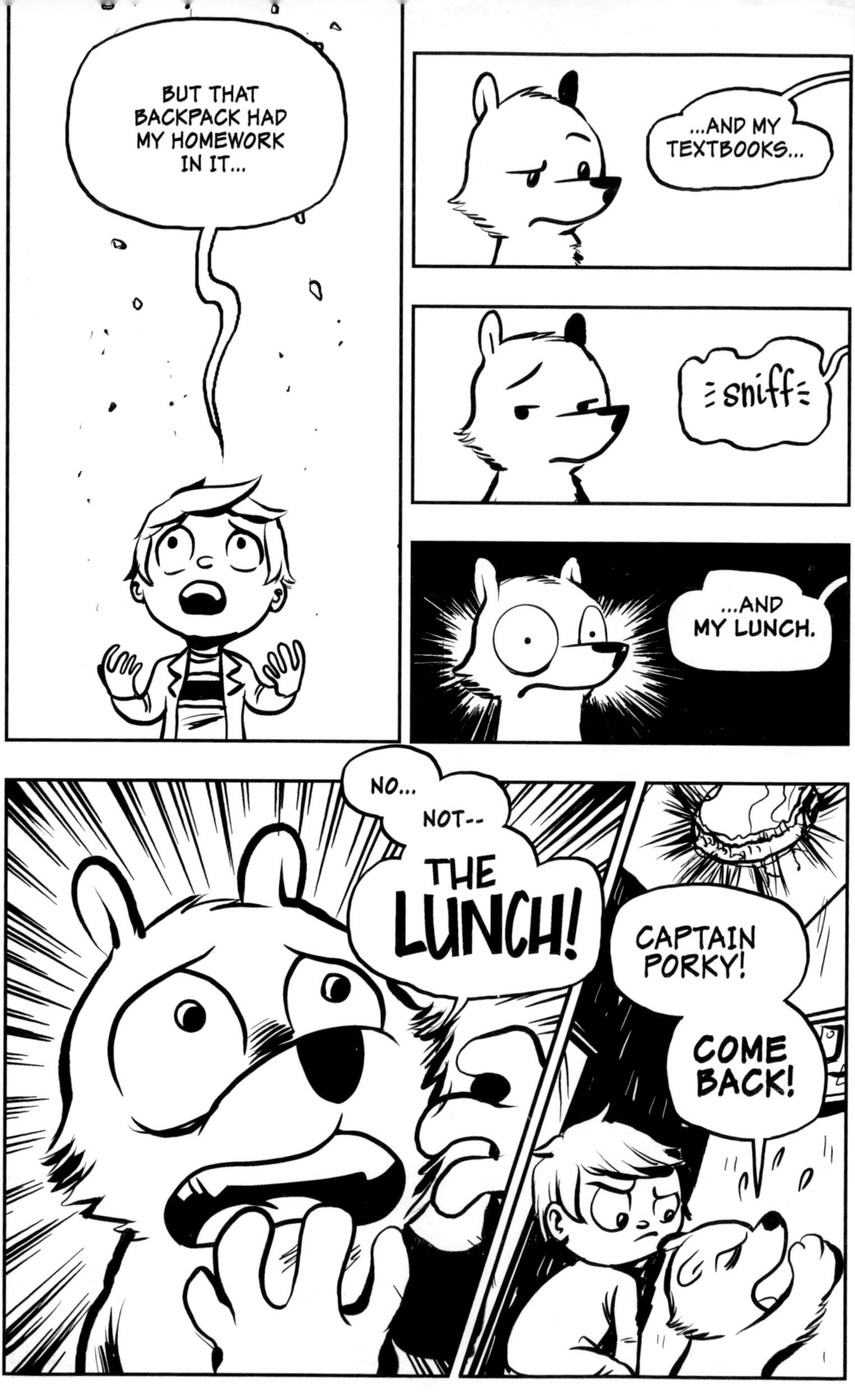
BUT THAT BACKPACK HAD MY HOMEWORK IN IT...
...AND MY TEXTBOOKS...
sniff
...AND MY LUNCH.
NO...
NOT--
THE LUNCH!
CAPTAIN PORKY!
COME BACK!

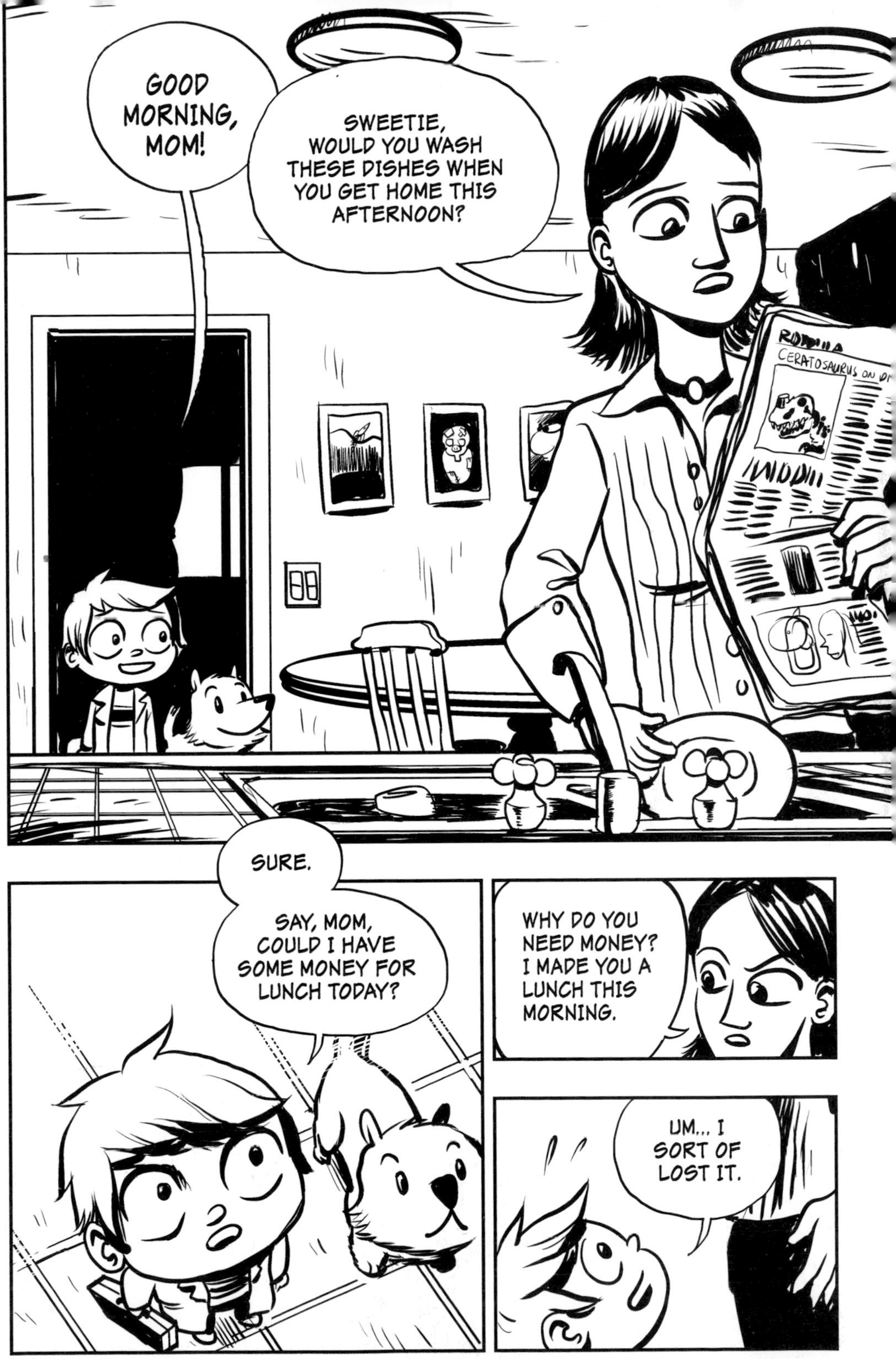
GOOD MORNING, MOM!
SWEETIE, WOULD YOU WASH THESE DISHES WHEN YOU GET HOME THIS AFTERNOON?
CERATOSAURUS ON
SURE.
SAY, MOM, COULD I HAVE SOME MONEY FOR LUNCH TODAY?
WHY DO YOU NEED MONEY? I MADE YOU A LUNCH THIS MORNING.
UM... I SORT OF LOST IT.

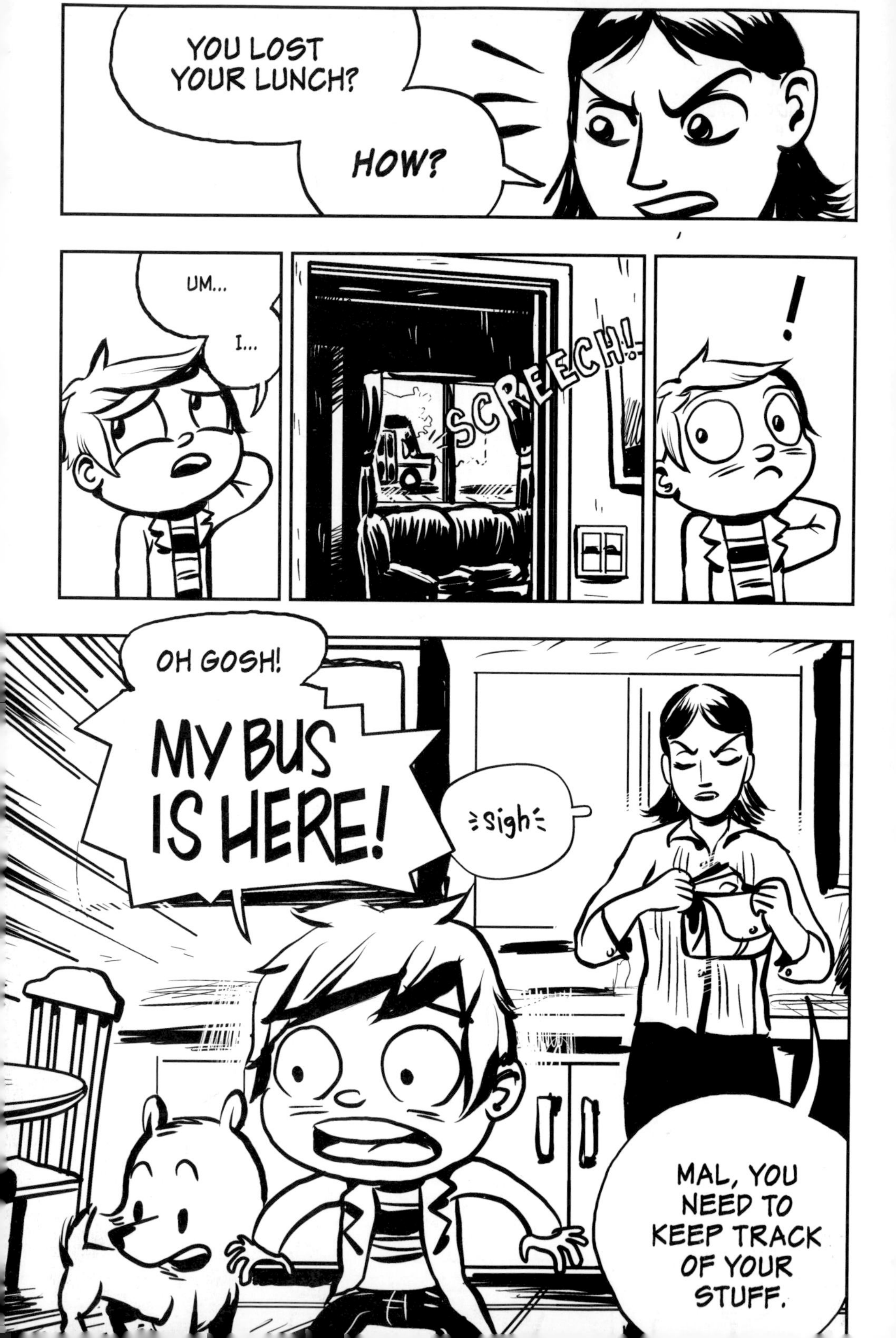
YOU LOST YOUR LUNCH?
HOW?
UM...
I...
SCREECH!
!
OH GOSH!
MY BUS IS HERE!
sigh
MAL, YOU NEED TO KEEP TRACK OF YOUR STUFF.

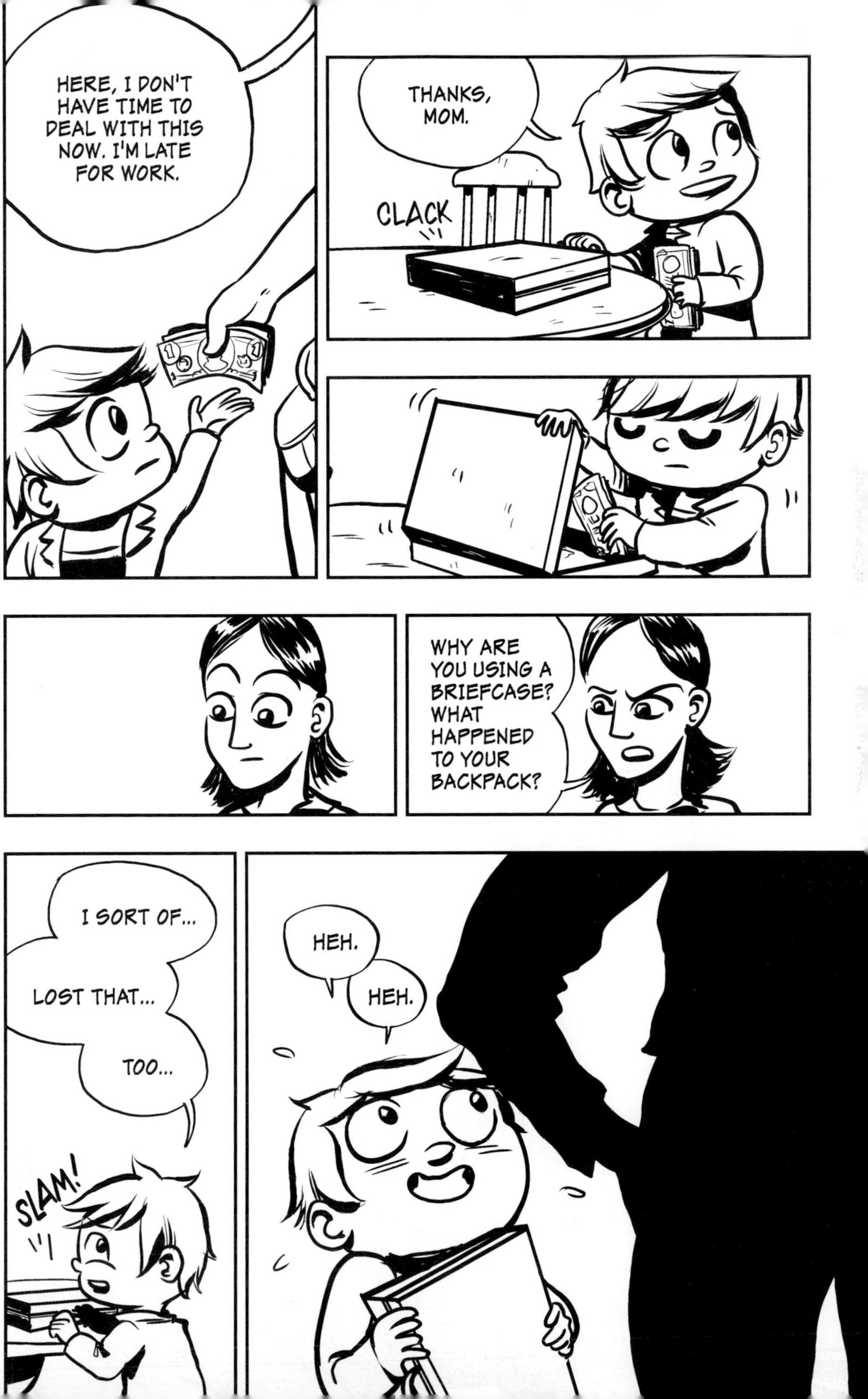
HERE, I DON'T HAVE TIME TO DEAL WITH THIS NOW. I'M LATE FOR WORK.
THANKS, MOM.
CLACK
WHY ARE YOU USING A BRIEFCASE? WHAT HAPPENED TO YOUR BACKPACK?
I SORT OF...
LOST THAT...
TOO...
SLAM!
HEH.
HEH.

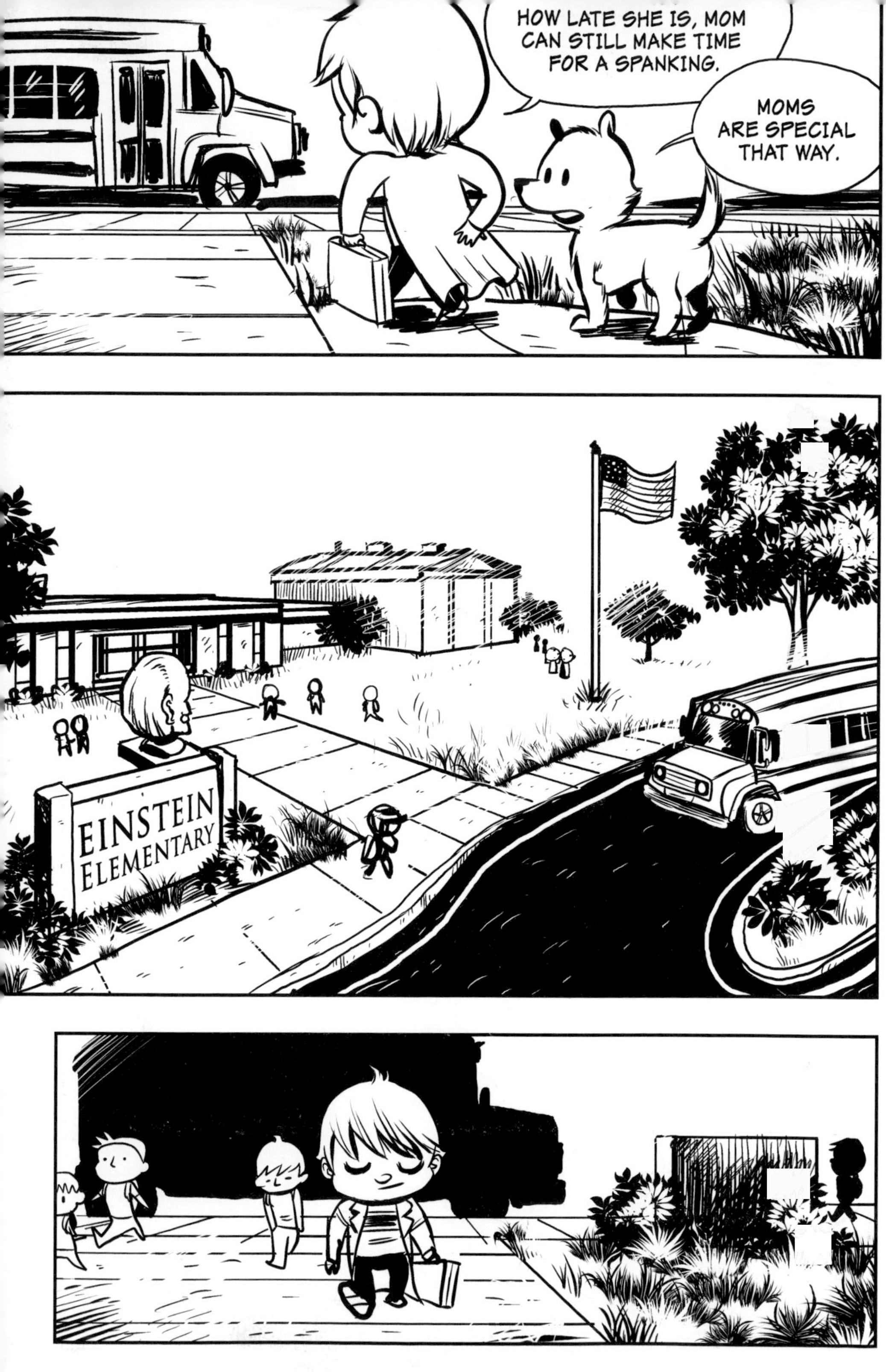
HOW LATE SHE IS, MOM CAN STILL MAKE TIME FOR A SPANKING.
MOMS ARE SPECIAL THAT WAY.
EINSTEIN ELEMENTARY

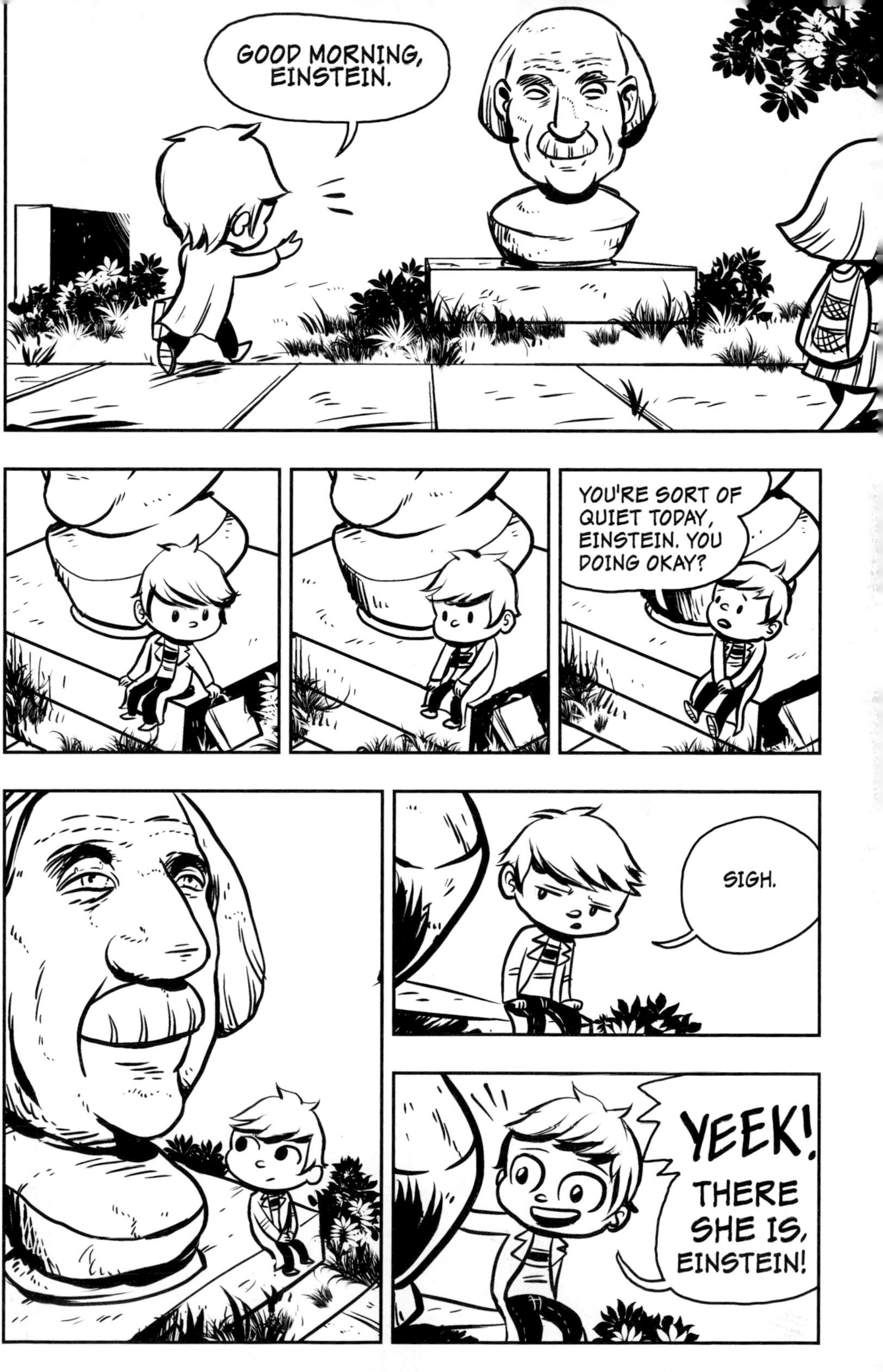
GOOD MORNING, EINSTEIN.
YOU'RE SORT OF QUIET TODAY, EINSTEIN. YOU DOING OKAY?
SIGH.
YEEK! THERE SHE IS, EINSTEIN!

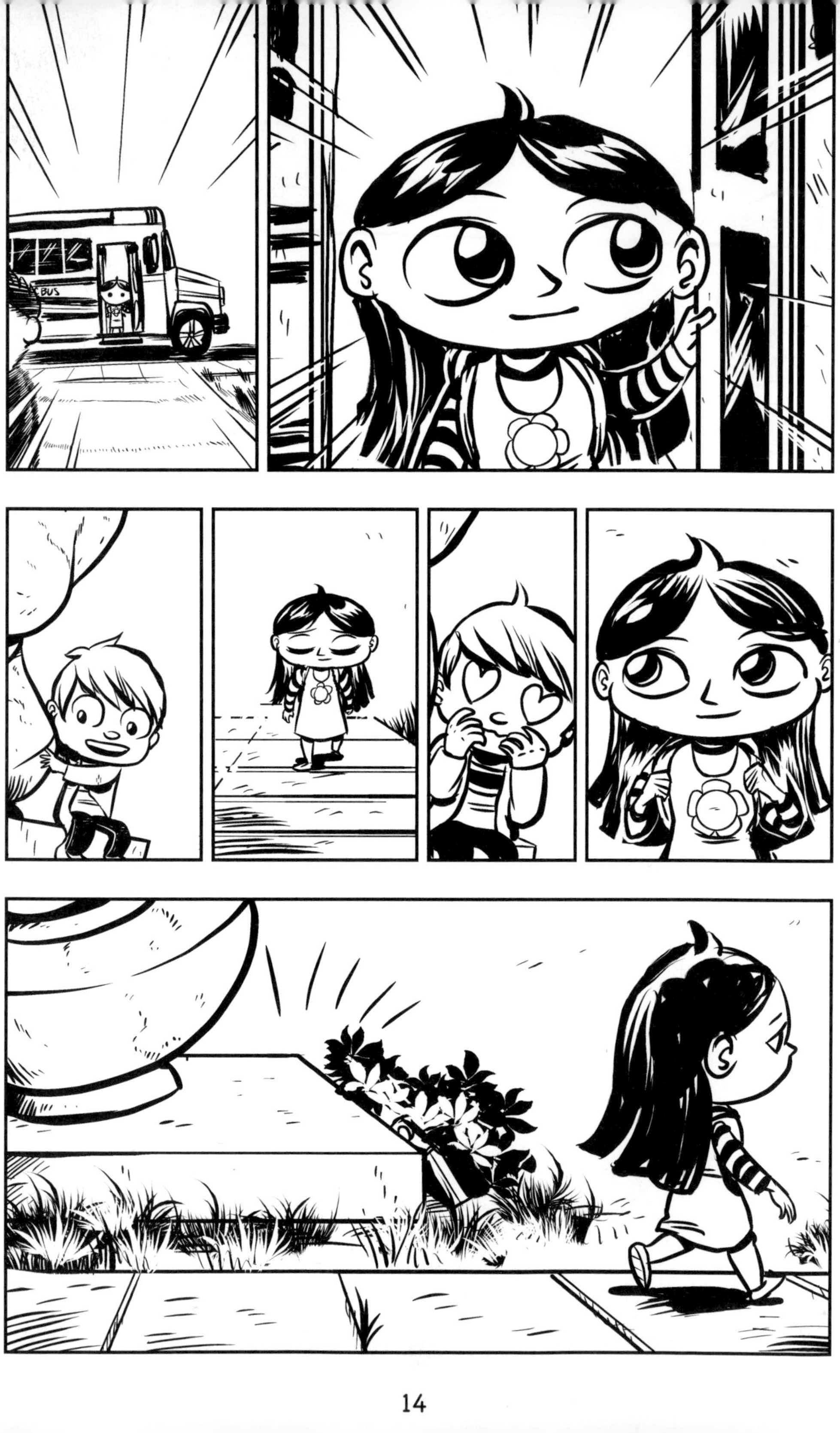
BUS

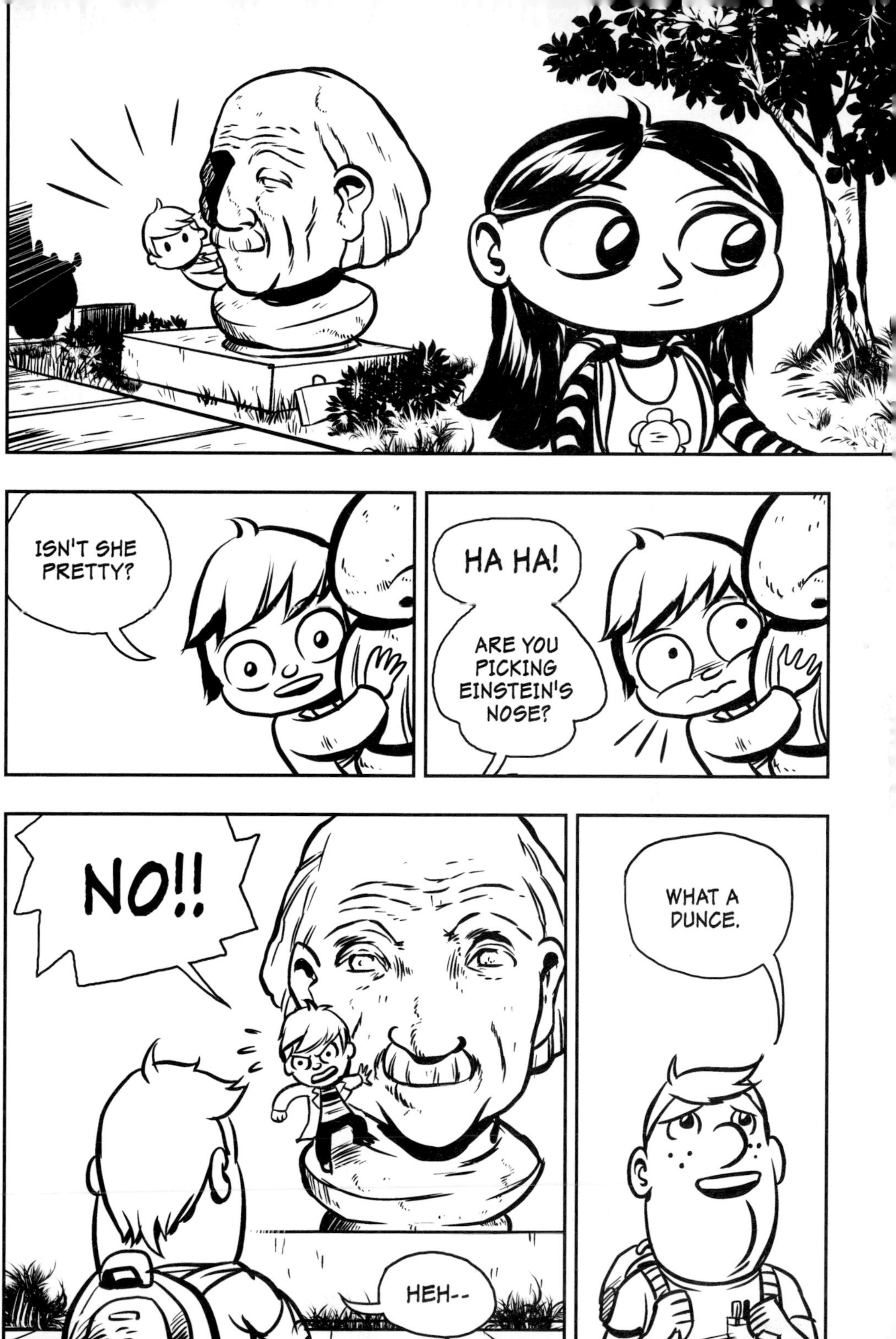
ISN'T SHE PRETTY?
HA HA!
ARE YOU PICKING EINSTEIN'S NOSE?
NO!!
HEH--
WHAT A DUNCE.

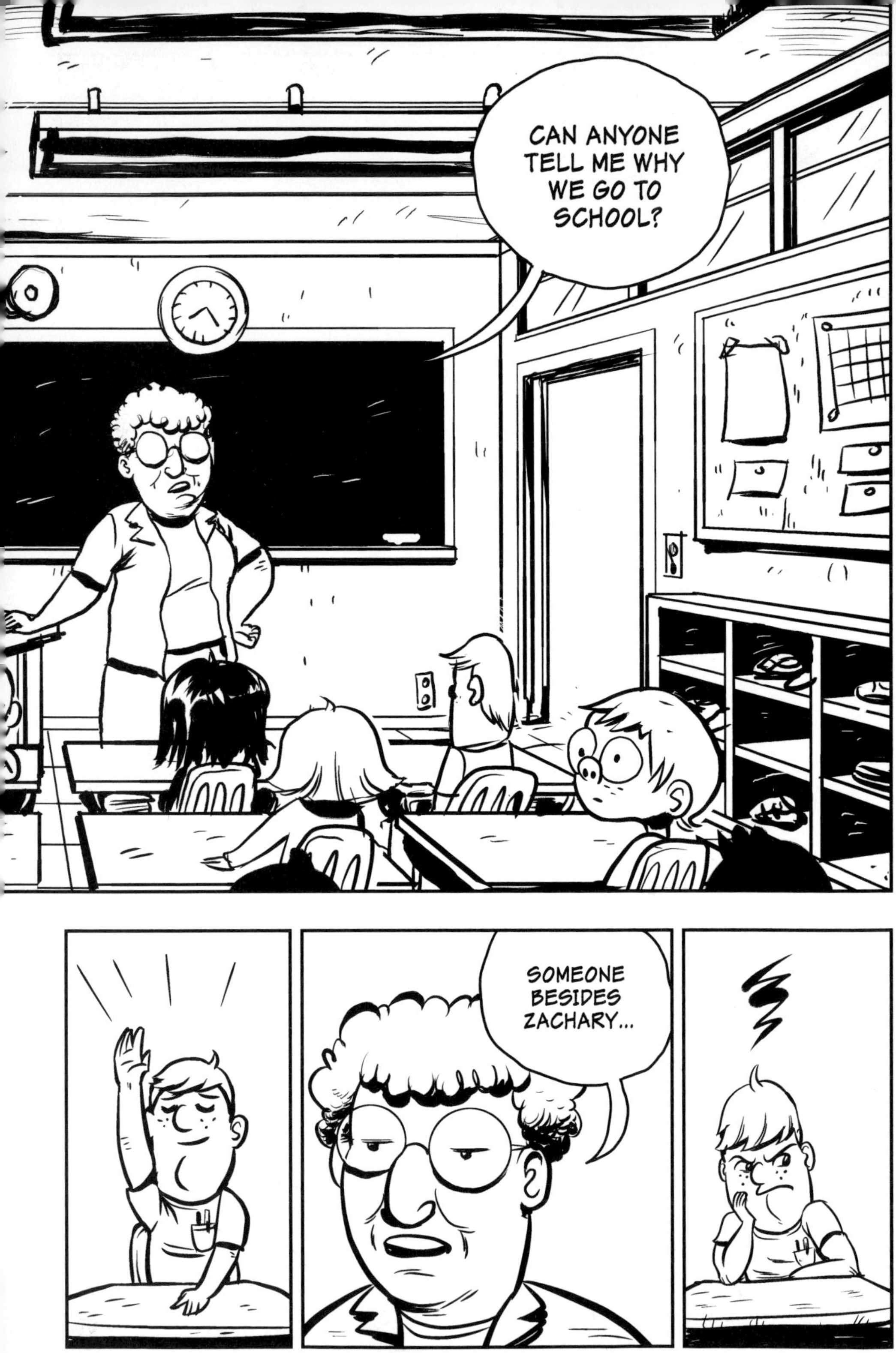
CAN ANYONE TELL ME WHY WE GO TO SCHOOL?
SOMEONE BESIDES ZACHARY...

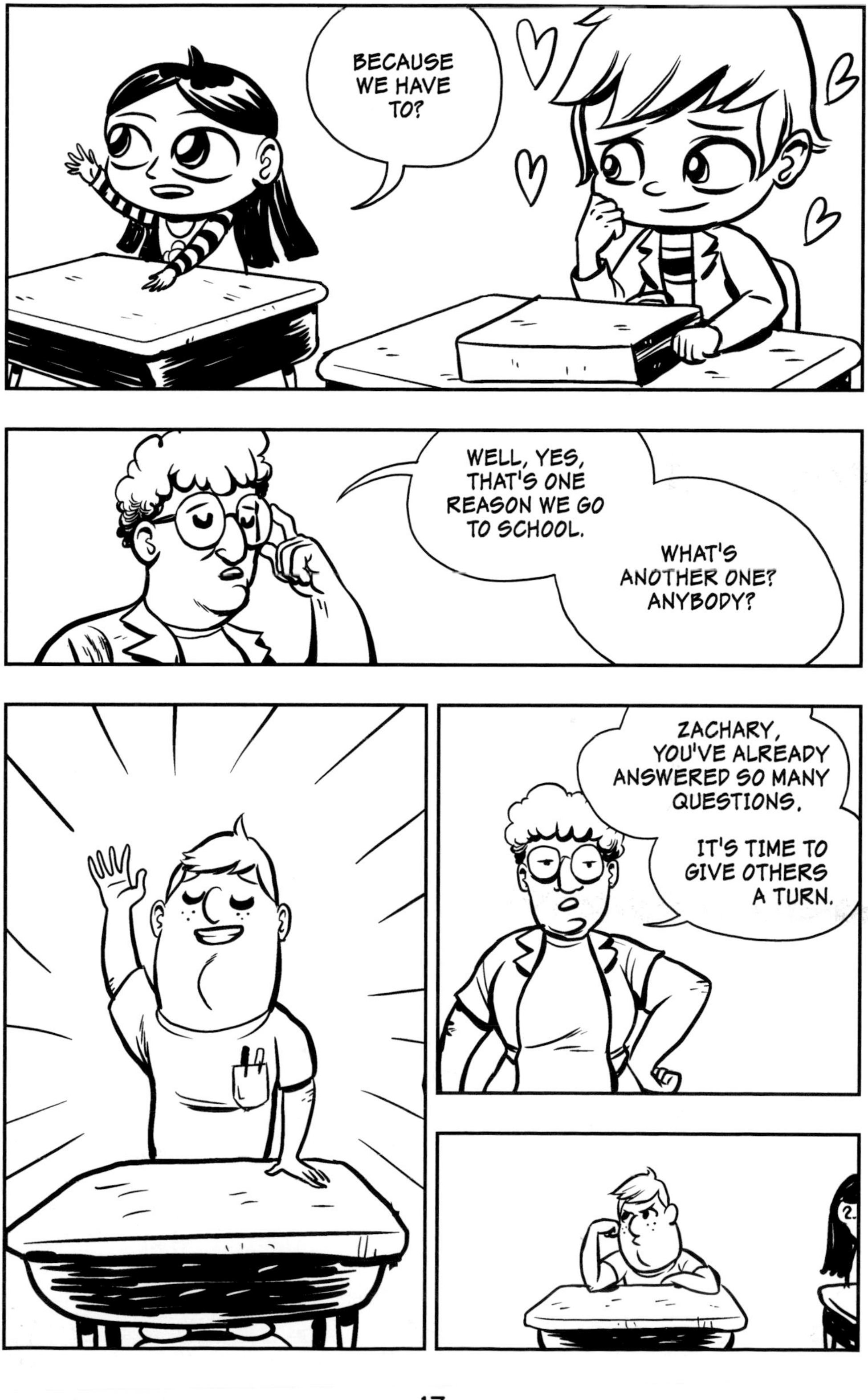
BECAUSE WE HAVE TO?
WELL, YES, THAT'S ONE REASON WE GO TO SCHOOL.
WHAT'S ANOTHER ONE? ANYBODY?
ZACHARY, YOU'VE ALREADY ANSWERED SO MANY QUESTIONS.
IT'S TIME TO GIVE OTHERS A TURN.

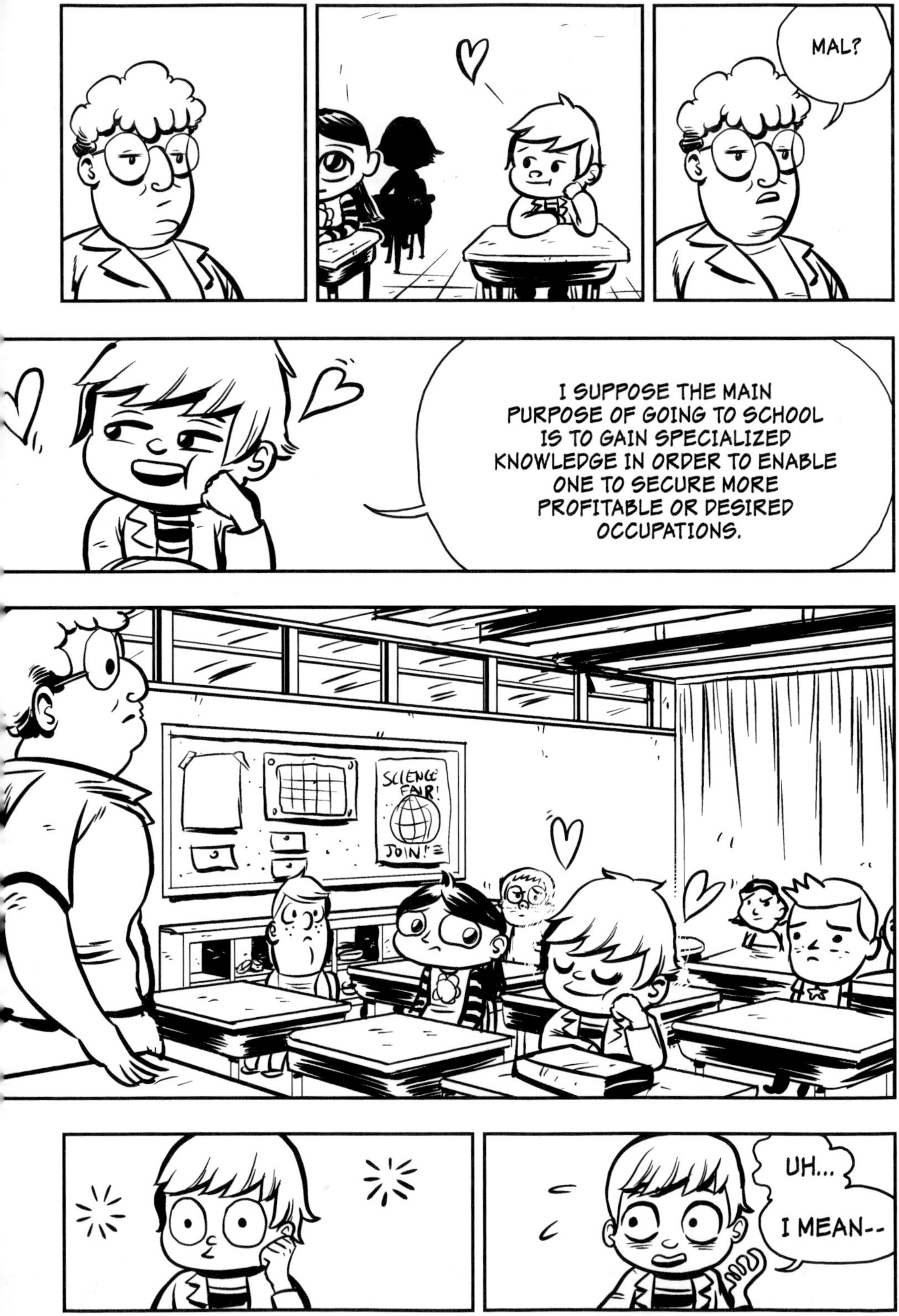
MAL?
I SUPPOSE THE MAIN PURPOSE OF GOING TO SCHOOL IS TO GAIN SPECIALIZED KNOWLEDGE IN ORDER TO ENABLE ONE TO SECURE MORE PROFITABLE OR DESIRED OCCUPATIONS.
SCIENCE FAIR!
JOIN!
UH...
I MEAN--

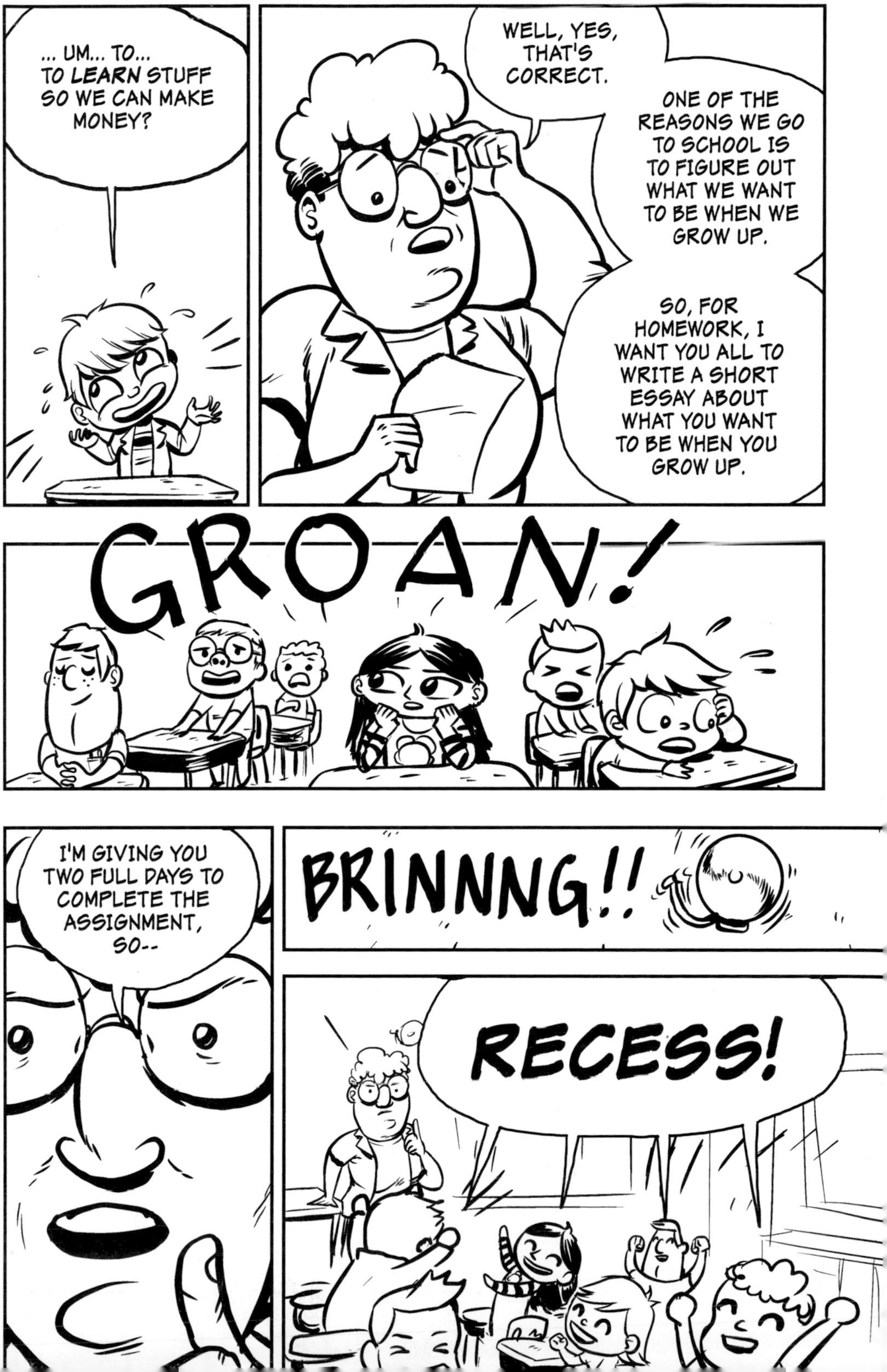
... UM... TO... TO LEARN STUFF SO WE CAN MAKE MONEY?
WELL, YES, THAT'S CORRECT.
ONE OF THE REASONS WE GO TO SCHOOL IS TO FIGURE OUT WHAT WE WANT TO BE WHEN WE GROW UP.
SO, FOR HOMEWORK, I WANT YOU ALL TO WRITE A SHORT ESSAY ABOUT WHAT YOU WANT TO BE WHEN YOU GROW UP.
GROAN!
I'M GIVING YOU TWO FULL DAYS TO COMPLETE THE ASSIGNMENT, SO--
BRINNNG!!
RECESS!

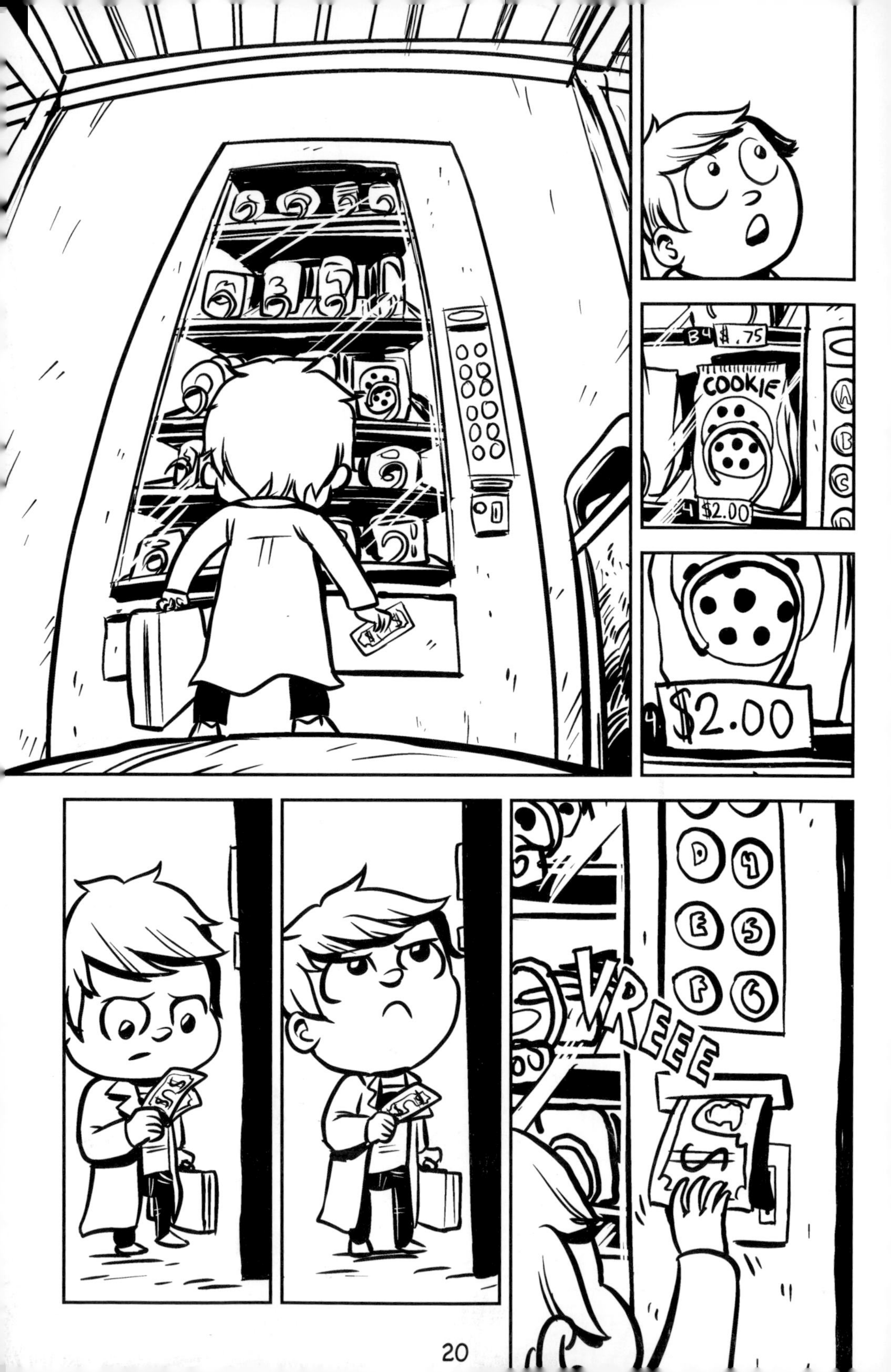
B4 $.75
COOKIE
4 $2.00
$2.00
VREEEE

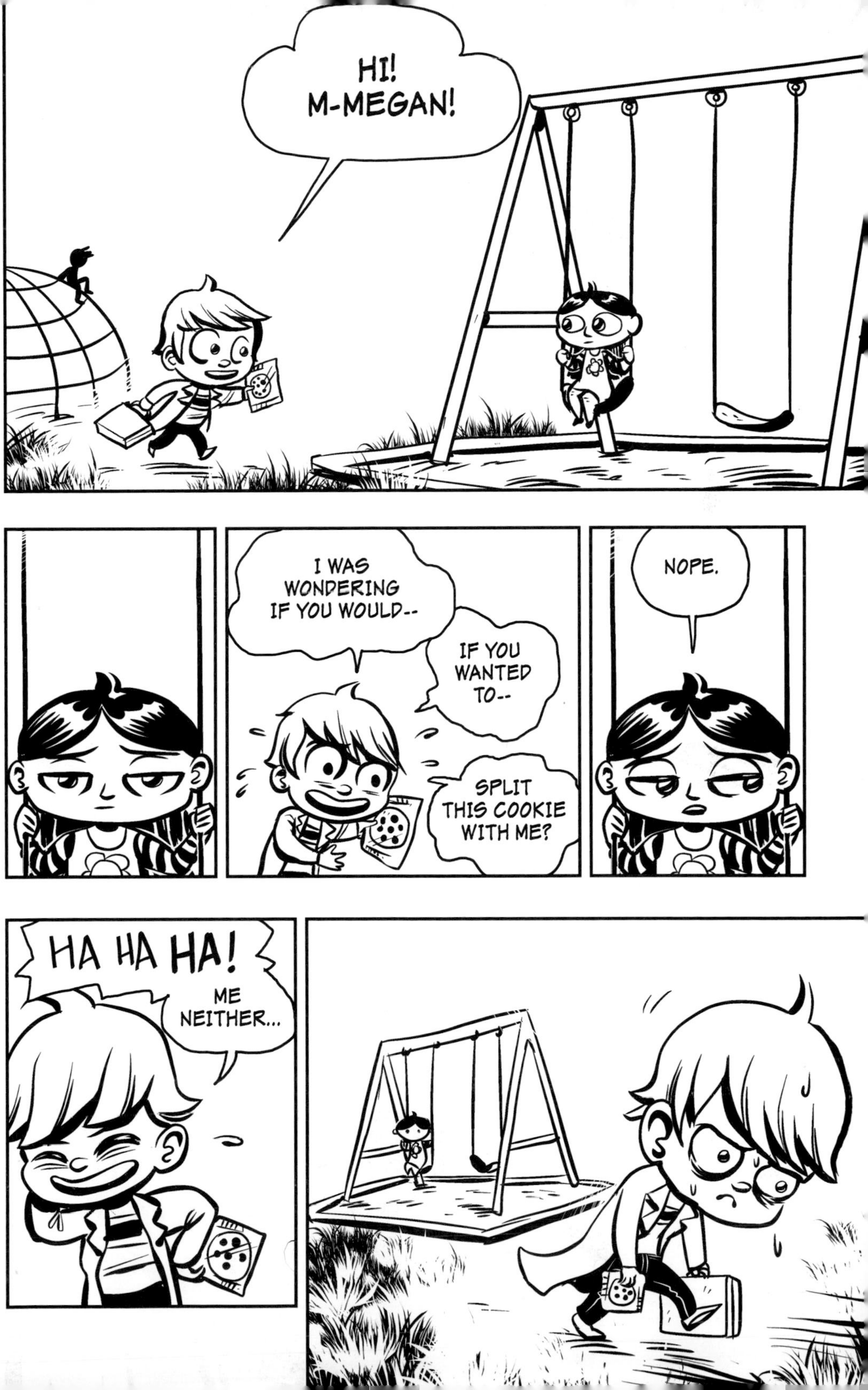
HI!
M-MEGAN!
I WAS WONDERING IF YOU WOULD--
IF YOU WANTED TO--
SPLIT THIS COOKIE WITH ME?
NOPE.
HA HA HA!
ME NEITHER...

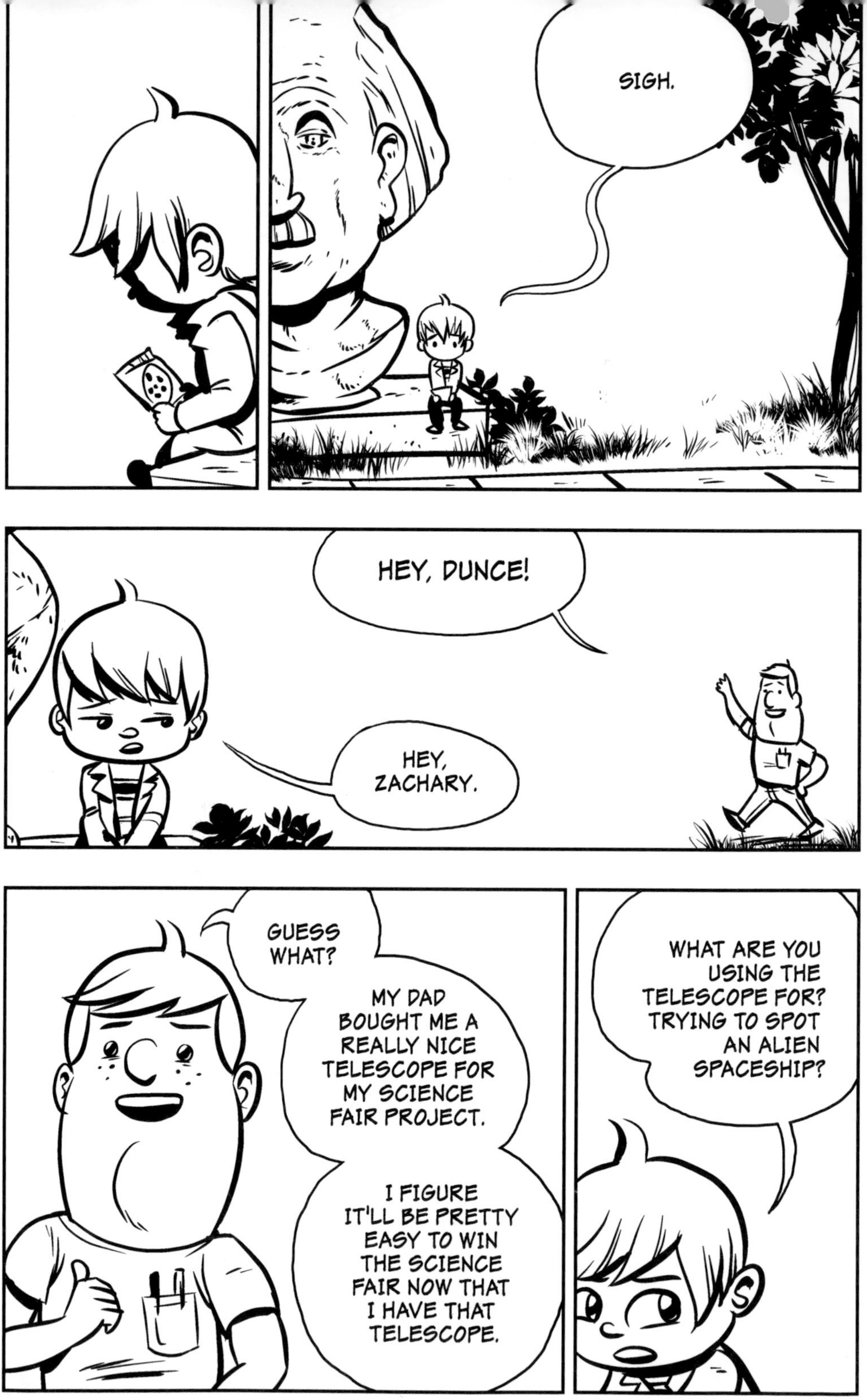
SIGH.
HEY, DUNCE!
HEY,
ZACHARY.
GUESS
WHAT?
MY DAD
BOUGHT ME A
REALLY NICE
TELESCOPE FOR
MY SCIENCE
FAIR PROJECT.
I FIGURE
IT'LL BE PRETTY
EASY TO WIN
THE SCIENCE
FAIR NOW THAT
I HAVE THAT
TELESCOPE.
WHAT ARE YOU
USING THE
TELESCOPE FOR?
TRYING TO SPOT
AN ALIEN
SPACESHIP?

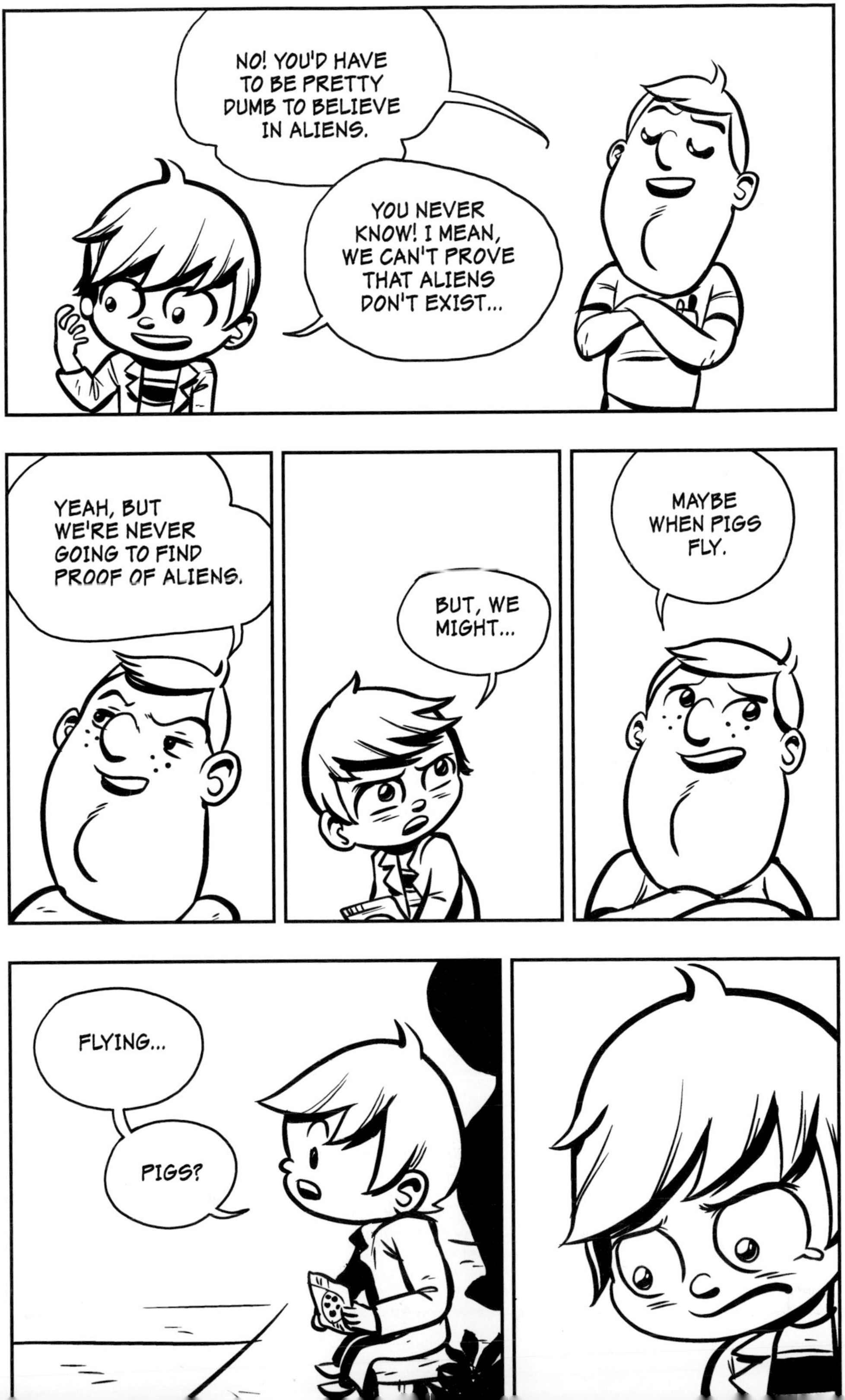
NO! YOU'D HAVE TO BE PRETTY DUMB TO BELIEVE IN ALIENS.
YOU NEVER KNOW! I MEAN, WE CAN'T PROVE THAT ALIENS DON'T EXIST...
YEAH, BUT WE'RE NEVER GOING TO FIND PROOF OF ALIENS.
BUT, WE MIGHT...
MAYBE WHEN PIGS FLY.
FLYING...
PIGS?

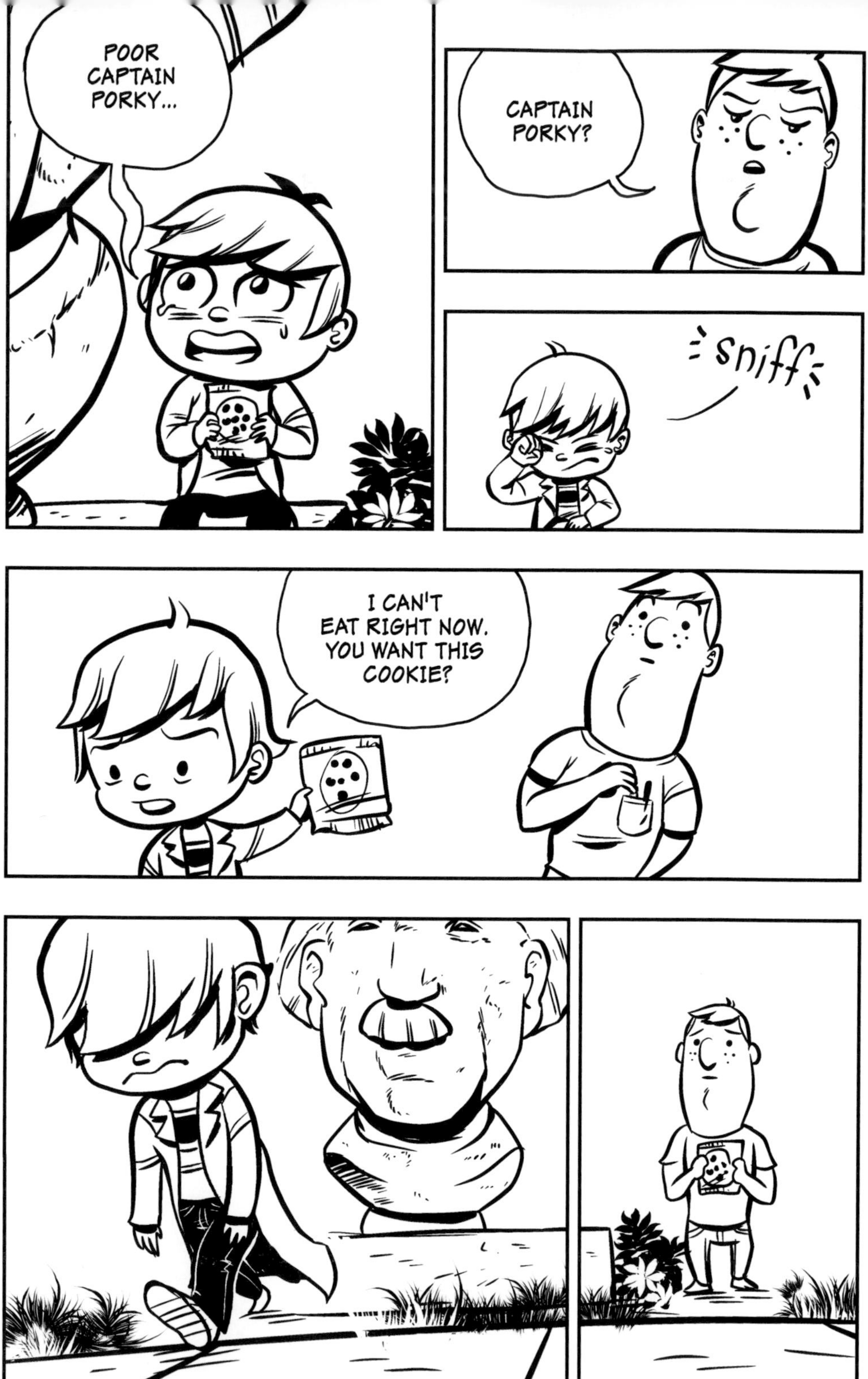
POOR CAPTAIN PORKY...
CAPTAIN PORKY?
sniff
I CAN'T EAT RIGHT NOW. YOU WANT THIS COOKIE?

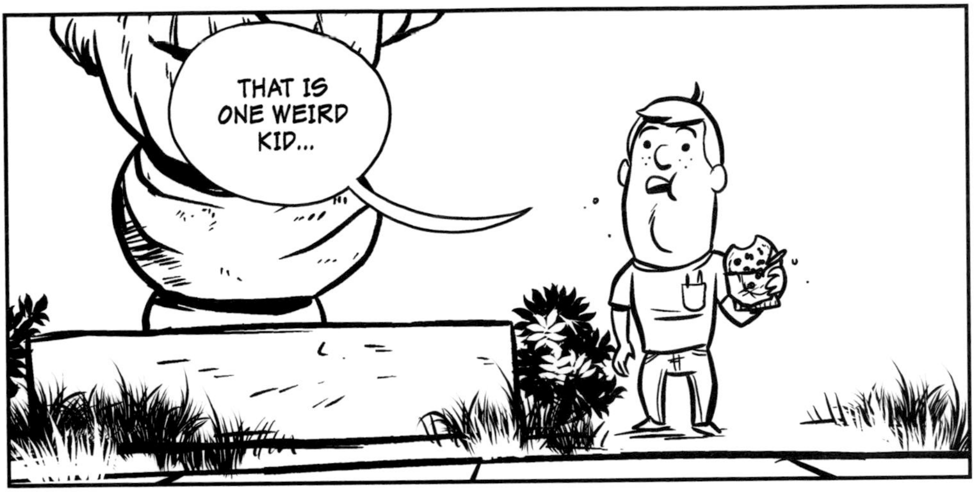
THAT IS ONE WEIRD KID...

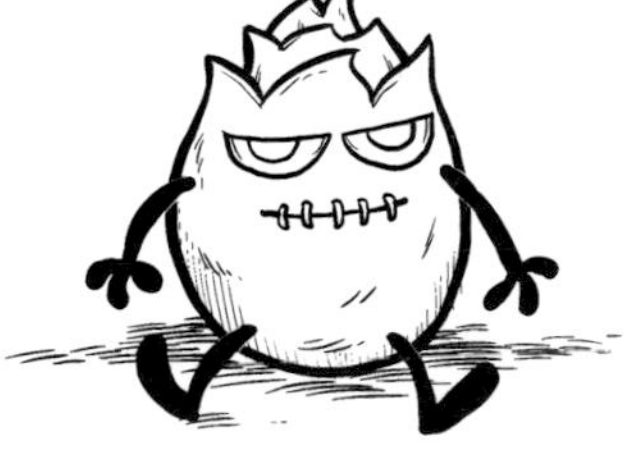

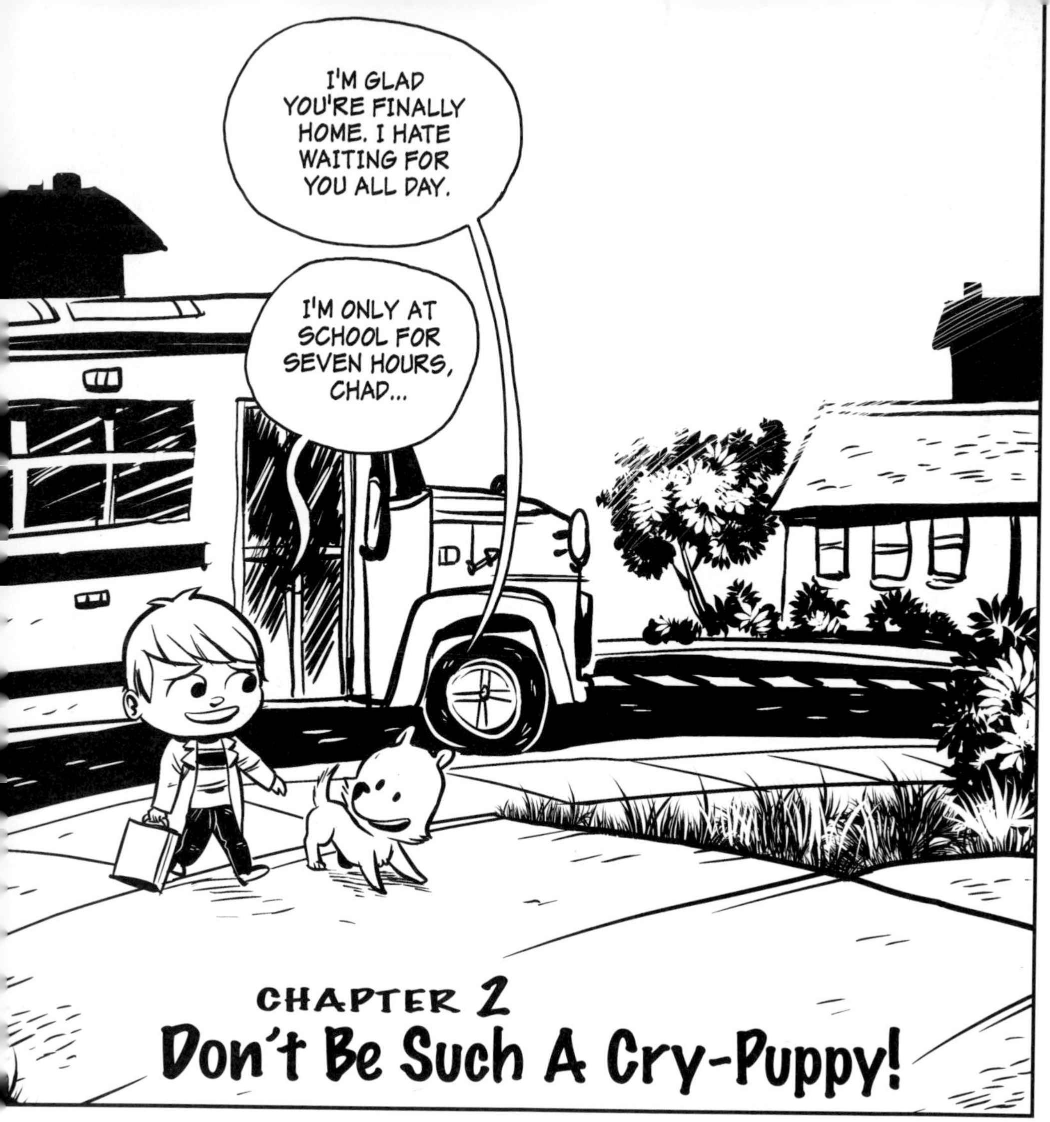
I'M GLAD YOU'RE FINALLY HOME. I HATE WAITING FOR YOU ALL DAY.
I'M ONLY AT SCHOOL FOR SEVEN HOURS, CHAD...
CHAPTER 2
Don't Be Such A Cry-Puppy!

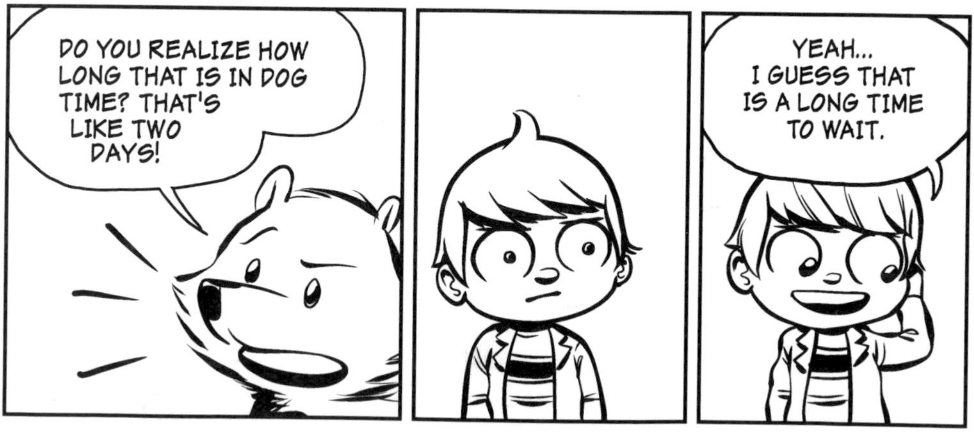
DO YOU REALIZE HOW LONG THAT IS IN DOG TIME? THAT'S LIKE TWO DAYS!
YEAH... I GUESS THAT IS A LONG TIME TO WAIT.

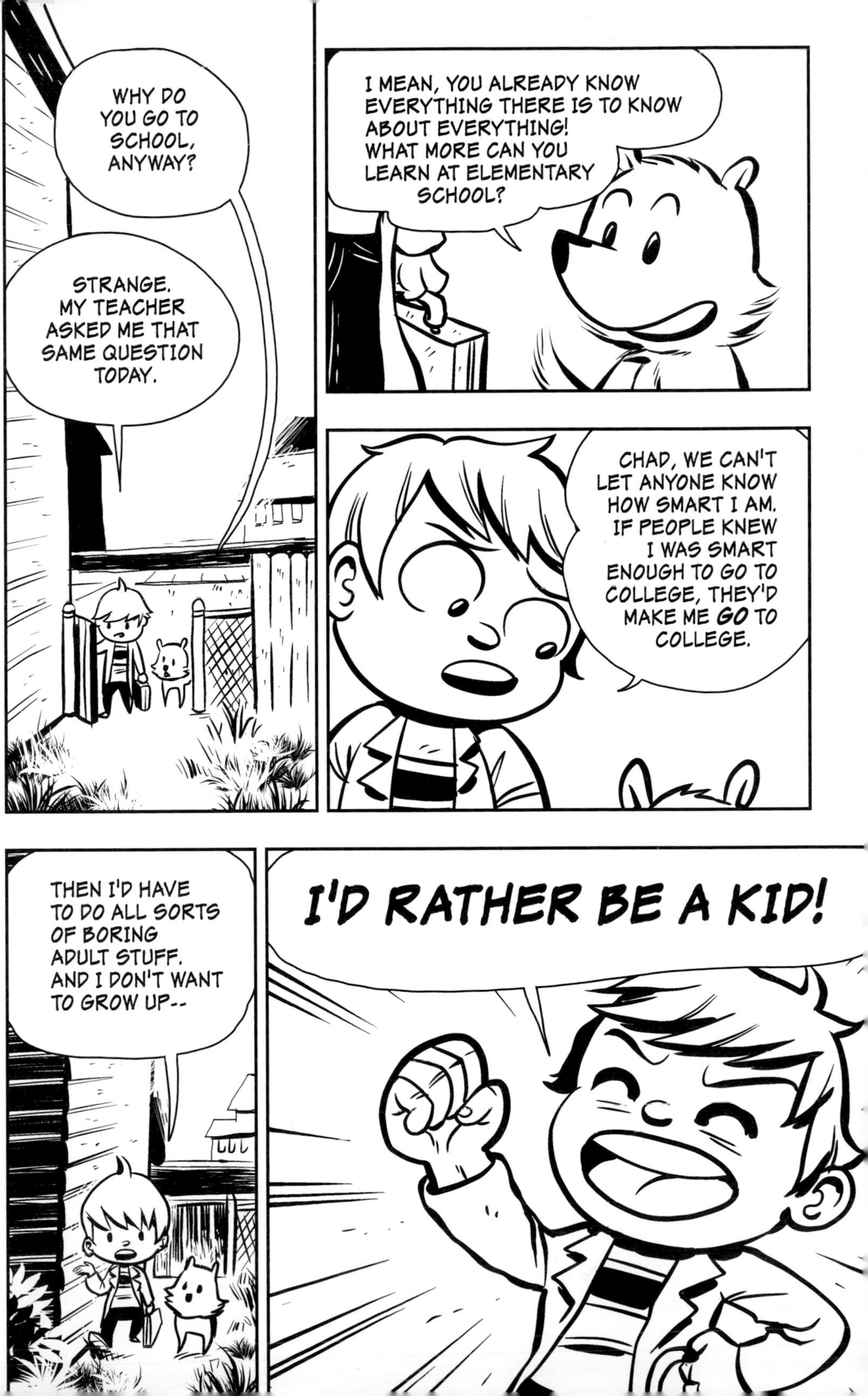
WHY DO YOU GO TO SCHOOL, ANYWAY?
STRANGE. MY TEACHER ASKED ME THAT SAME QUESTION TODAY.
I MEAN, YOU ALREADY KNOW EVERYTHING THERE IS TO KNOW ABOUT EVERYTHING! WHAT MORE CAN YOU LEARN AT ELEMENTARY SCHOOL?
CHAD, WE CAN'T LET ANYONE KNOW HOW SMART I AM. IF PEOPLE KNEW I WAS SMART ENOUGH TO GO TO COLLEGE, THEY'D MAKE ME GO TO COLLEGE.
THEN I'D HAVE TO DO ALL SORTS OF BORING ADULT STUFF. AND I DON'T WANT TO GROW UP--
I'D RATHER BE A KID!

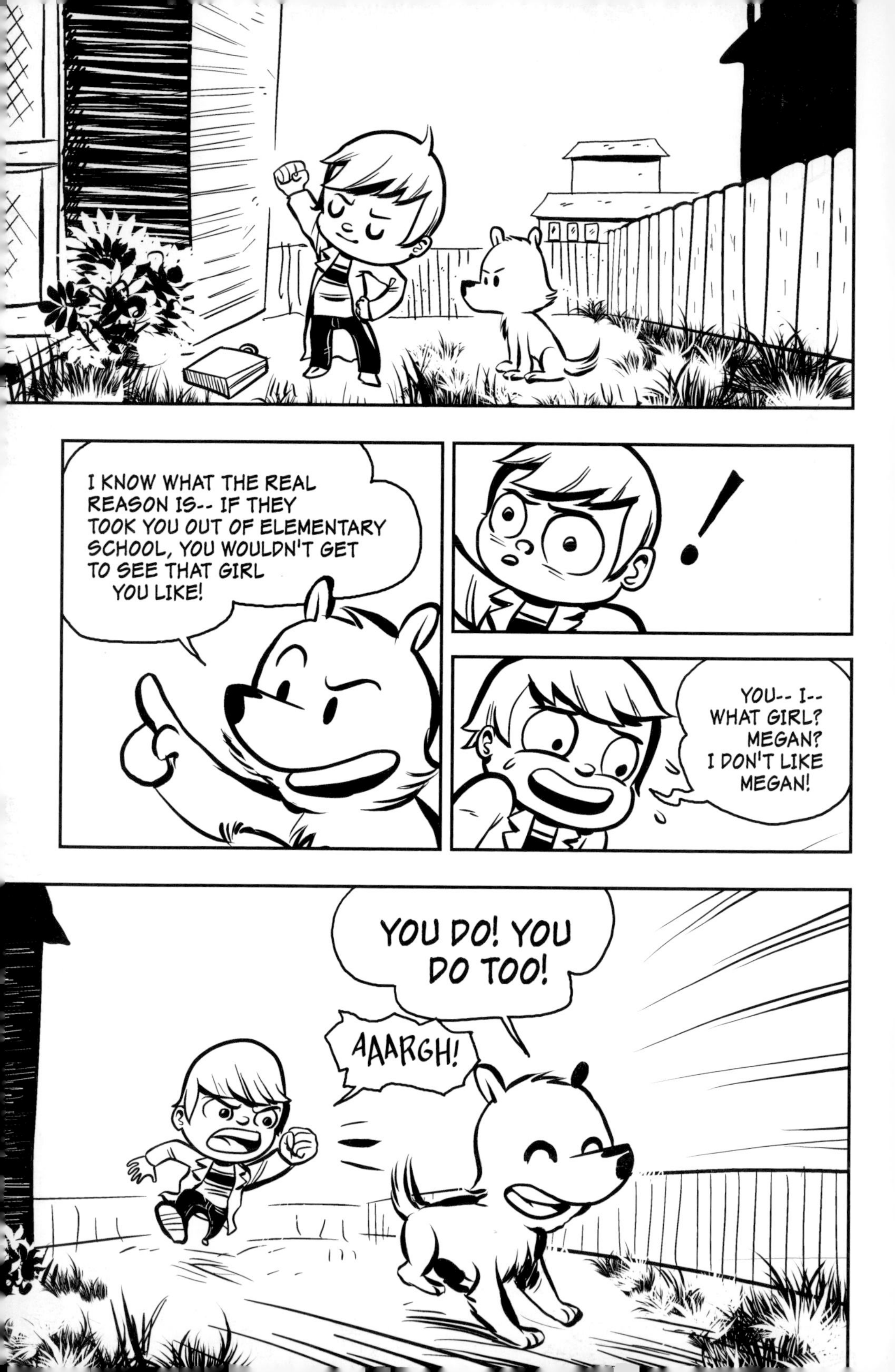

I KNOW WHAT THE REAL REASON IS-- IF THEY TOOK YOU OUT OF ELEMENTARY SCHOOL, YOU WOULDN'T GET TO SEE THAT GIRL YOU LIKE!
!
YOU-- I-- WHAT GIRL? MEGAN? I DON'T LIKE MEGAN!
YOU DO! YOU DO TOO!
AAARGH!

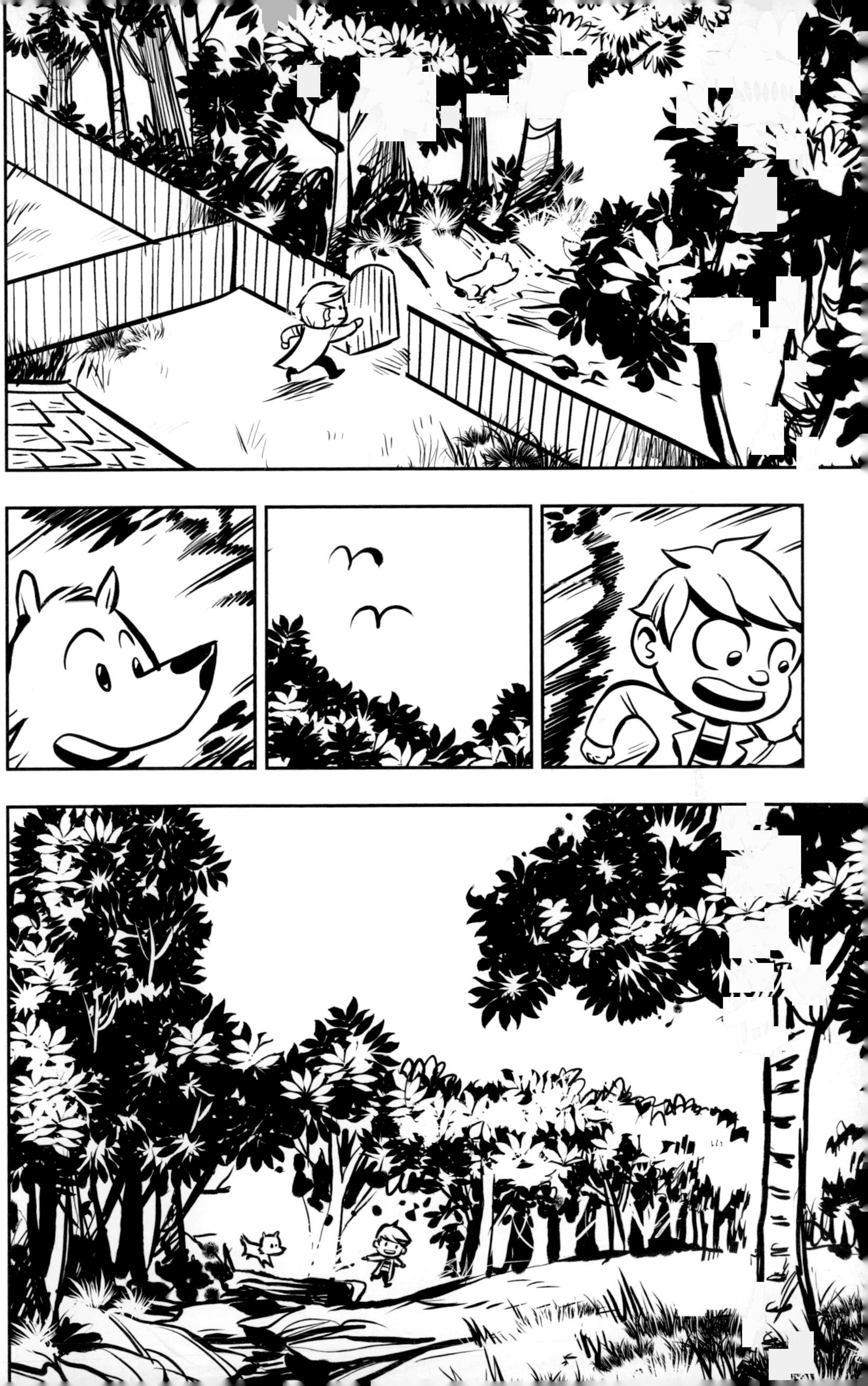

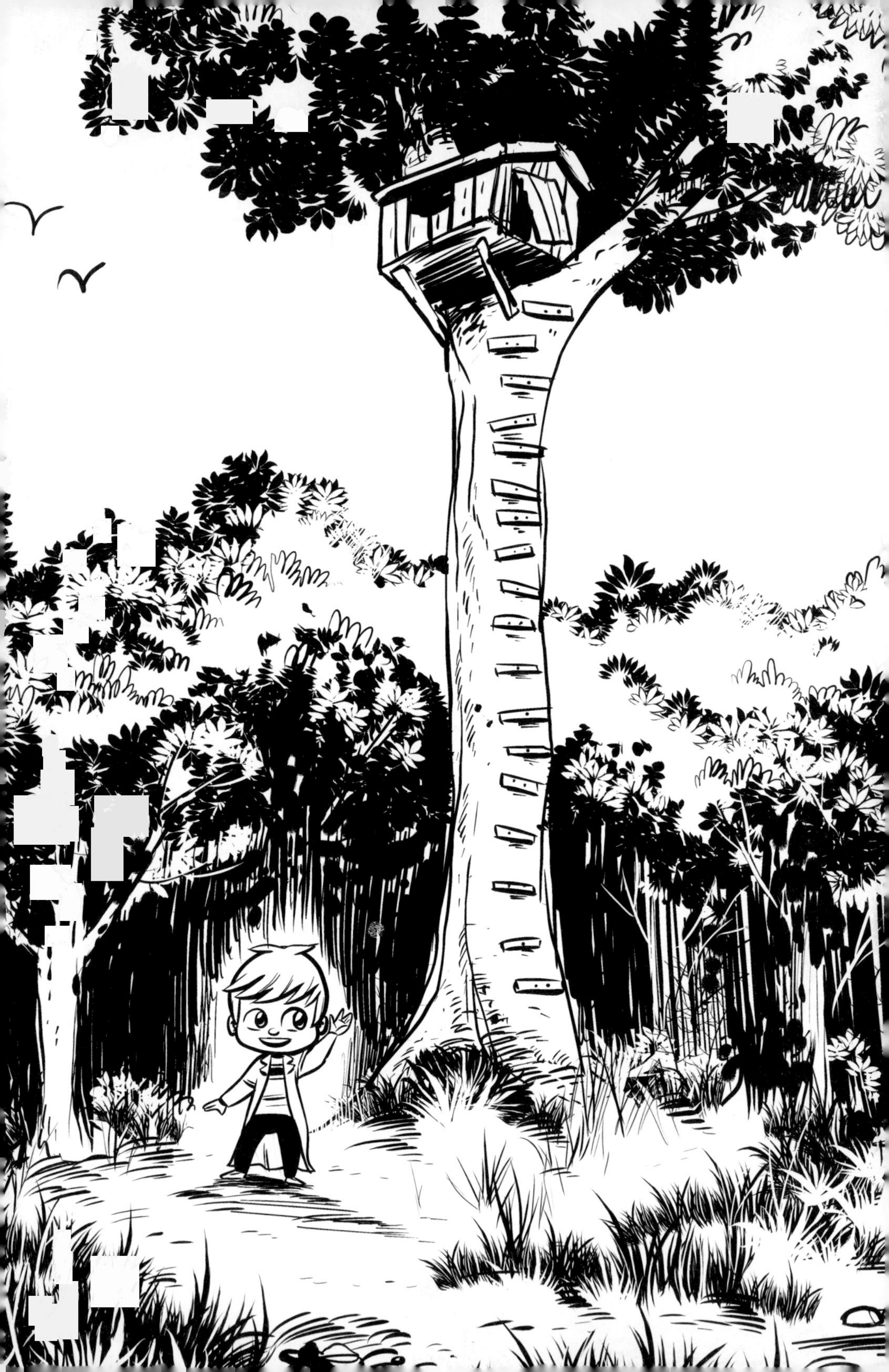

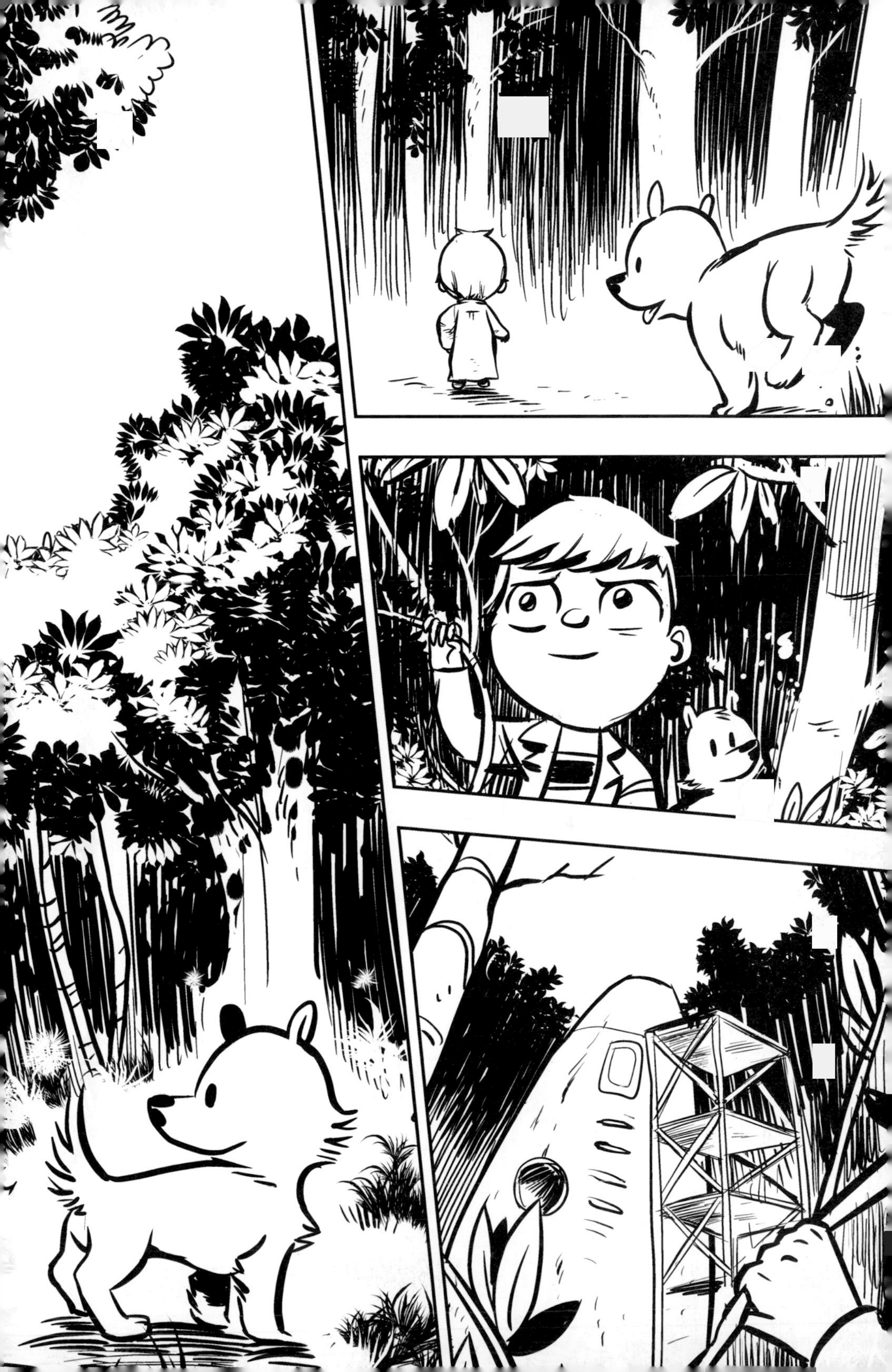

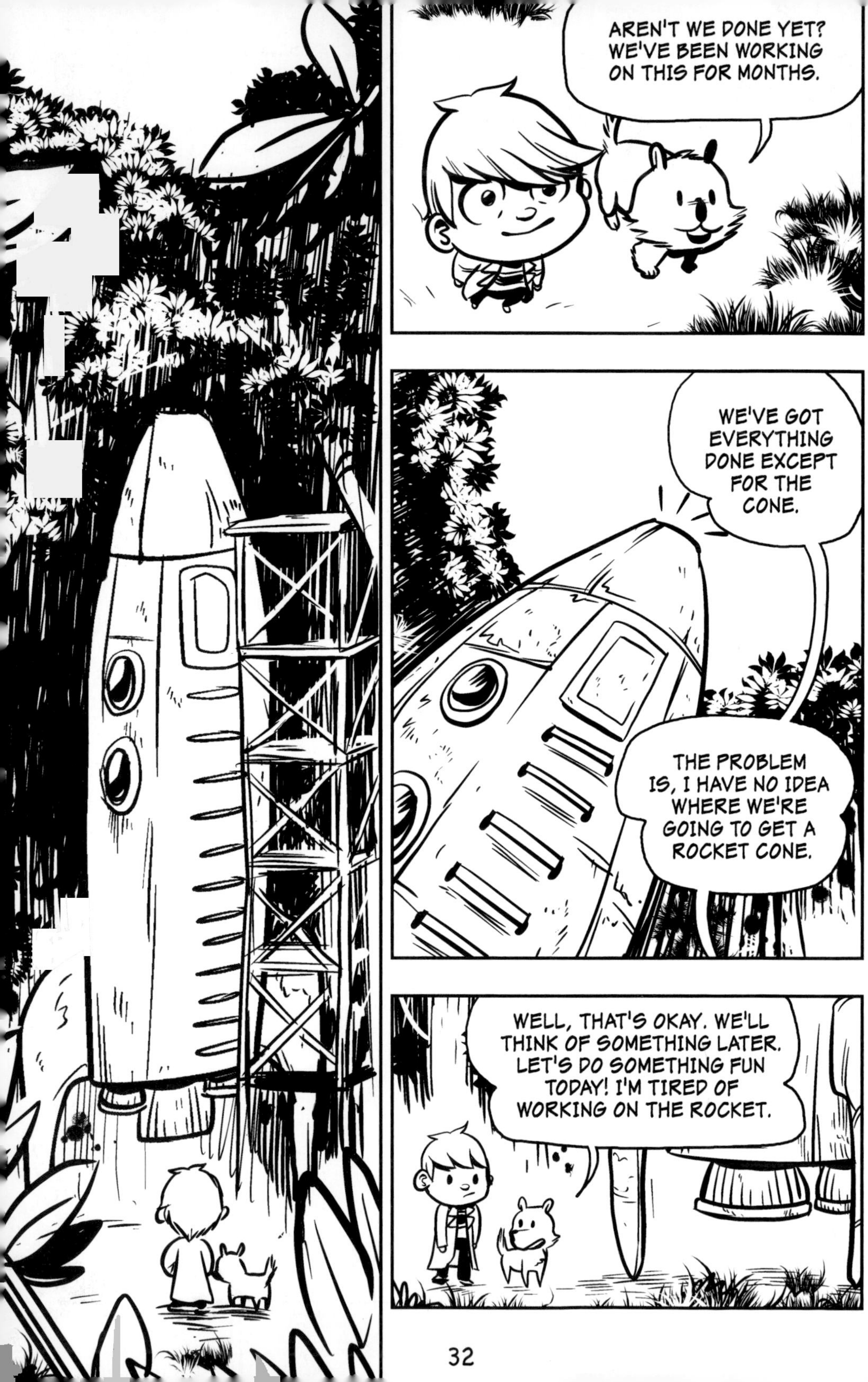

AREN'T WE DONE YET? WE'VE BEEN WORKING ON THIS FOR MONTHS.
WE'VE GOT EVERYTHING DONE EXCEPT FOR THE CONE.
THE PROBLEM IS, I HAVE NO IDEA WHERE WE'RE GOING TO GET A ROCKET CONE.
WELL, THAT'S OKAY. WE'LL THINK OF SOMETHING LATER. LET'S DO SOMETHING FUN TODAY! I'M TIRED OF WORKING ON THE ROCKET.

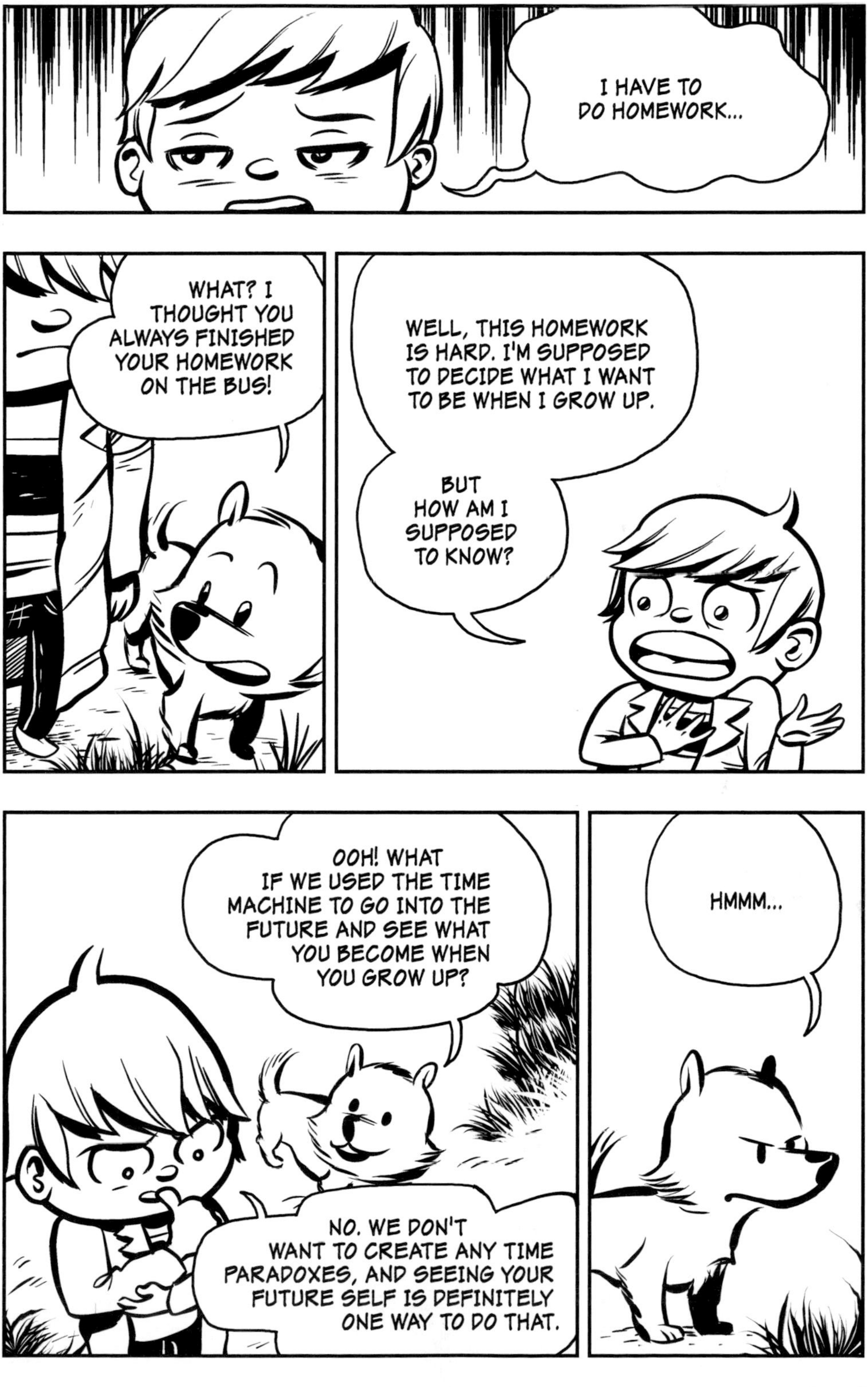
I HAVE TO DO HOMEWORK...
WHAT? I THOUGHT YOU ALWAYS FINISHED YOUR HOMEWORK ON THE BUS!
WELL, THIS HOMEWORK IS HARD. I'M SUPPOSED TO DECIDE WHAT I WANT TO BE WHEN I GROW UP.
BUT HOW AM I SUPPOSED TO KNOW?
OOH! WHAT IF WE USED THE TIME MACHINE TO GO INTO THE FUTURE AND SEE WHAT YOU BECOME WHEN YOU GROW UP?
NO. WE DON'T WANT TO CREATE ANY TIME PARADOXES, AND SEEING YOUR FUTURE SELF IS DEFINITELY ONE WAY TO DO THAT.
HMMM...

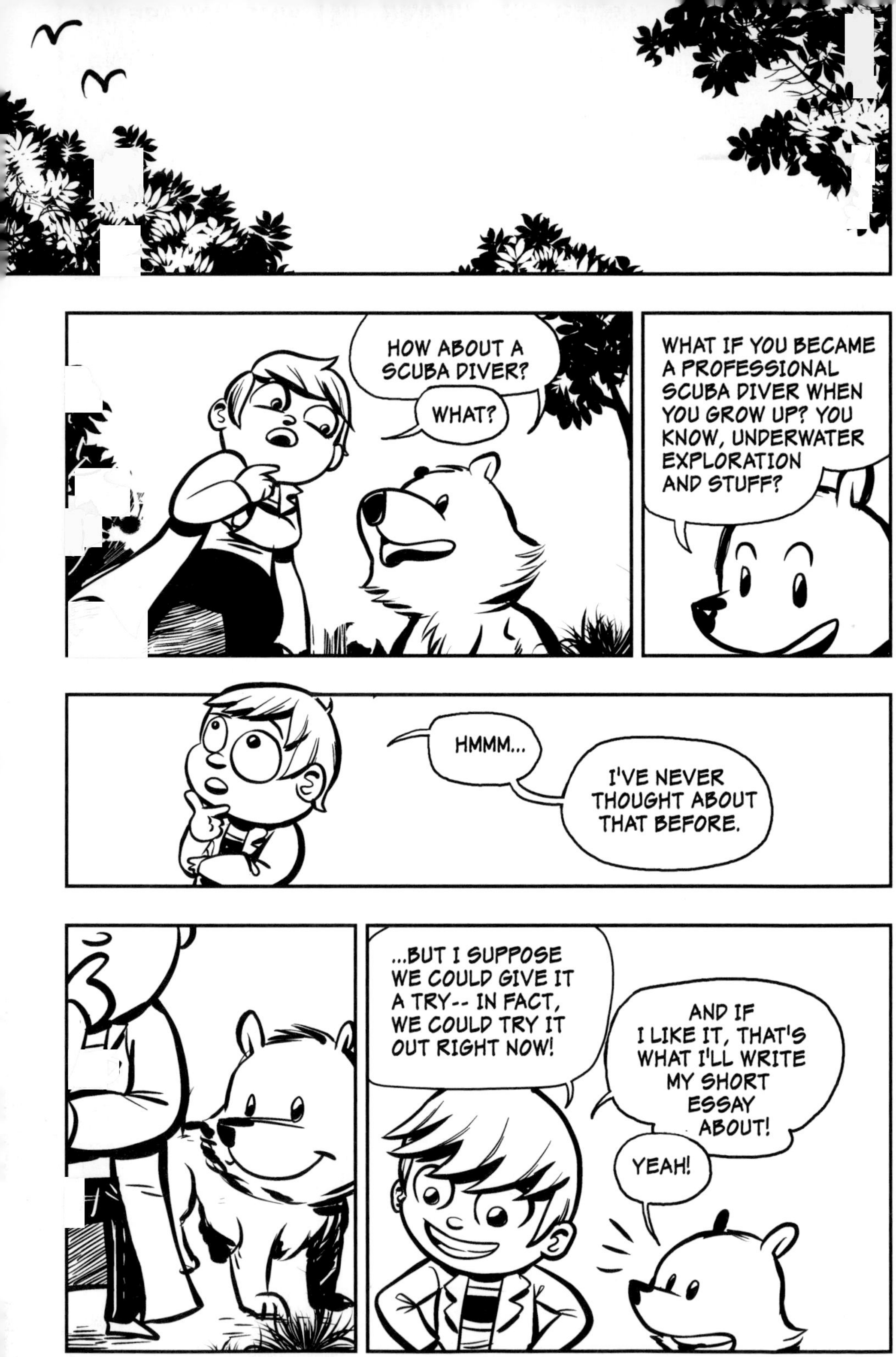
HOW ABOUT A SCUBA DIVER?
WHAT?
WHAT IF YOU BECAME A PROFESSIONAL SCUBA DIVER WHEN YOU GROW UP? YOU KNOW, UNDERWATER EXPLORATION AND STUFF?
HMMM...
I'VE NEVER THOUGHT ABOUT THAT BEFORE.
...BUT I SUPPOSE WE COULD GIVE IT A TRY-- IN FACT, WE COULD TRY IT OUT RIGHT NOW!
AND IF I LIKE IT, THAT'S WHAT I'LL WRITE MY SHORT ESSAY ABOUT!
YEAH!

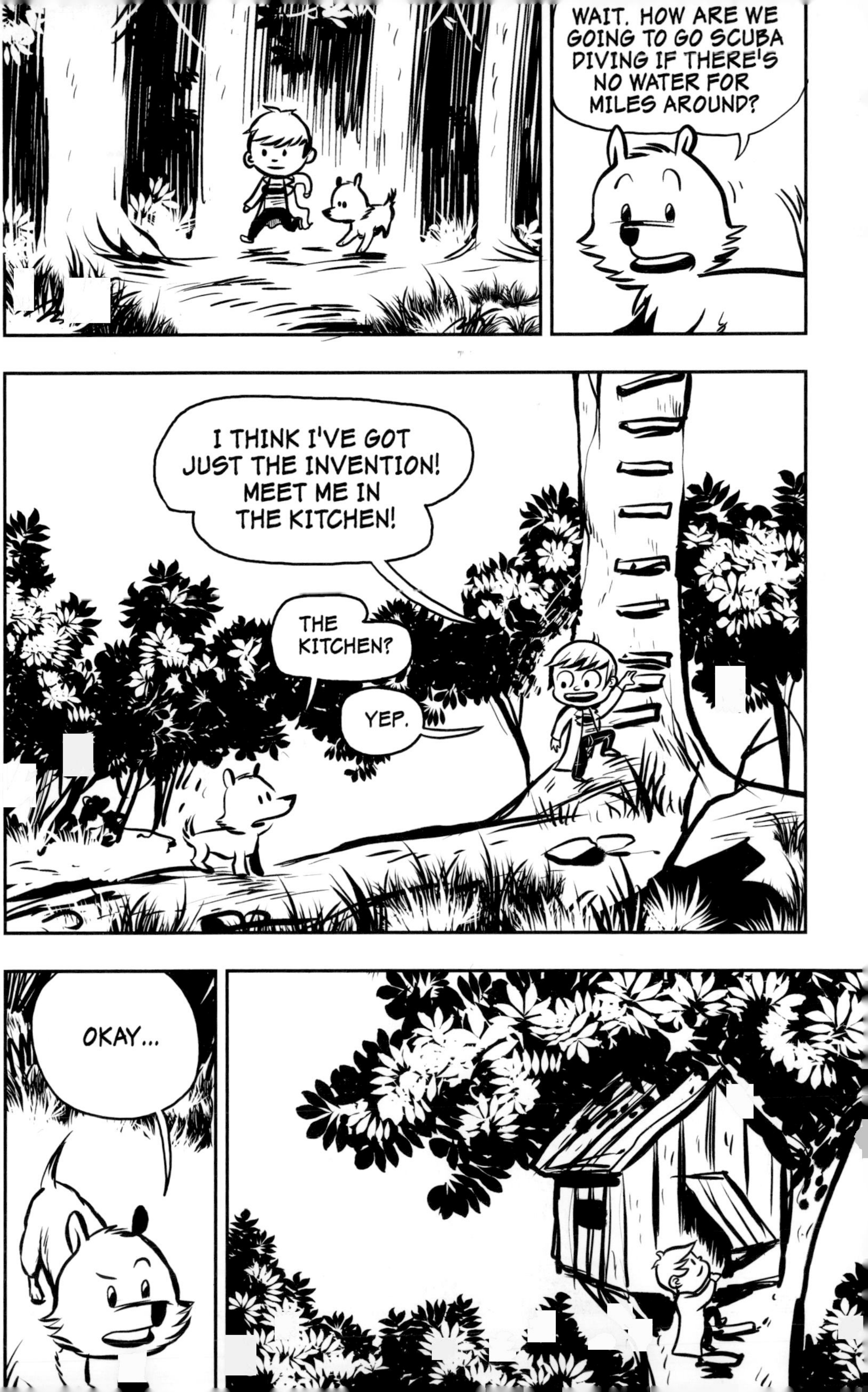
WAIT. HOW ARE WE GOING TO GO SCUBA DIVING IF THERE'S NO WATER FOR MILES AROUND?
I THINK I'VE GOT JUST THE INVENTION! MEET ME IN THE KITCHEN!
THE KITCHEN?
YEP.
OKAY...

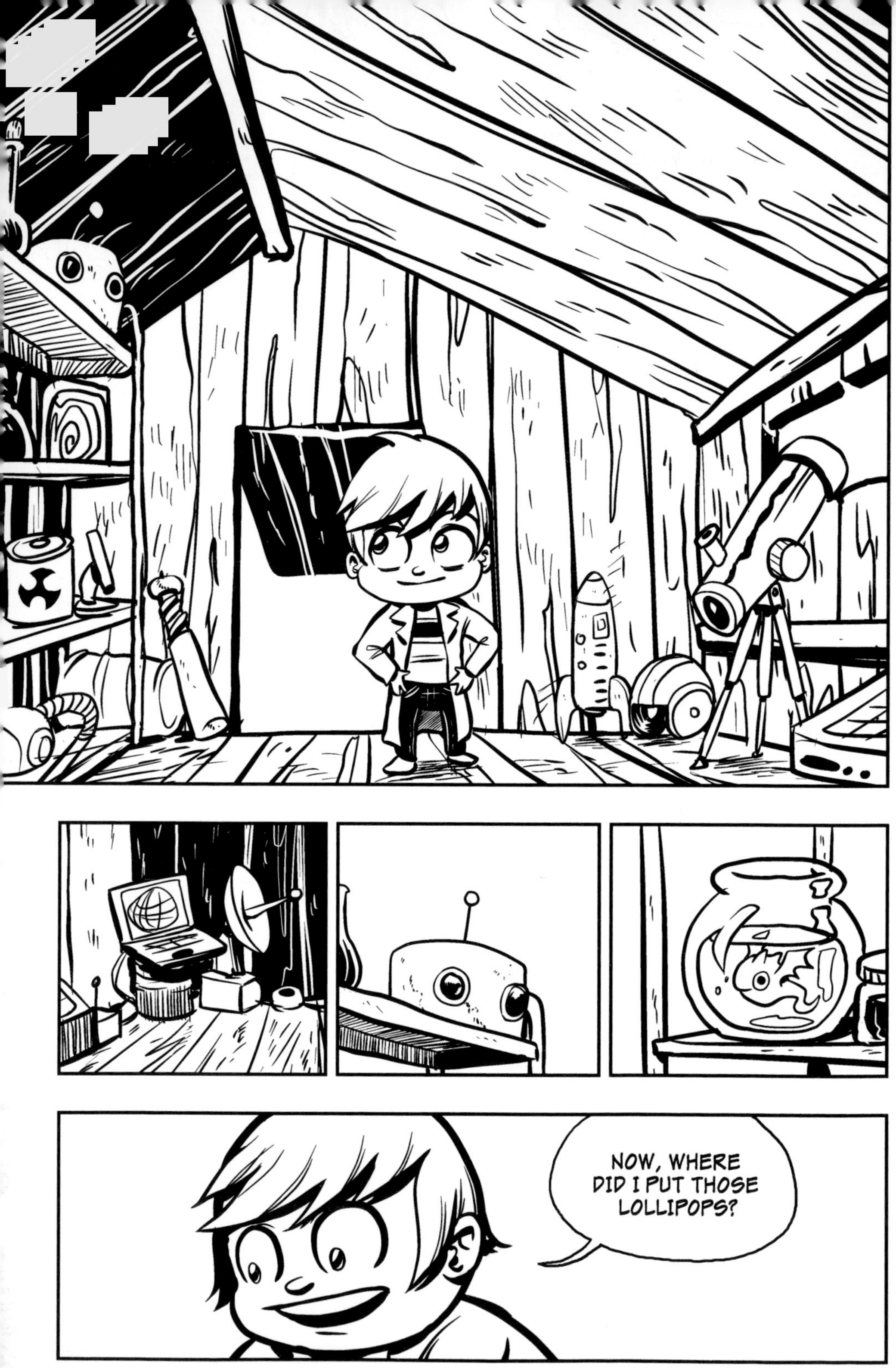
NOW, WHERE DID I PUT THOSE LOLLIPOPS?

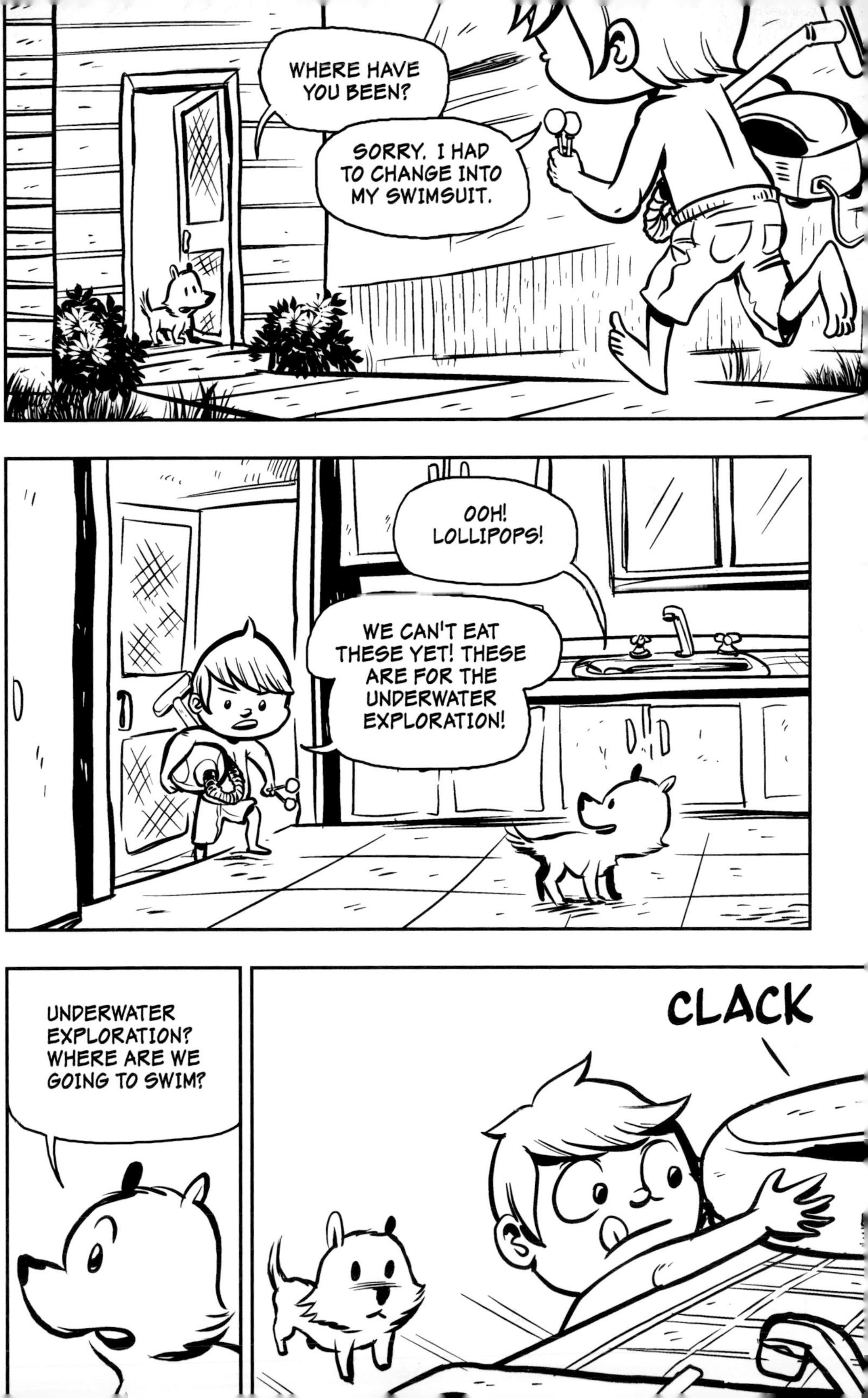
WHERE HAVE YOU BEEN?
SORRY. I HAD TO CHANGE INTO MY SWIMSUIT.
OOH! LOLLIPOPS!
WE CAN'T EAT THESE YET! THESE ARE FOR THE UNDERWATER EXPLORATION!
UNDERWATER EXPLORATION? WHERE ARE WE GOING TO SWIM?
CLACK

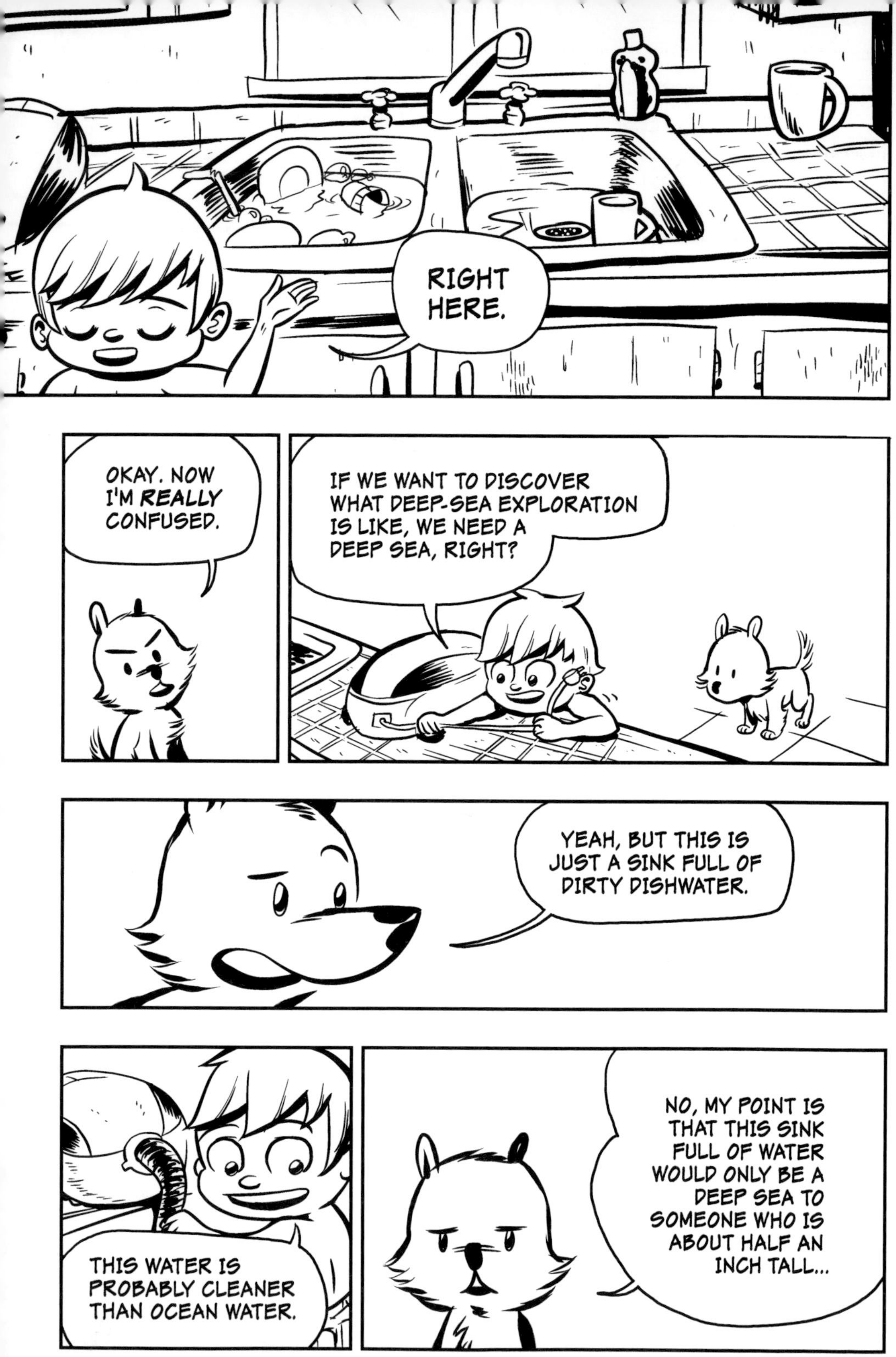
RIGHT HERE.
OKAY. NOW I'M *REALLY* CONFUSED.
IF WE WANT TO DISCOVER WHAT DEEP-SEA EXPLORATION IS LIKE, WE NEED A DEEP SEA, RIGHT?
YEAH, BUT THIS IS JUST A SINK FULL OF DIRTY DISHWATER.
THIS WATER IS PROBABLY CLEANER THAN OCEAN WATER.
NO, MY POINT IS THAT THIS SINK FULL OF WATER WOULD ONLY BE A DEEP SEA TO SOMEONE WHO IS ABOUT HALF AN INCH TALL...

EXACTLY! NOW, OBSERVE...

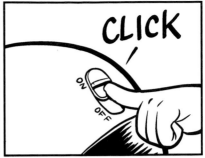

CLICK

ON
OFF

VREEEEEE

WHAT ARE YOU DOING WITH MOM'S OLD VACUUM CLEANER?

VREEEEEE

I MODIFIED IT. NOW IT'S A MINI-MEGA-MORPHER!

A WHAT?

JUST WATCH!

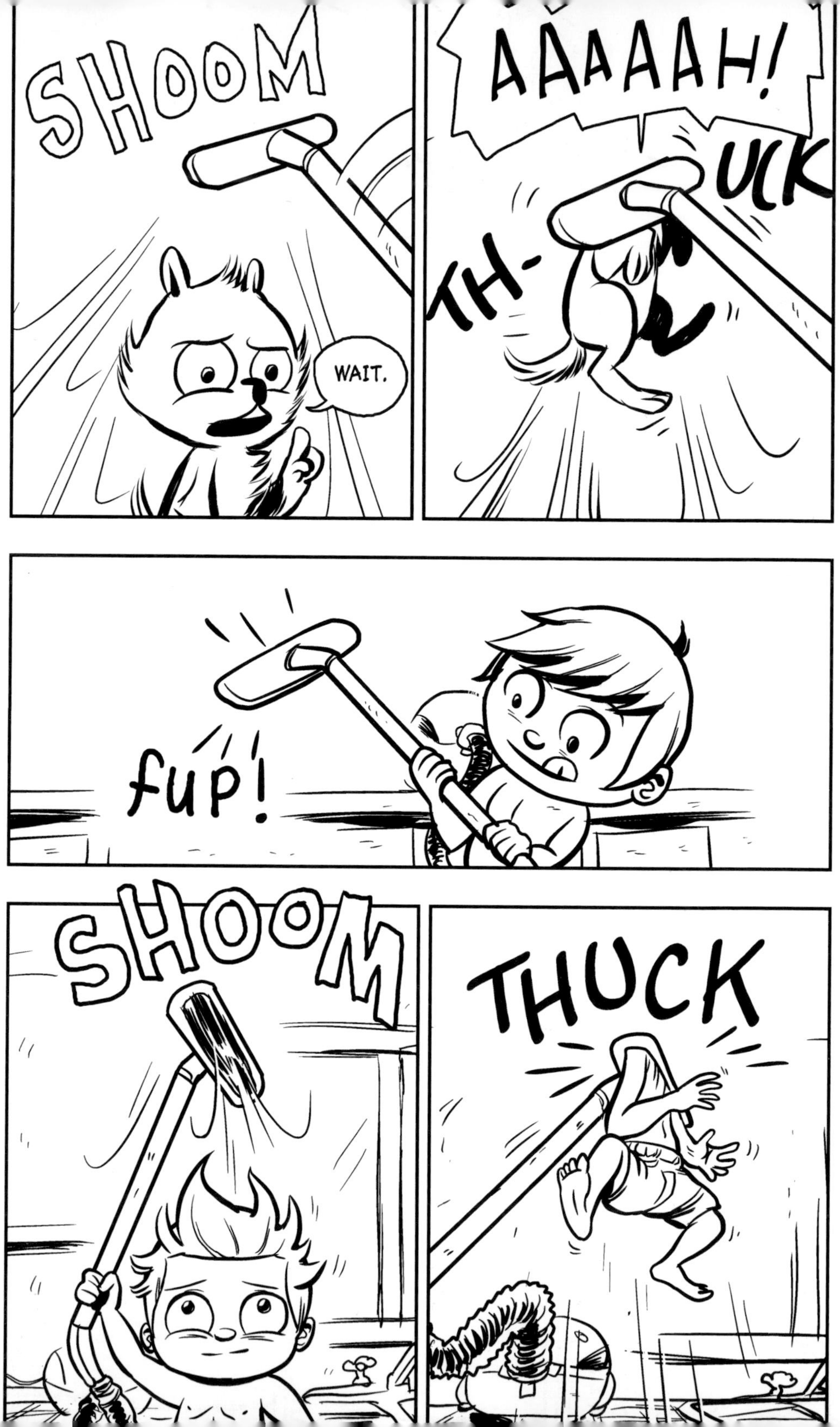
SHOOM
WAIT.
AAAAAH!
TH-
UCK
fup!
SHOOM
THUCK

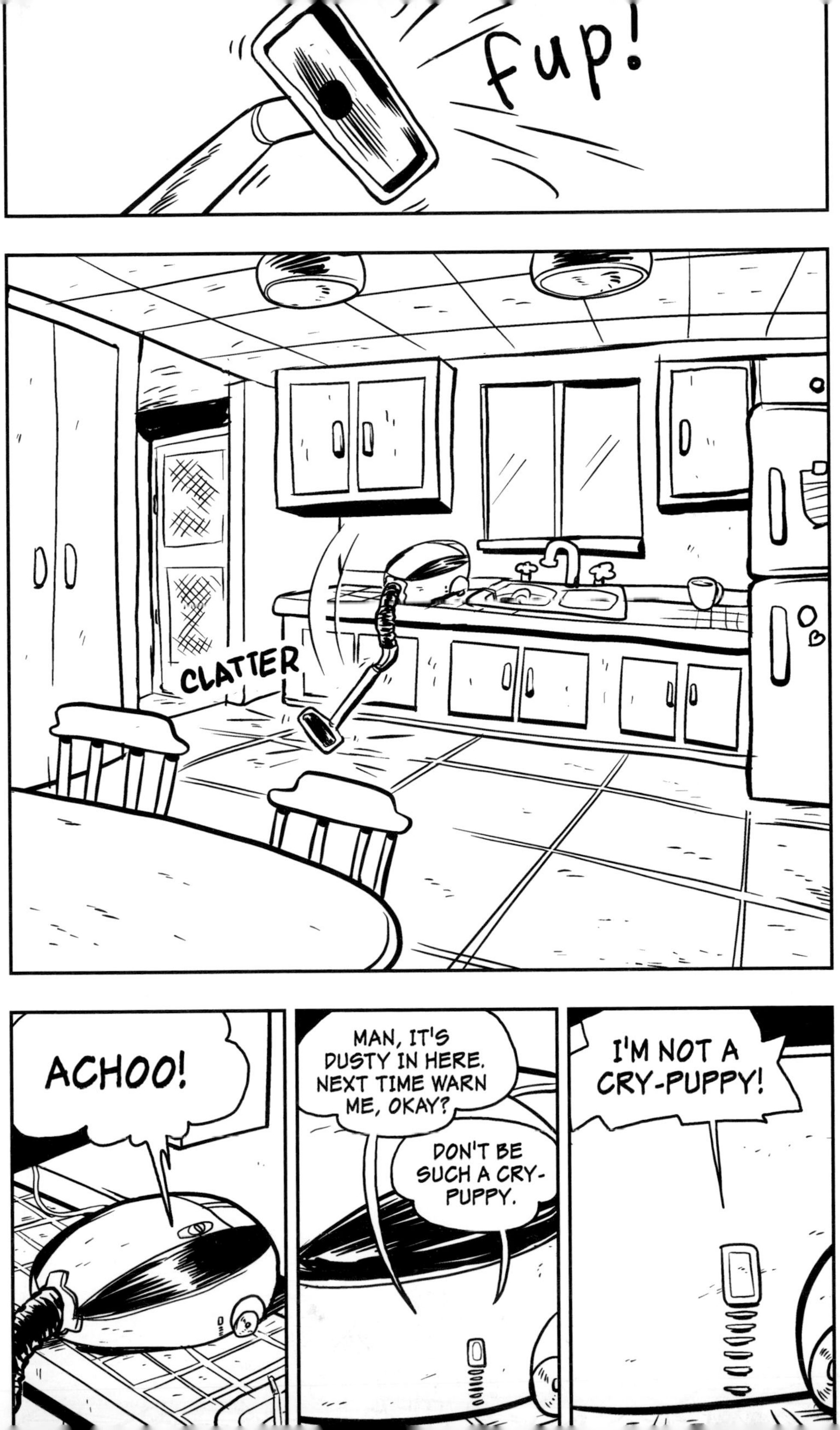
fup!
CLATTER
ACHOO!
MAN, IT'S DUSTY IN HERE. NEXT TIME WARN ME, OKAY?
DON'T BE SUCH A CRY-PUPPY.
I'M NOT A CRY-PUPPY!

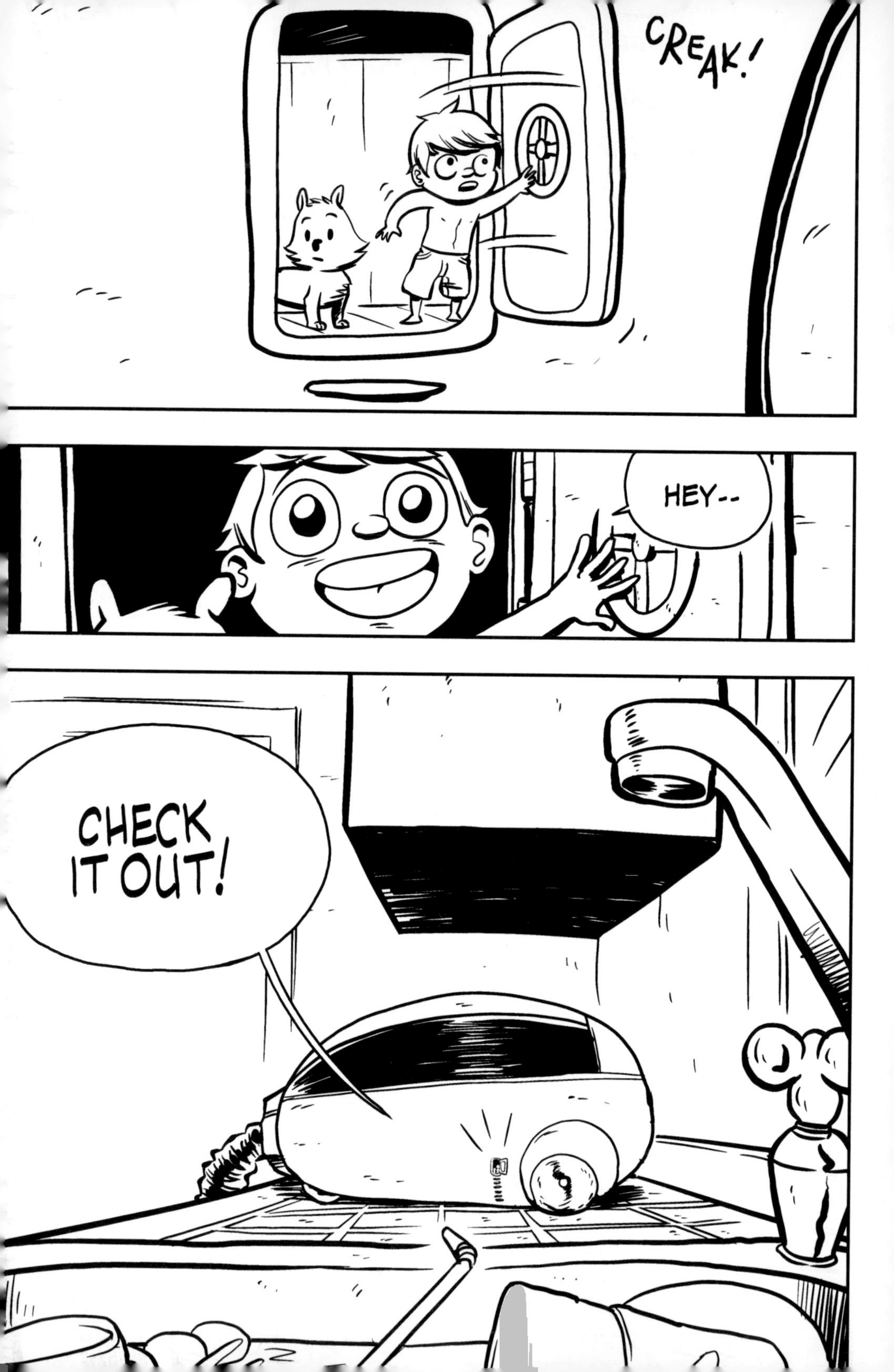
CREAK!
HEY--
CHECK IT OUT!

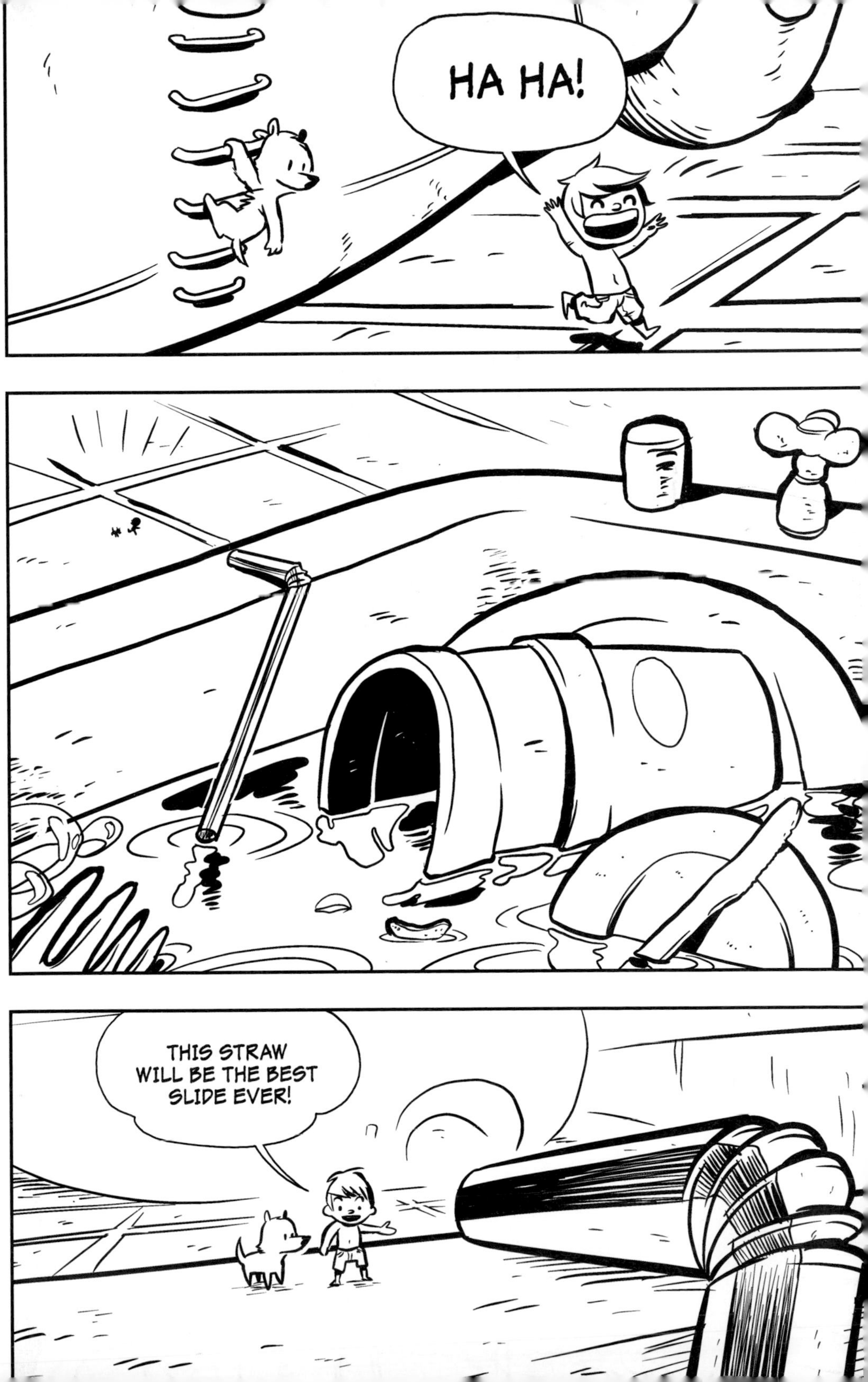
HA HA!
THIS STRAW WILL BE THE BEST SLIDE EVER!

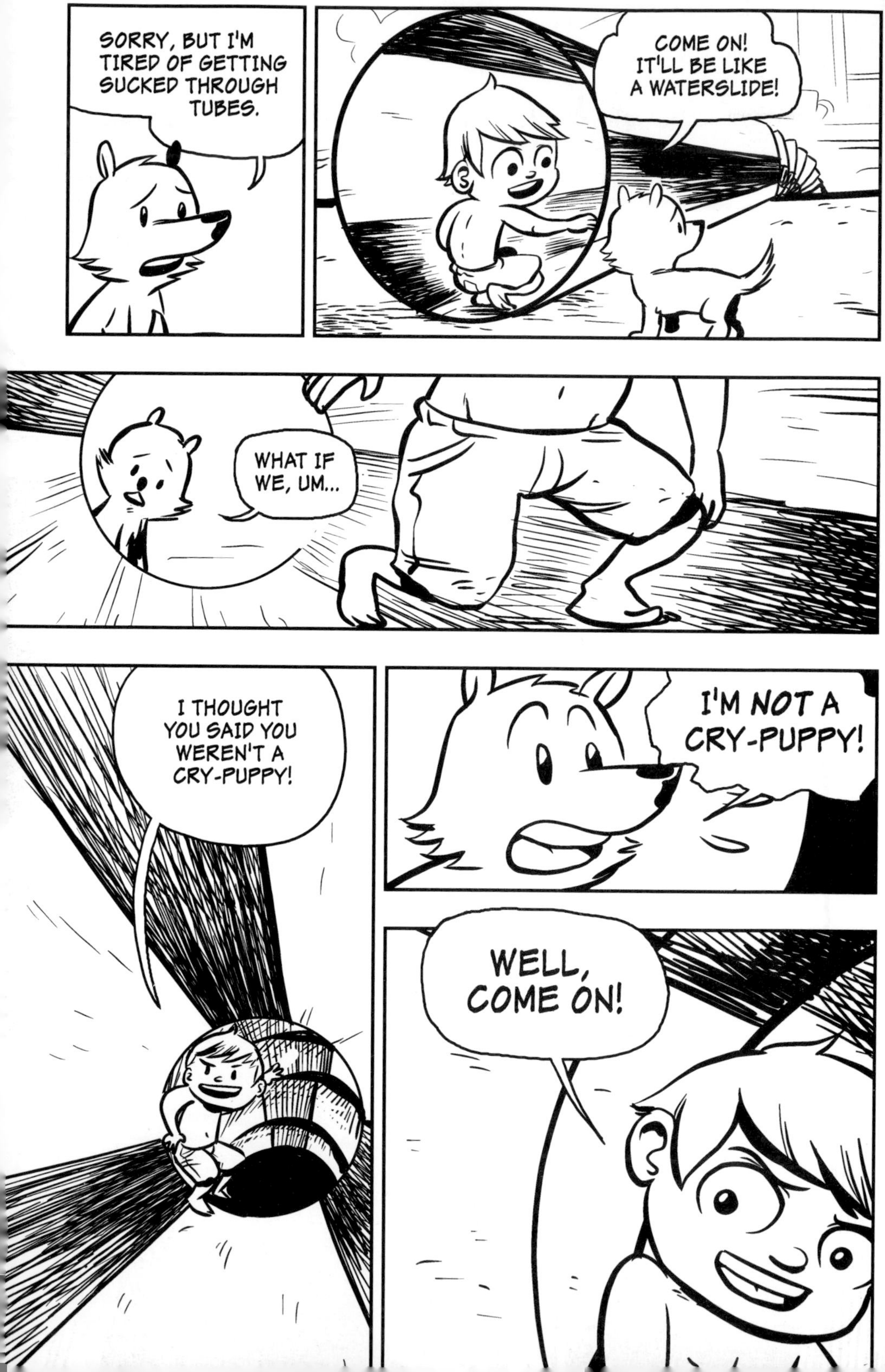
SORRY, BUT I'M TIRED OF GETTING SUCKED THROUGH TUBES.
COME ON! IT'LL BE LIKE A WATERSLIDE!
WHAT IF WE, UM...
I THOUGHT YOU SAID YOU WEREN'T A CRY-PUPPY!
I'M *NOT* A CRY-PUPPY!
WELL, COME ON!

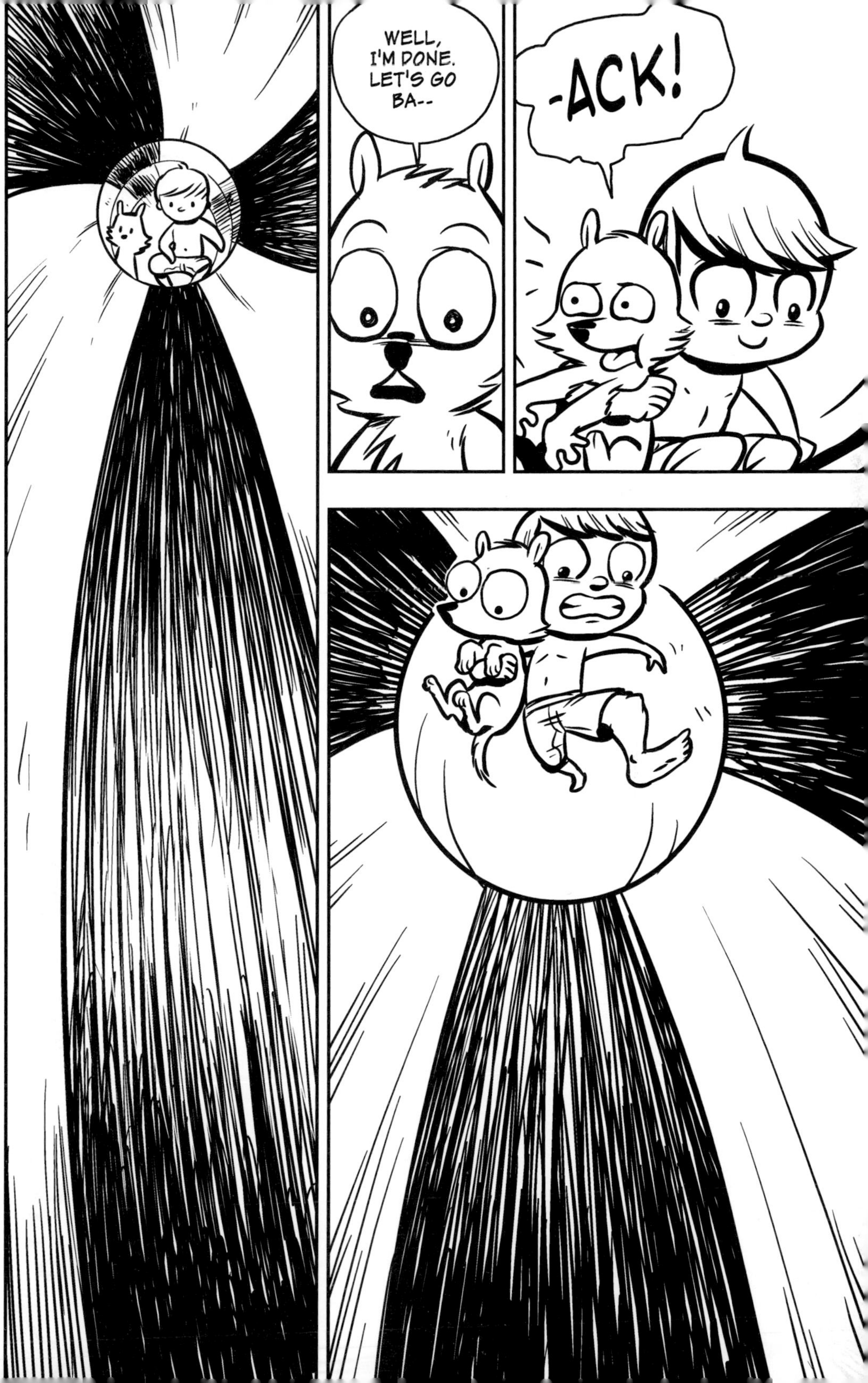
WELL, I'M DONE. LET'S GO BA--
-ACK!

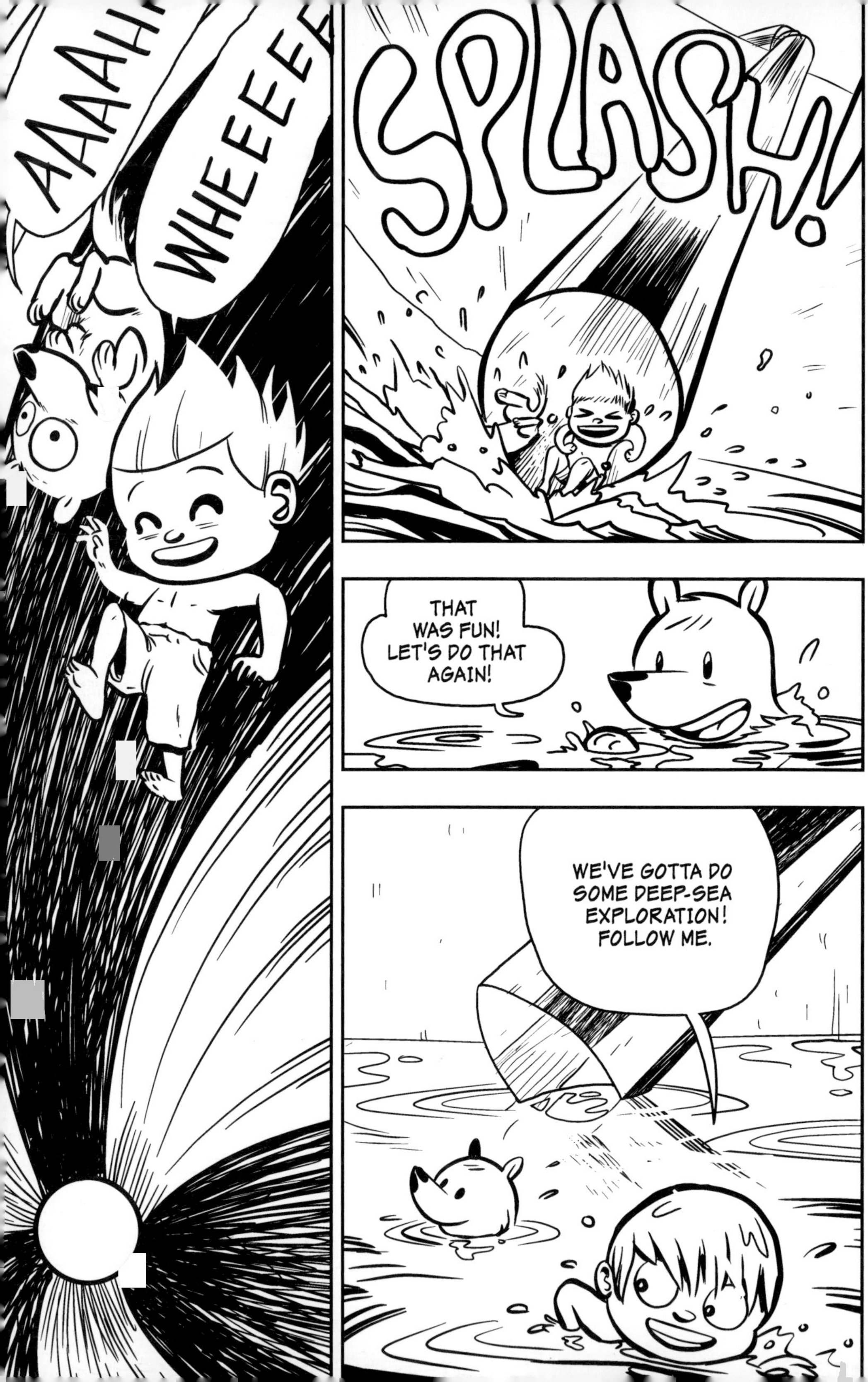
AAAAH!
WHEEEEE
SPLASH!
THAT WAS FUN! LET'S DO THAT AGAIN!
WE'VE GOTTA DO SOME DEEP-SEA EXPLORATION! FOLLOW ME.

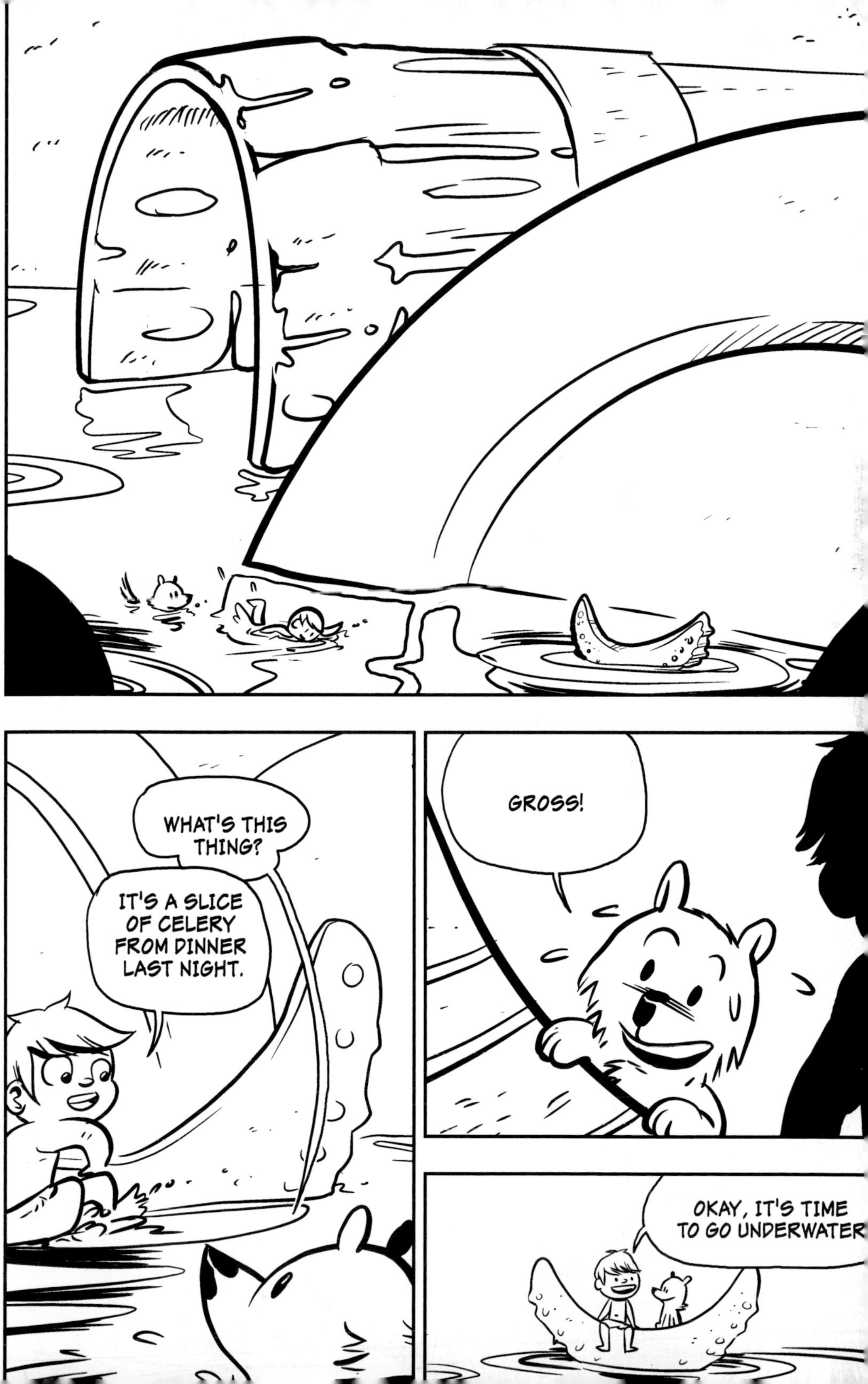
WHAT'S THIS THING?
IT'S A SLICE OF CELERY FROM DINNER LAST NIGHT.
GROSS!
OKAY, IT'S TIME TO GO UNDERWATER

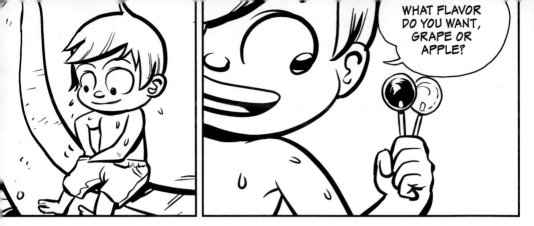

WHAT FLAVOR DO YOU WANT, GRAPE OR APPLE?

I'LL HAVE APPLE.

NOW, THESE LOLLIPOPS ARE MADE OUT OF CHEMICAL M, A SUBSTANCE I MADE THAT WILL ALLOW YOU TO HOLD YOUR BREATH FOR UP TO AN HOUR!

ACTUALLY, I'LL HAVE GRAPE. I'M IN KIND OF A GRAPEY MOOD.

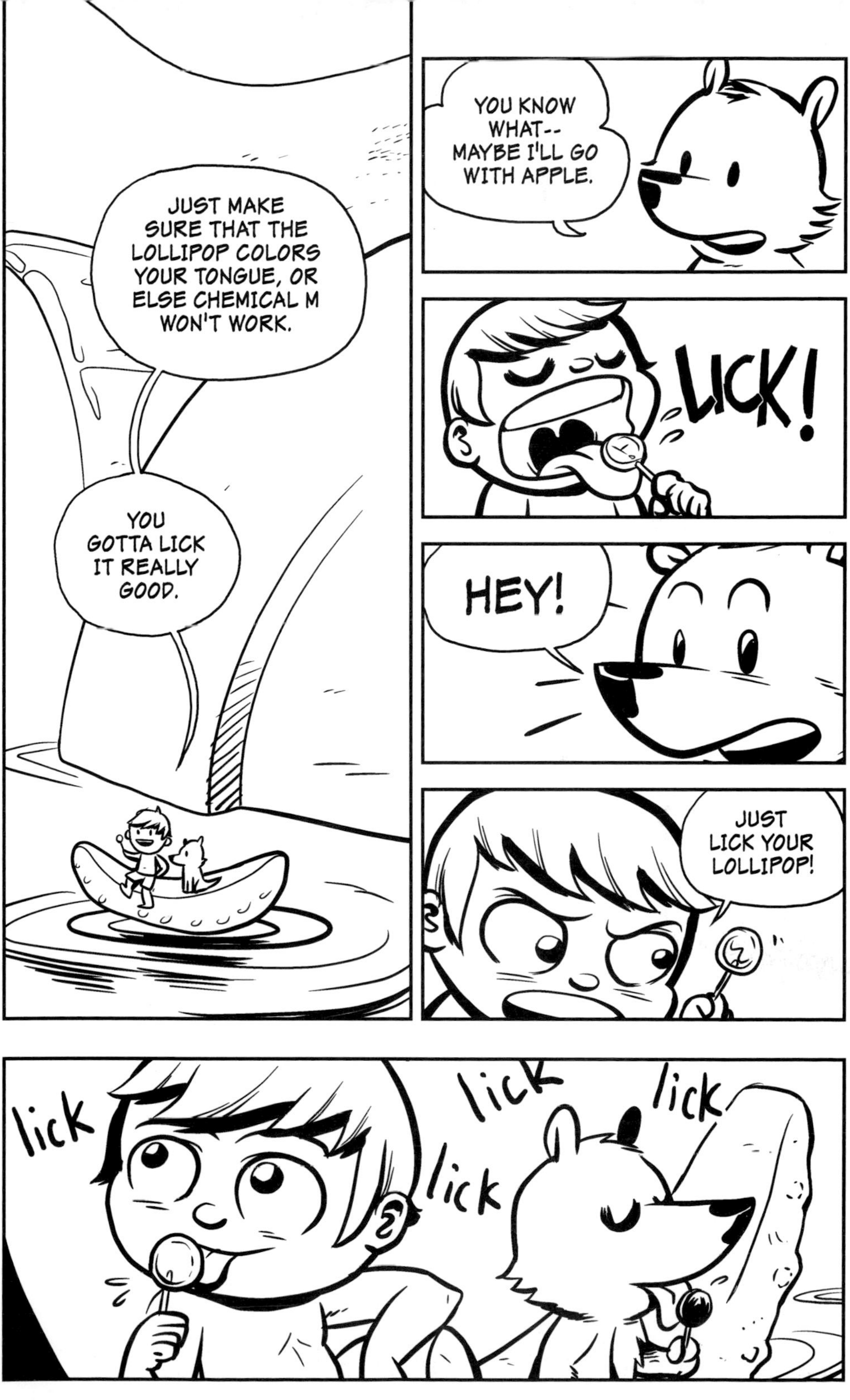
JUST MAKE SURE THAT THE LOLLIPOP COLORS YOUR TONGUE, OR ELSE CHEMICAL M WON'T WORK.
YOU GOTTA LICK IT REALLY GOOD.
YOU KNOW WHAT-- MAYBE I'LL GO WITH APPLE.
LICK!
HEY!
JUST LICK YOUR LOLLIPOP!
lick
lick
lick
lick

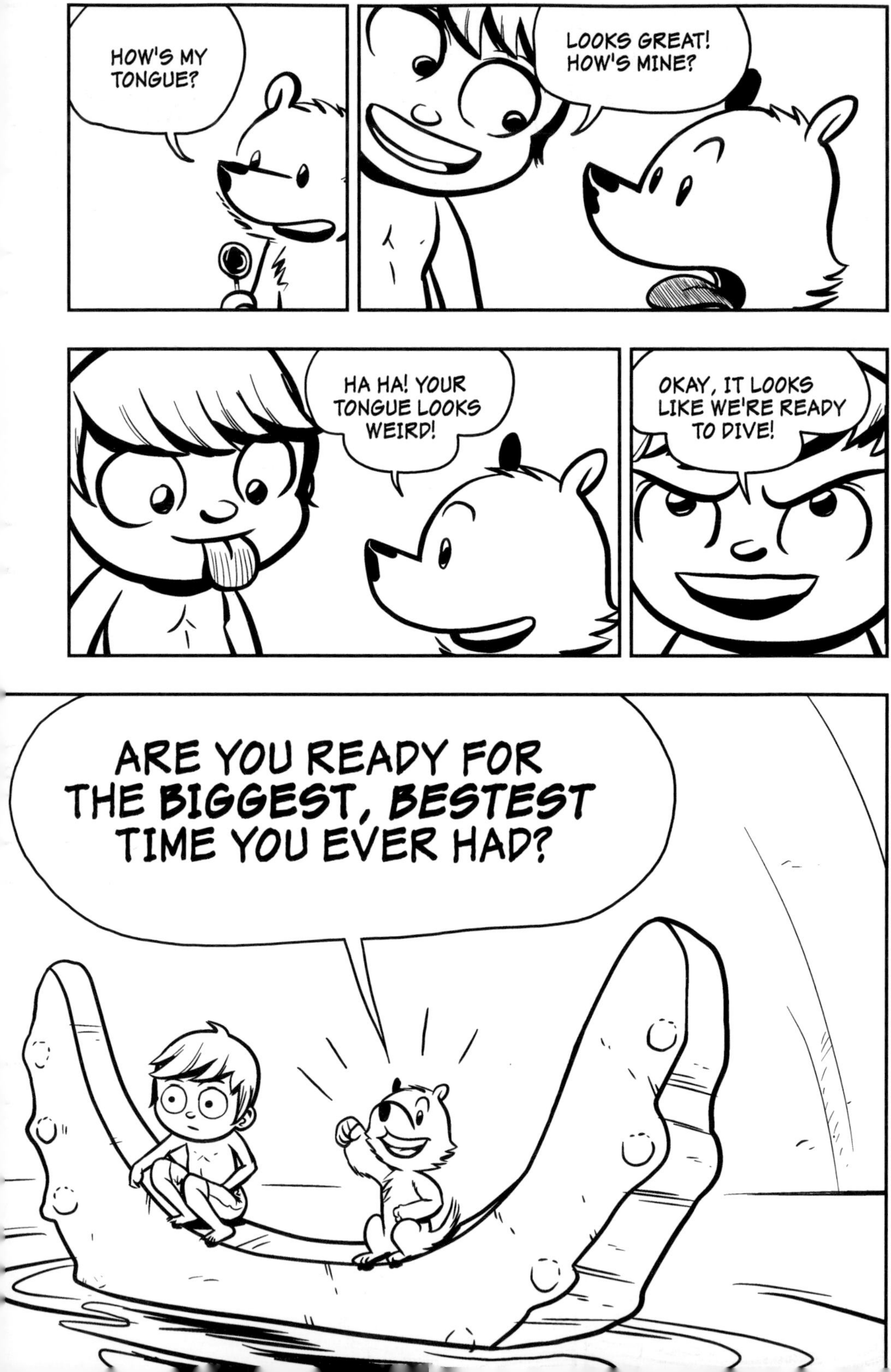
HOW'S MY TONGUE?
LOOKS GREAT! HOW'S MINE?
HA HA! YOUR TONGUE LOOKS WEIRD!
OKAY, IT LOOKS LIKE WE'RE READY TO DIVE!
ARE YOU READY FOR THE BIGGEST, BESTEST TIME YOU EVER HAD?

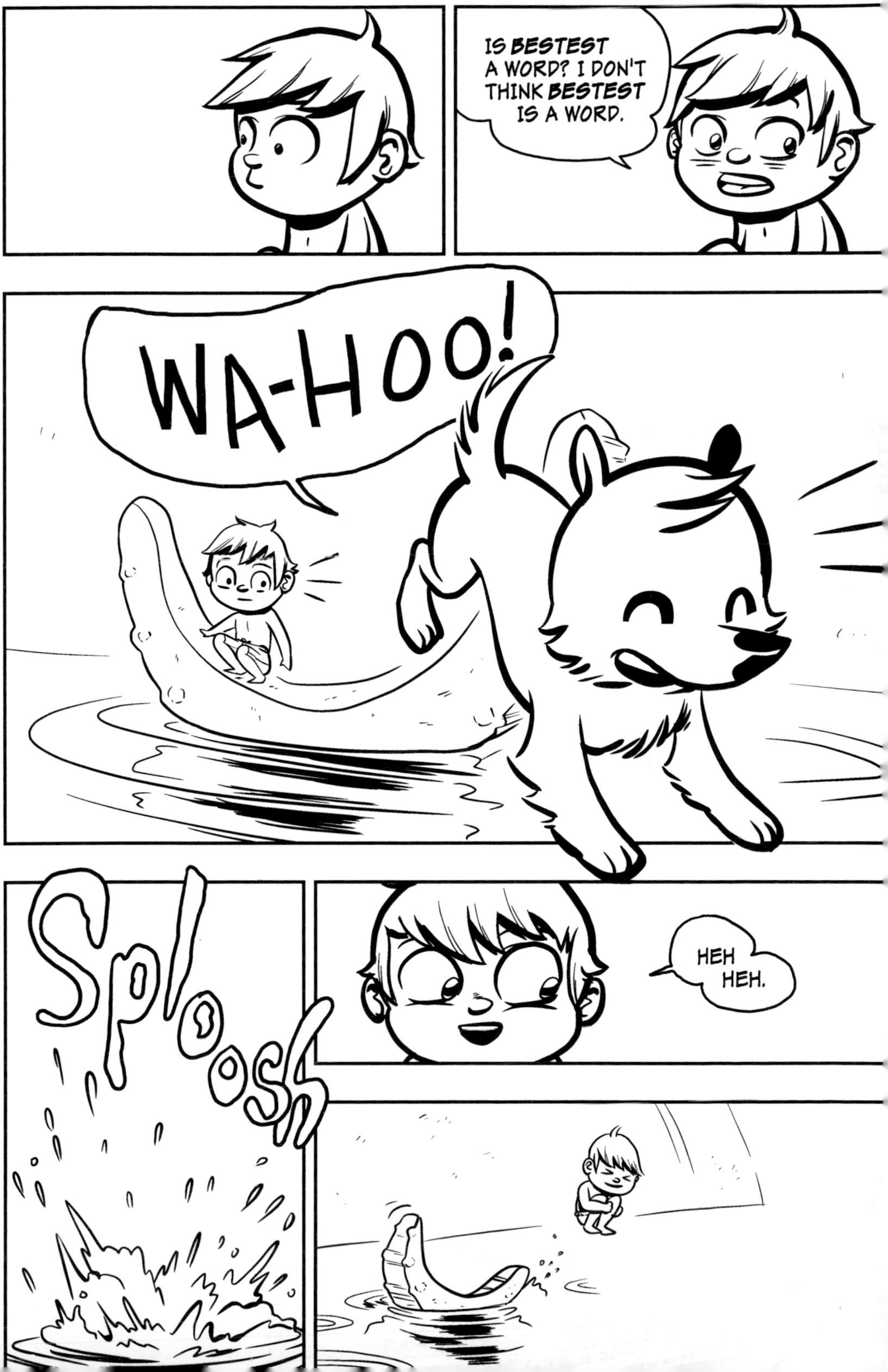
IS BESTEST A WORD? I DON'T THINK BESTEST IS A WORD.
WA-HOO!
SPLOOSH
HEH HEH.

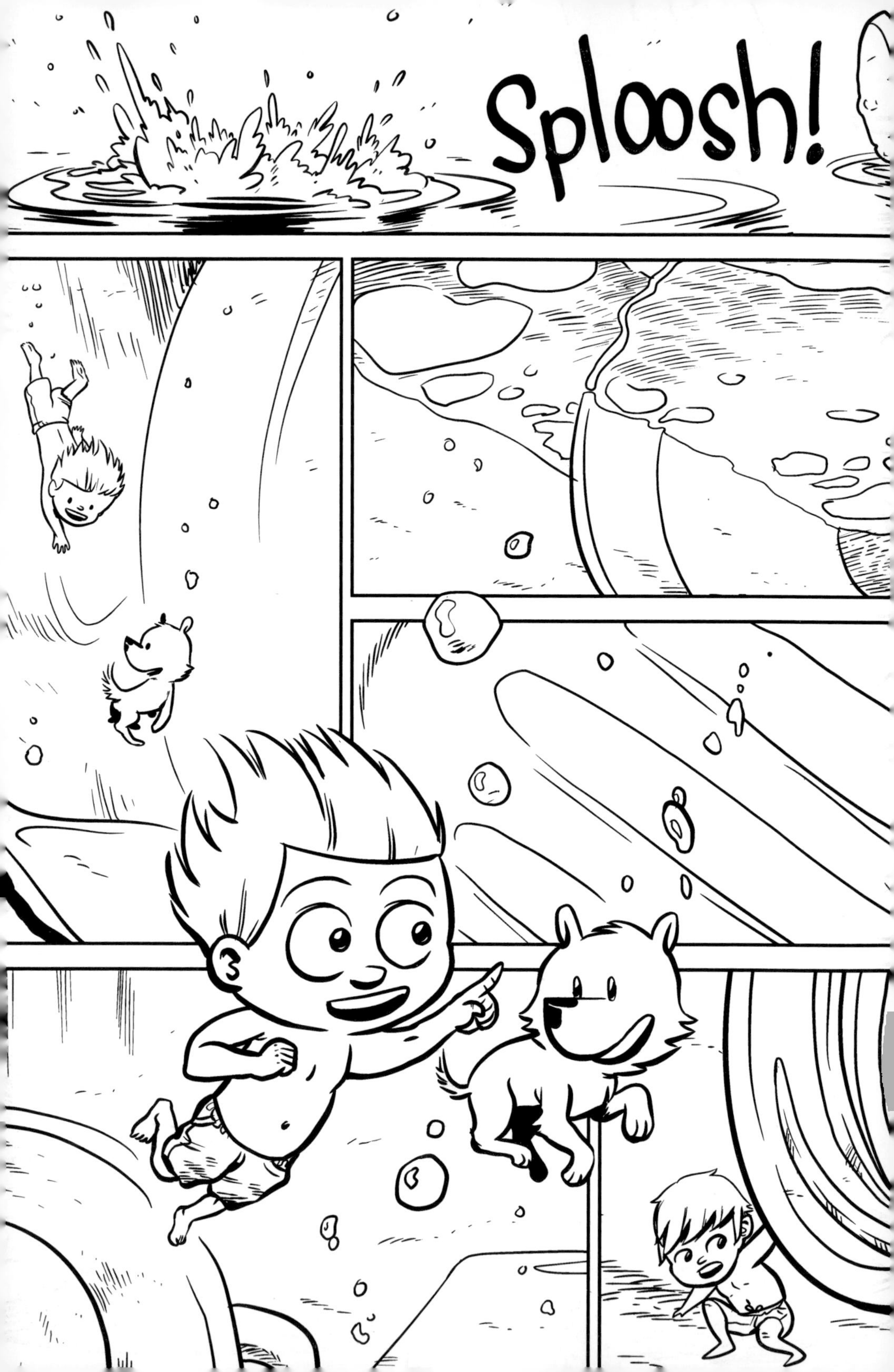
Sploosh!

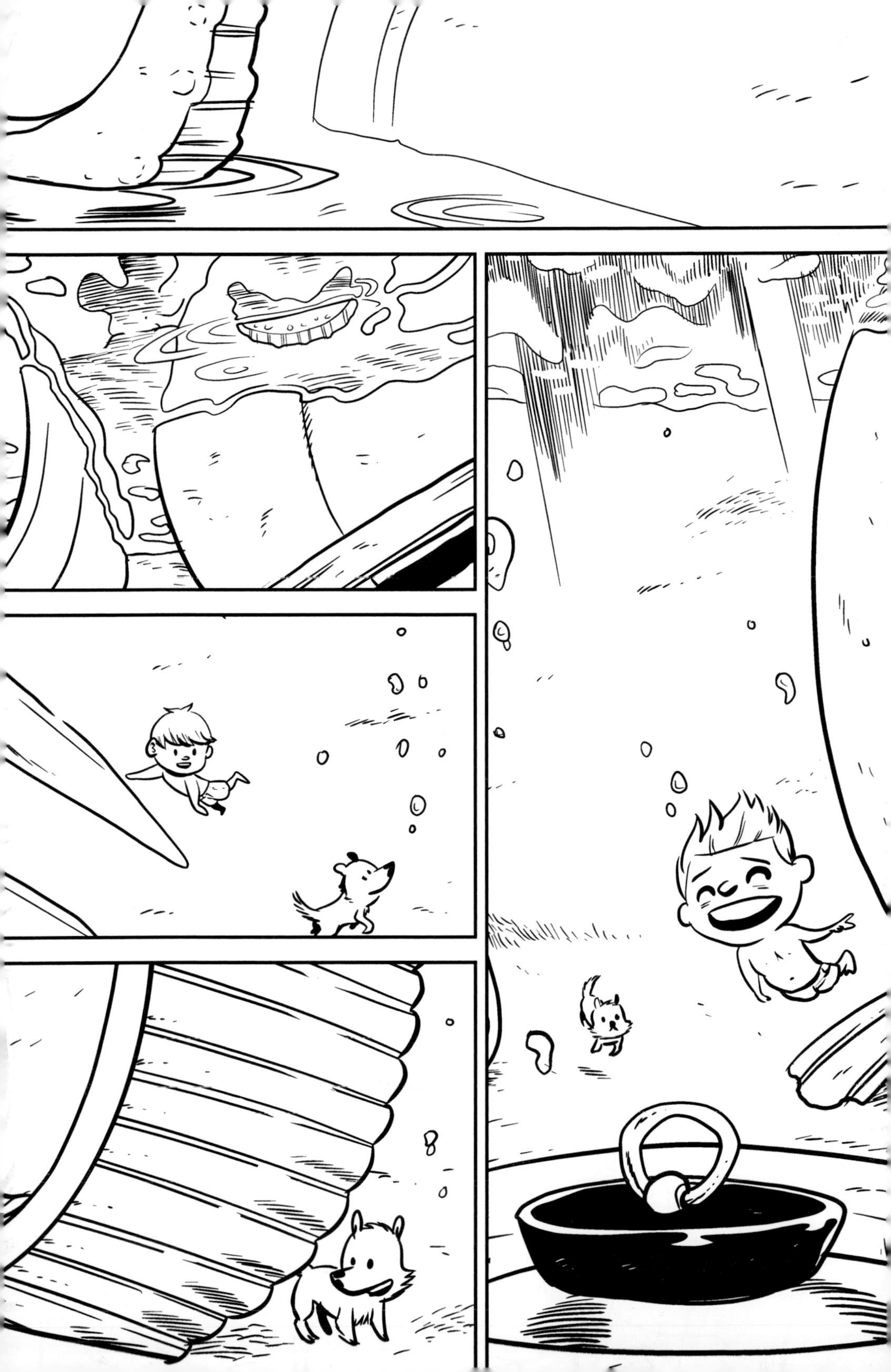

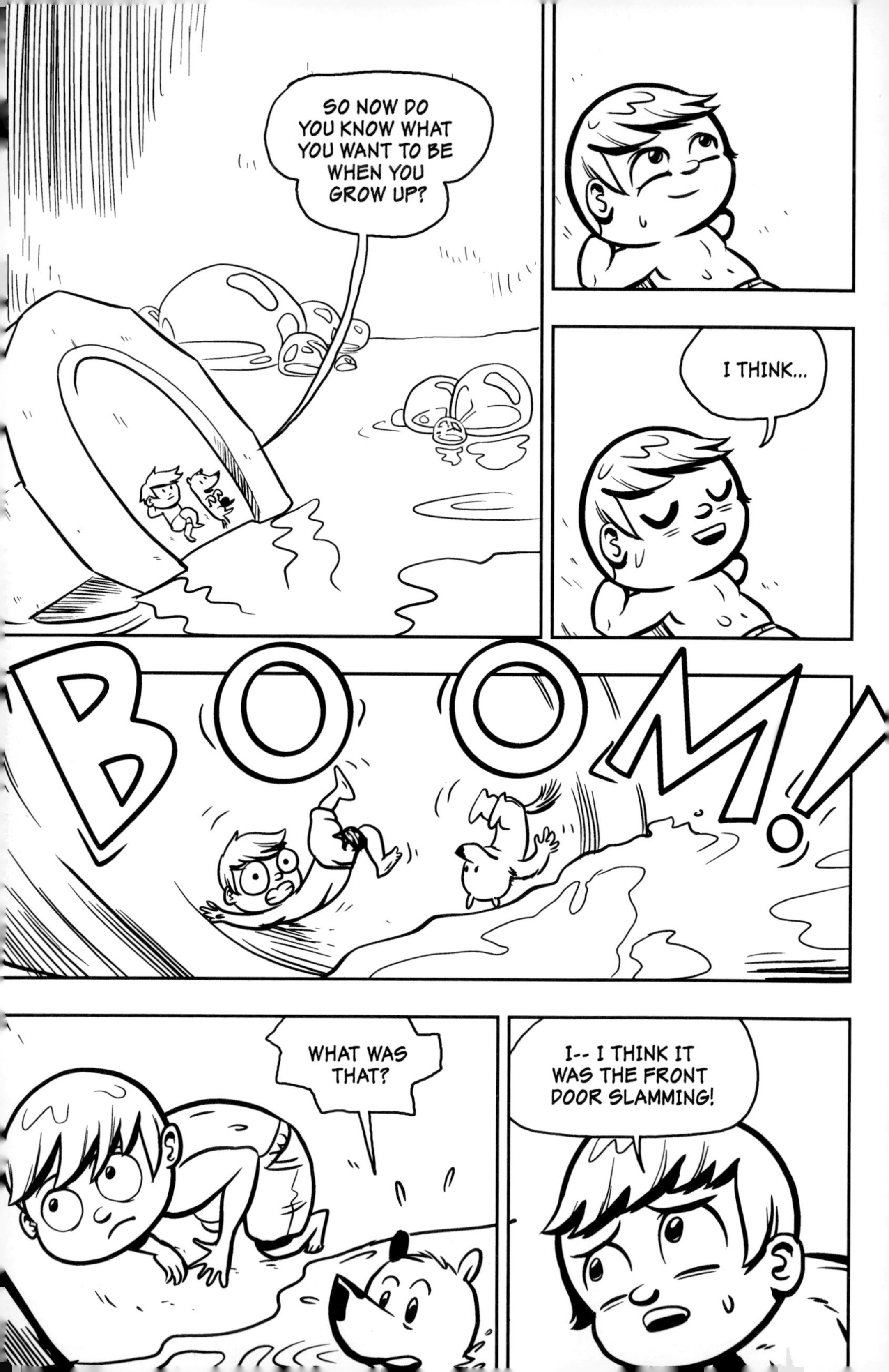
SO NOW DO YOU KNOW WHAT YOU WANT TO BE WHEN YOU GROW UP?
I THINK...
BOOM!!
WHAT WAS THAT?
I-- I THINK IT WAS THE FRONT DOOR SLAMMING!

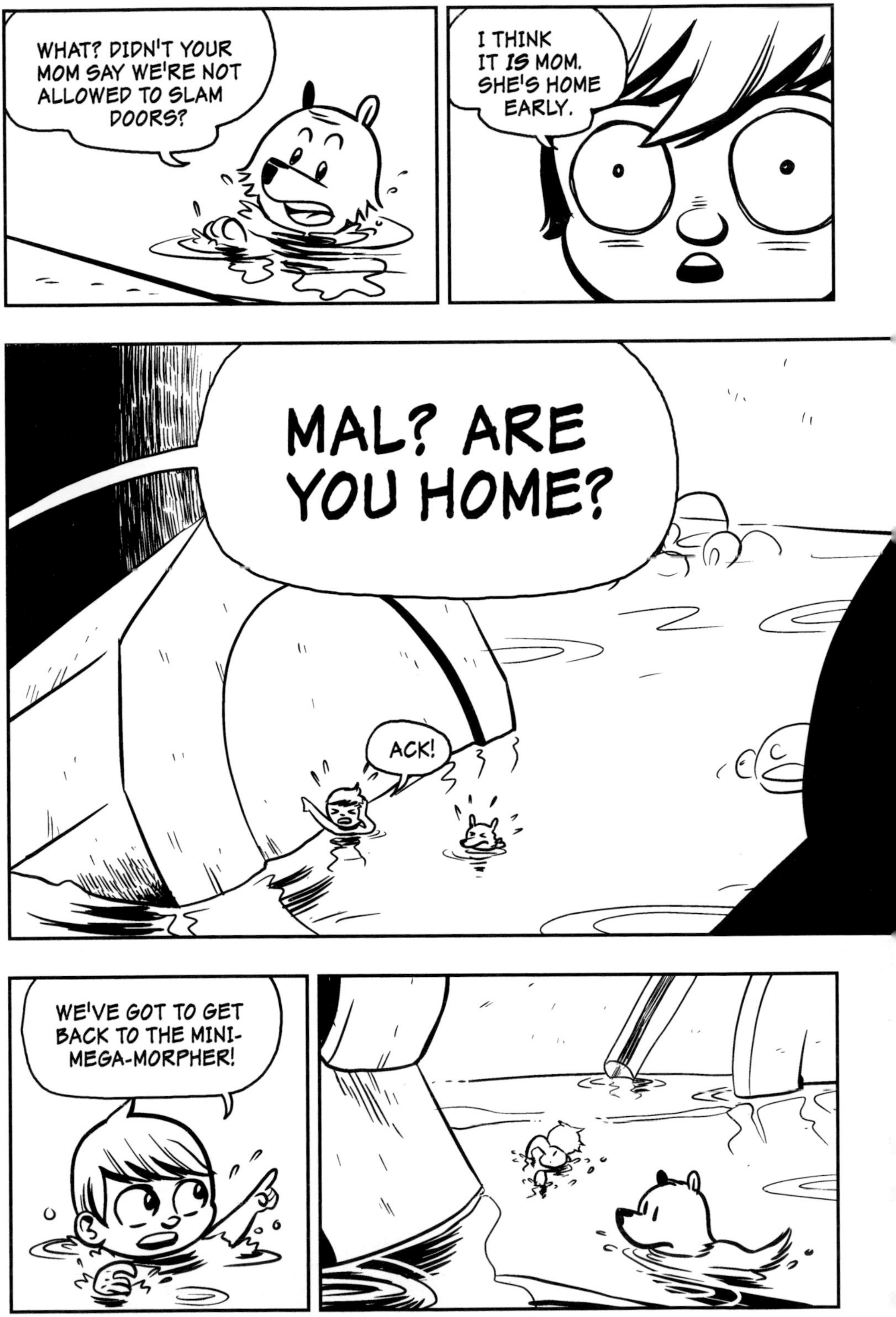
WHAT? DIDN'T YOUR MOM SAY WE'RE NOT ALLOWED TO SLAM DOORS?
I THINK IT IS MOM. SHE'S HOME EARLY.
MAL? ARE YOU HOME?
ACK!
WE'VE GOT TO GET BACK TO THE MINI-MEGA-MORPHER!

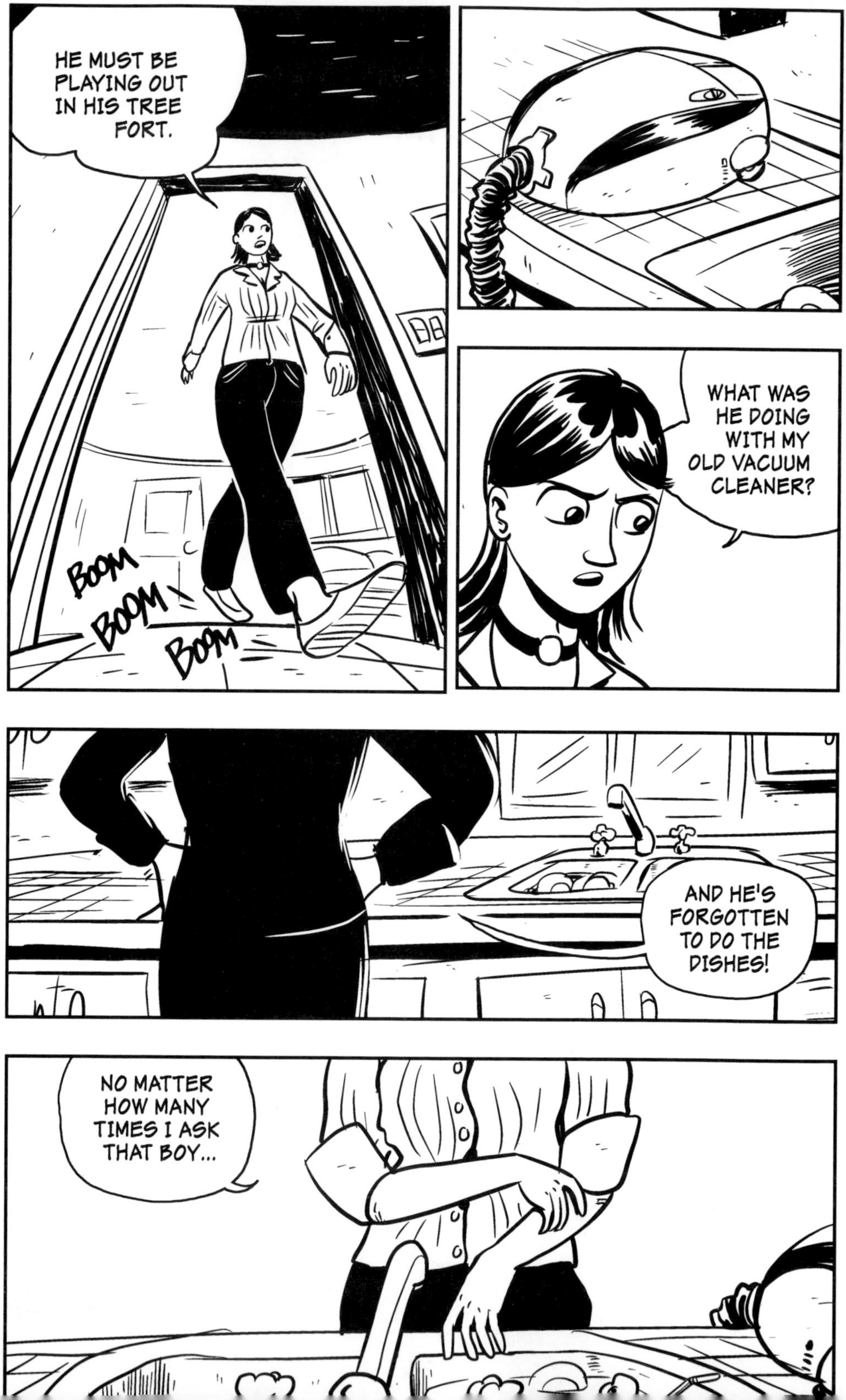
HE MUST BE PLAYING OUT IN HIS TREE FORT.
BOOM BOOM BOOM
WHAT WAS HE DOING WITH MY OLD VACUUM CLEANER?
AND HE'S FORGOTTEN TO DO THE DISHES!
NO MATTER HOW MANY TIMES I ASK THAT BOY...

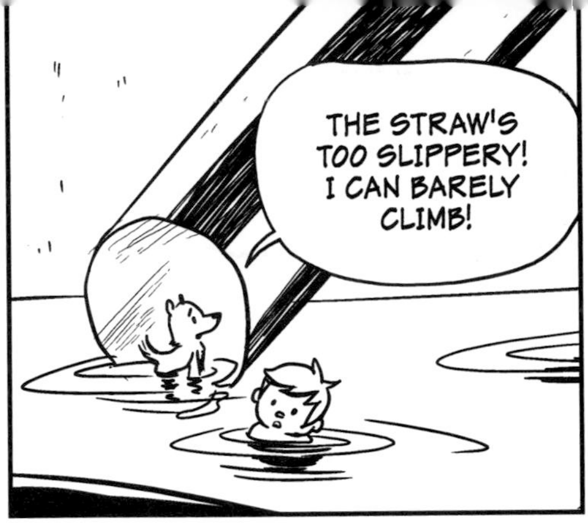
THE STRAW'S TOO SLIPPERY! I CAN BARELY CLIMB!

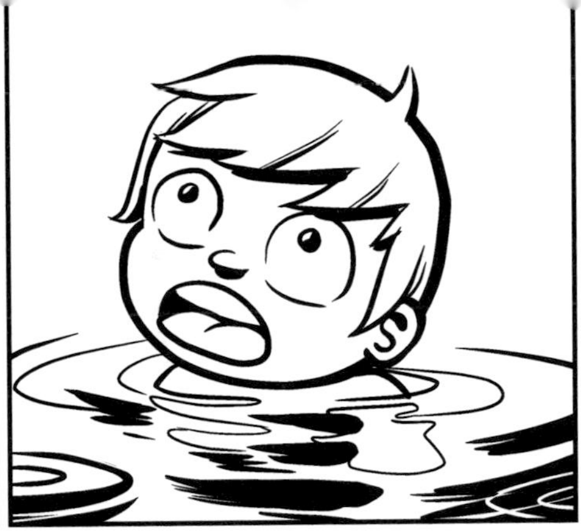

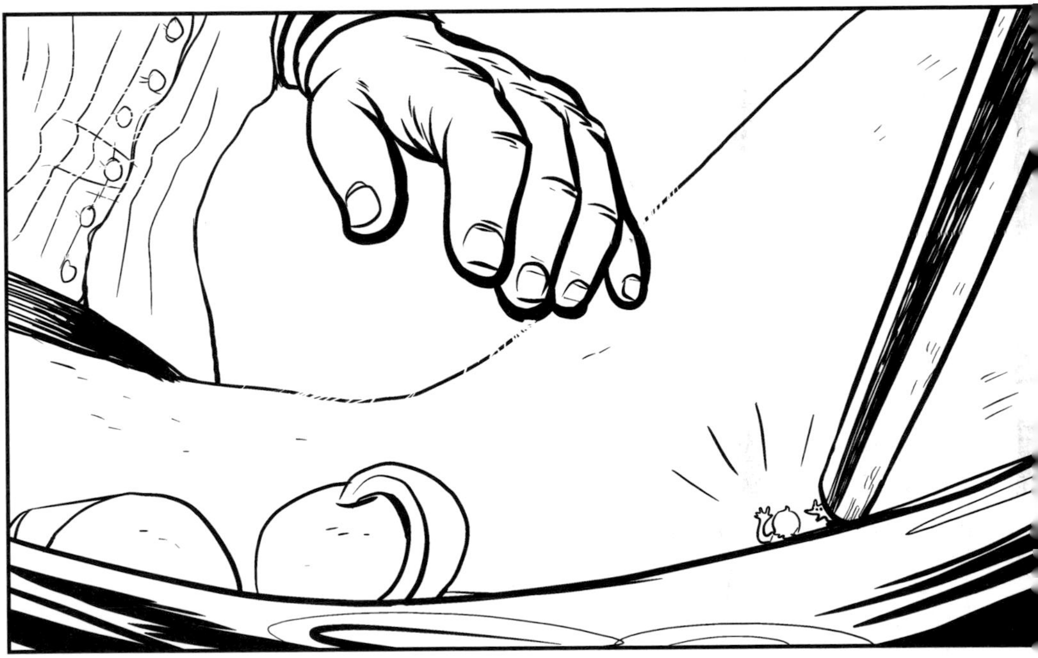

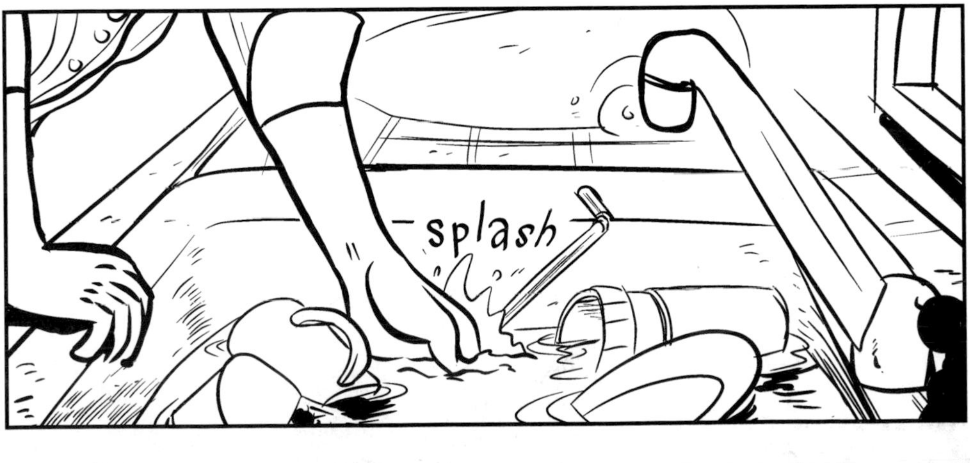
splash

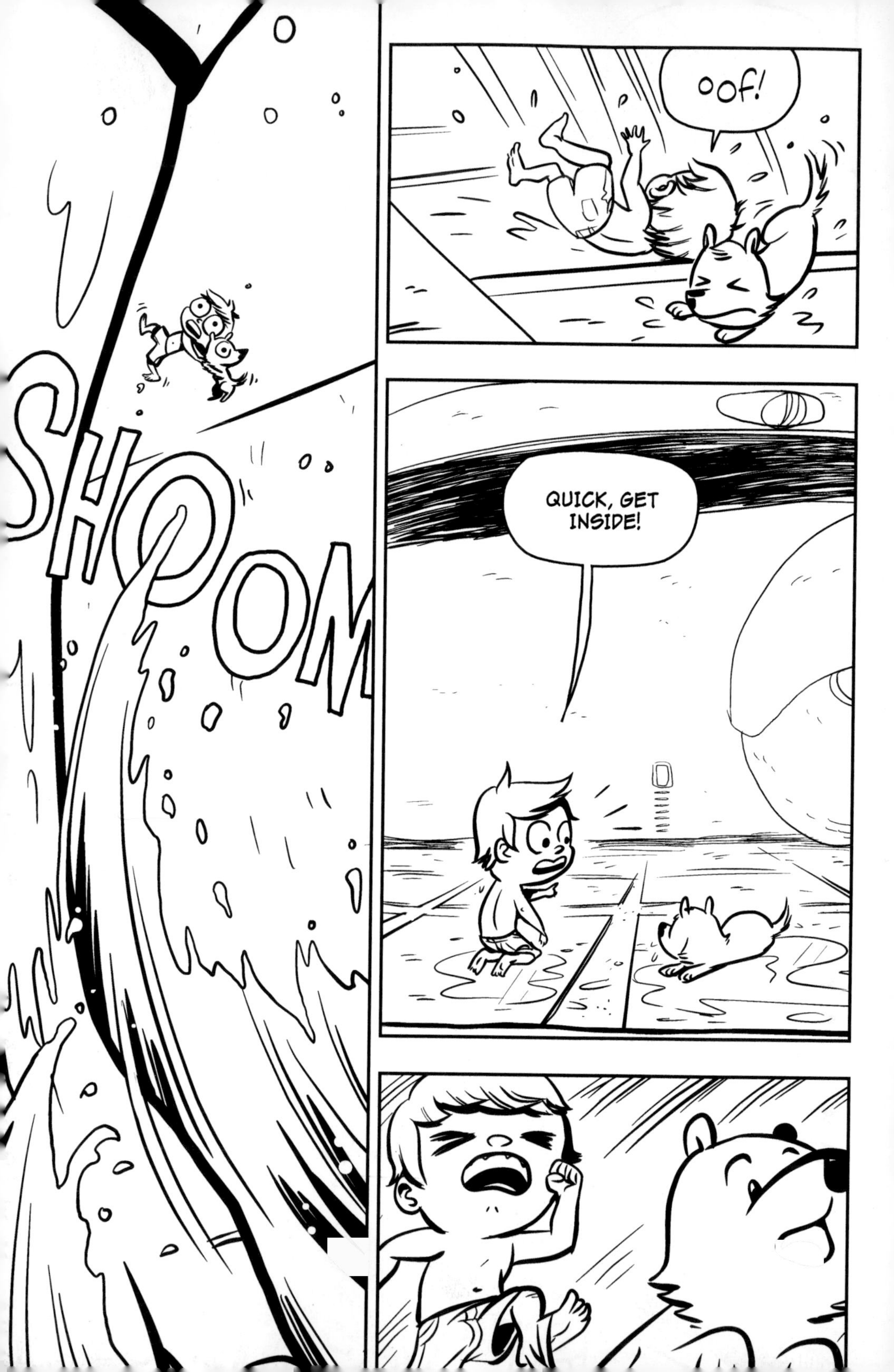
SHOOOM
OOF!
QUICK, GET INSIDE!

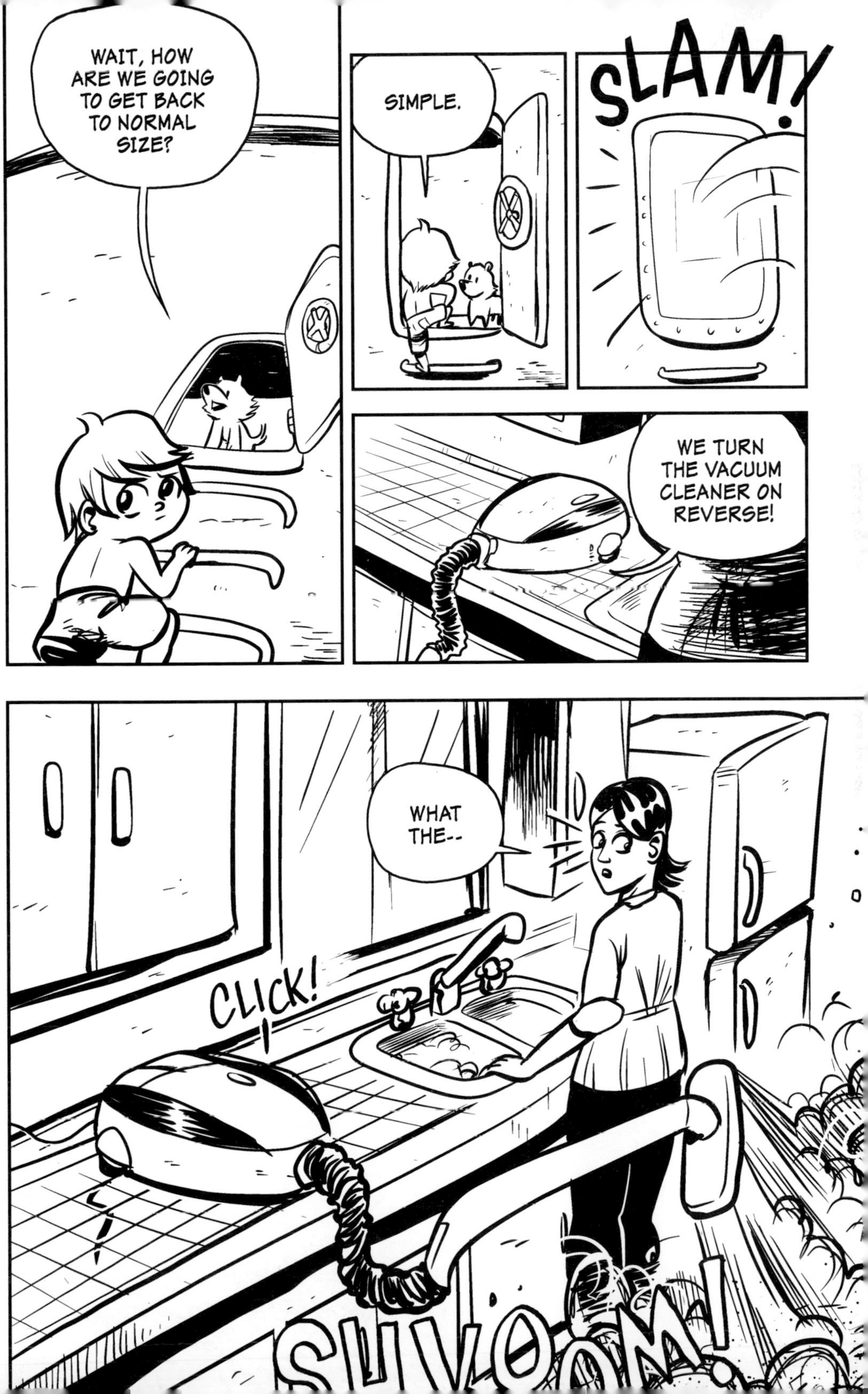
WAIT, HOW ARE WE GOING TO GET BACK TO NORMAL SIZE?
SIMPLE.
SLAM!
WE TURN THE VACUUM CLEANER ON REVERSE!
WHAT THE--
CLICK!
SHVOOM!

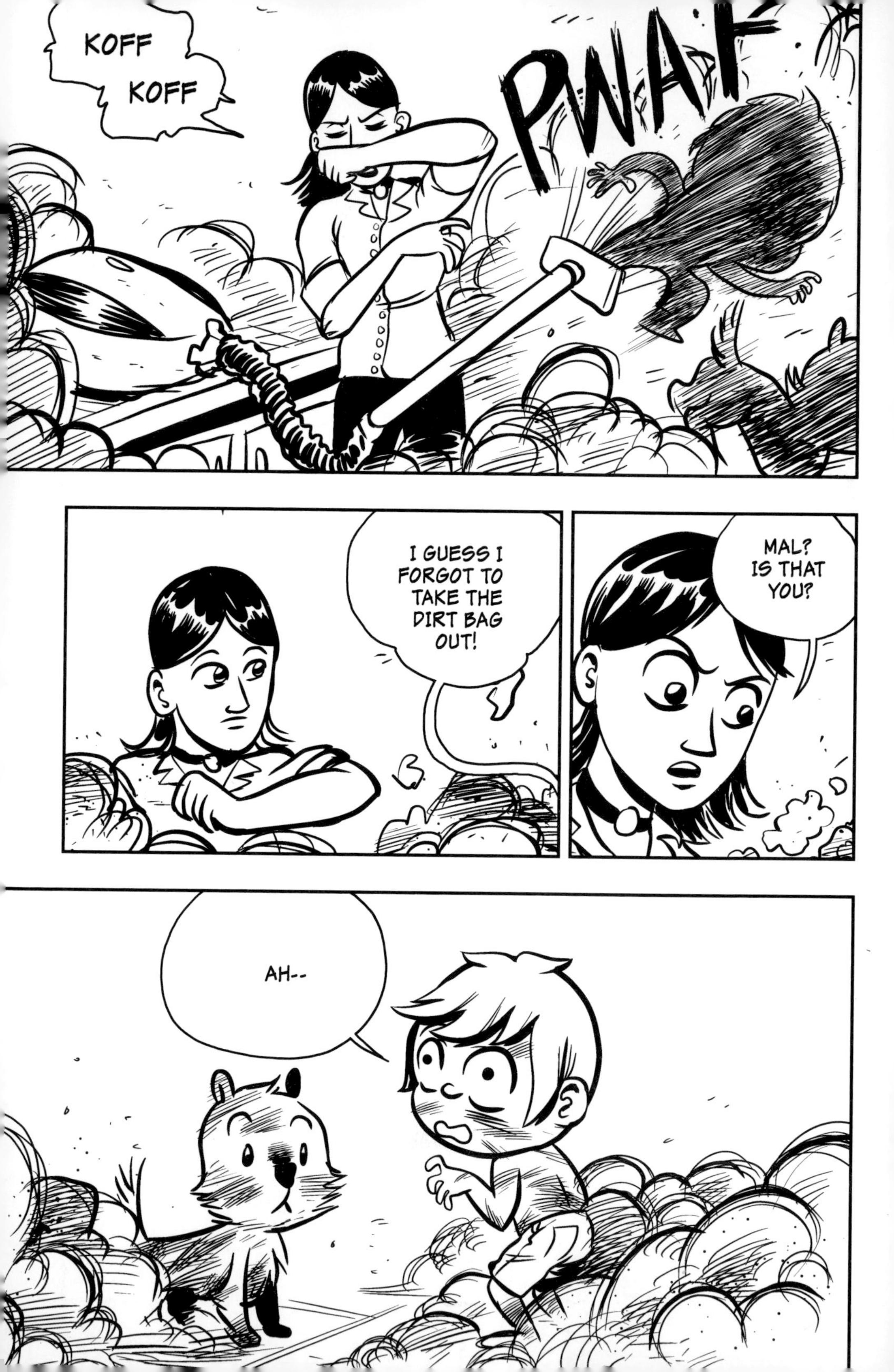
KOFF
KOFF
PWAF
I GUESS I FORGOT TO TAKE THE DIRT BAG OUT!
MAL? IS THAT YOU?
AH--

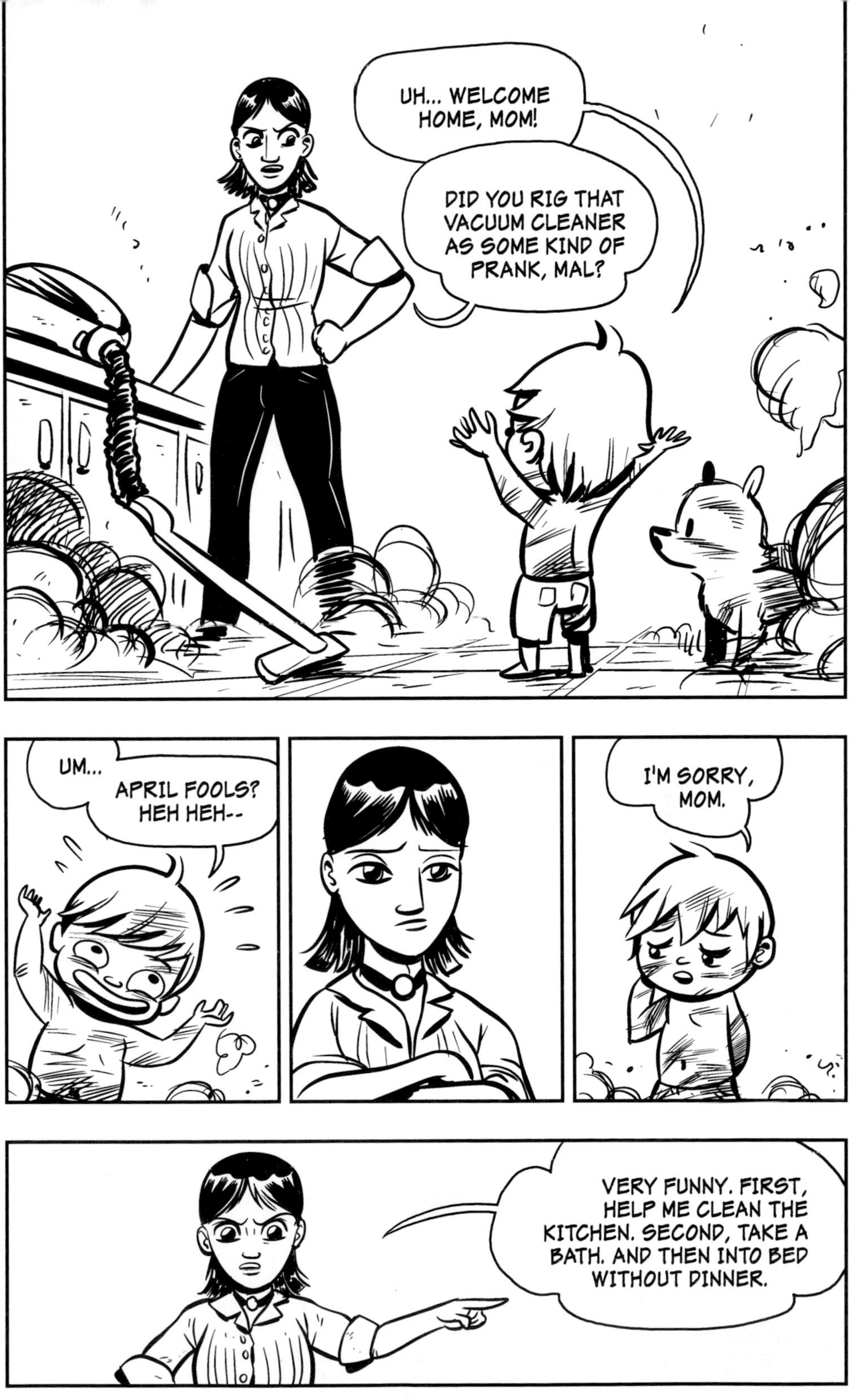
UH... WELCOME HOME, MOM!
DID YOU RIG THAT VACUUM CLEANER AS SOME KIND OF PRANK, MAL?
UM...
APRIL FOOLS? HEH HEH--
I'M SORRY, MOM.
VERY FUNNY. FIRST, HELP ME CLEAN THE KITCHEN. SECOND, TAKE A BATH. AND THEN INTO BED WITHOUT DINNER.

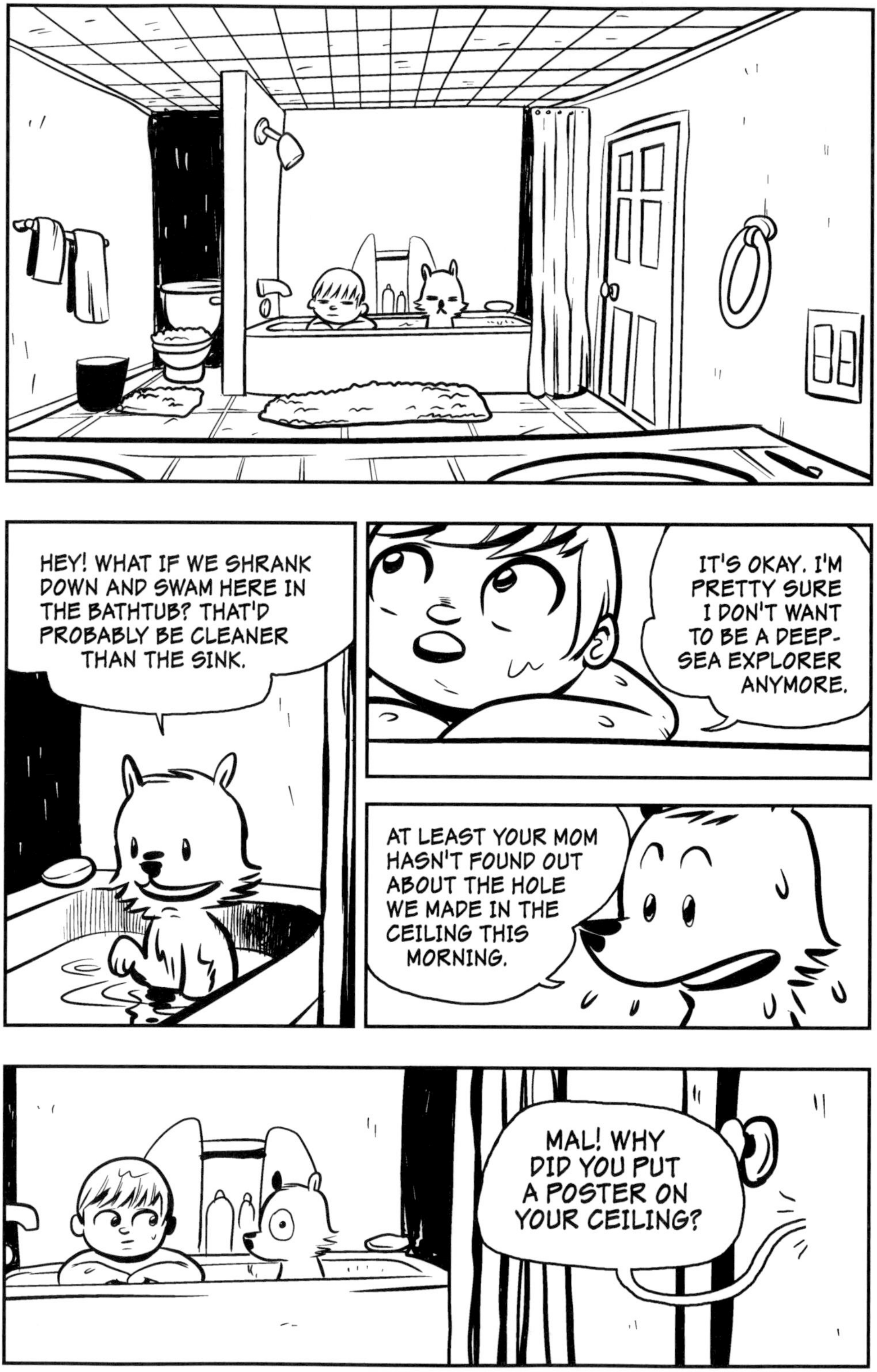
HEY! WHAT IF WE SHRANK DOWN AND SWAM HERE IN THE BATHTUB? THAT'D PROBABLY BE CLEANER THAN THE SINK.
IT'S OKAY. I'M PRETTY SURE I DON'T WANT TO BE A DEEP-SEA EXPLORER ANYMORE.
AT LEAST YOUR MOM HASN'T FOUND OUT ABOUT THE HOLE WE MADE IN THE CEILING THIS MORNING.
MAL! WHY DID YOU PUT A POSTER ON YOUR CEILING?

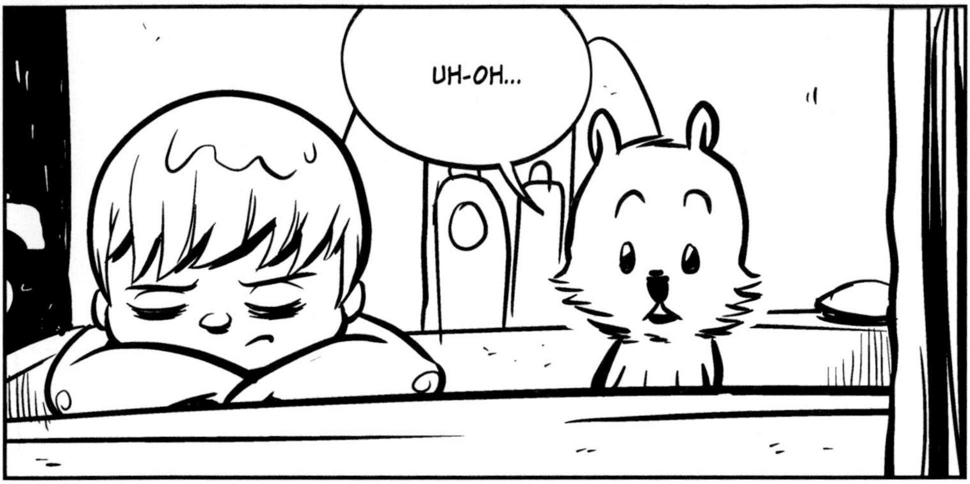
UH-OH...

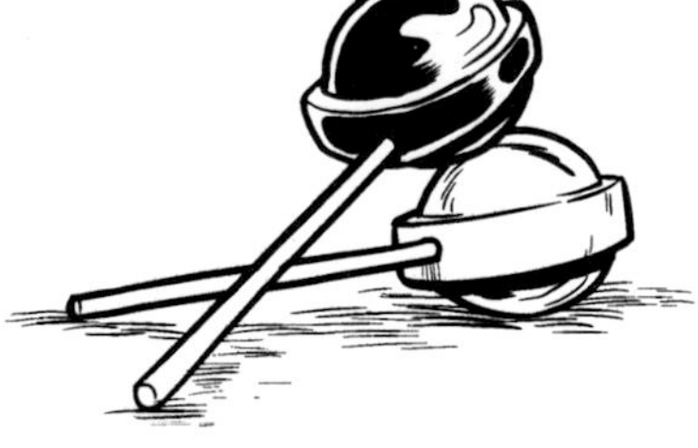

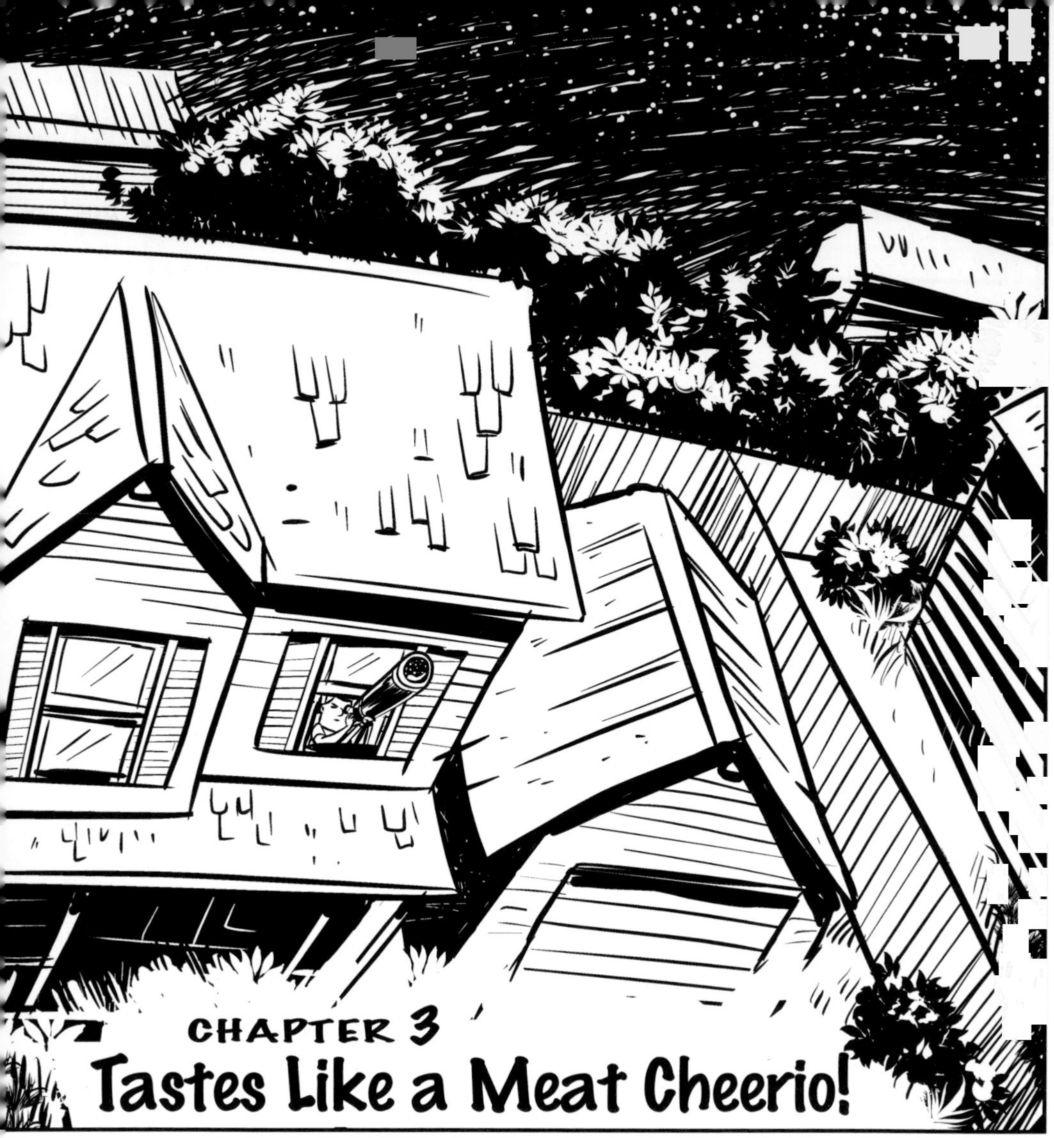
CHAPTER 3
Tastes Like a Meat Cheerio!

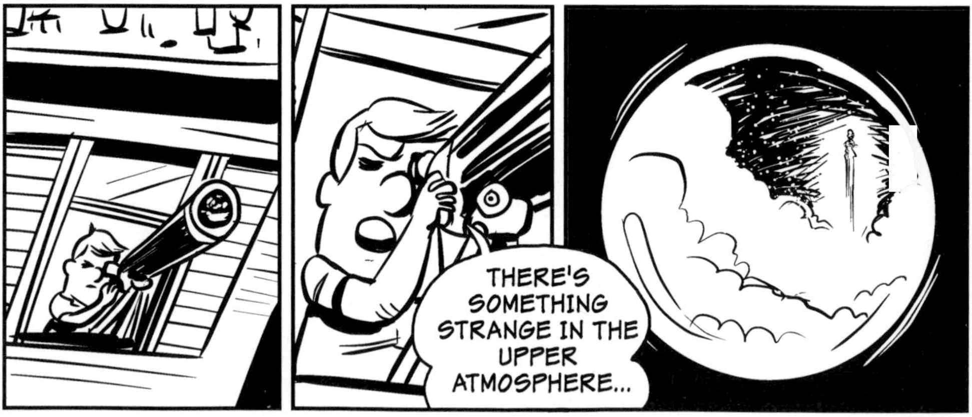
THERE'S SOMETHING STRANGE IN THE UPPER ATMOSPHERE...

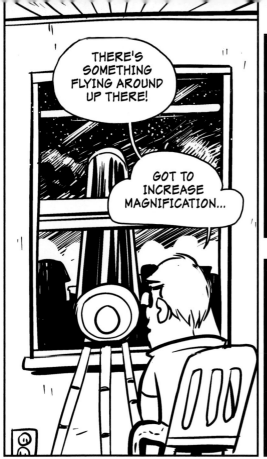

THERE'S SOMETHING FLYING AROUND UP THERE!

GOT TO INCREASE MAGNIFICATION...

IS THAT A--

ALIEN!

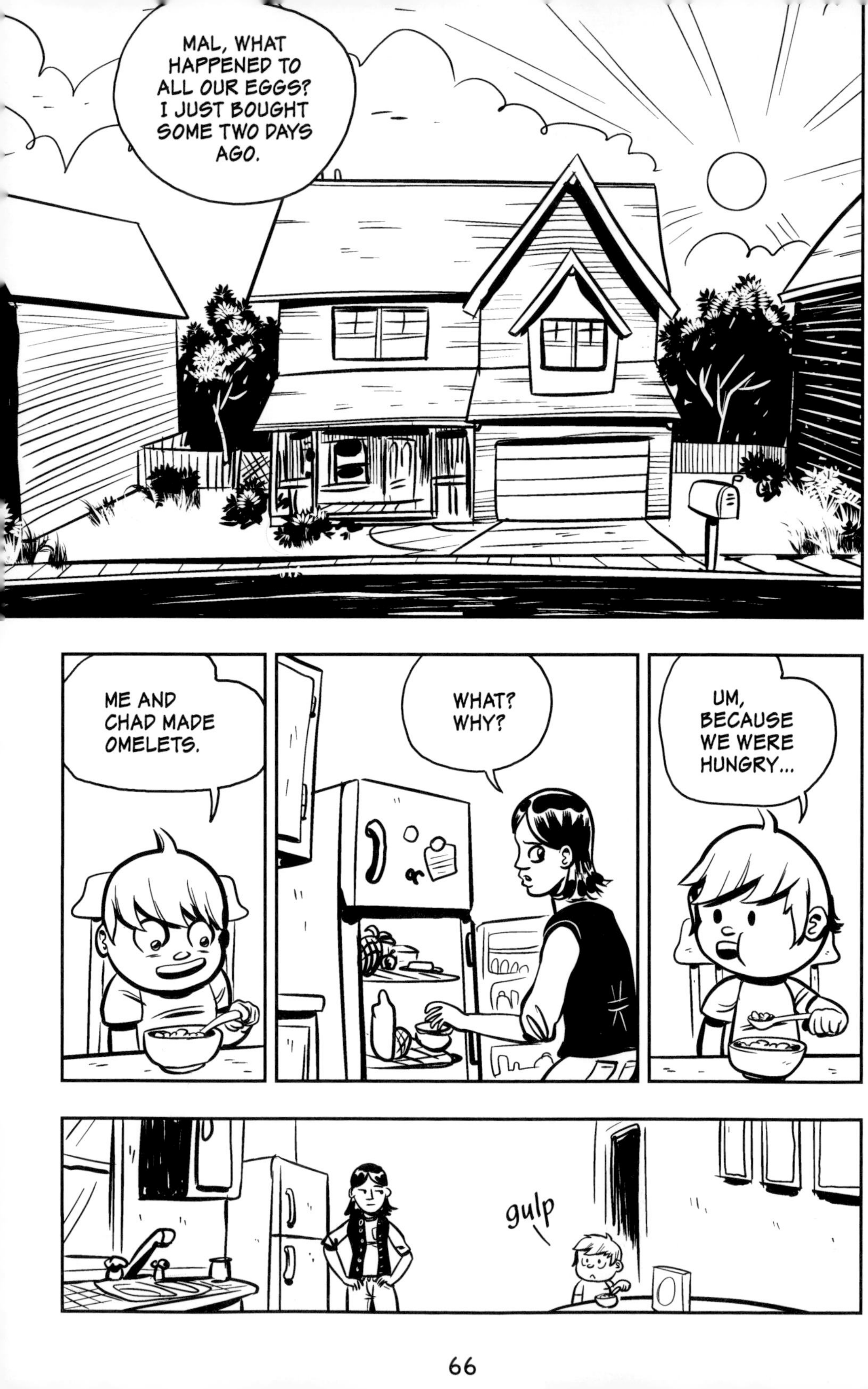
MAL, WHAT HAPPENED TO ALL OUR EGGS? I JUST BOUGHT SOME TWO DAYS AGO.
ME AND CHAD MADE OMELETS.
WHAT? WHY?
UM, BECAUSE WE WERE HUNGRY...
gulp

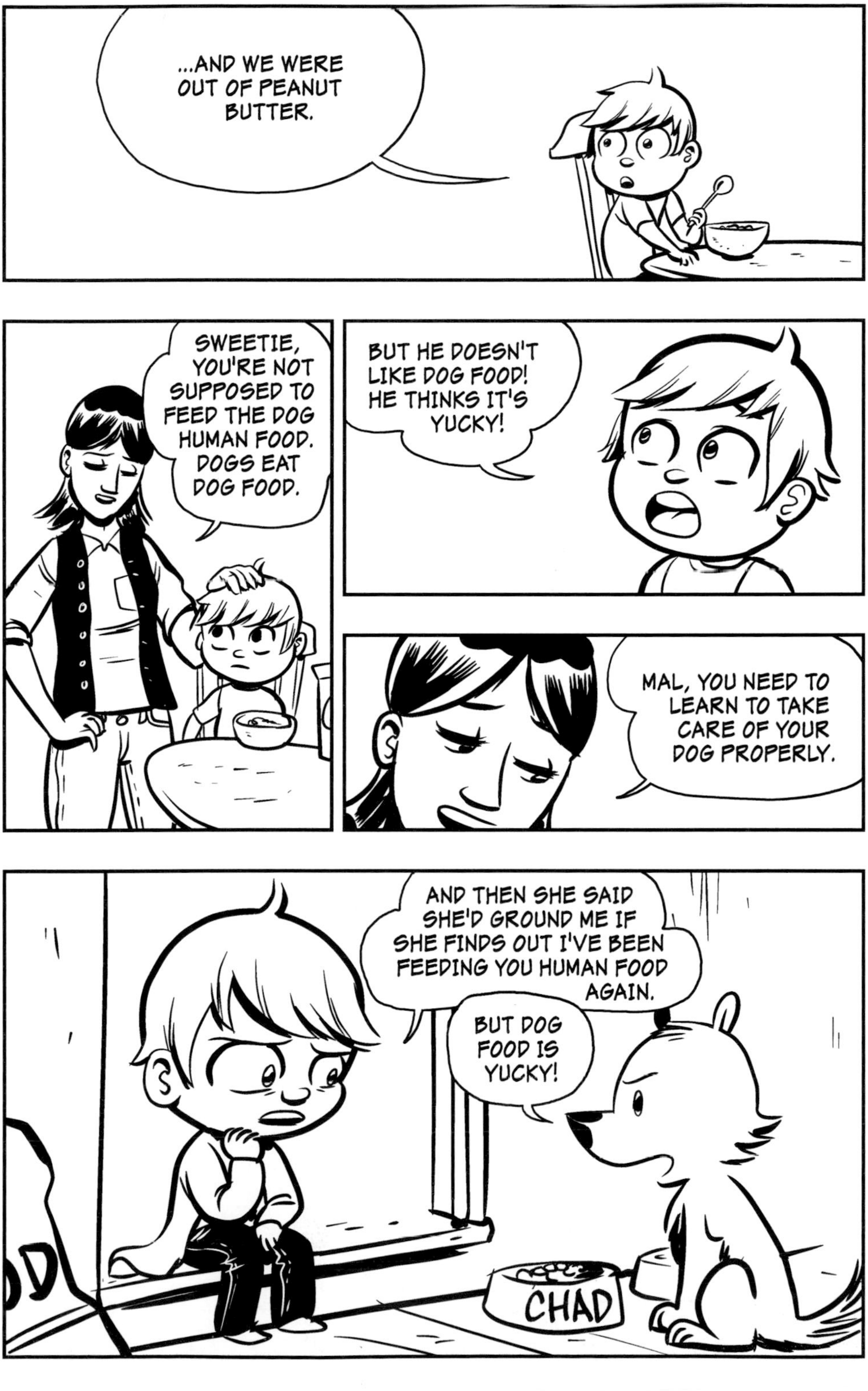
...AND WE WERE OUT OF PEANUT BUTTER.
SWEETIE, YOU'RE NOT SUPPOSED TO FEED THE DOG HUMAN FOOD. DOGS EAT DOG FOOD.
BUT HE DOESN'T LIKE DOG FOOD! HE THINKS IT'S YUCKY!
MAL, YOU NEED TO LEARN TO TAKE CARE OF YOUR DOG PROPERLY.
AND THEN SHE SAID SHE'D GROUND ME IF SHE FINDS OUT I'VE BEEN FEEDING YOU HUMAN FOOD AGAIN.
BUT DOG FOOD IS YUCKY!
CHAD

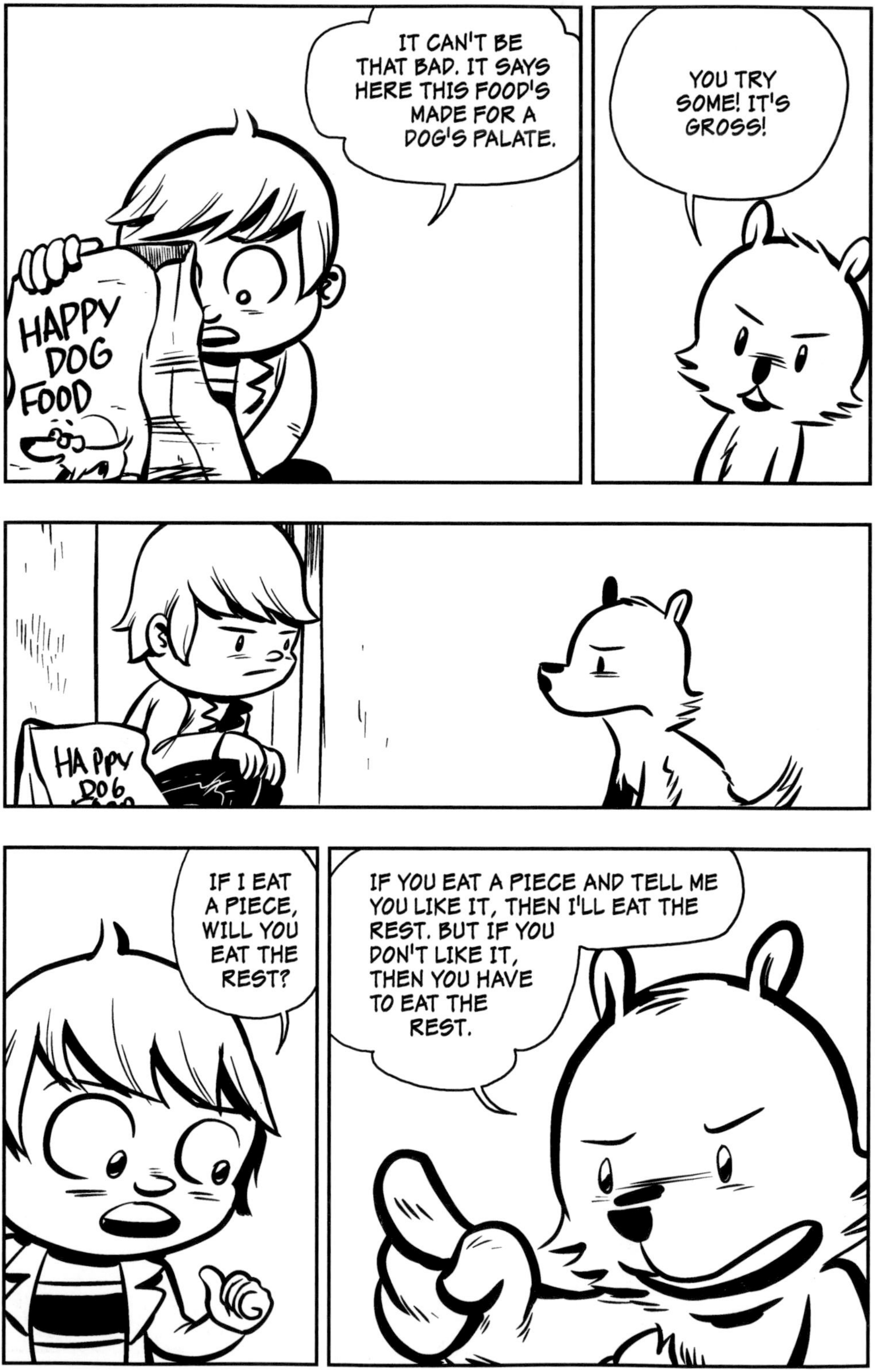
HAPPY DOG FOOD
IT CAN'T BE THAT BAD. IT SAYS HERE THIS FOOD'S MADE FOR A DOG'S PALATE.
YOU TRY SOME! IT'S GROSS!
HAPPY DOG
IF I EAT A PIECE, WILL YOU EAT THE REST?
IF YOU EAT A PIECE AND TELL ME YOU LIKE IT, THEN I'LL EAT THE REST. BUT IF YOU DON'T LIKE IT, THEN YOU HAVE TO EAT THE REST.

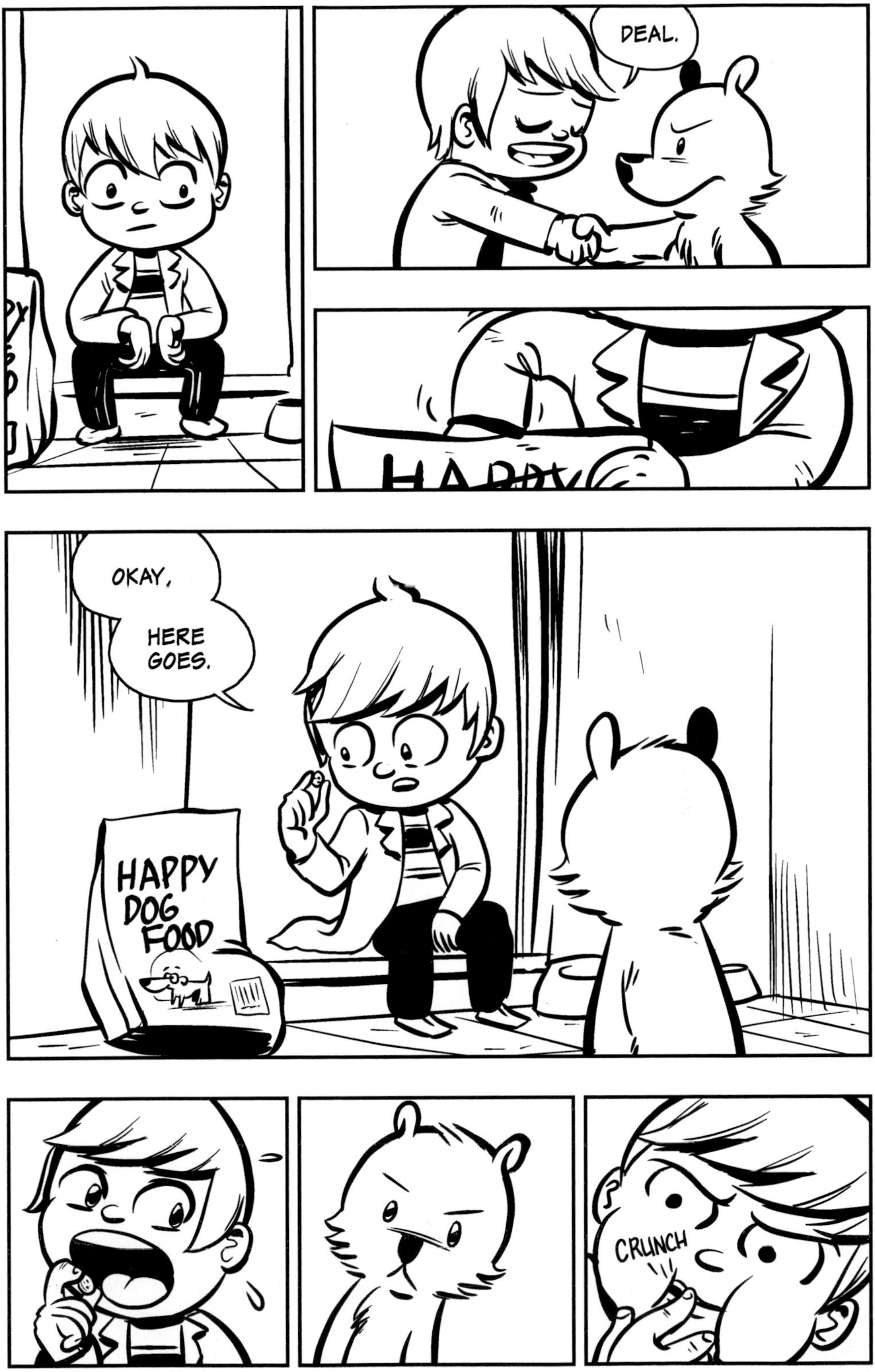
DEAL.
HAPPY
OKAY,
HERE GOES.
HAPPY DOG FOOD
CRUNCH

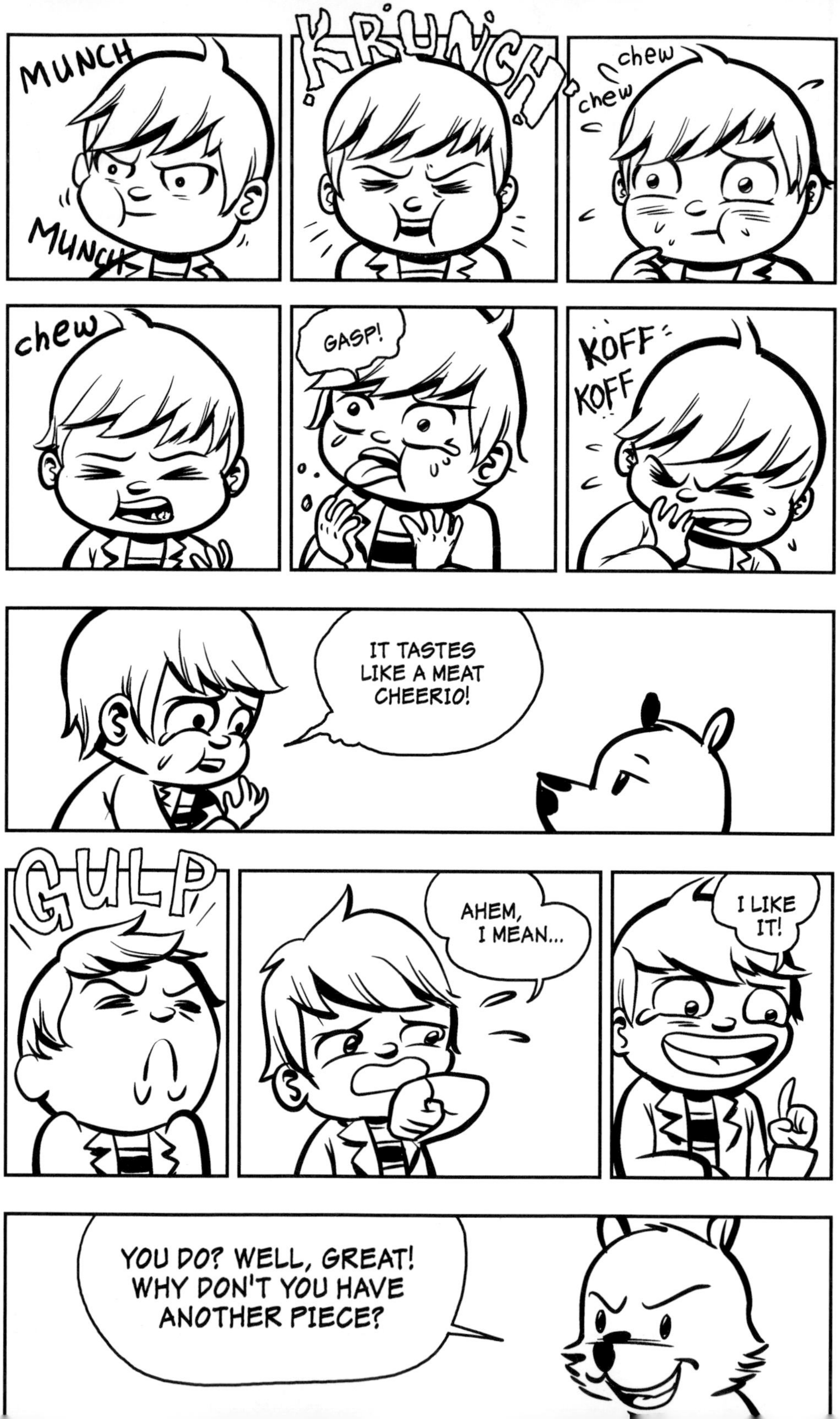
MUNCH
MUNCH
KRUNCH
chew
chew
chew
GASP!
KOFF
KOFF
IT TASTES LIKE A MEAT CHEERIO!
GULP
AHEM, I MEAN...
I LIKE IT!
YOU DO? WELL, GREAT! WHY DON'T YOU HAVE ANOTHER PIECE?

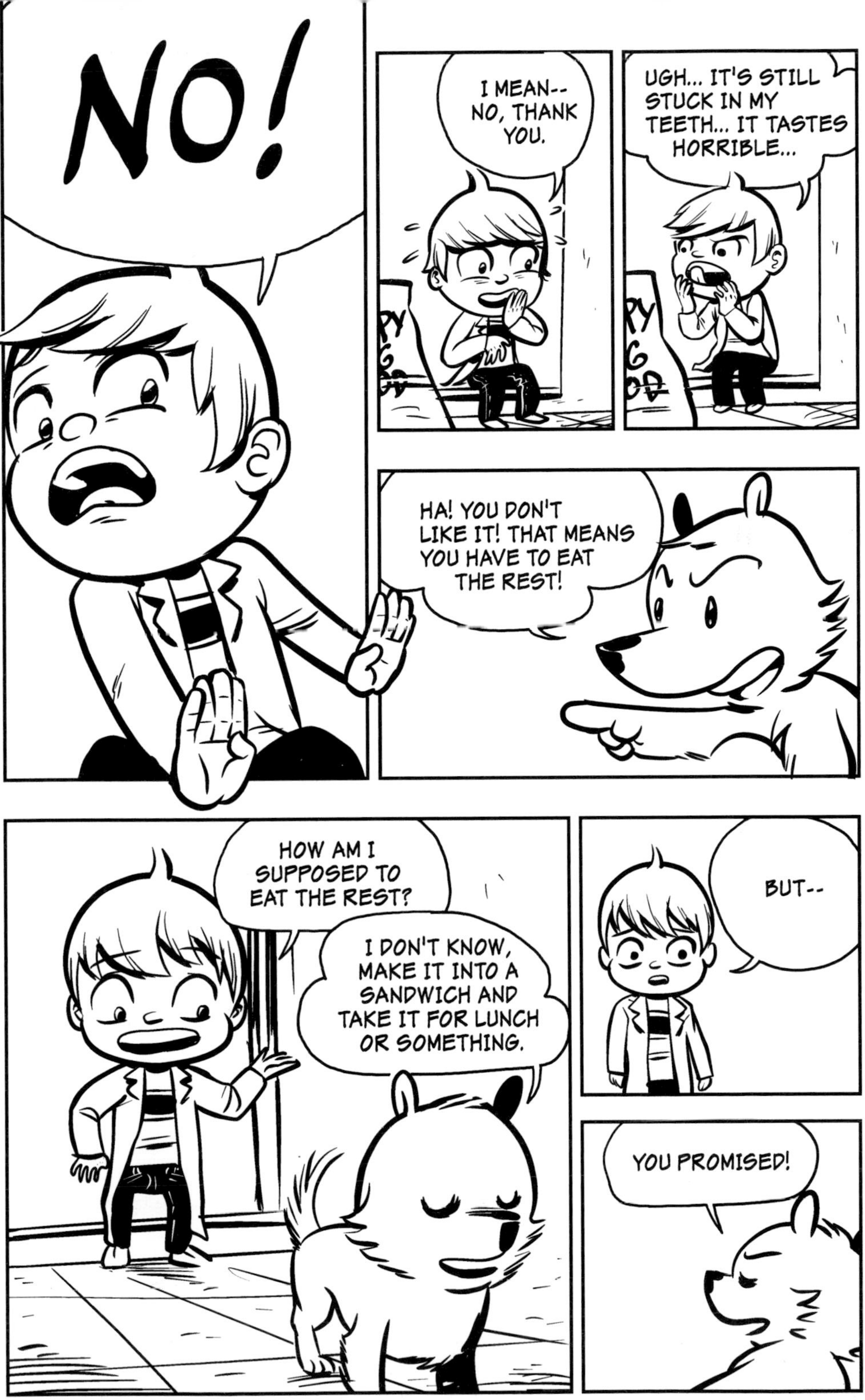
NO!
I MEAN-- NO, THANK YOU.
UGH... IT'S STILL STUCK IN MY TEETH... IT TASTES HORRIBLE...
HA! YOU DON'T LIKE IT! THAT MEANS YOU HAVE TO EAT THE REST!
HOW AM I SUPPOSED TO EAT THE REST?
I DON'T KNOW, MAKE IT INTO A SANDWICH AND TAKE IT FOR LUNCH OR SOMETHING.
BUT--
YOU PROMISED!

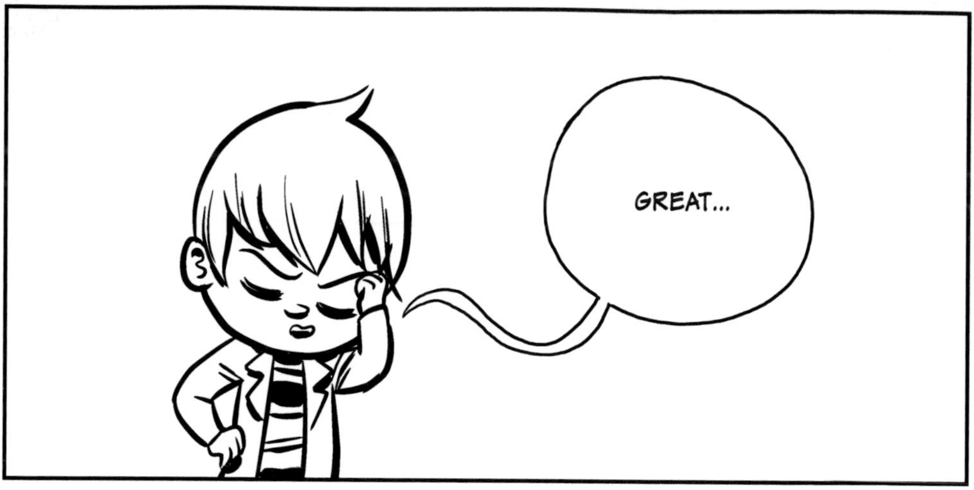
GREAT...

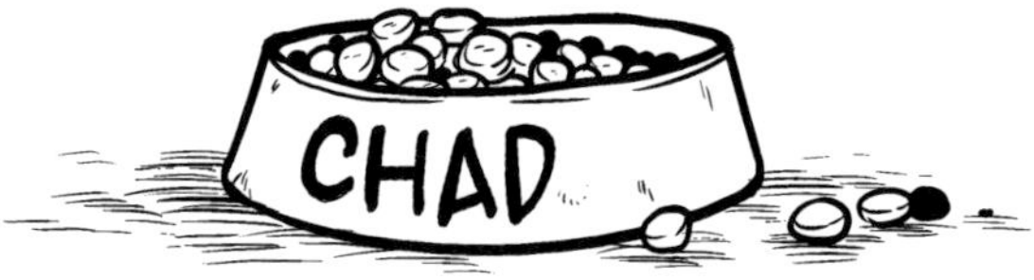
CHAD

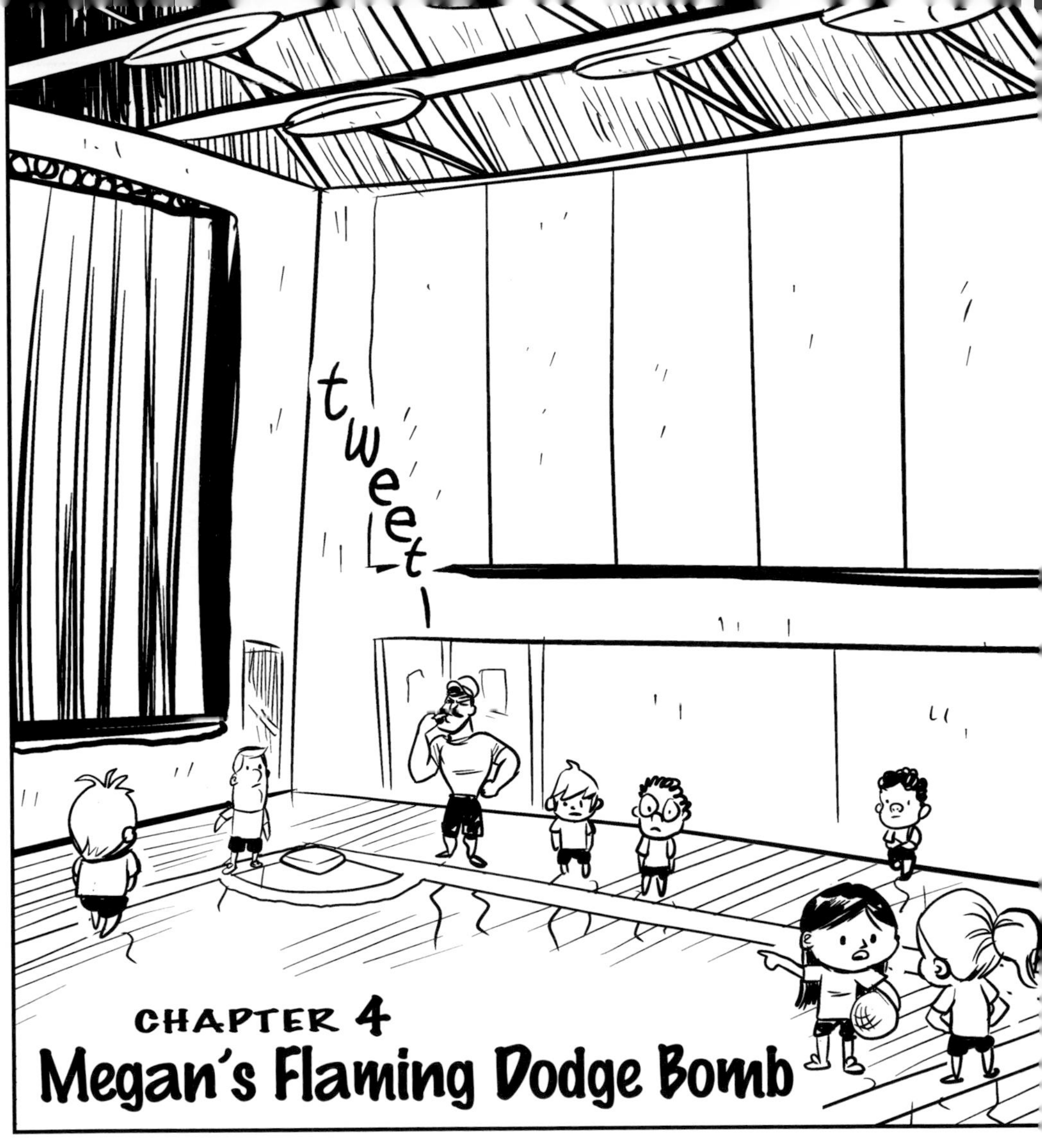
tweet

CHAPTER 4
Megan's Flaming Dodge Bomb

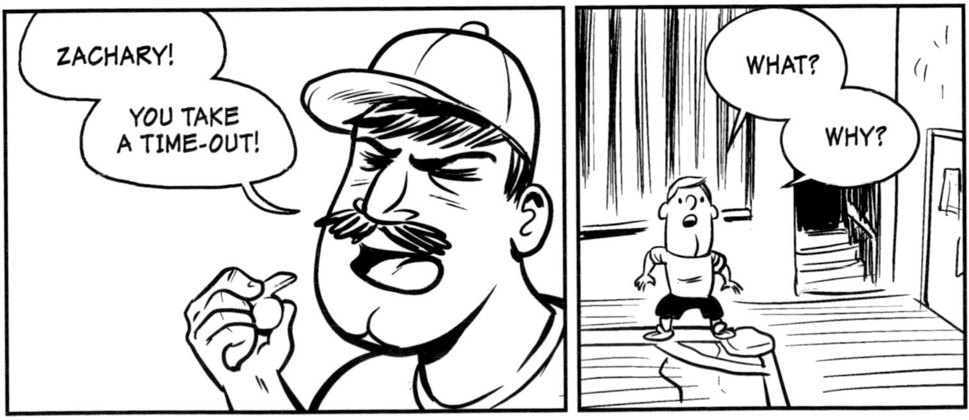
ZACHARY!
YOU TAKE A TIME-OUT!
WHAT?
WHY?

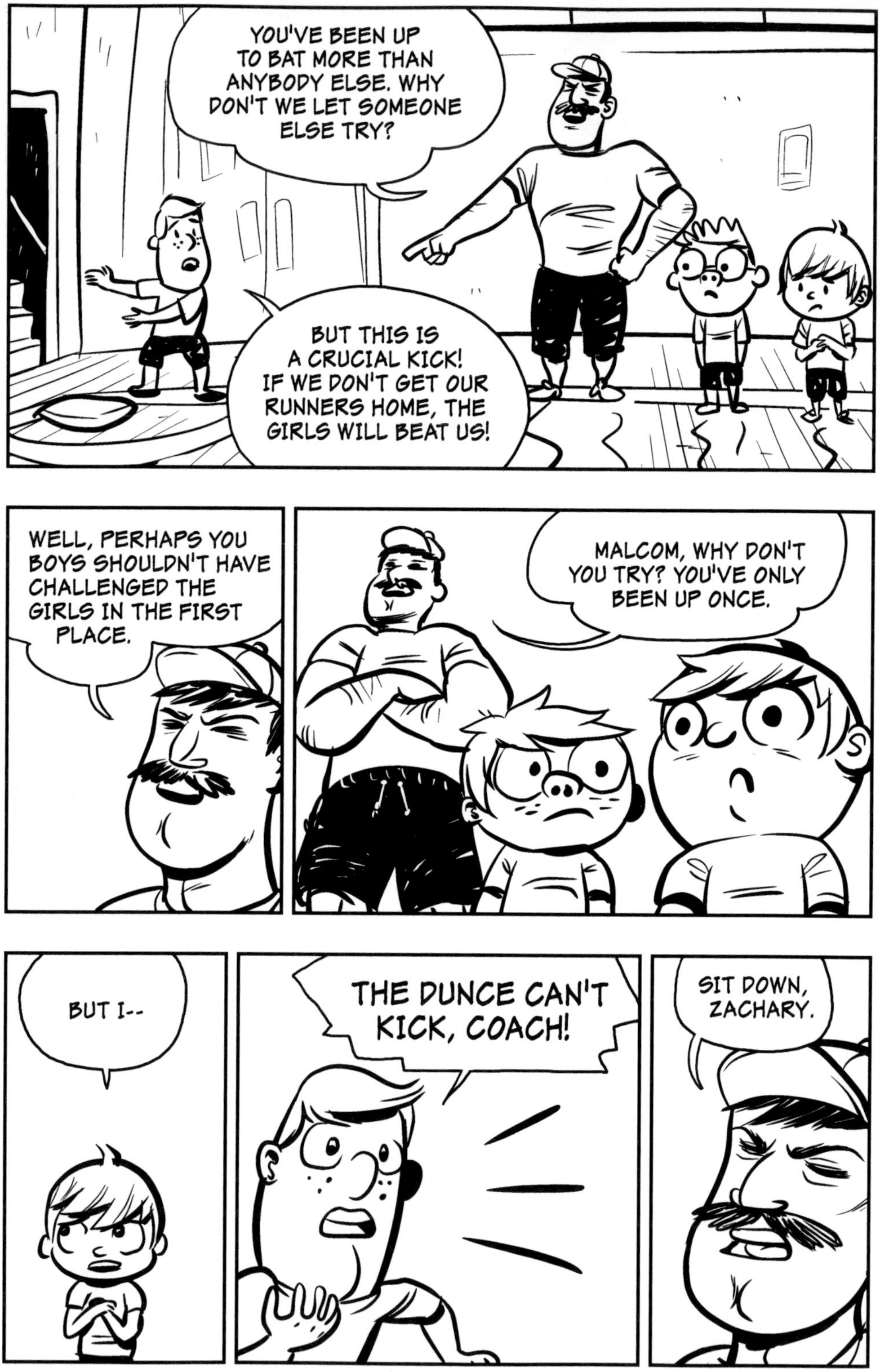
YOU'VE BEEN UP TO BAT MORE THAN ANYBODY ELSE. WHY DON'T WE LET SOMEONE ELSE TRY?
BUT THIS IS A CRUCIAL KICK! IF WE DON'T GET OUR RUNNERS HOME, THE GIRLS WILL BEAT US!
WELL, PERHAPS YOU BOYS SHOULDN'T HAVE CHALLENGED THE GIRLS IN THE FIRST PLACE.
MALCOM, WHY DON'T YOU TRY? YOU'VE ONLY BEEN UP ONCE.
BUT I--
THE DUNCE CAN'T KICK, COACH!
SIT DOWN, ZACHARY.

WAVE

VWOOSH!

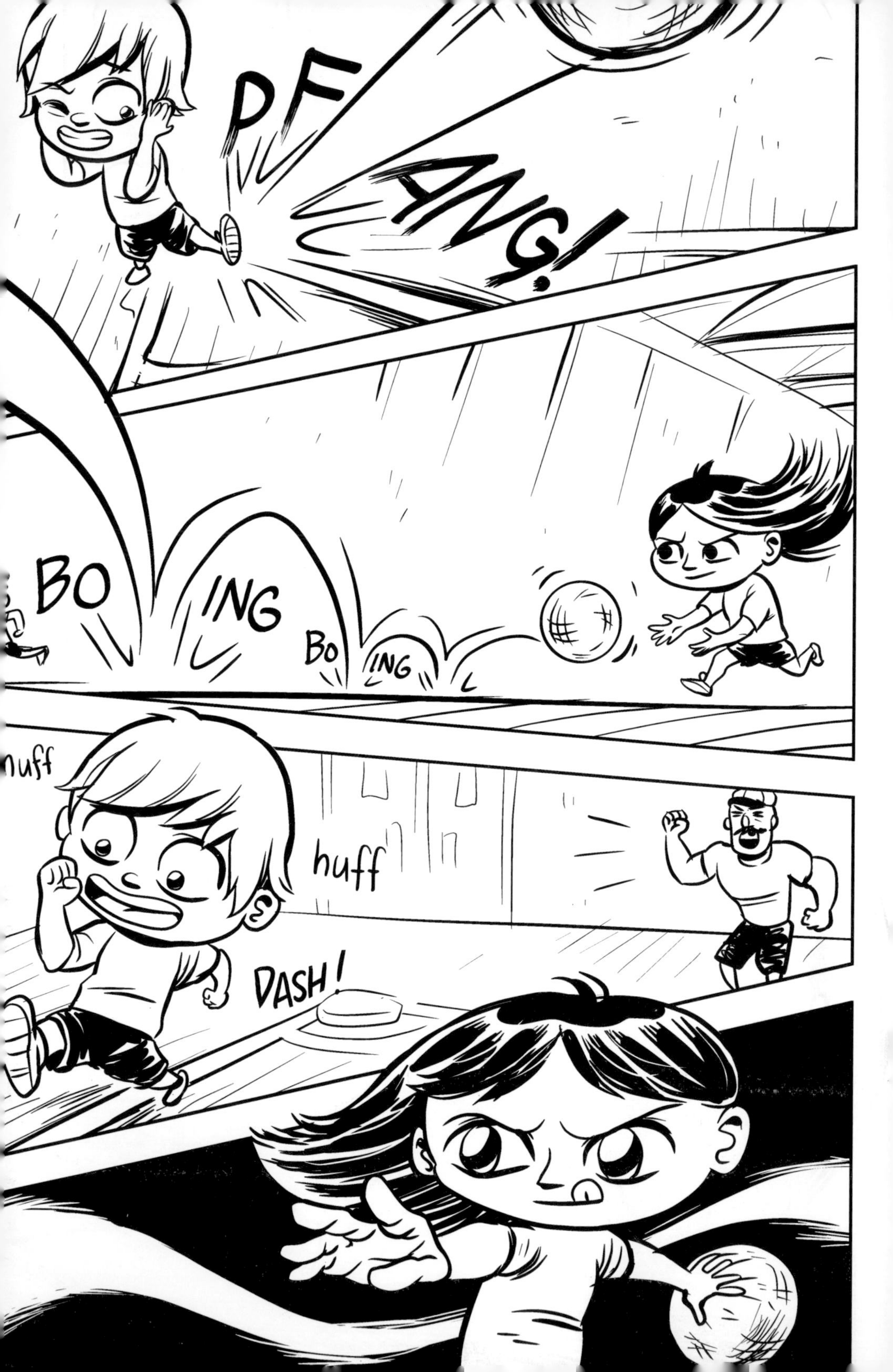
PF
ANG!
BO
ING
Bo
ING
huff
huff
DASH!

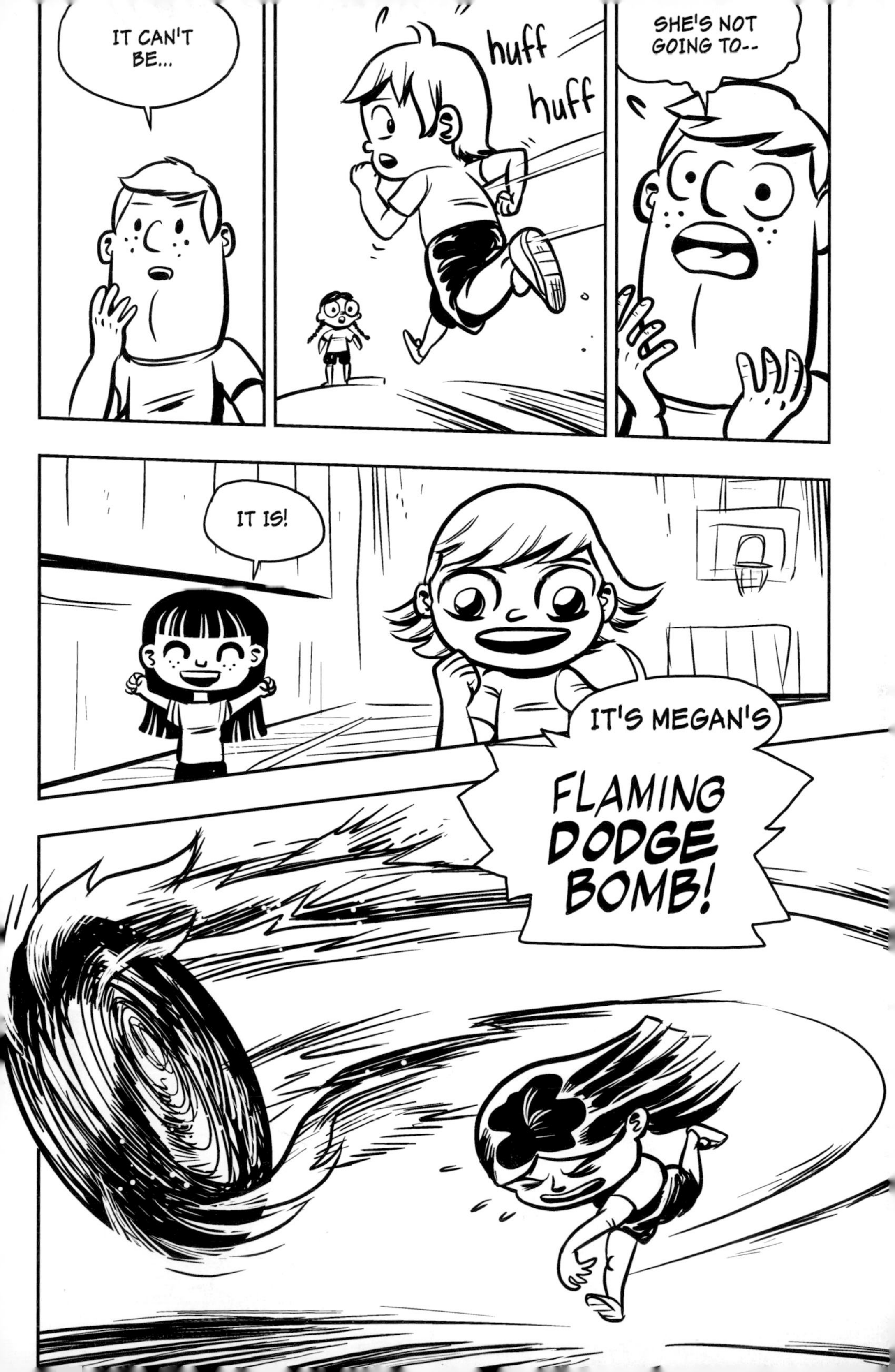
IT CAN'T BE...
huff
huff
SHE'S NOT GOING TO--
IT IS!
IT'S MEGAN'S
FLAMING DODGE BOMB!

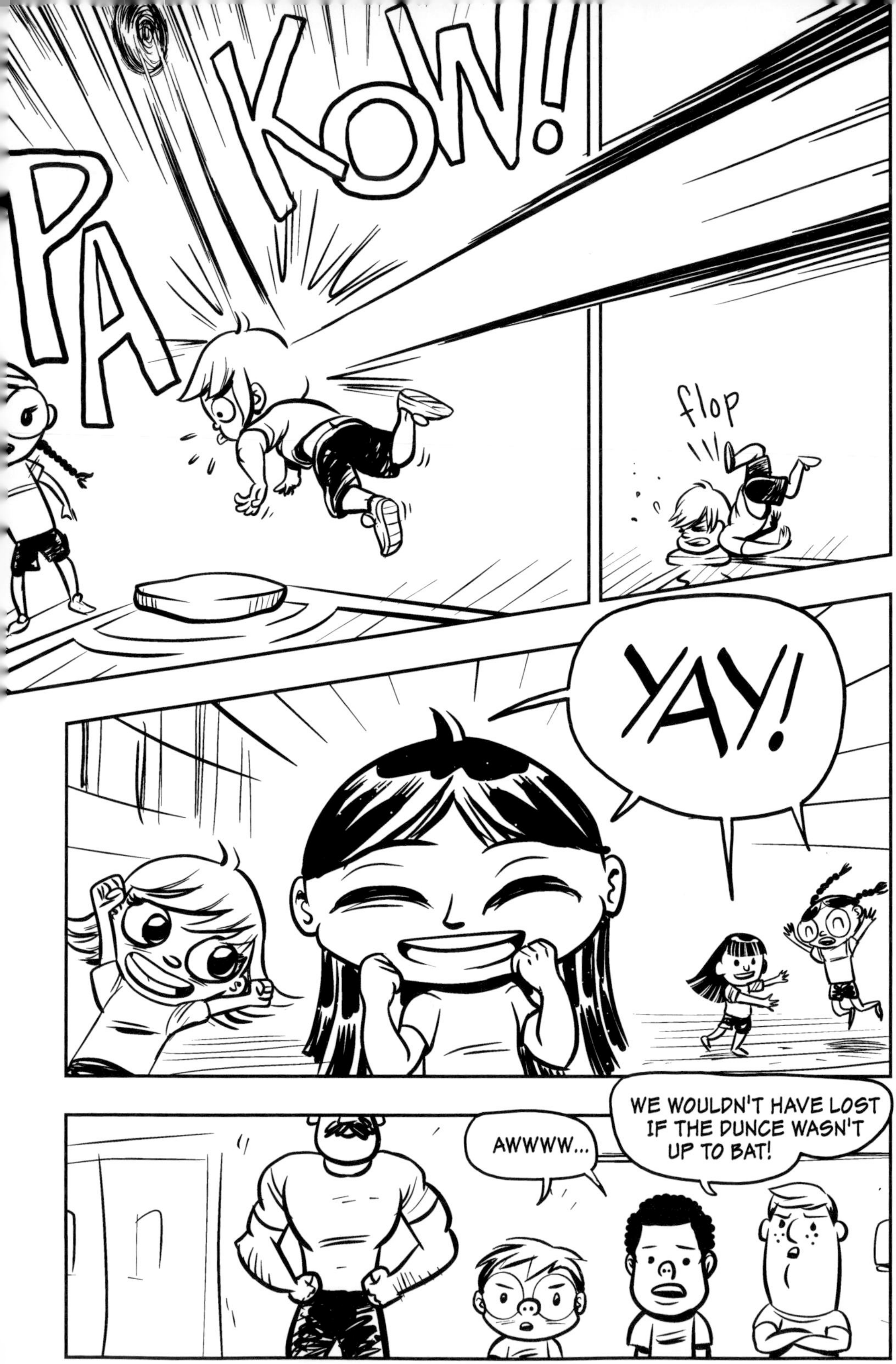
PA KOW!
flop
YAY!
AWWWW...
WE WOULDN'T HAVE LOST IF THE DUNCE WASN'T UP TO BAT!

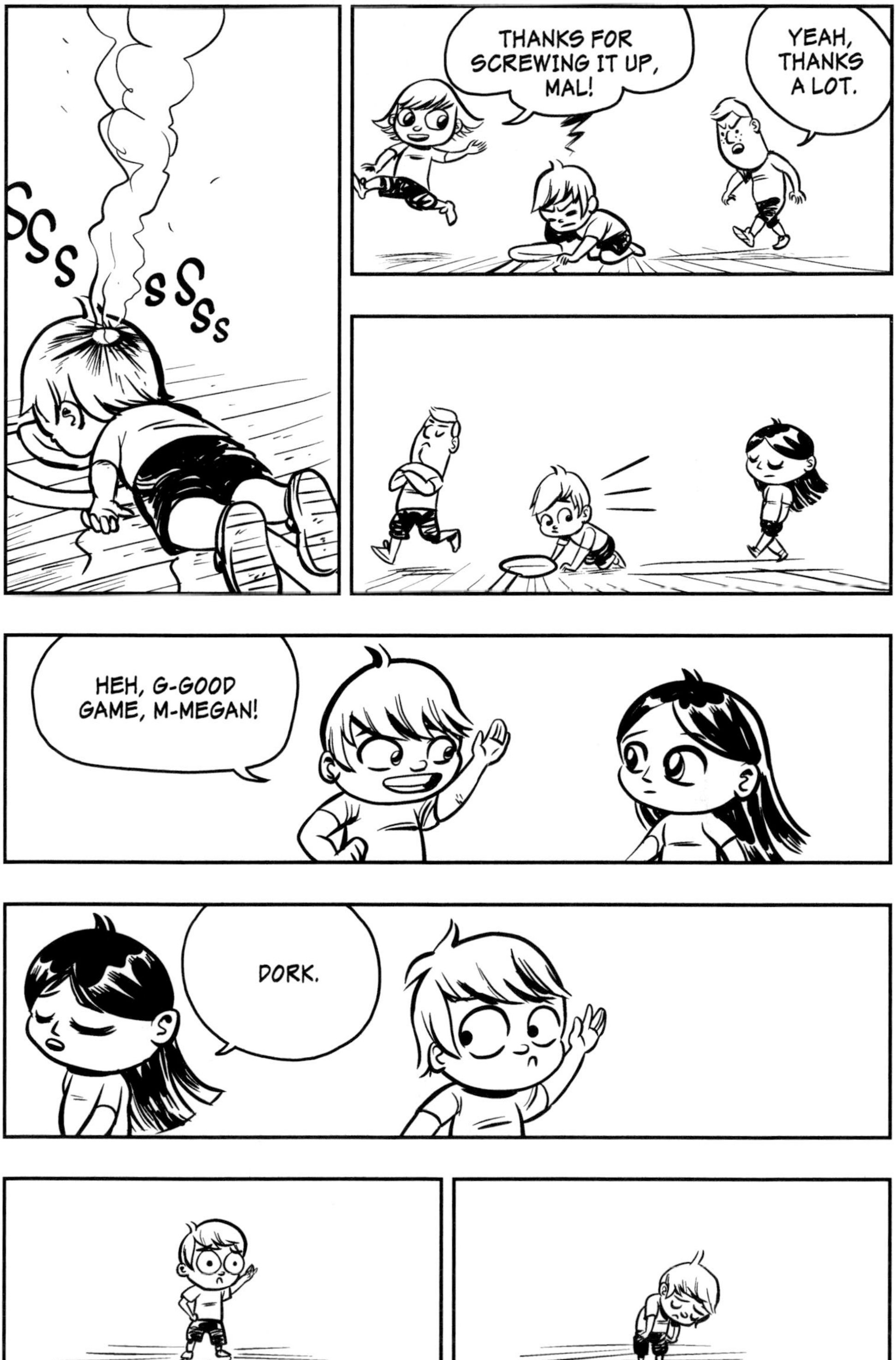
SSSs
sSSs
THANKS FOR SCREWING IT UP, MAL!
YEAH, THANKS A LOT.
HEH, G-GOOD GAME, M-MEGAN!
DORK.

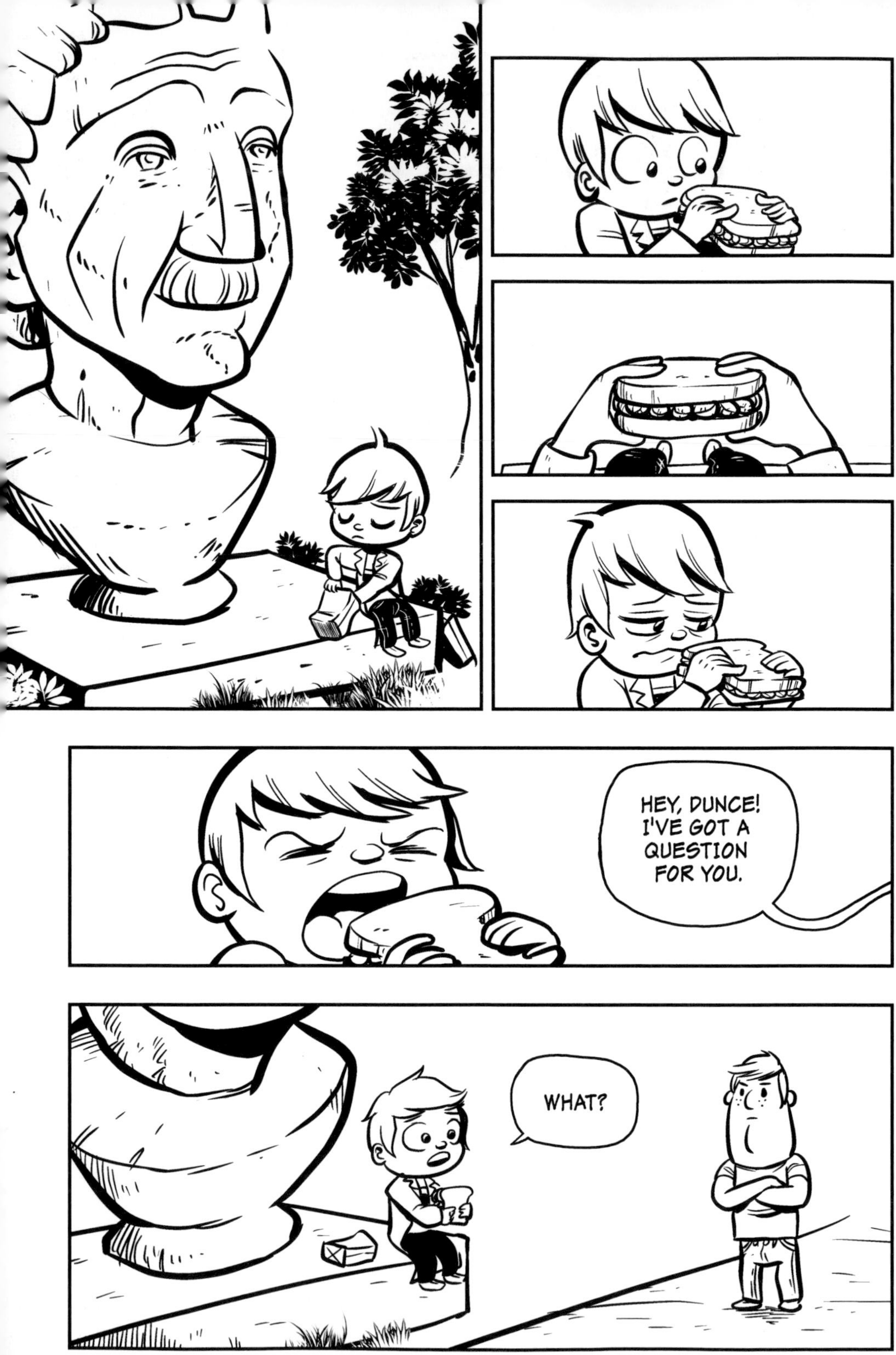
HEY, DUNCE! I'VE GOT A QUESTION FOR YOU.
WHAT?

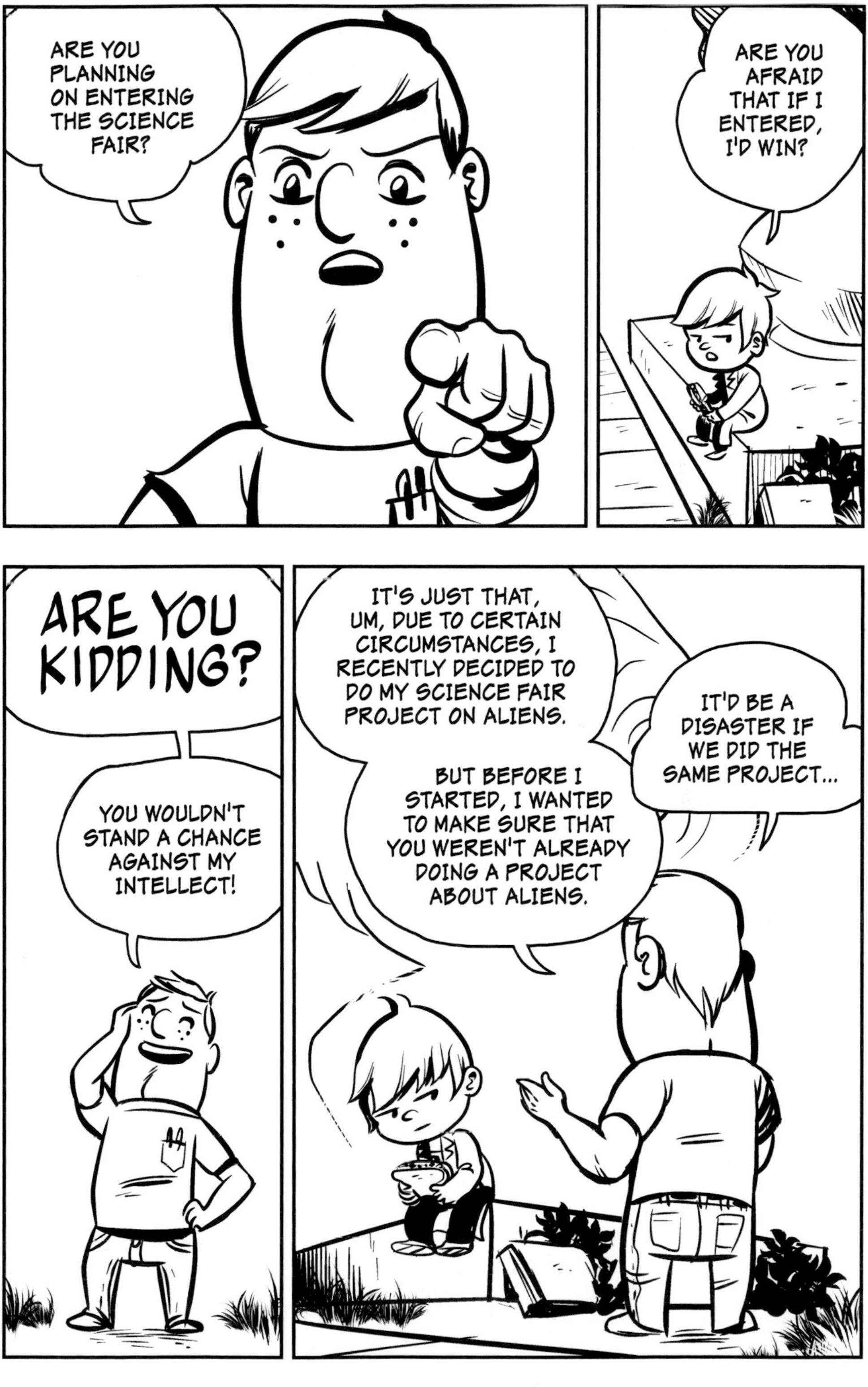

ARE YOU PLANNING ON ENTERING THE SCIENCE FAIR?
ARE YOU AFRAID THAT IF I ENTERED, I'D WIN?
ARE YOU KIDDING?
YOU WOULDN'T STAND A CHANCE AGAINST MY INTELLECT!
IT'S JUST THAT, UM, DUE TO CERTAIN CIRCUMSTANCES, I RECENTLY DECIDED TO DO MY SCIENCE FAIR PROJECT ON ALIENS.
BUT BEFORE I STARTED, I WANTED TO MAKE SURE THAT YOU WEREN'T ALREADY DOING A PROJECT ABOUT ALIENS.
IT'D BE A DISASTER IF WE DID THE SAME PROJECT...

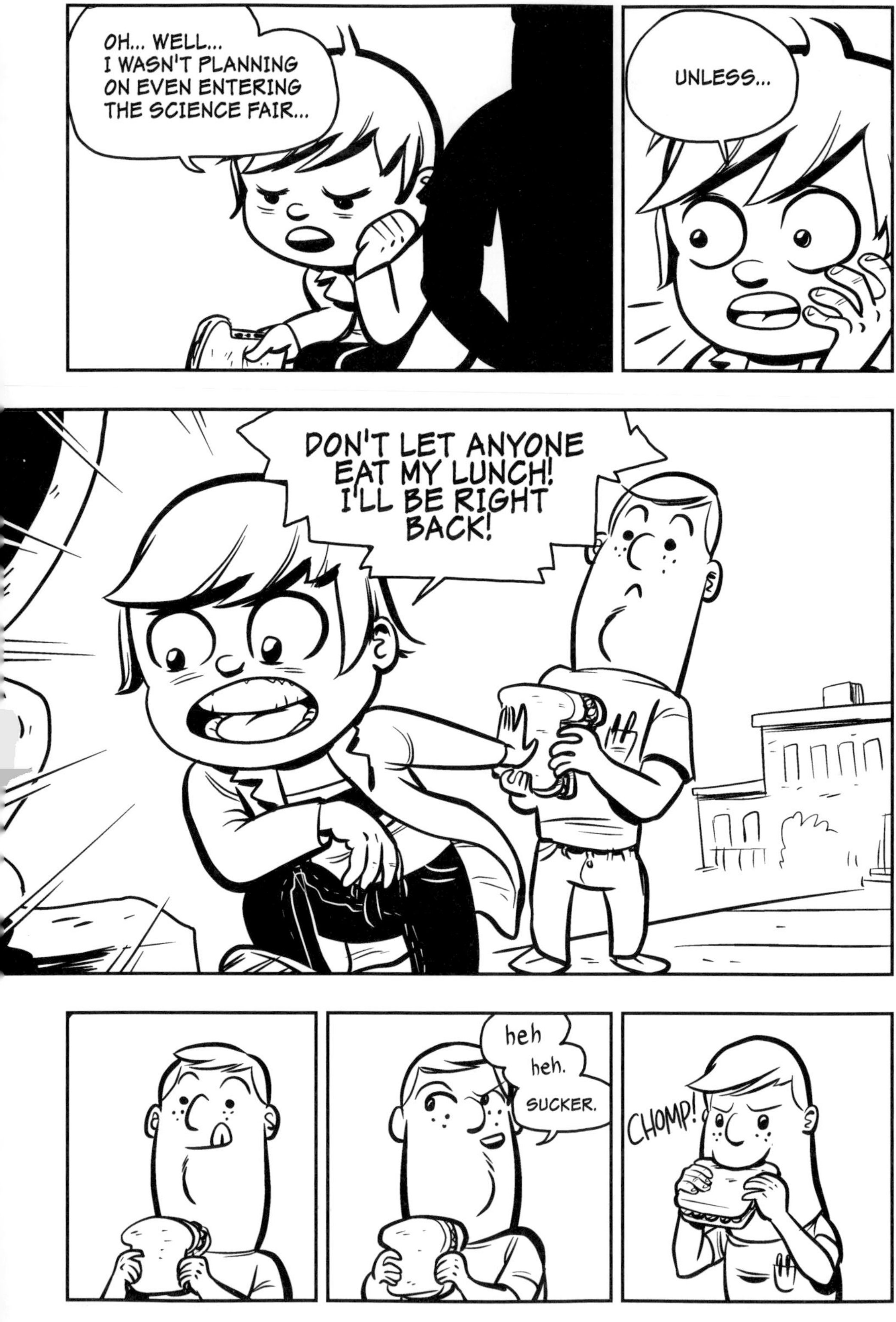
OH... WELL... I WASN'T PLANNING ON EVEN ENTERING THE SCIENCE FAIR...
UNLESS...
DON'T LET ANYONE EAT MY LUNCH! I'LL BE RIGHT BACK!
heh
heh.
SUCKER.
CHOMP!

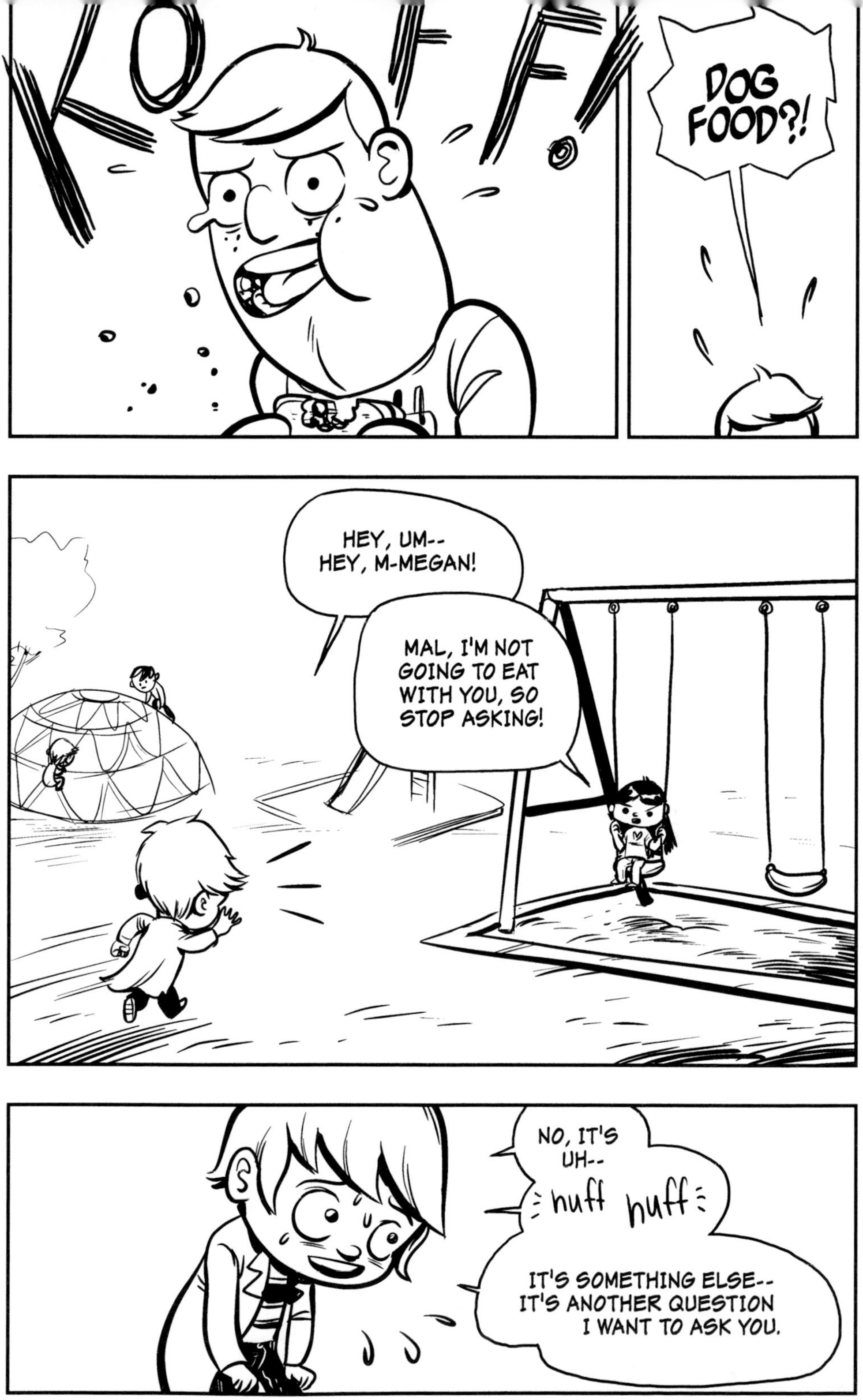
KOFF!
DOG FOOD?!
HEY, UM--
HEY, M-MEGAN!
MAL, I'M NOT GOING TO EAT WITH YOU, SO STOP ASKING!
NO, IT'S UH--
huff huff
IT'S SOMETHING ELSE-- IT'S ANOTHER QUESTION I WANT TO ASK YOU.

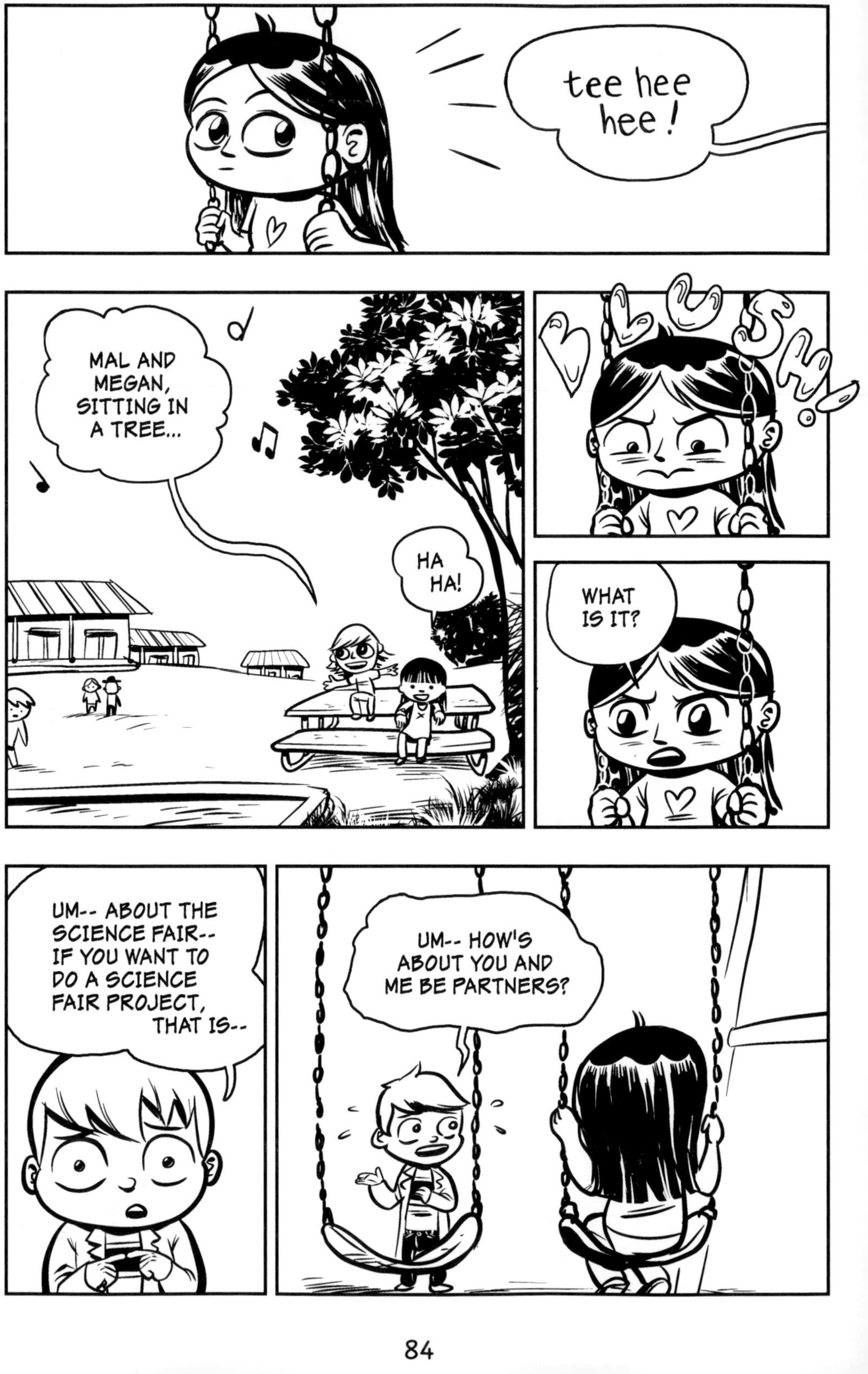
tee hee hee!
MAL AND MEGAN, SITTING IN A TREE...
HA HA!
BLUSH!
WHAT IS IT?
UM-- ABOUT THE SCIENCE FAIR-- IF YOU WANT TO DO A SCIENCE FAIR PROJECT, THAT IS--
UM-- HOW'S ABOUT YOU AND ME BE PARTNERS?

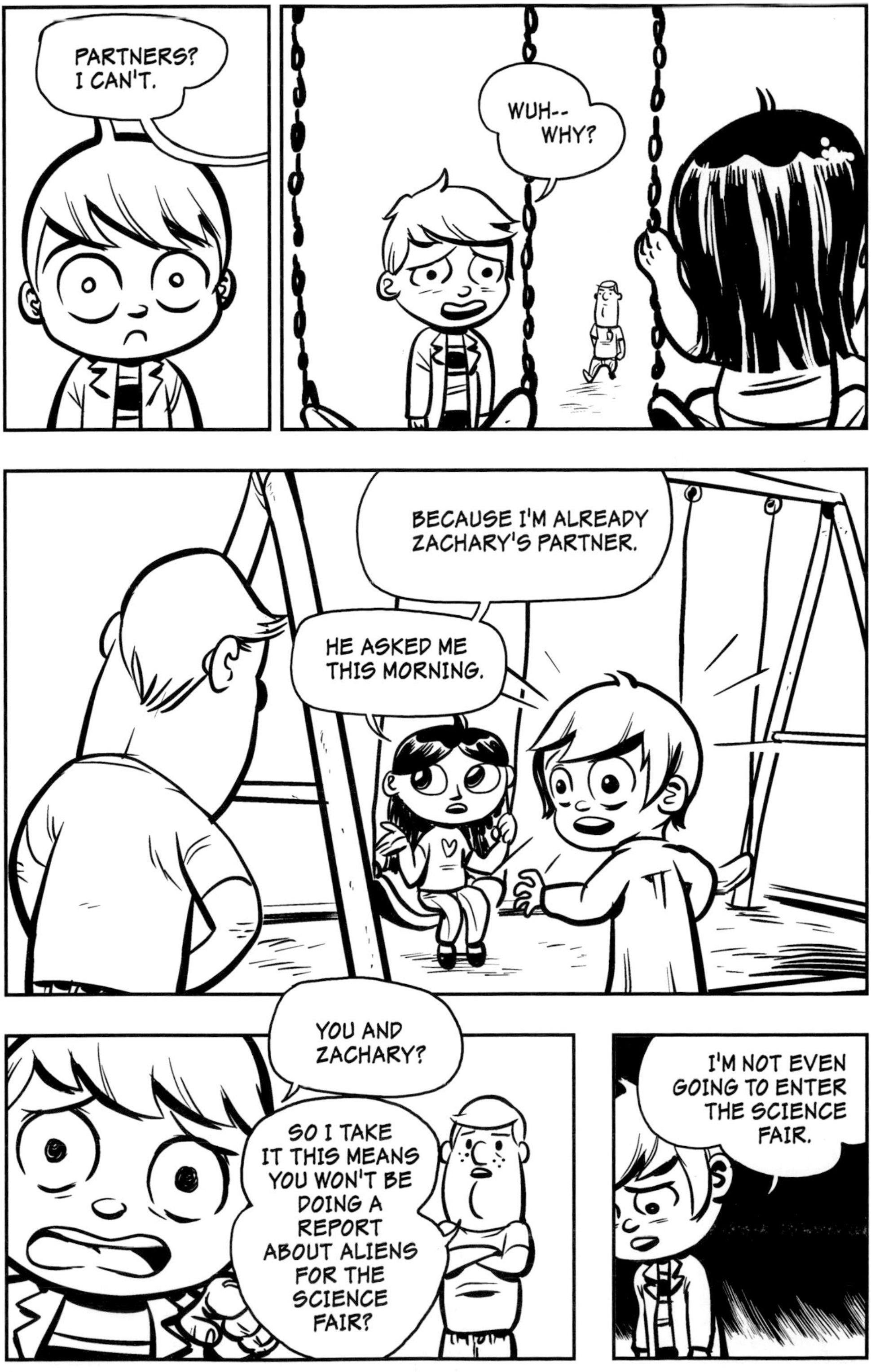
PARTNERS? I CAN'T.
WUH-- WHY?
BECAUSE I'M ALREADY ZACHARY'S PARTNER.
HE ASKED ME THIS MORNING.
YOU AND ZACHARY?
SO I TAKE IT THIS MEANS YOU WON'T BE DOING A REPORT ABOUT ALIENS FOR THE SCIENCE FAIR?
I'M NOT EVEN GOING TO ENTER THE SCIENCE FAIR.

THAT IS ONE WEIRD KID... DO YOU KNOW WHAT HE BROUGHT FOR LUNCH TODAY?

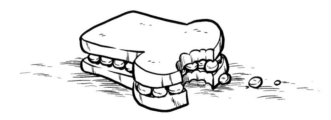

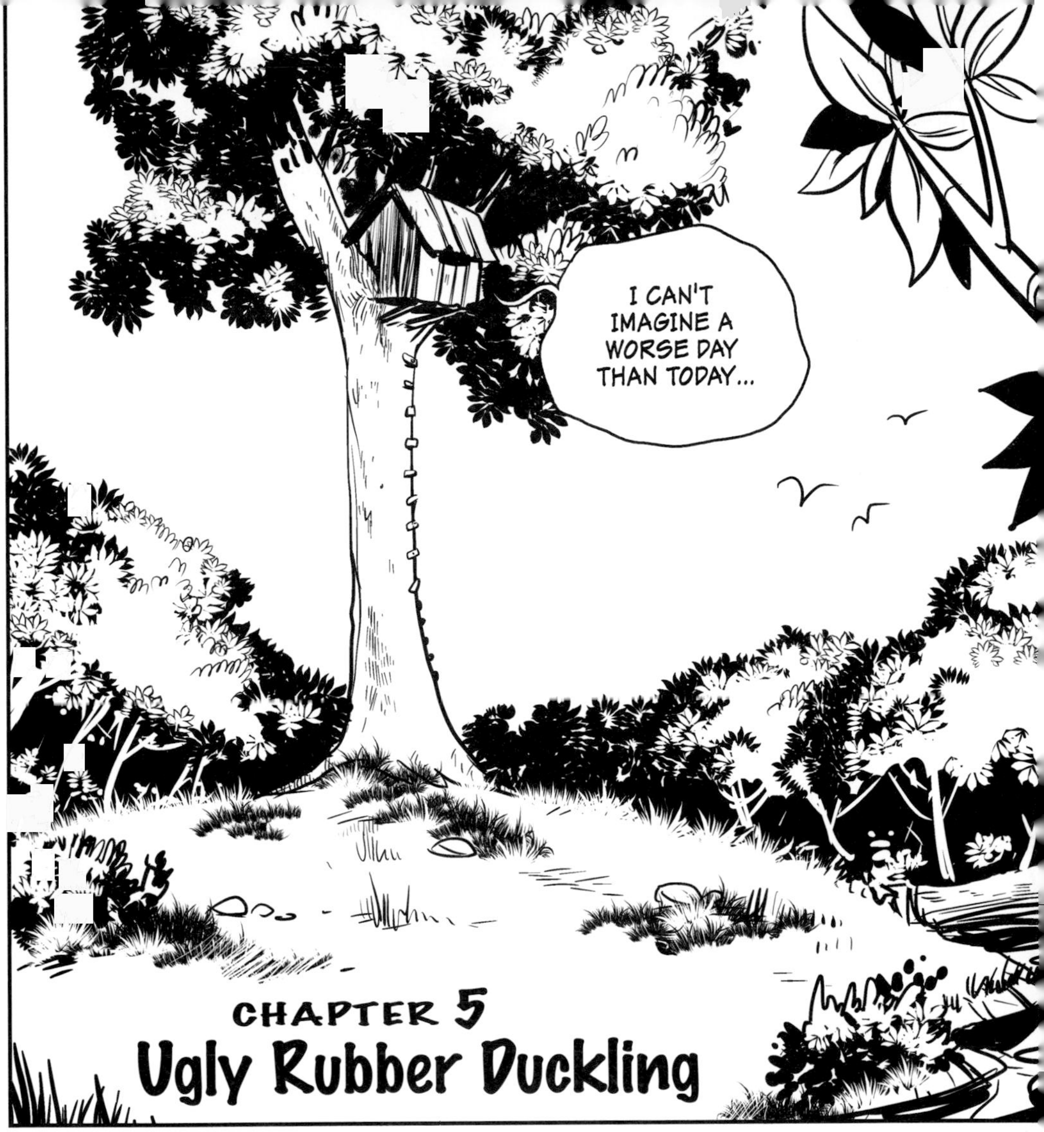
I CAN'T IMAGINE A WORSE DAY THAN TODAY...

CHAPTER 5
Ugly Rubber Duckling

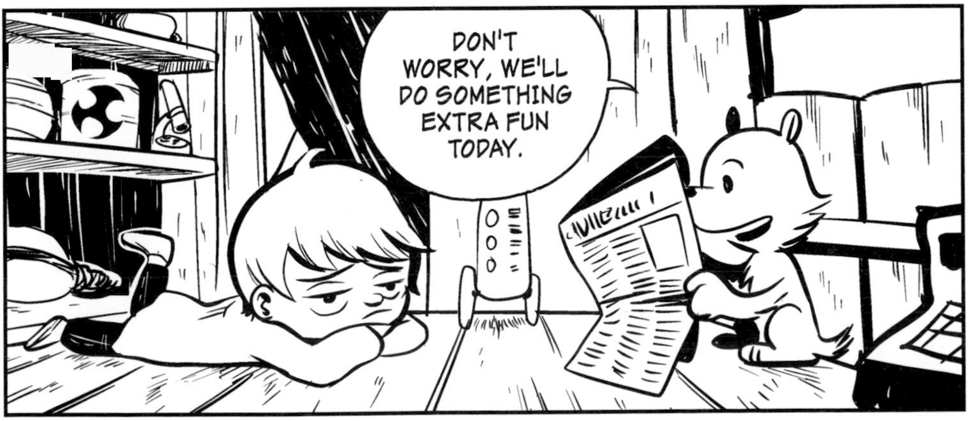
DON'T WORRY, WE'LL DO SOMETHING EXTRA FUN TODAY.

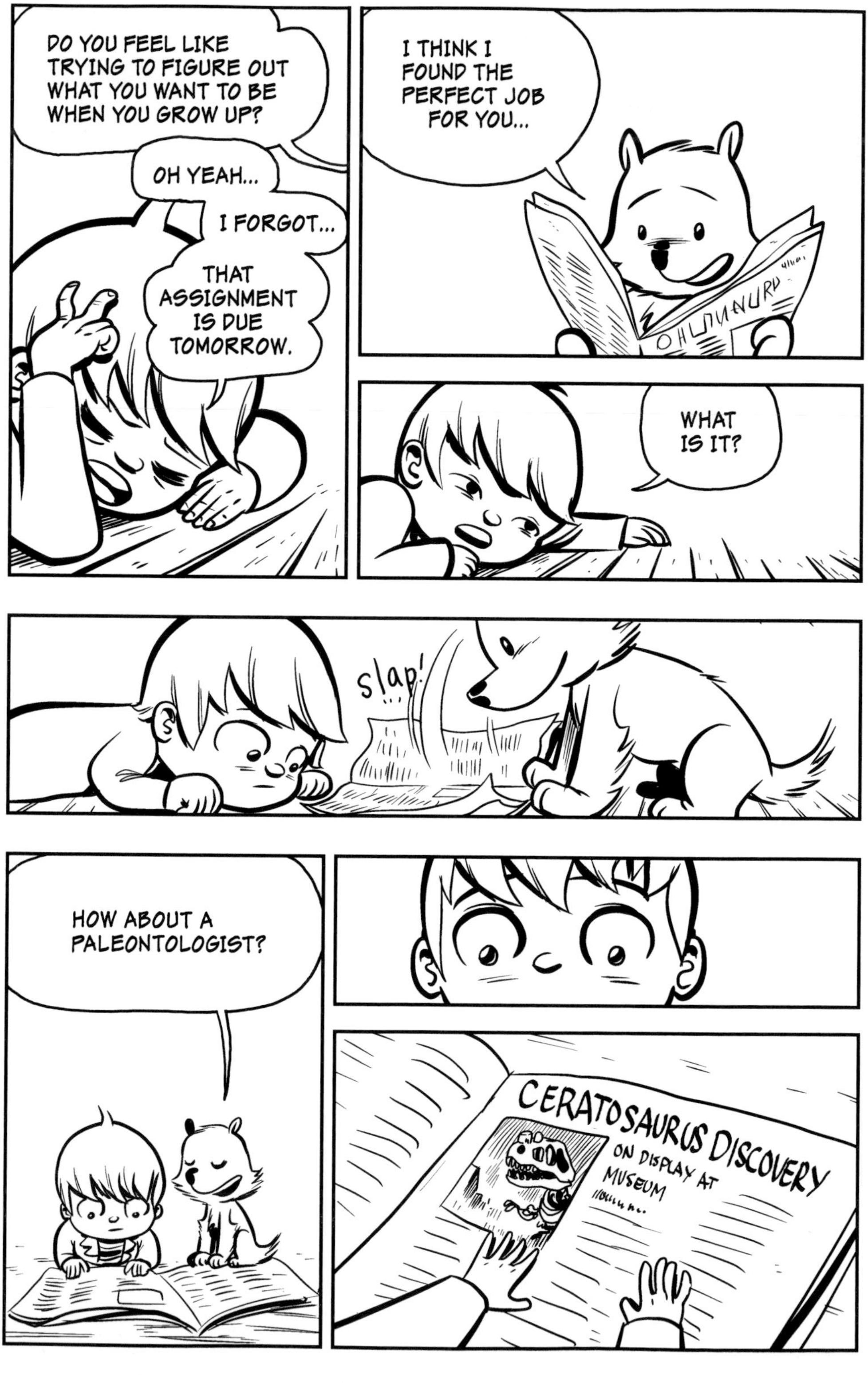
DO YOU FEEL LIKE TRYING TO FIGURE OUT WHAT YOU WANT TO BE WHEN YOU GROW UP?
OH YEAH...
I FORGOT...
THAT ASSIGNMENT IS DUE TOMORROW.
I THINK I FOUND THE PERFECT JOB FOR YOU...
WHAT IS IT?
slap!
HOW ABOUT A PALEONTOLOGIST?
CERATOSAURUS DISCOVERY
ON DISPLAY AT MUSEUM

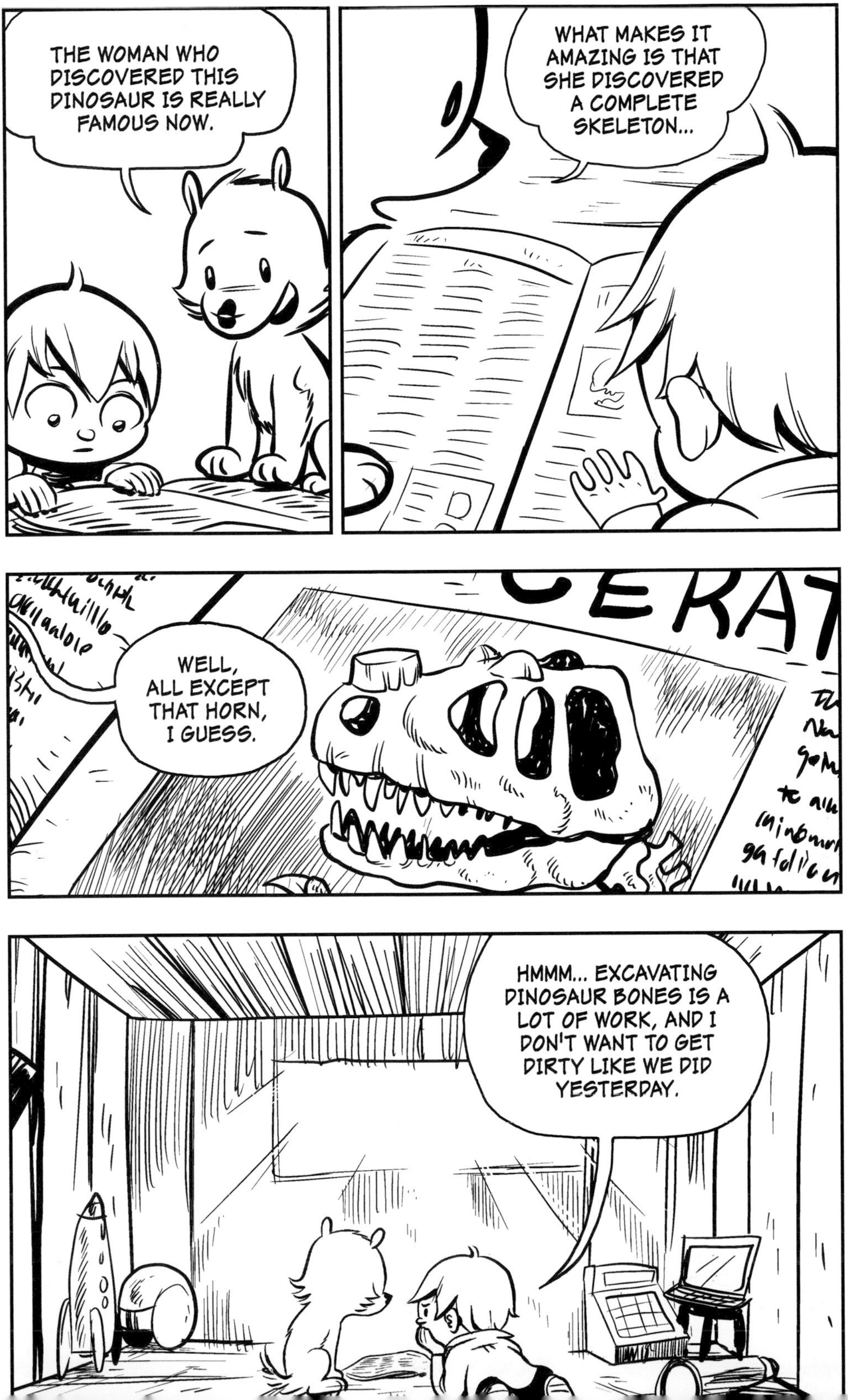

THE WOMAN WHO DISCOVERED THIS DINOSAUR IS REALLY FAMOUS NOW.
WHAT MAKES IT AMAZING IS THAT SHE DISCOVERED A COMPLETE SKELETON...
CERAT
WELL, ALL EXCEPT THAT HORN, I GUESS.
HMMM... EXCAVATING DINOSAUR BONES IS A LOT OF WORK, AND I DON'T WANT TO GET DIRTY LIKE WE DID YESTERDAY.

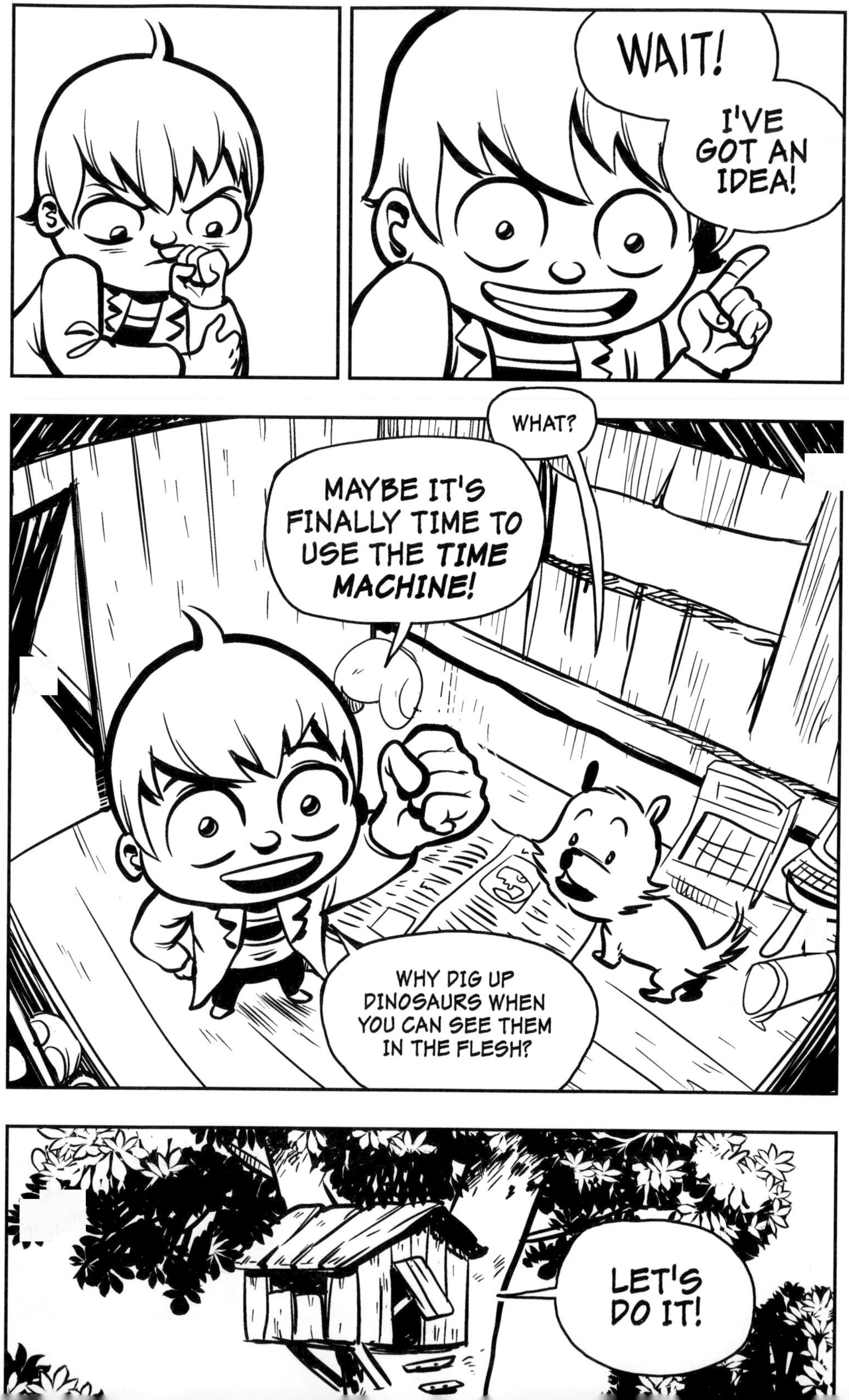
WAIT!
I'VE GOT AN IDEA!
WHAT?
MAYBE IT'S FINALLY TIME TO USE THE *TIME MACHINE!*
WHY DIG UP DINOSAURS WHEN YOU CAN SEE THEM IN THE FLESH?
LET'S DO IT!

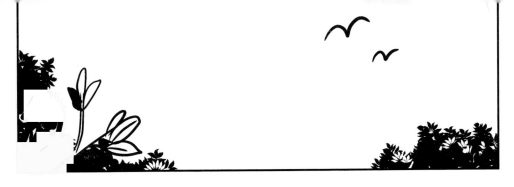

THIS ELEVATOR HAS COME A LONG WAY SINCE WE FOUND IT IN THE JUNKYARD.

I PACKED THE FOOD. ARE YOU READY?

YEP! LET'S GO!

1 10 100
TIME JUMP
CLICK
CLOSE

bing!

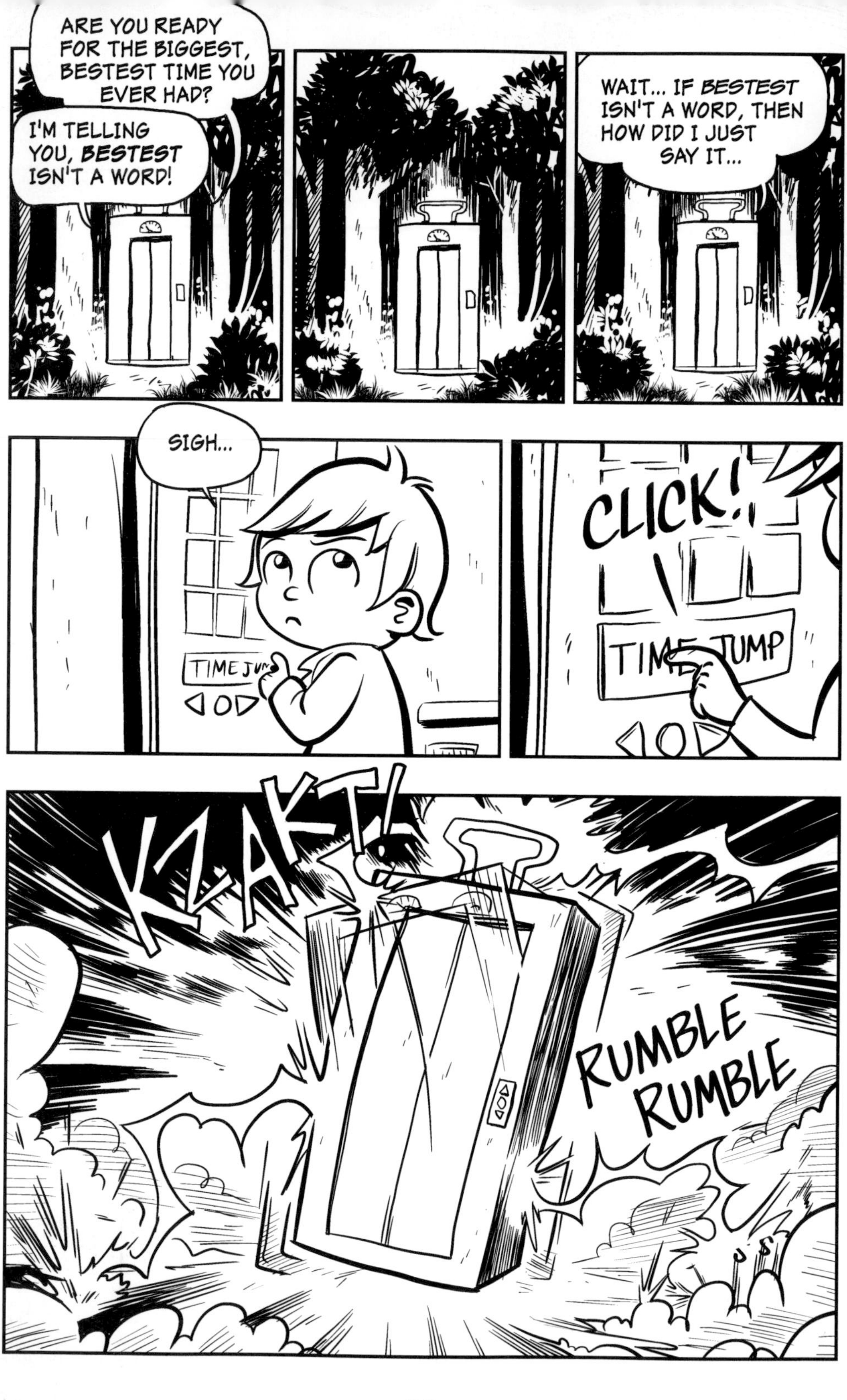
ARE YOU READY FOR THE BIGGEST, BESTEST TIME YOU EVER HAD?
I'M TELLING YOU, BESTEST ISN'T A WORD!
WAIT... IF BESTEST ISN'T A WORD, THEN HOW DID I JUST SAY IT...
SIGH...
TIME JUMP
CLICK!
TIME JUMP
KZAKT!
RUMBLE RUMBLE

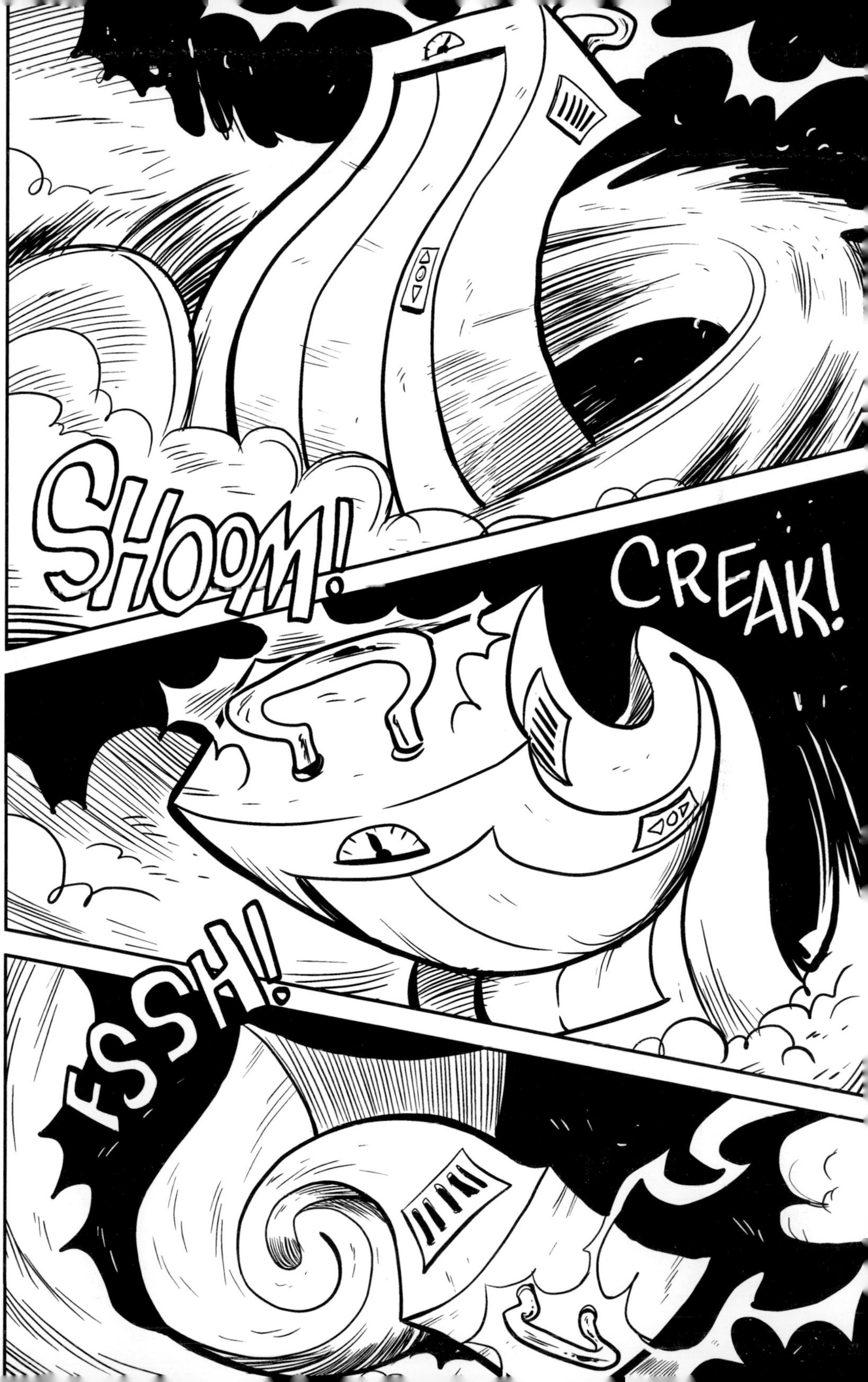
SHOOM!
CREAK!
FSSH!

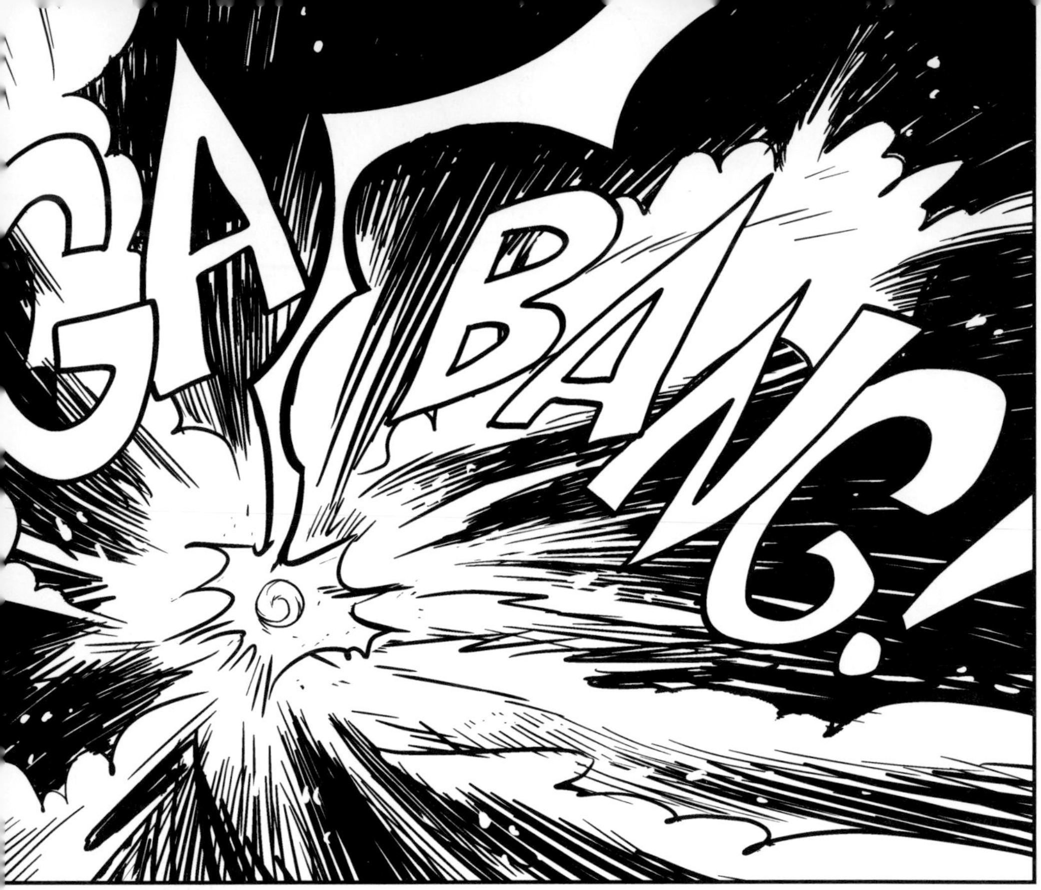
GABANG!

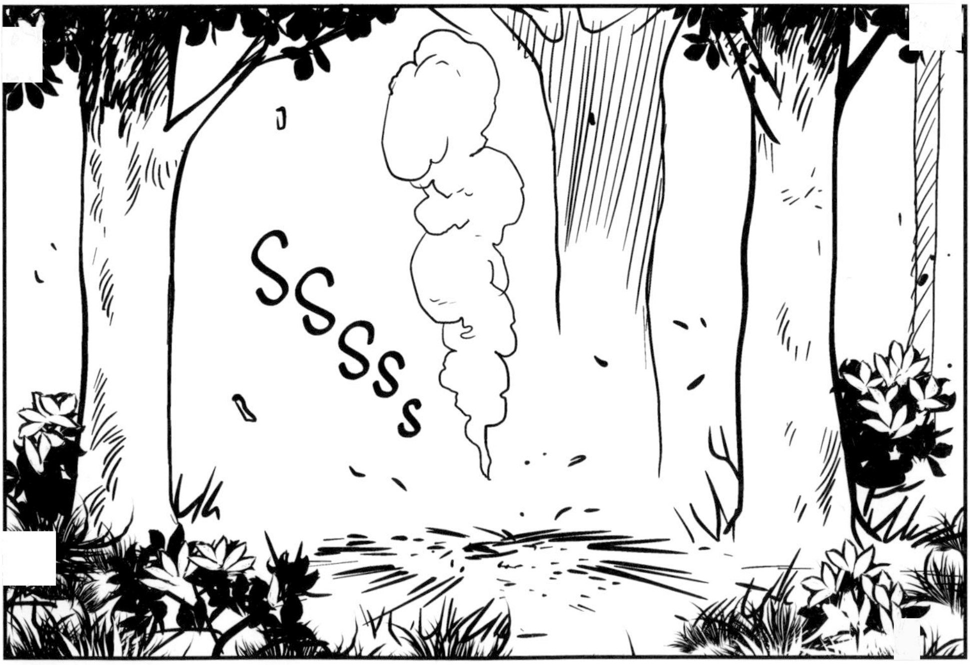
SSSSSs

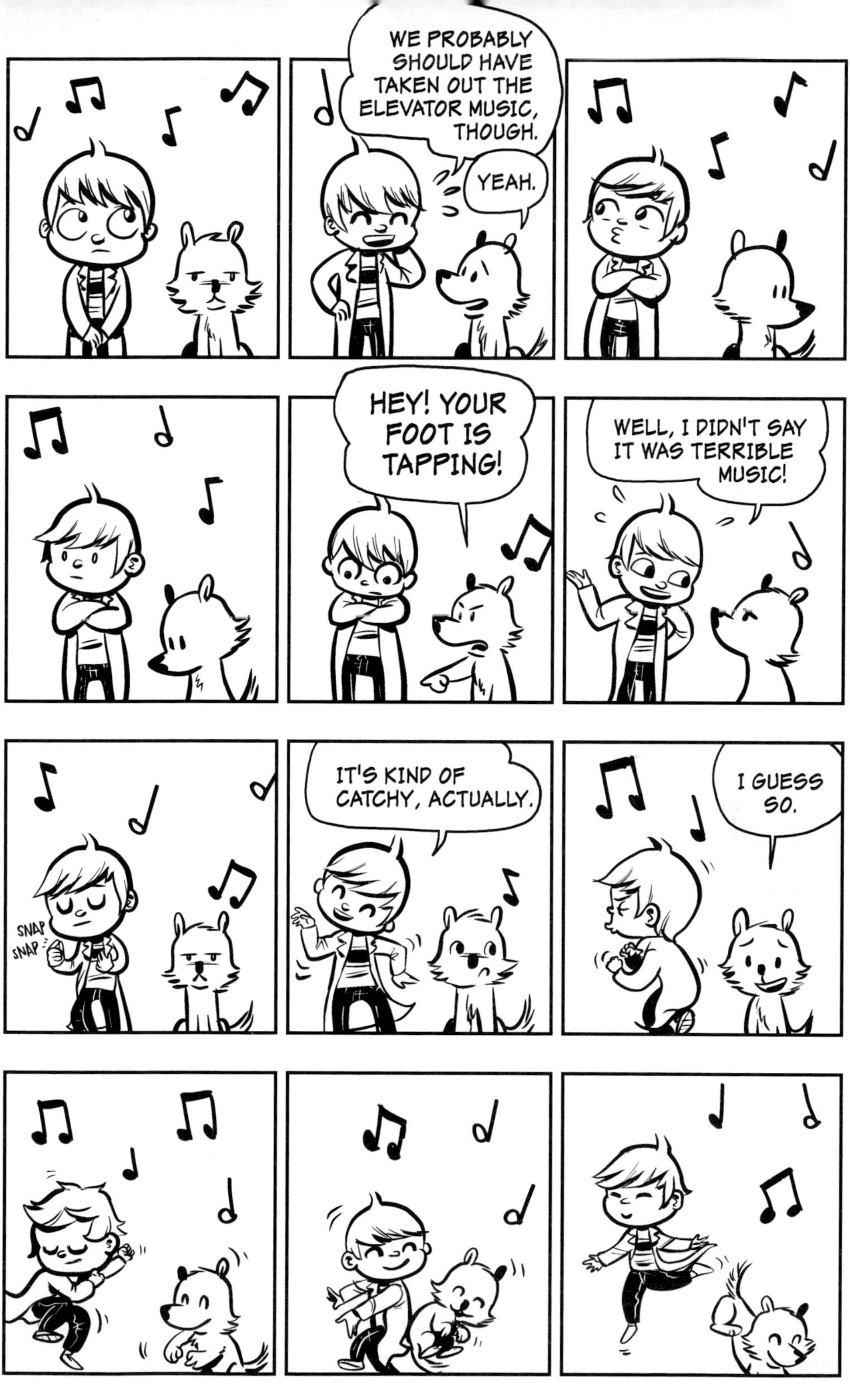
WE PROBABLY SHOULD HAVE TAKEN OUT THE ELEVATOR MUSIC, THOUGH.
YEAH.
HEY! YOUR FOOT IS TAPPING!
WELL, I DIDN'T SAY IT WAS TERRIBLE MUSIC!
SNAP SNAP
IT'S KIND OF CATCHY, ACTUALLY.
I GUESS SO.

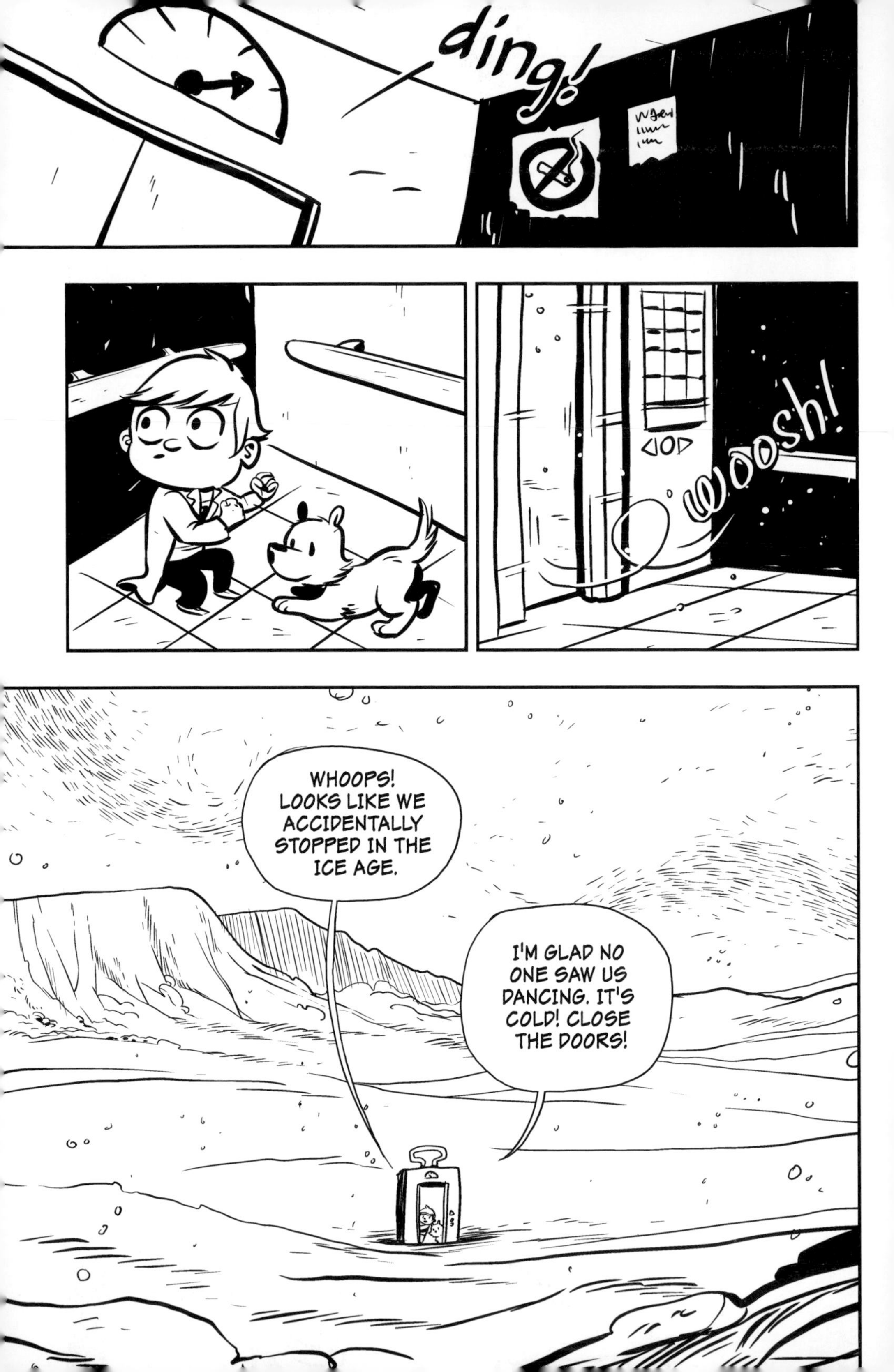
ding!
WOOSH!
WHOOPS! LOOKS LIKE WE ACCIDENTALLY STOPPED IN THE ICE AGE.
I'M GLAD NO ONE SAW US DANCING. IT'S COLD! CLOSE THE DOORS!

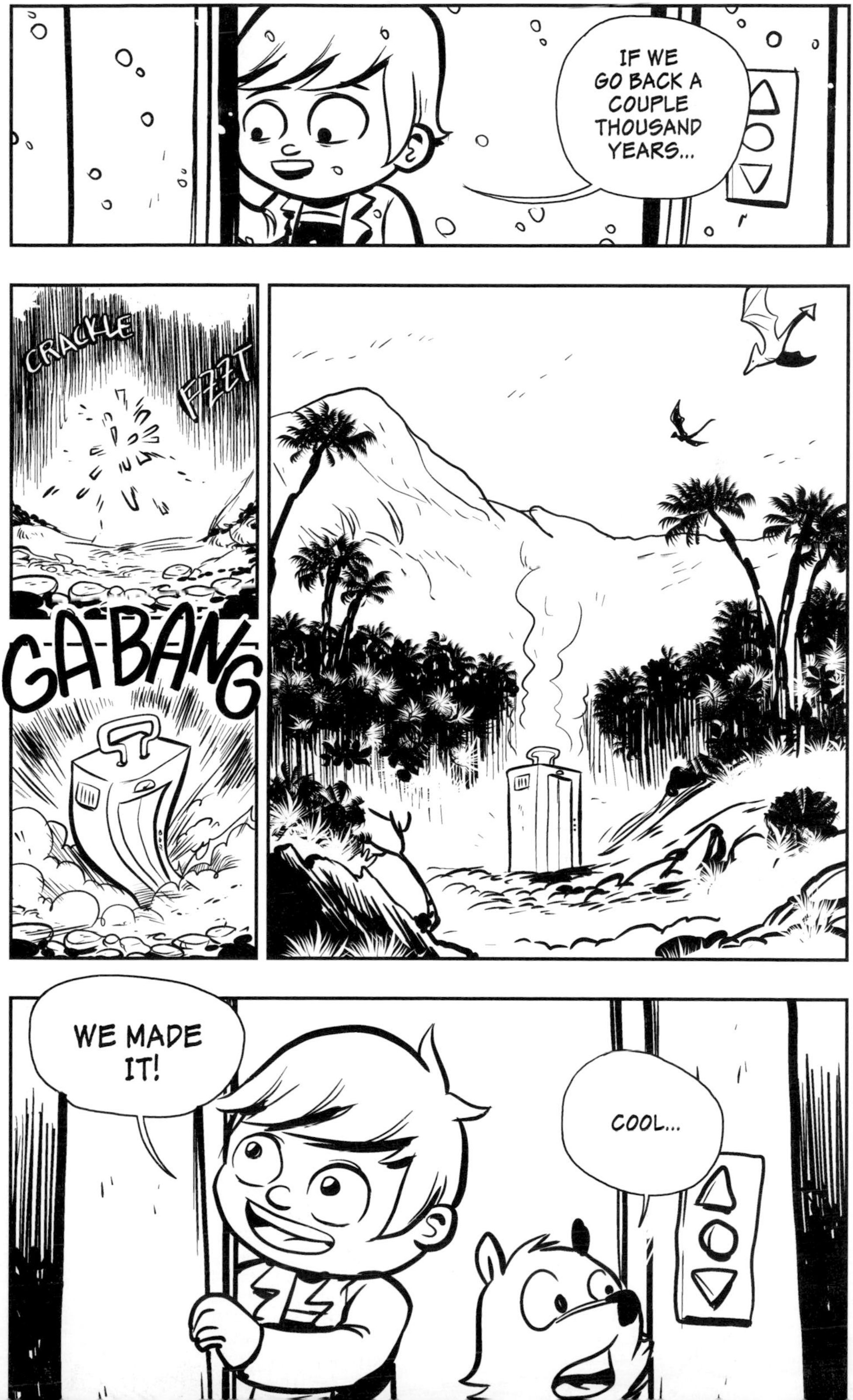
IF WE GO BACK A COUPLE THOUSAND YEARS...
CRACKLE
FZZT
GA BANG
WE MADE IT!
COOL...

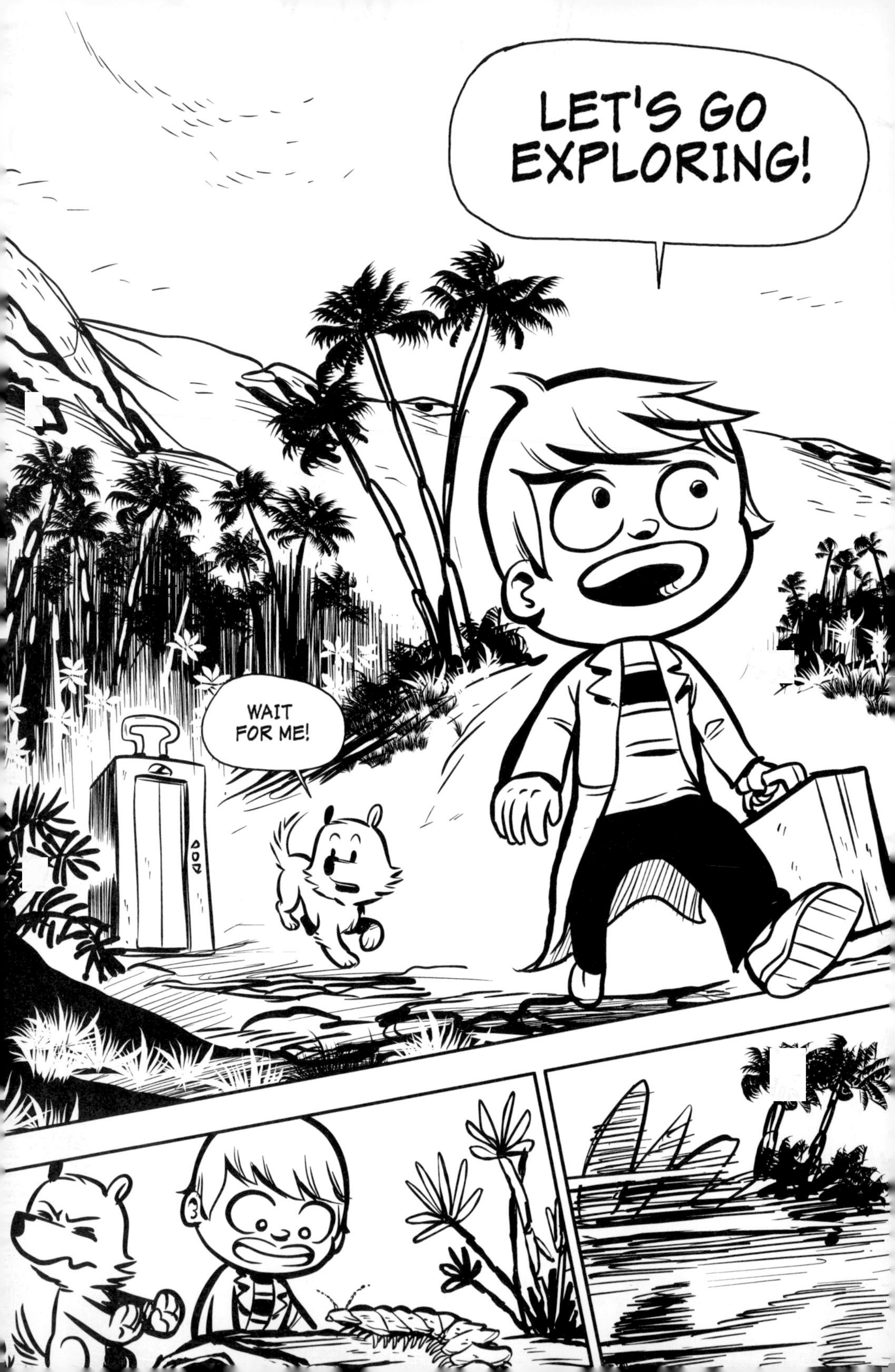
LET'S GO EXPLORING!
WAIT FOR ME!

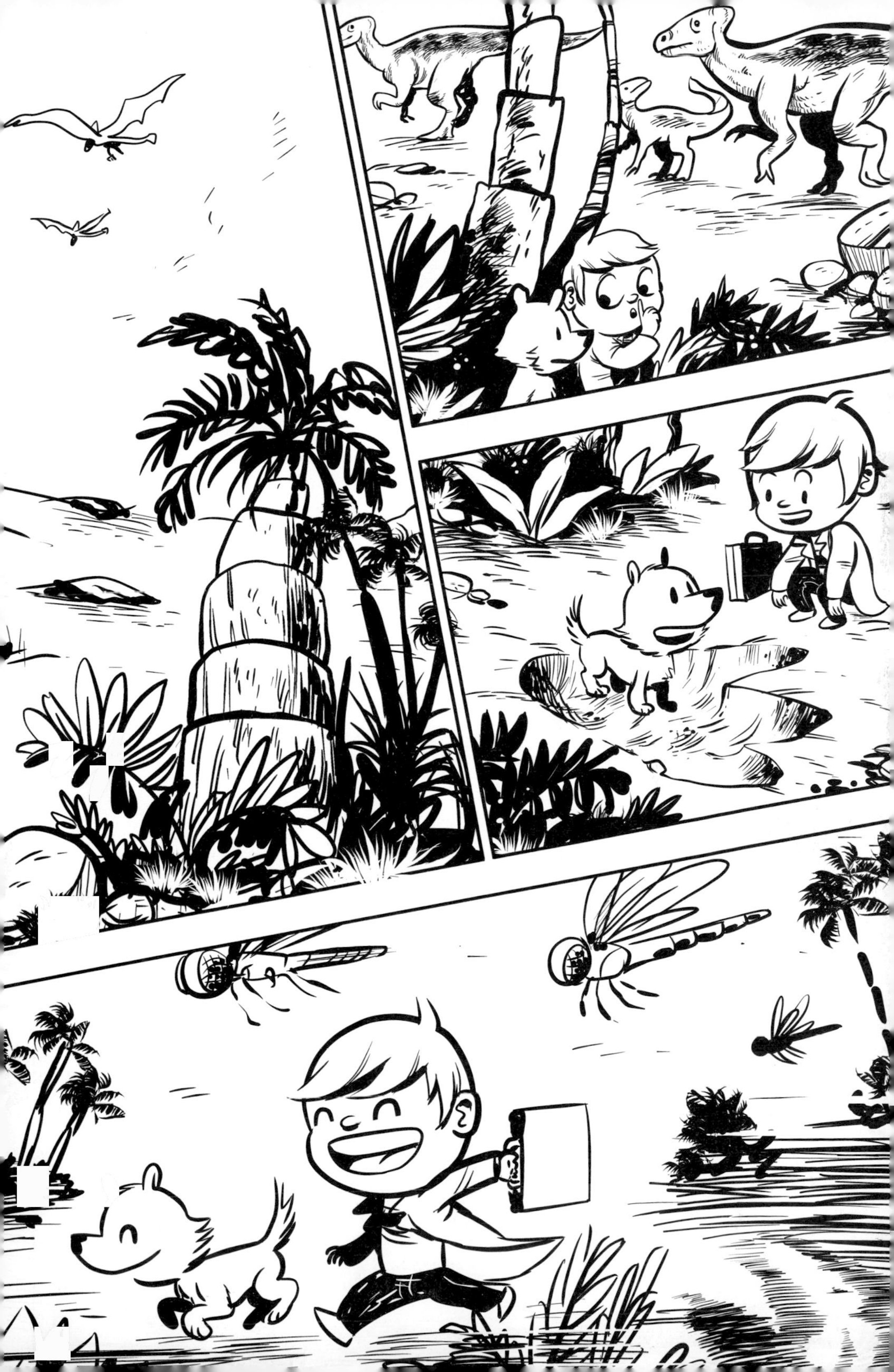

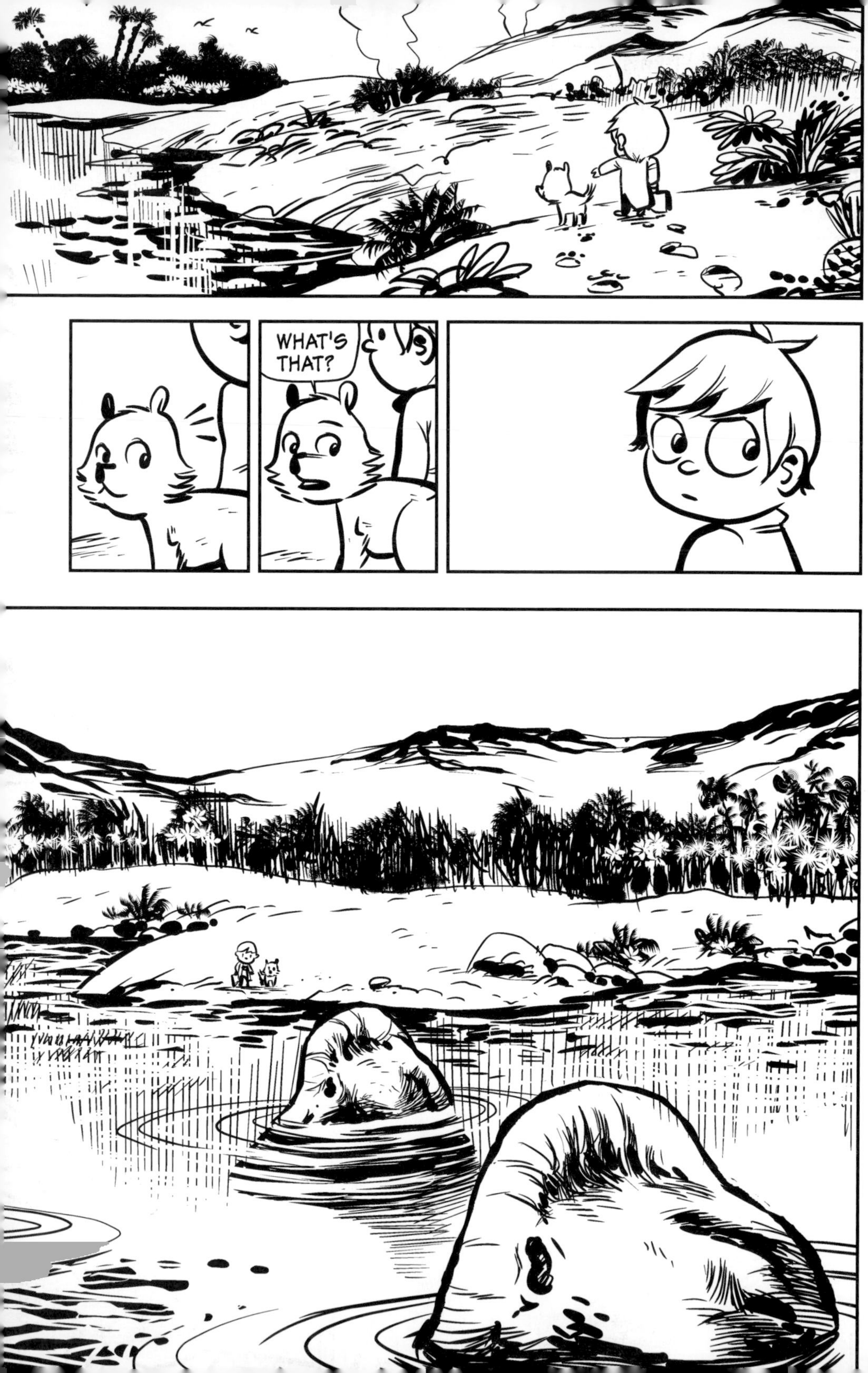
WHAT'S THAT?

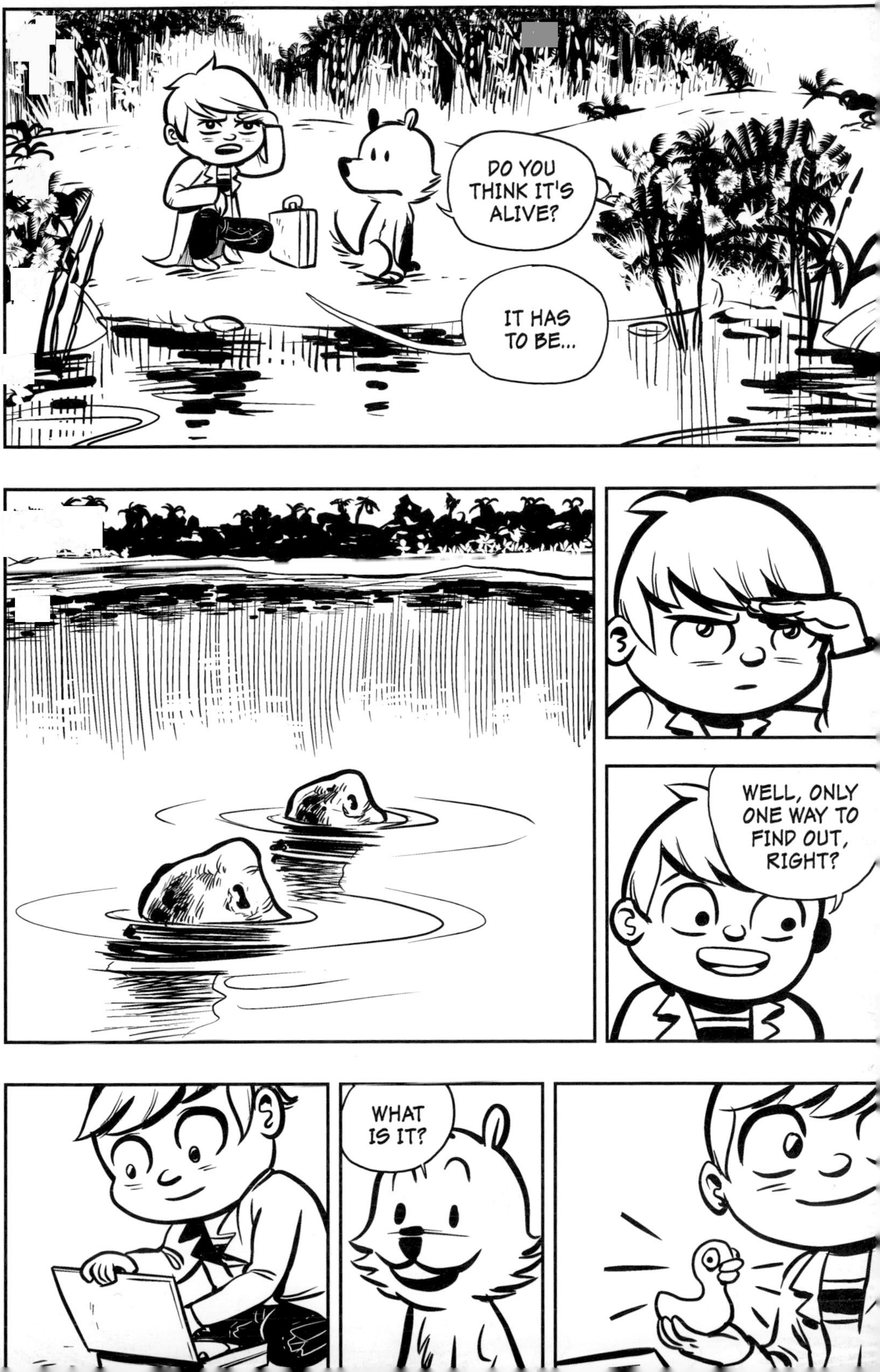
DO YOU THINK IT'S ALIVE?
IT HAS TO BE...
WELL, ONLY ONE WAY TO FIND OUT, RIGHT?
WHAT IS IT?

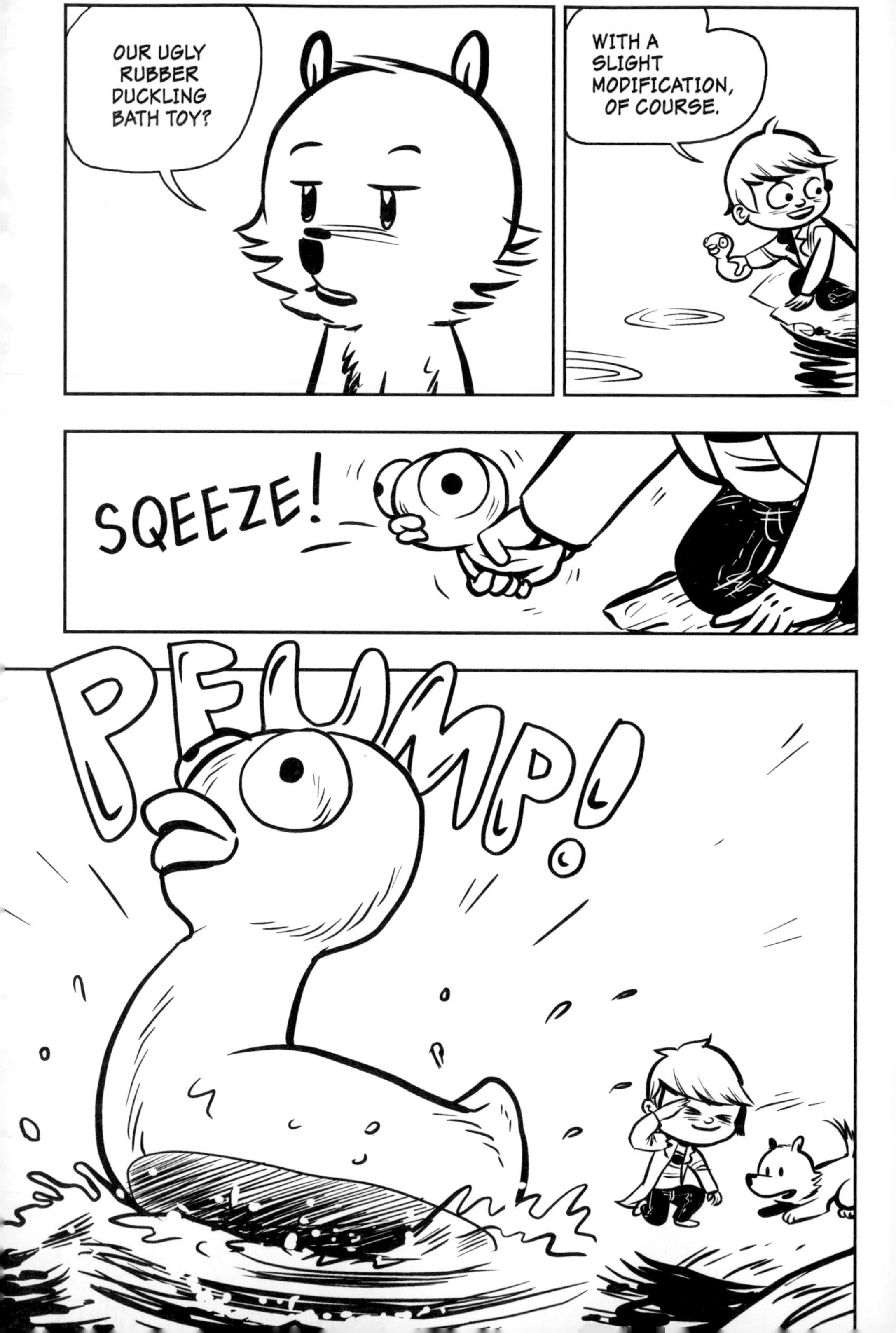
OUR UGLY RUBBER DUCKLING BATH TOY?
WITH A SLIGHT MODIFICATION, OF COURSE.
SQEEZE!
PFUMP!

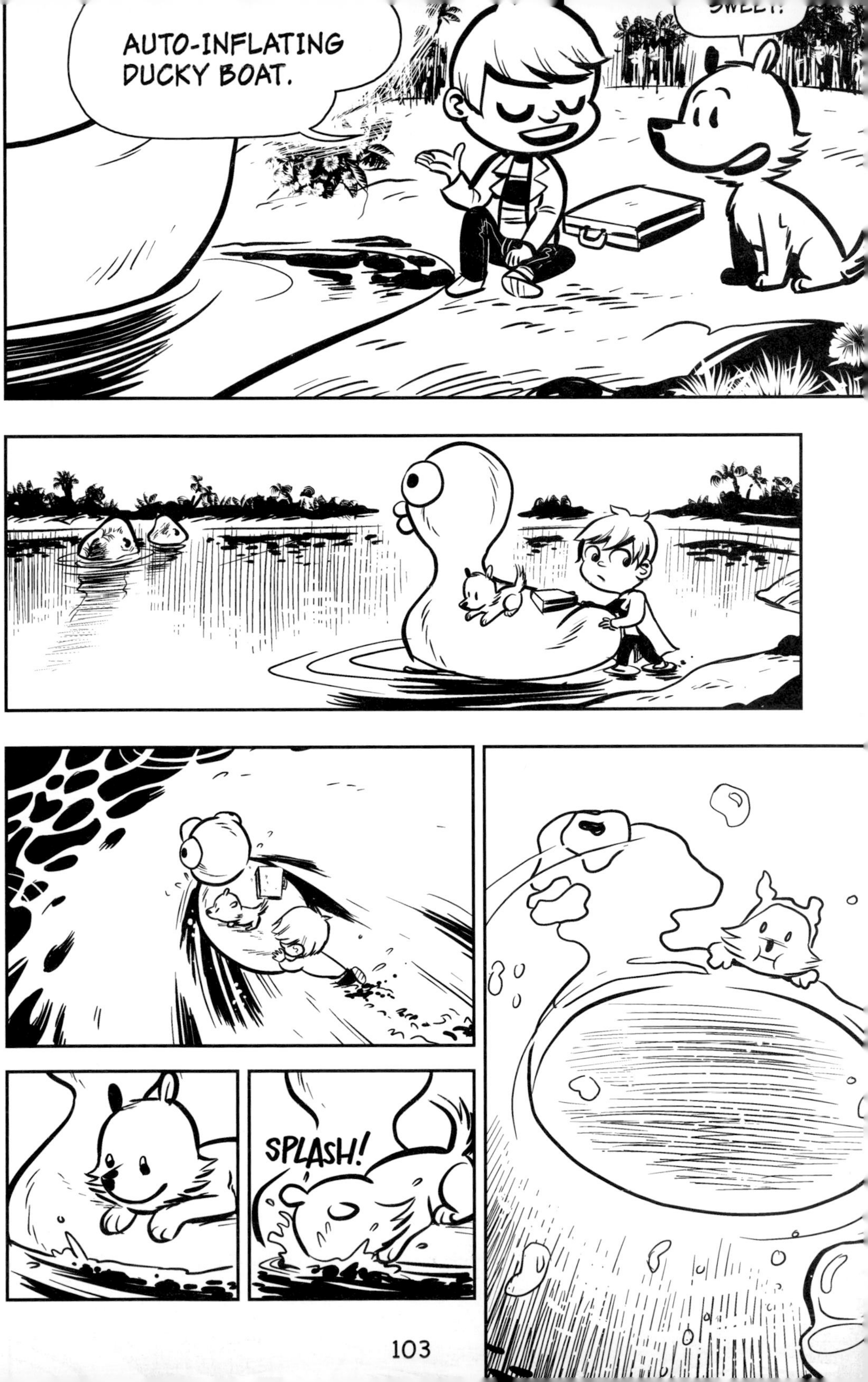
AUTO-INFLATING DUCKY BOAT.
SPLASH!

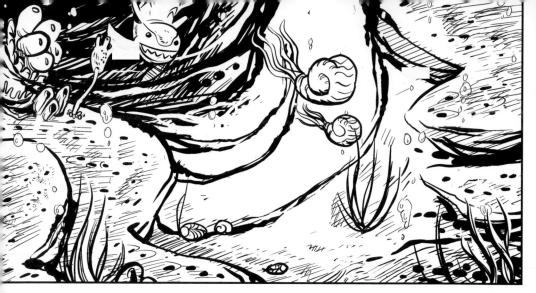

THERE ARE SOME AMAZING CREATURES DOWN THERE!

WE'RE GETTING CLOSE. CAN YOU LOOK DOWN THERE AND SEE WHAT THOSE THINGS ARE?

OH YEAH! I'LL CHECK.

sploosh!

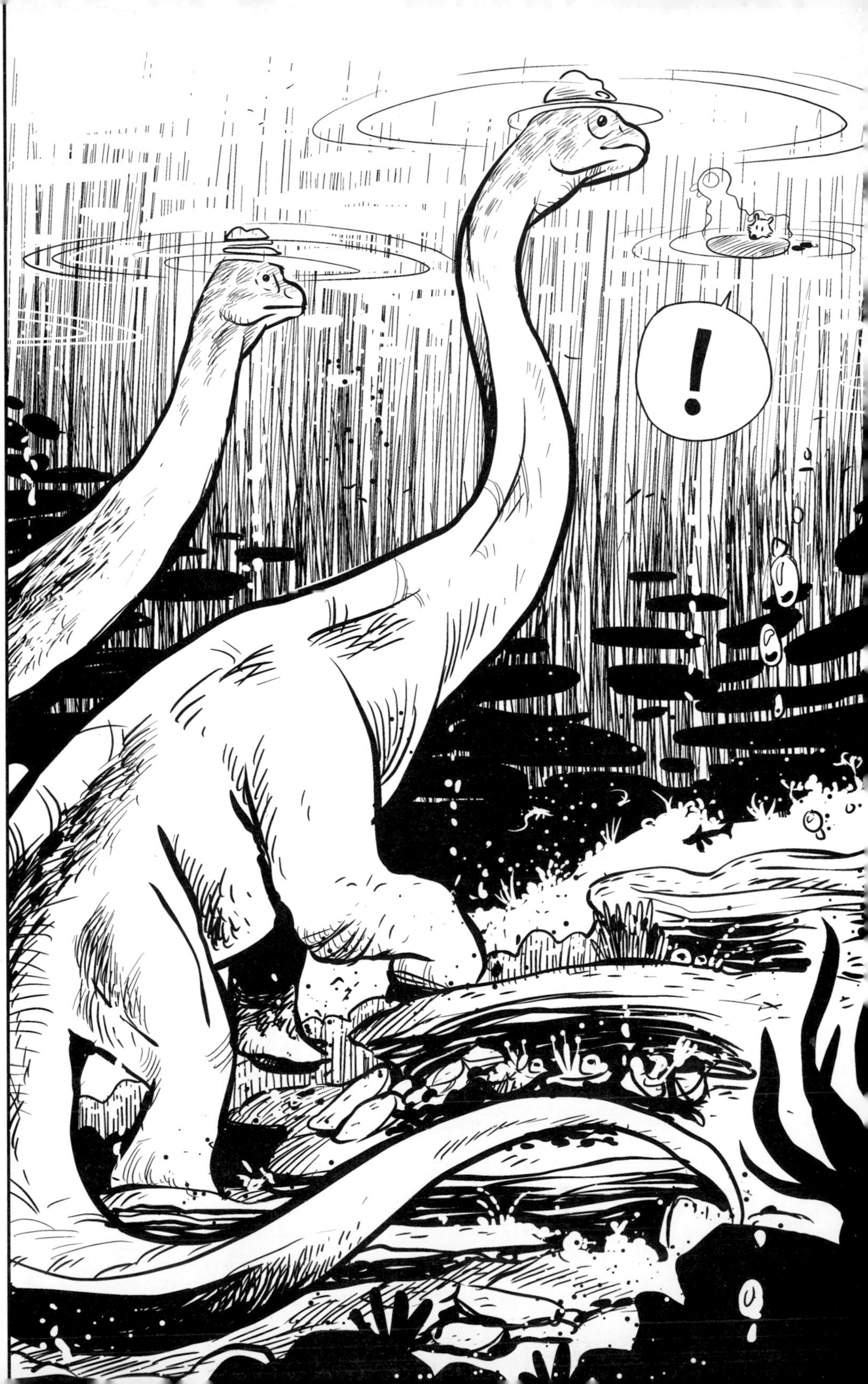
!

SWIM FOR YOUR LIFE!

THERE ARE HUGE DINOSAURS DOWN THERE, LIKE GIANT UNDERWATER LIZARD GIRAFFES!

GIRAFFES? OH, WHY DIDN'T I SEE IT BEFORE!

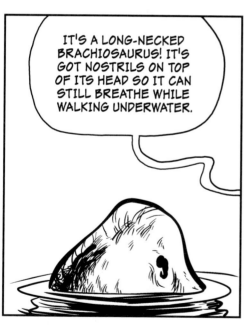

IT'S A LONG-NECKED BRACHIOSAURUS! IT'S GOT NOSTRILS ON TOP OF ITS HEAD SO IT CAN STILL BREATHE WHILE WALKING UNDERWATER.

BOOSH!

AAAHH! IT'S GOING TO EAT US!

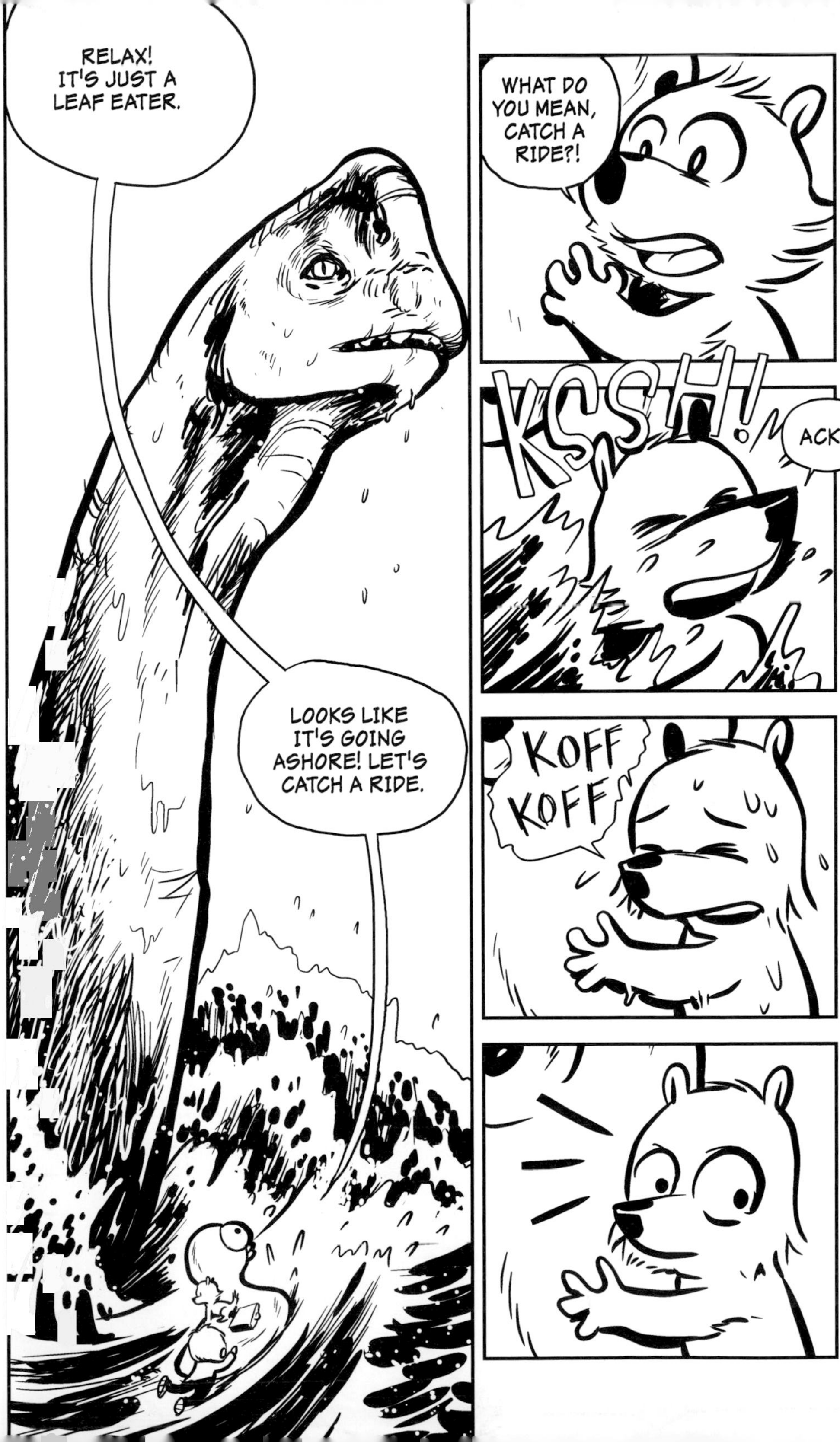
RELAX! IT'S JUST A LEAF EATER.
LOOKS LIKE IT'S GOING ASHORE! LET'S CATCH A RIDE.
WHAT DO YOU MEAN, CATCH A RIDE?!
KSSH!
ACK!
KOFF KOFF

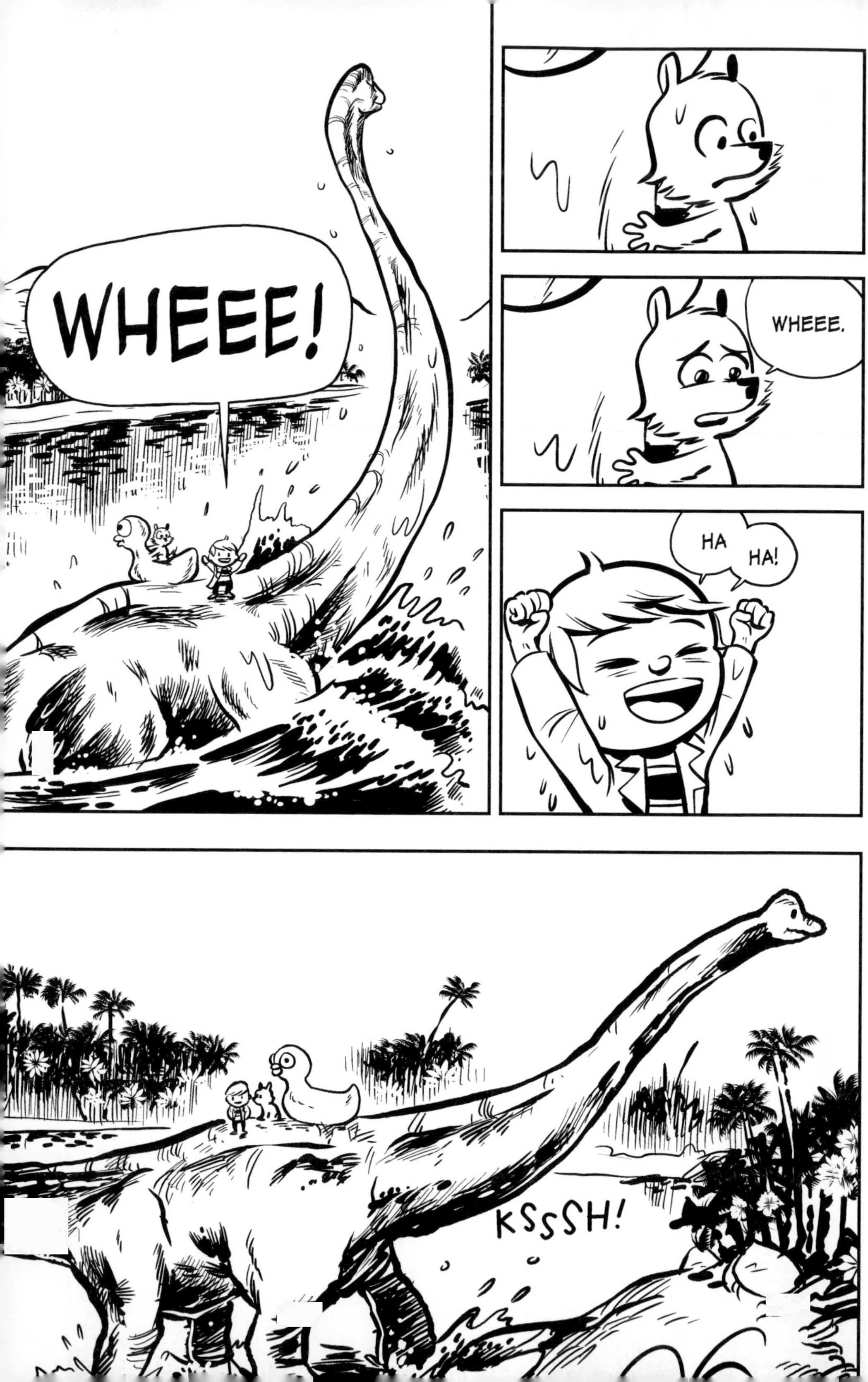

WHEEE!
WHEEE.
HA
HA!
KSSSH!

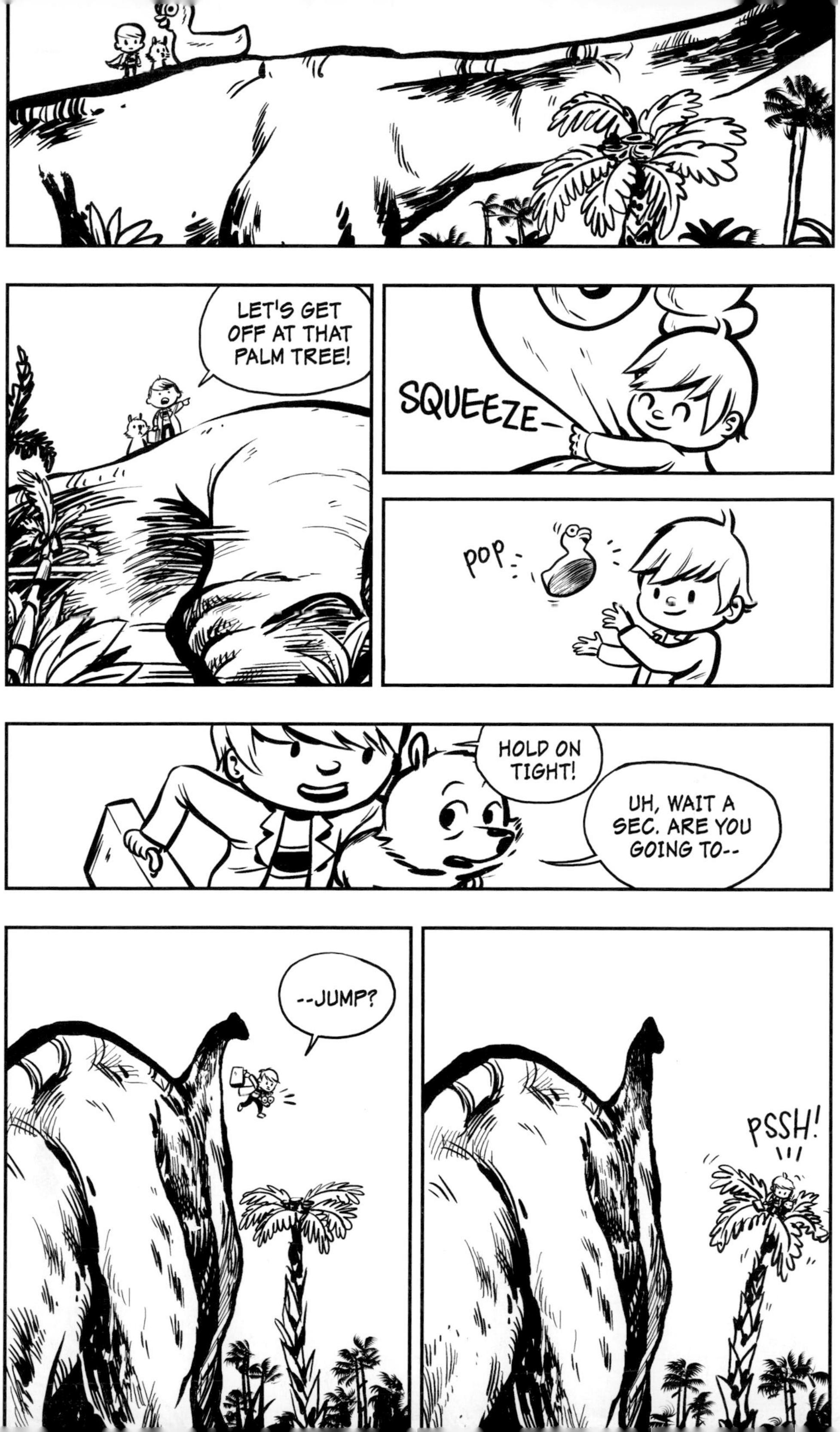
LET'S GET OFF AT THAT PALM TREE!
SQUEEZE
pop
HOLD ON TIGHT!
UH, WAIT A SEC. ARE YOU GOING TO--
--JUMP?
PSSH!

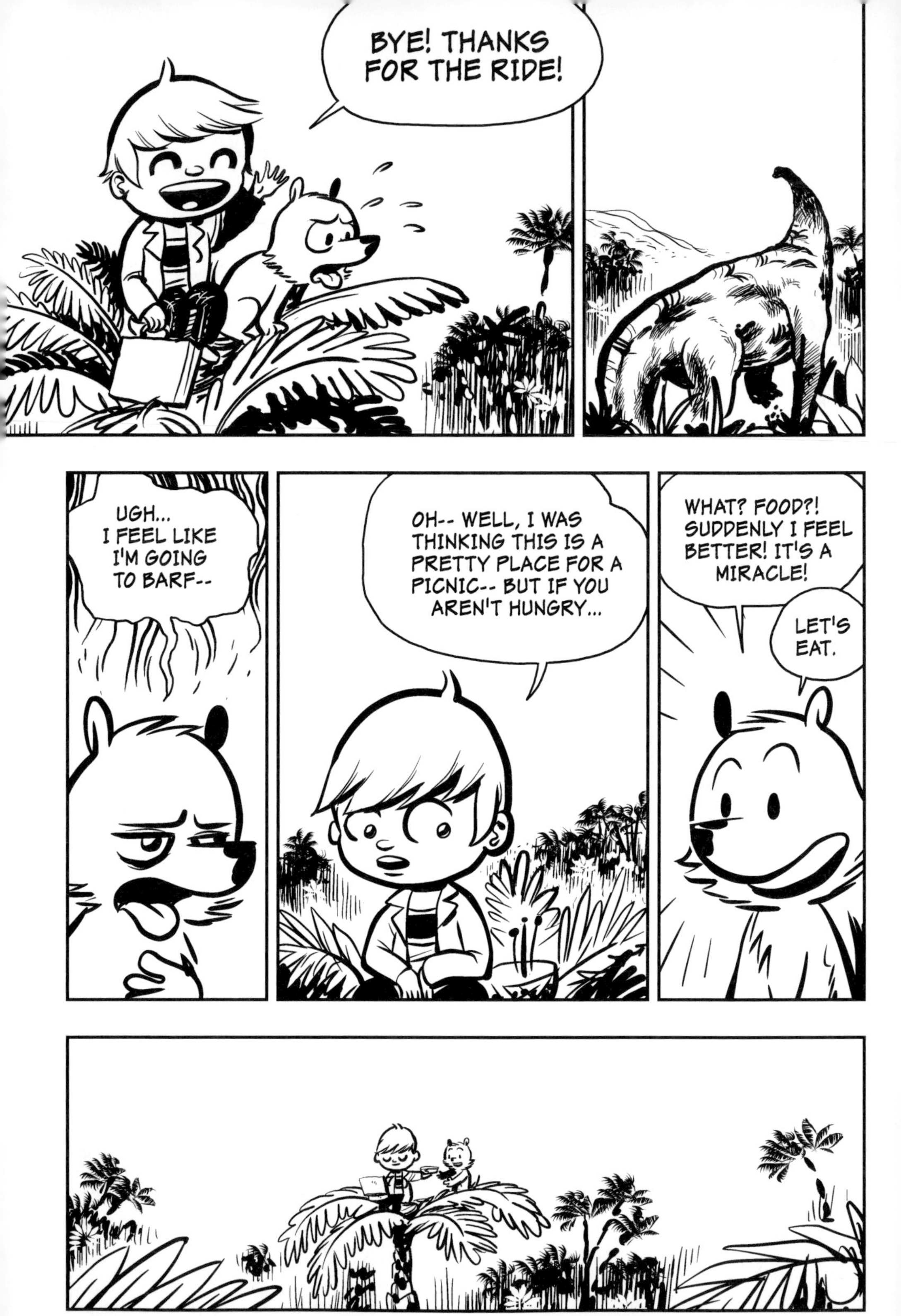
BYE! THANKS FOR THE RIDE!
UGH... I FEEL LIKE I'M GOING TO BARF--
OH-- WELL, I WAS THINKING THIS IS A PRETTY PLACE FOR A PICNIC-- BUT IF YOU AREN'T HUNGRY...
WHAT? FOOD?! SUDDENLY I FEEL BETTER! IT'S A MIRACLE!
LET'S EAT.

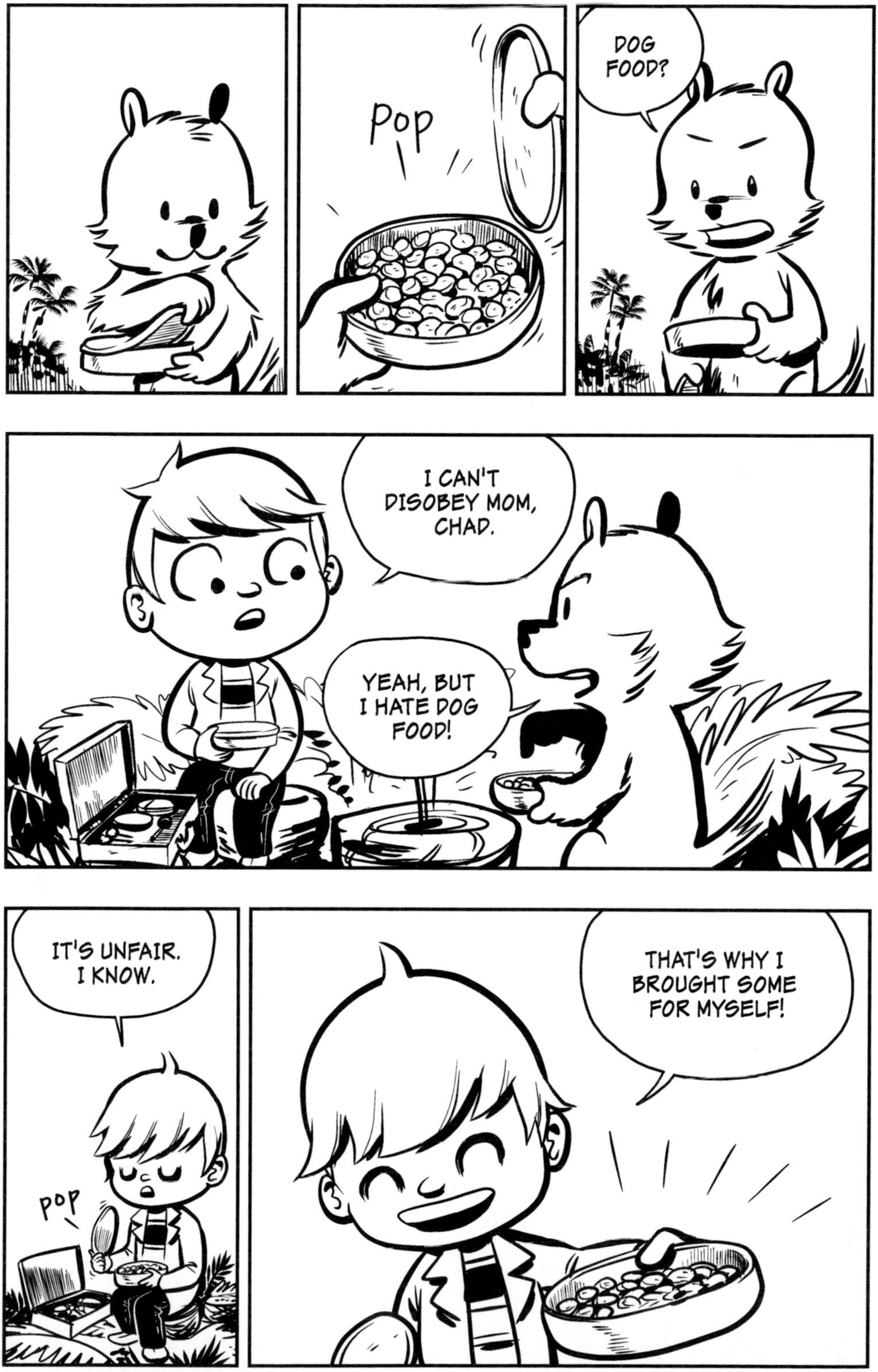
POP
DOG FOOD?
I CAN'T DISOBEY MOM, CHAD.
YEAH, BUT I HATE DOG FOOD!
IT'S UNFAIR. I KNOW.
POP
THAT'S WHY I BROUGHT SOME FOR MYSELF!

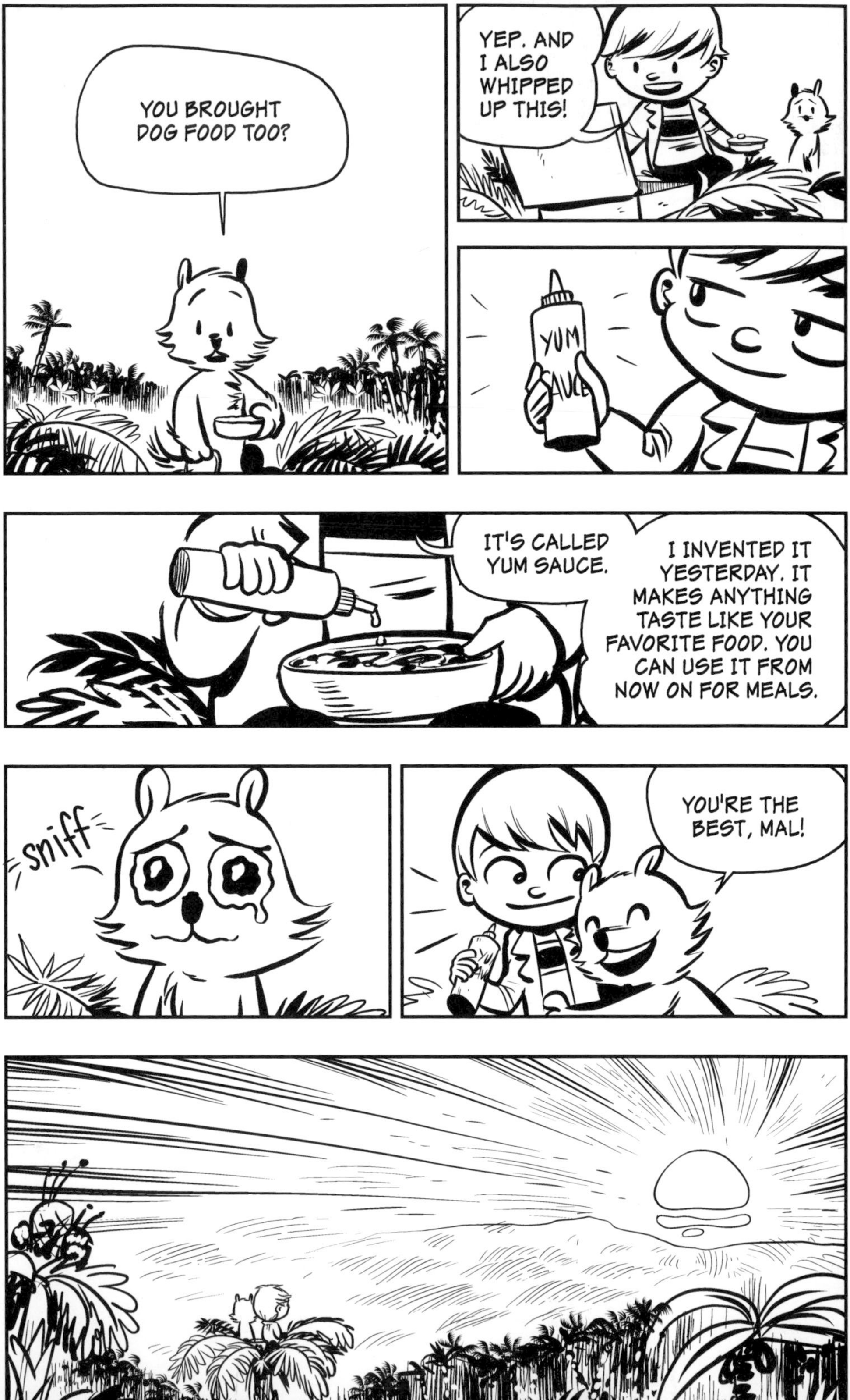
YOU BROUGHT DOG FOOD TOO?
YEP. AND I ALSO WHIPPED UP THIS!
YUM SAUCE
IT'S CALLED YUM SAUCE.
I INVENTED IT YESTERDAY. IT MAKES ANYTHING TASTE LIKE YOUR FAVORITE FOOD. YOU CAN USE IT FROM NOW ON FOR MEALS.
sniff
YOU'RE THE BEST, MAL!

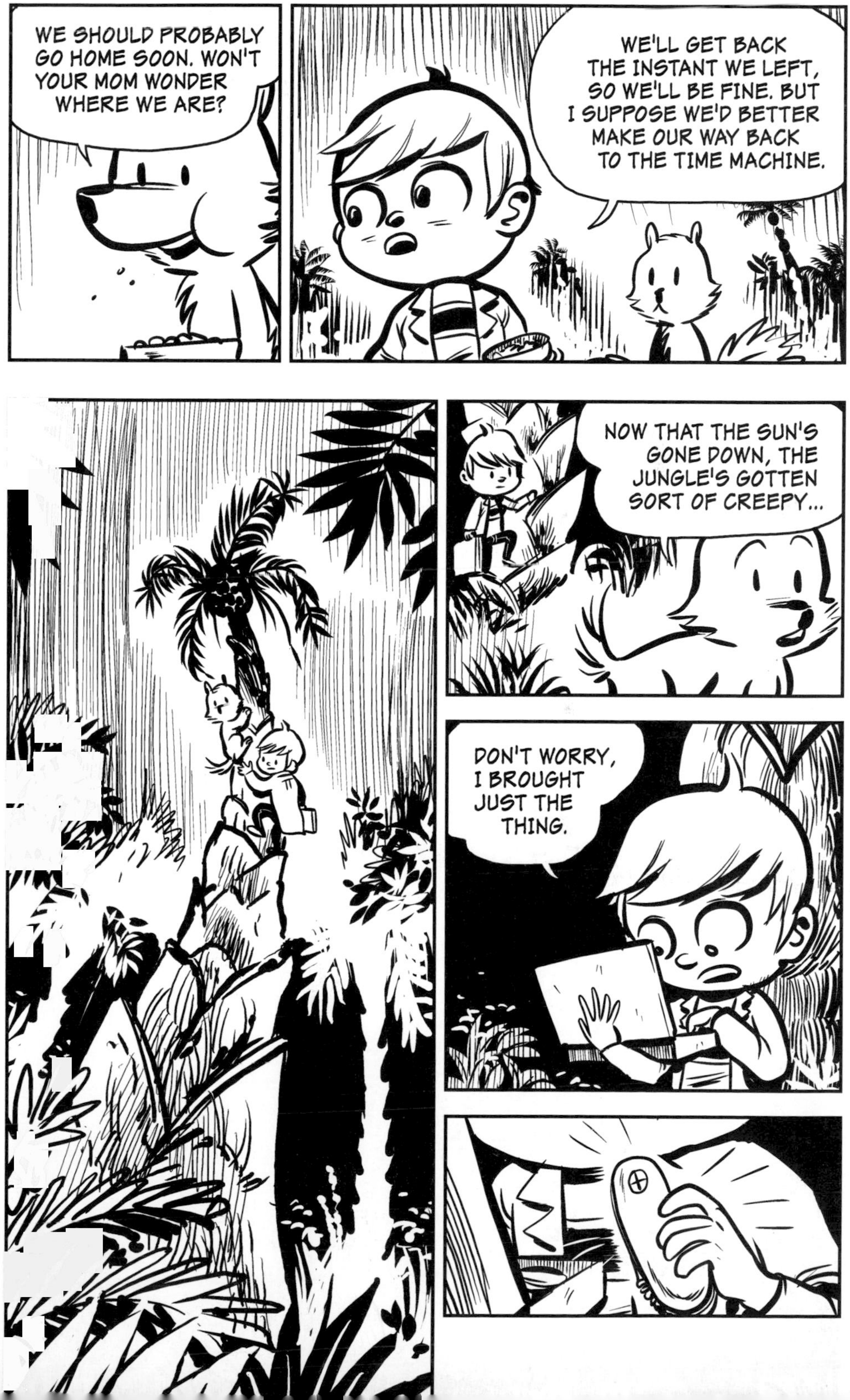
WE SHOULD PROBABLY GO HOME SOON. WON'T YOUR MOM WONDER WHERE WE ARE?
WE'LL GET BACK THE INSTANT WE LEFT, SO WE'LL BE FINE. BUT I SUPPOSE WE'D BETTER MAKE OUR WAY BACK TO THE TIME MACHINE.
NOW THAT THE SUN'S GONE DOWN, THE JUNGLE'S GOTTEN SORT OF CREEPY...
DON'T WORRY, I BROUGHT JUST THE THING.

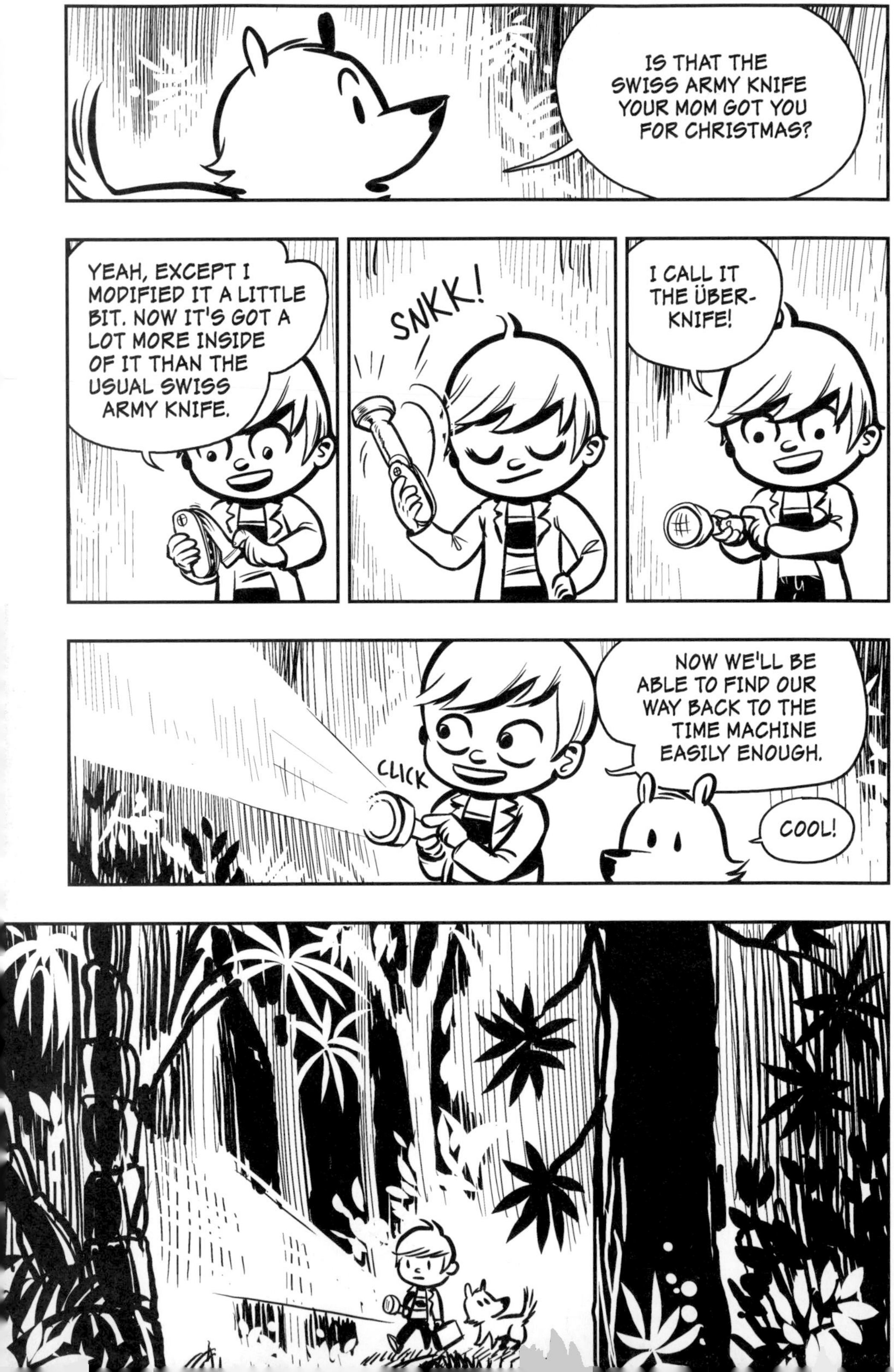
IS THAT THE SWISS ARMY KNIFE YOUR MOM GOT YOU FOR CHRISTMAS?
YEAH, EXCEPT I MODIFIED IT A LITTLE BIT. NOW IT'S GOT A LOT MORE INSIDE OF IT THAN THE USUAL SWISS ARMY KNIFE.
SNKK!
I CALL IT THE ÜBER-KNIFE!
CLICK
NOW WE'LL BE ABLE TO FIND OUR WAY BACK TO THE TIME MACHINE EASILY ENOUGH.
COOL!

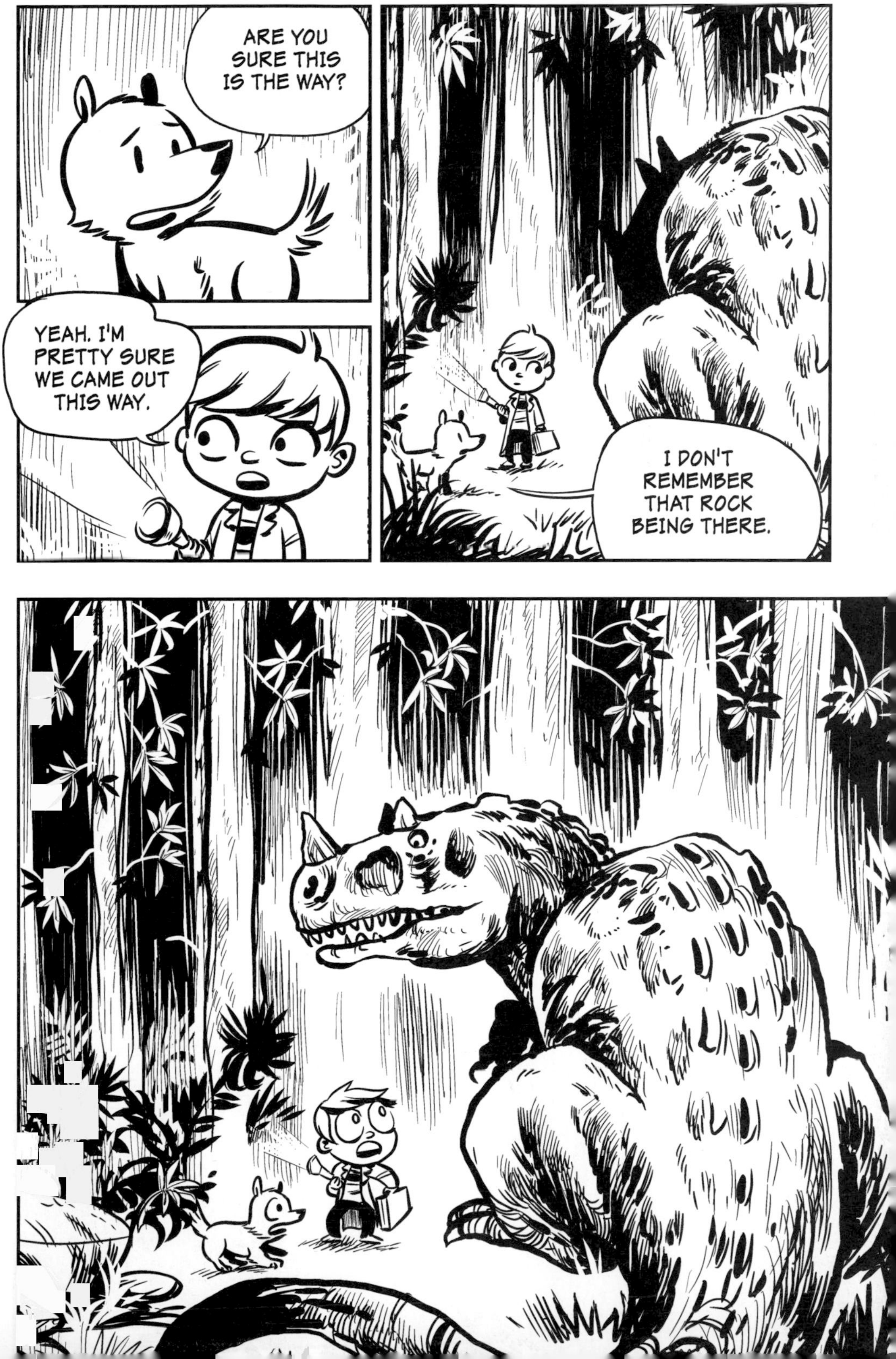
ARE YOU SURE THIS IS THE WAY?
YEAH. I'M PRETTY SURE WE CAME OUT THIS WAY.
I DON'T REMEMBER THAT ROCK BEING THERE.

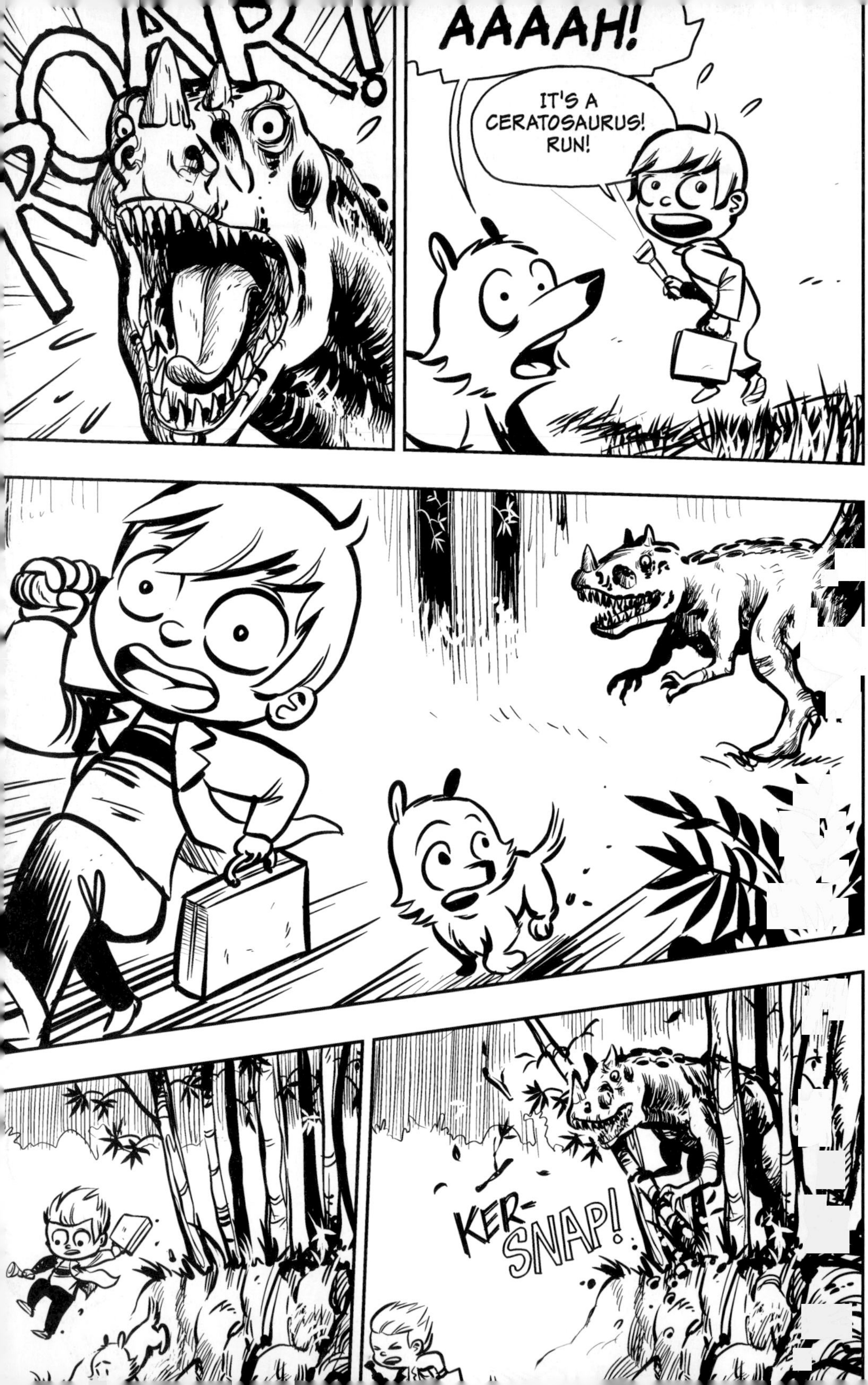

ROAR!
AAAAH!
IT'S A CERATOSAURUS! RUN!
KER-SNAP!

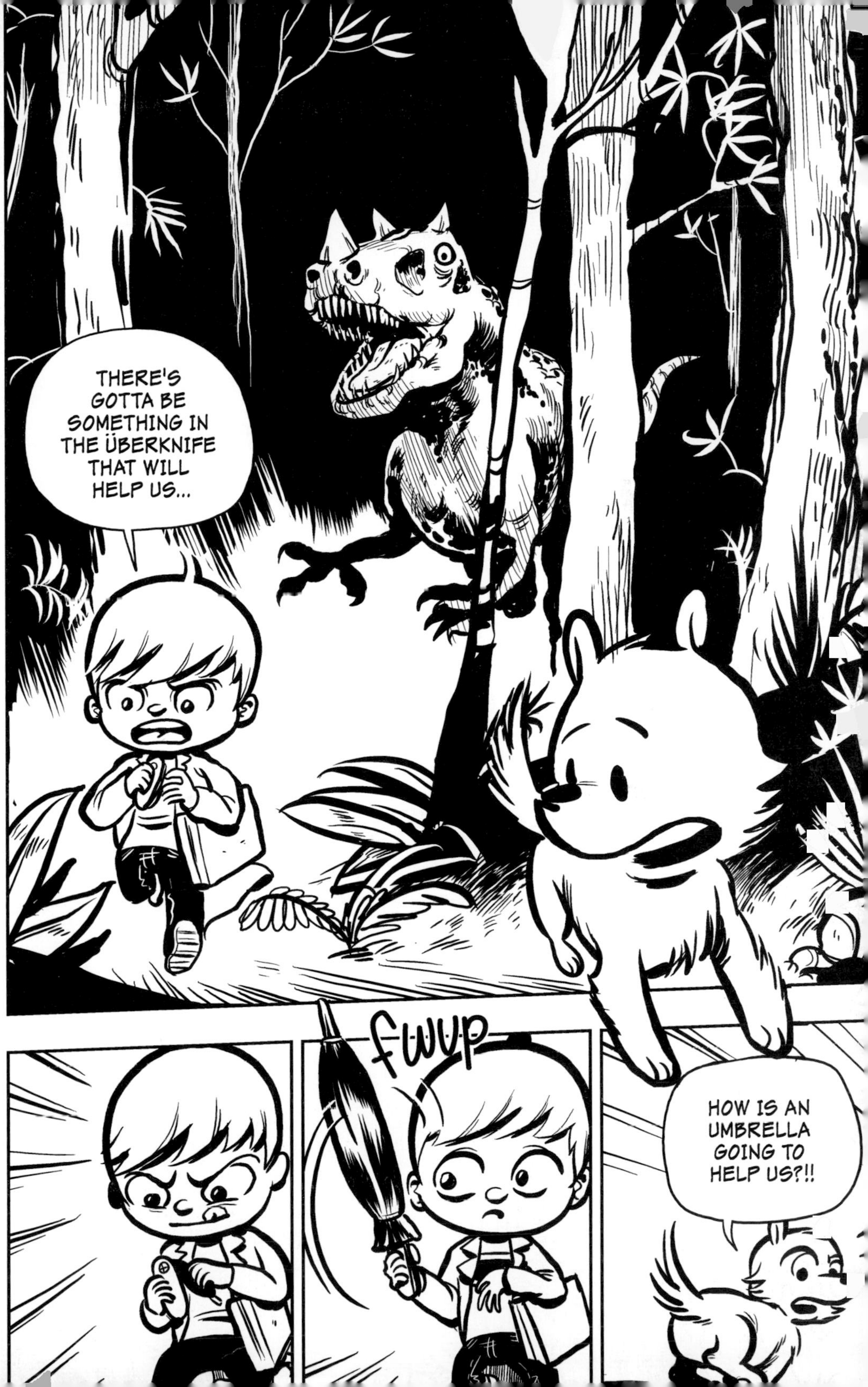
THERE'S GOTTA BE SOMETHING IN THE ÜBERKNIFE THAT WILL HELP US...
fwup
HOW IS AN UMBRELLA GOING TO HELP US?!!

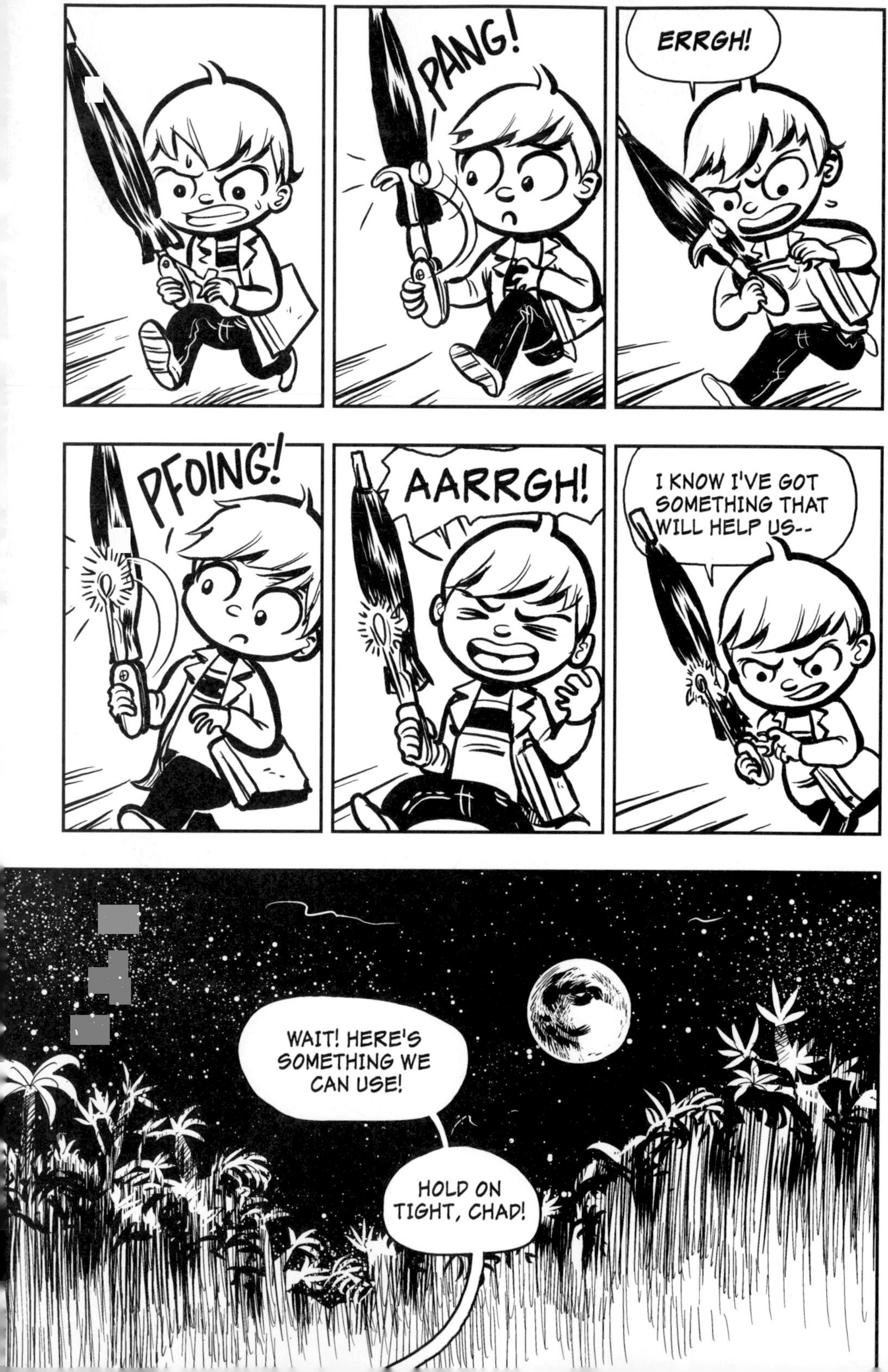
PANG!
ERRGH!
PFOING!
AARRGH!
I KNOW I'VE GOT SOMETHING THAT WILL HELP US--
WAIT! HERE'S SOMETHING WE CAN USE!
HOLD ON TIGHT, CHAD!

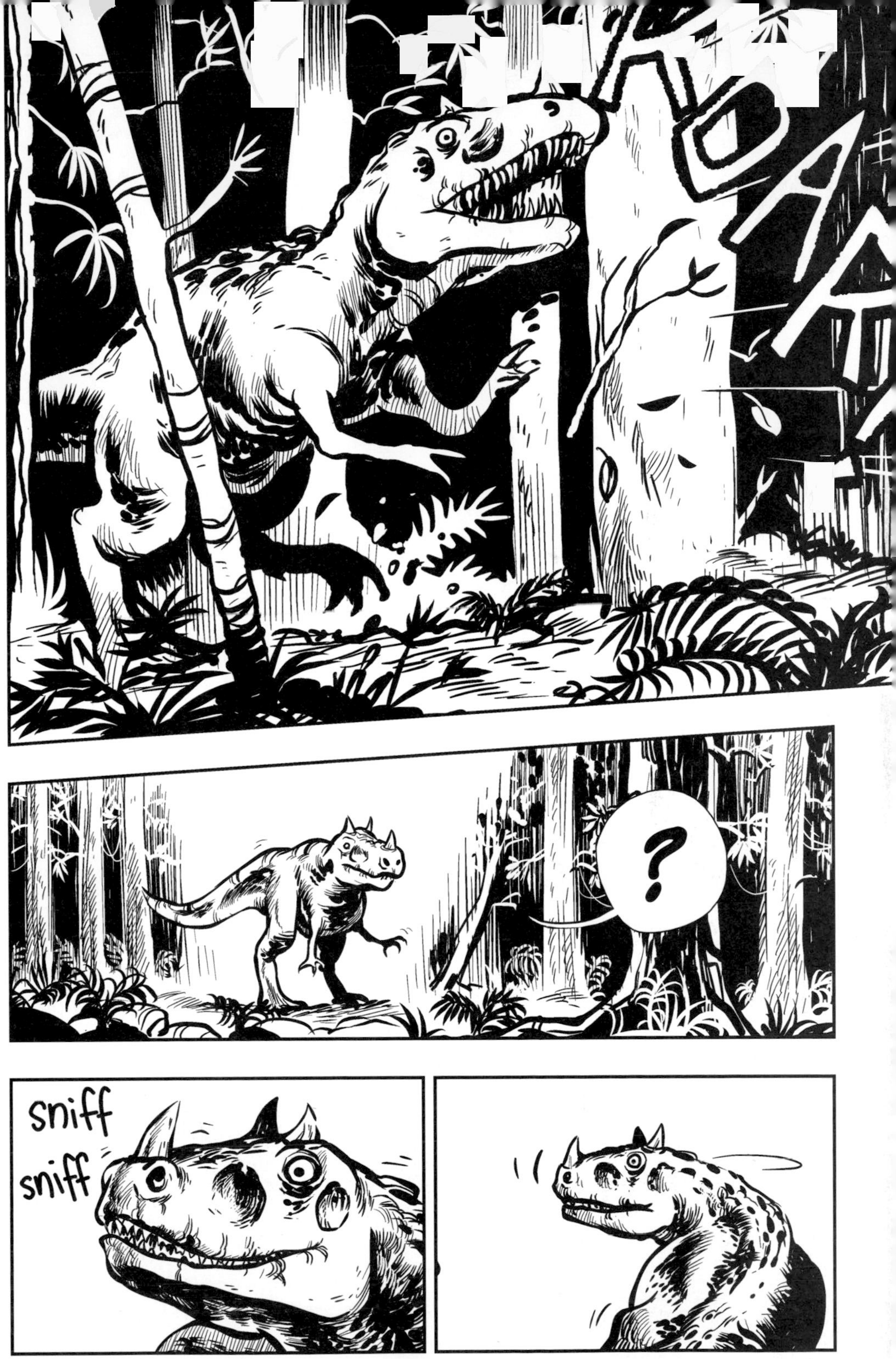
?
sniff
sniff

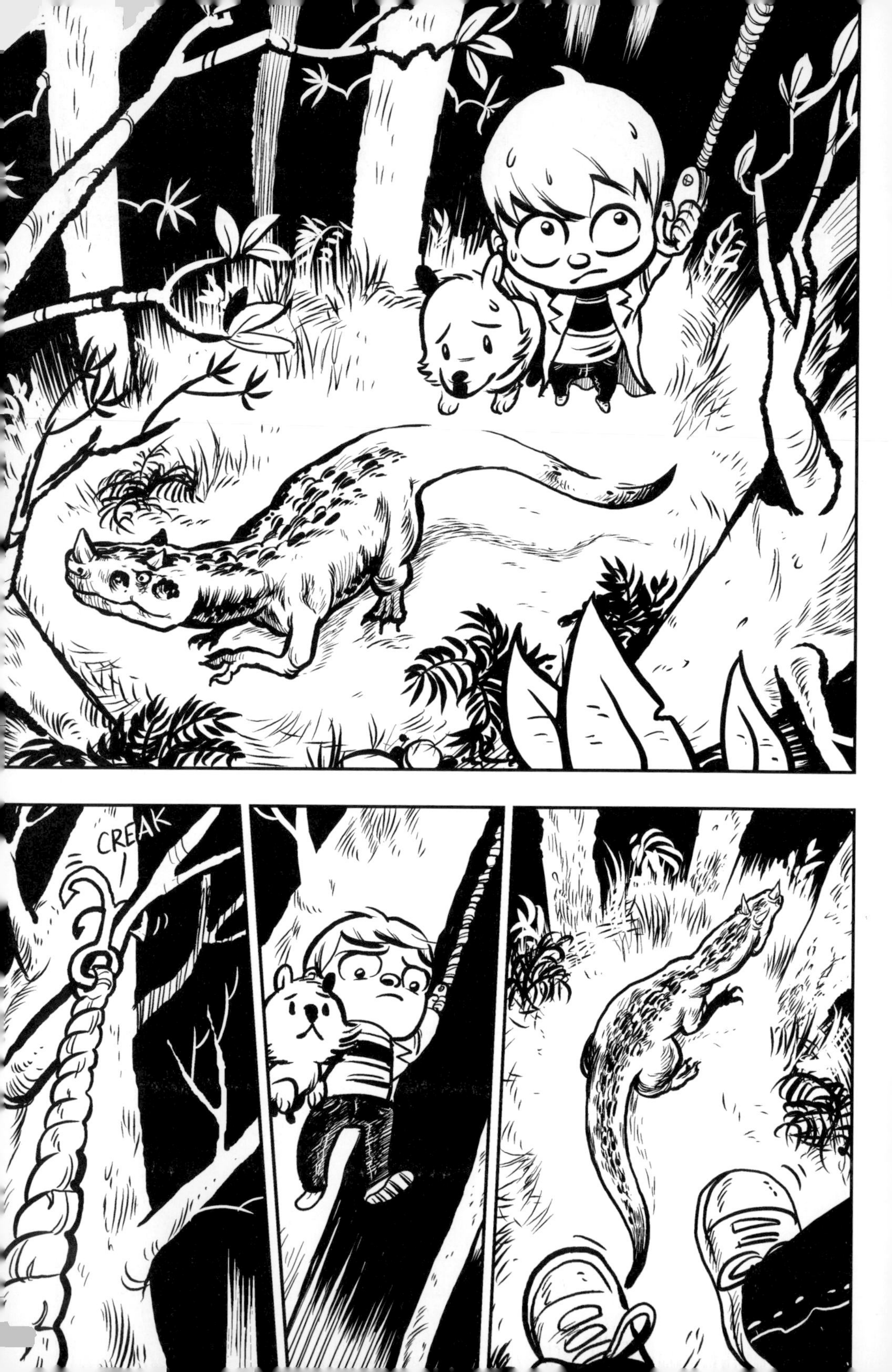
CREAK

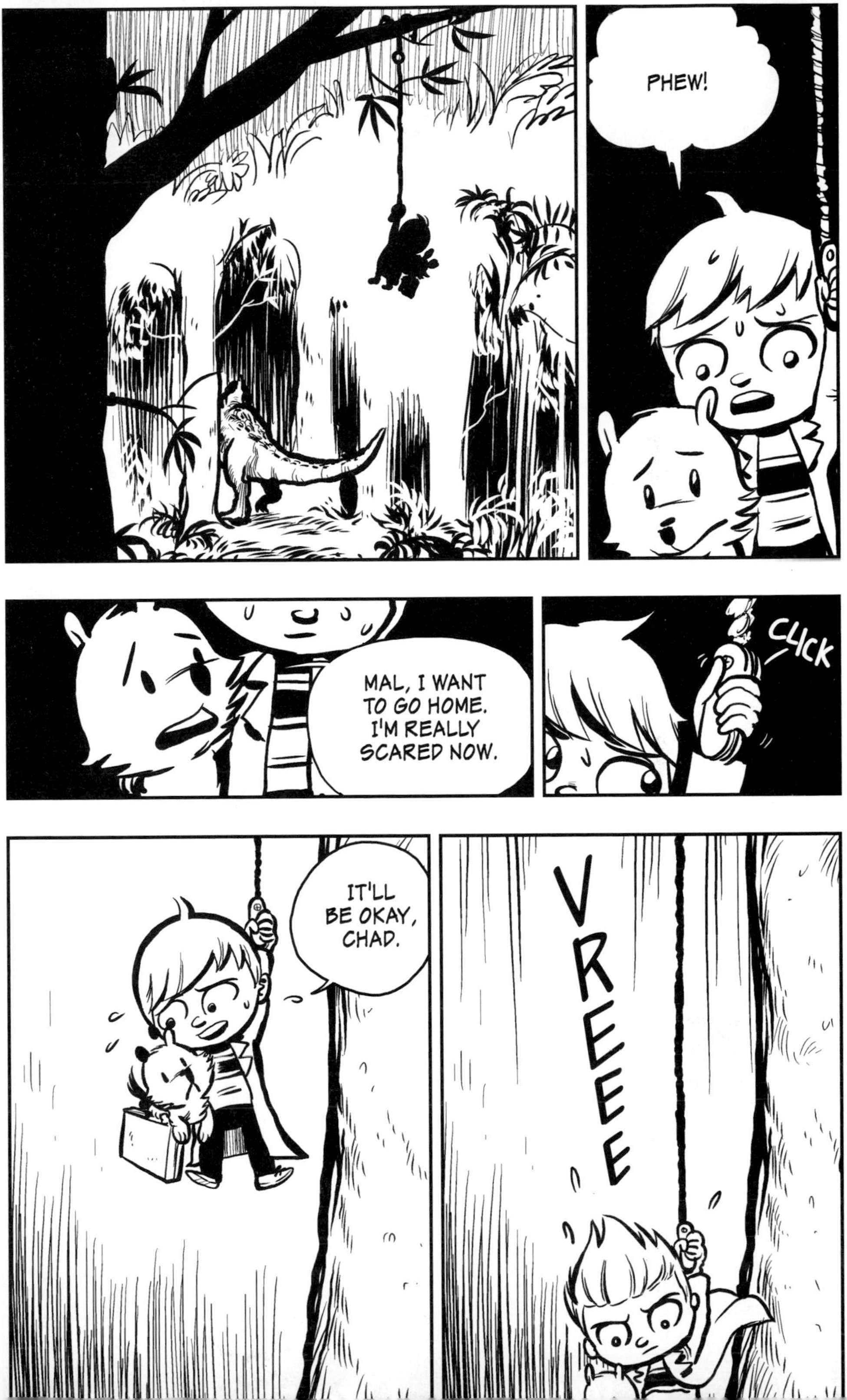
PHEW!
MAL, I WANT TO GO HOME. I'M REALLY SCARED NOW.
CLICK
IT'LL BE OKAY, CHAD.
VREEEE

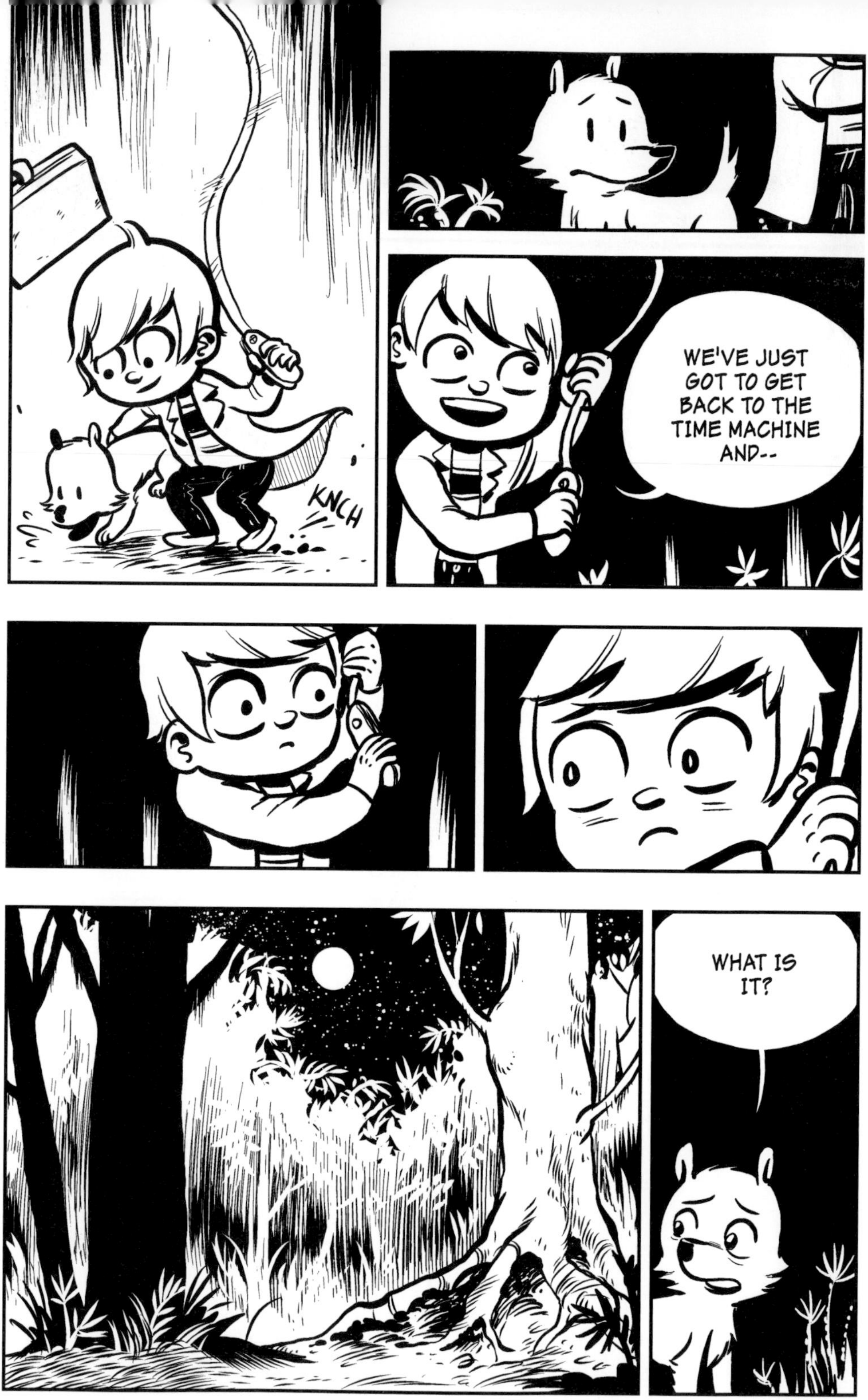
KNCH
WE'VE JUST GOT TO GET BACK TO THE TIME MACHINE AND--
WHAT IS IT?

WHERE ARE WE?

CHAPTER 6
But Mal, Think of the Omelets!

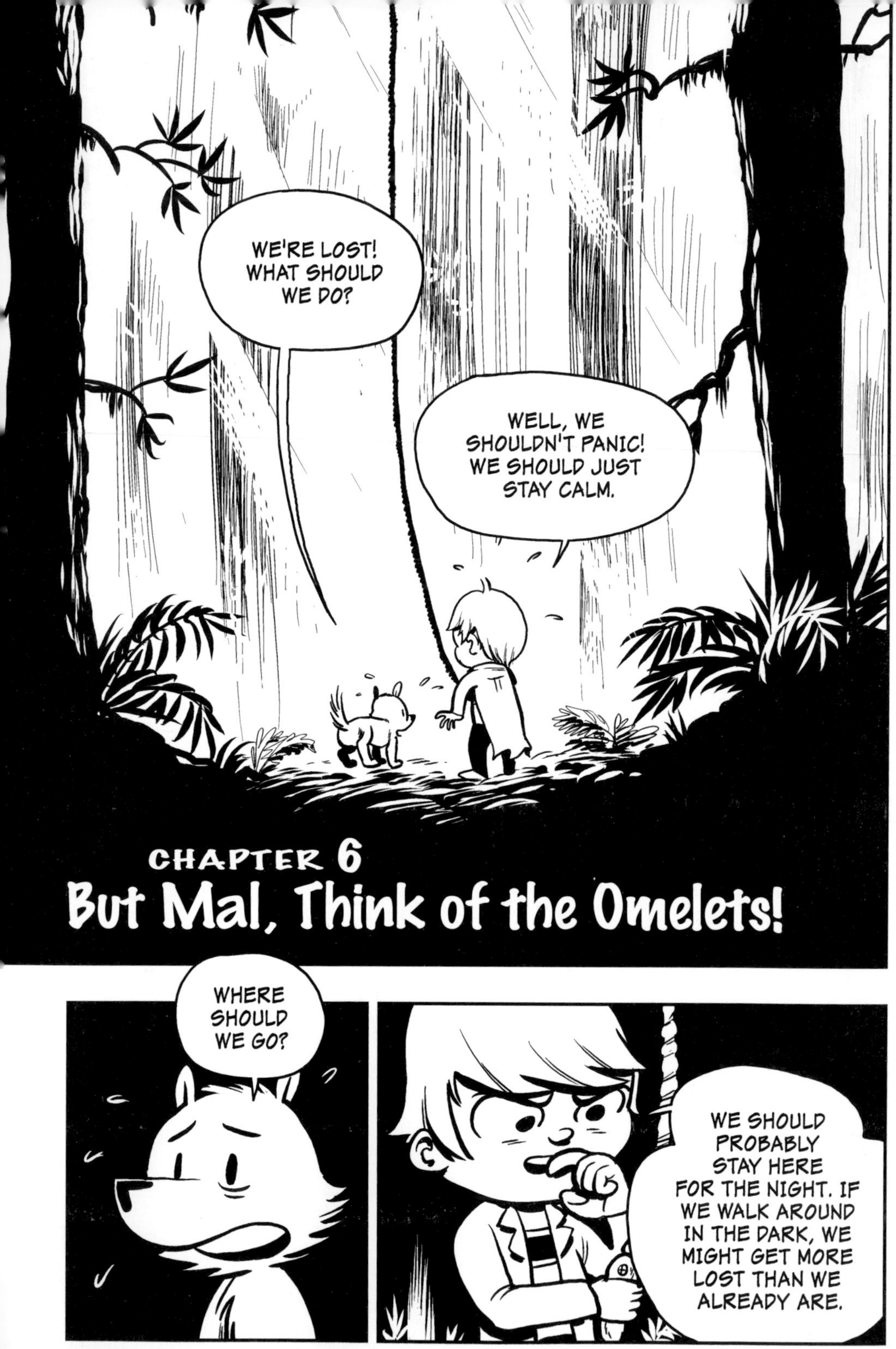
WE'RE LOST! WHAT SHOULD WE DO?
WELL, WE SHOULDN'T PANIC! WE SHOULD JUST STAY CALM.
WHERE SHOULD WE GO?
WE SHOULD PROBABLY STAY HERE FOR THE NIGHT. IF WE WALK AROUND IN THE DARK, WE MIGHT GET MORE LOST THAN WE ALREADY ARE.

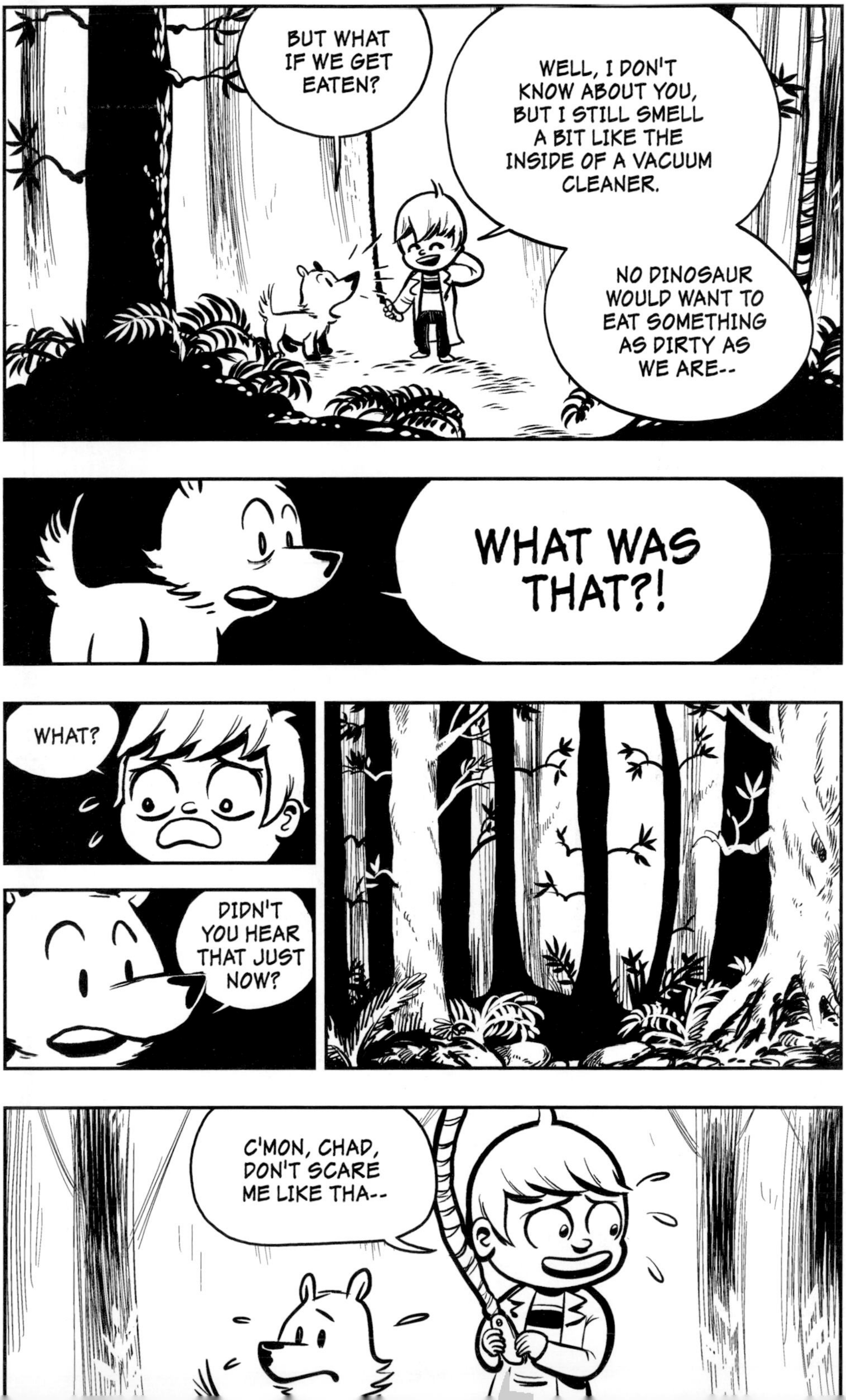

BUT WHAT IF WE GET EATEN?
WELL, I DON'T KNOW ABOUT YOU, BUT I STILL SMELL A BIT LIKE THE INSIDE OF A VACUUM CLEANER.
NO DINOSAUR WOULD WANT TO EAT SOMETHING AS DIRTY AS WE ARE--
WHAT WAS THAT?!
WHAT?
DIDN'T YOU HEAR THAT JUST NOW?
C'MON, CHAD, DON'T SCARE ME LIKE THA--

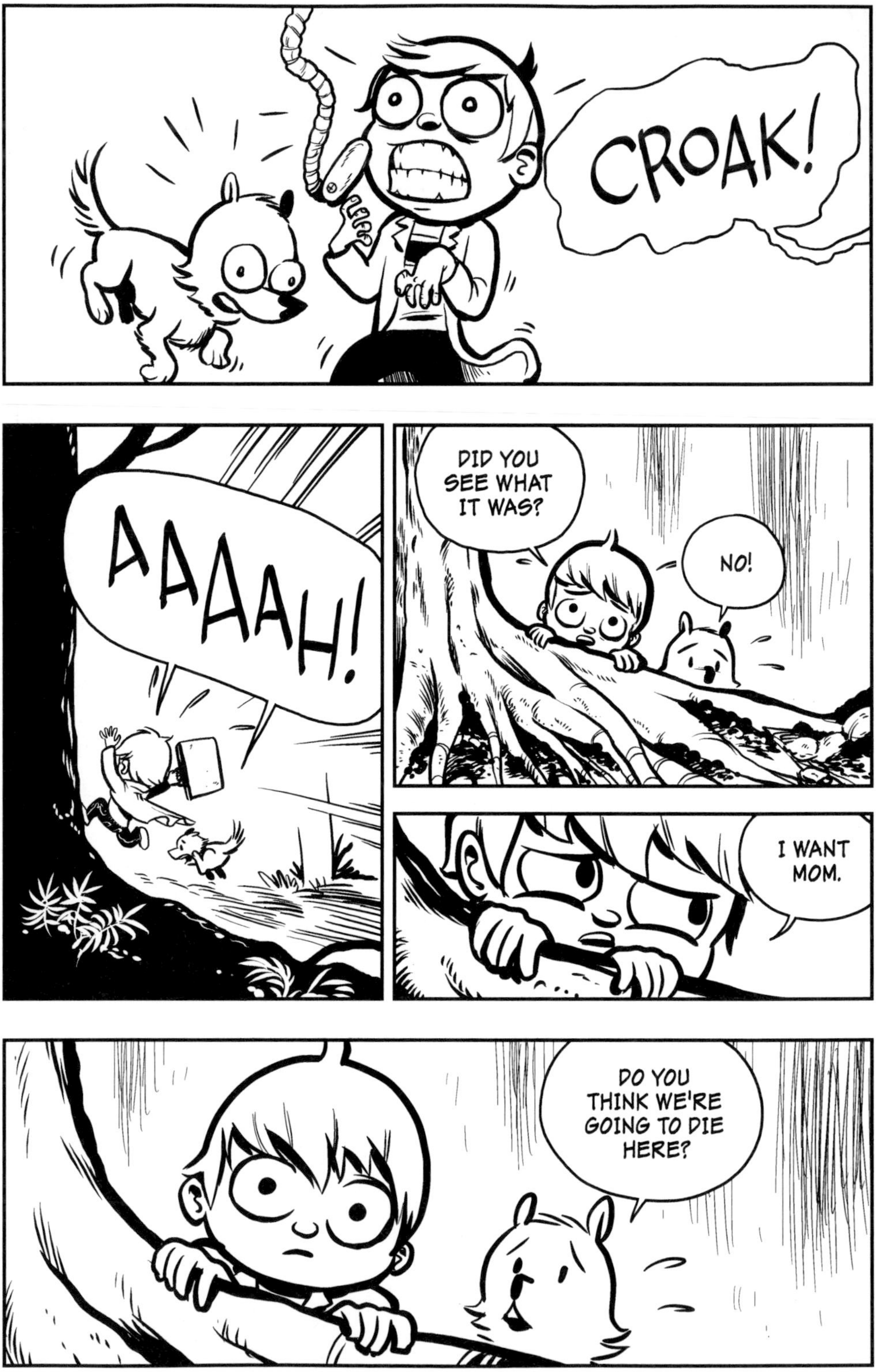
CROAK!
AAAAAH!
DID YOU SEE WHAT IT WAS?
NO!
I WANT MOM.
DO YOU THINK WE'RE GOING TO DIE HERE?

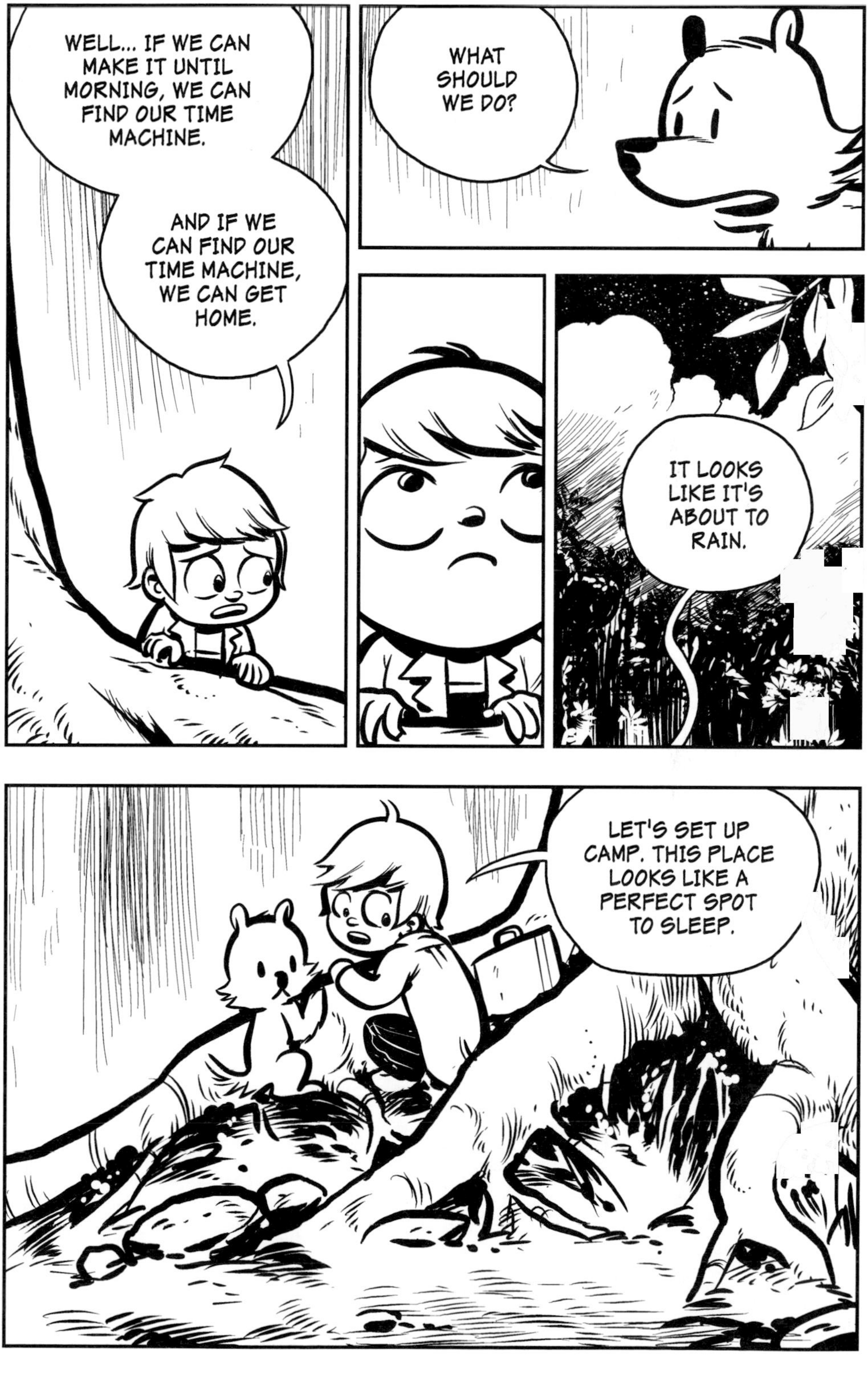
WELL... IF WE CAN MAKE IT UNTIL MORNING, WE CAN FIND OUR TIME MACHINE.
AND IF WE CAN FIND OUR TIME MACHINE, WE CAN GET HOME.
WHAT SHOULD WE DO?
IT LOOKS LIKE IT'S ABOUT TO RAIN.
LET'S SET UP CAMP. THIS PLACE LOOKS LIKE A PERFECT SPOT TO SLEEP.

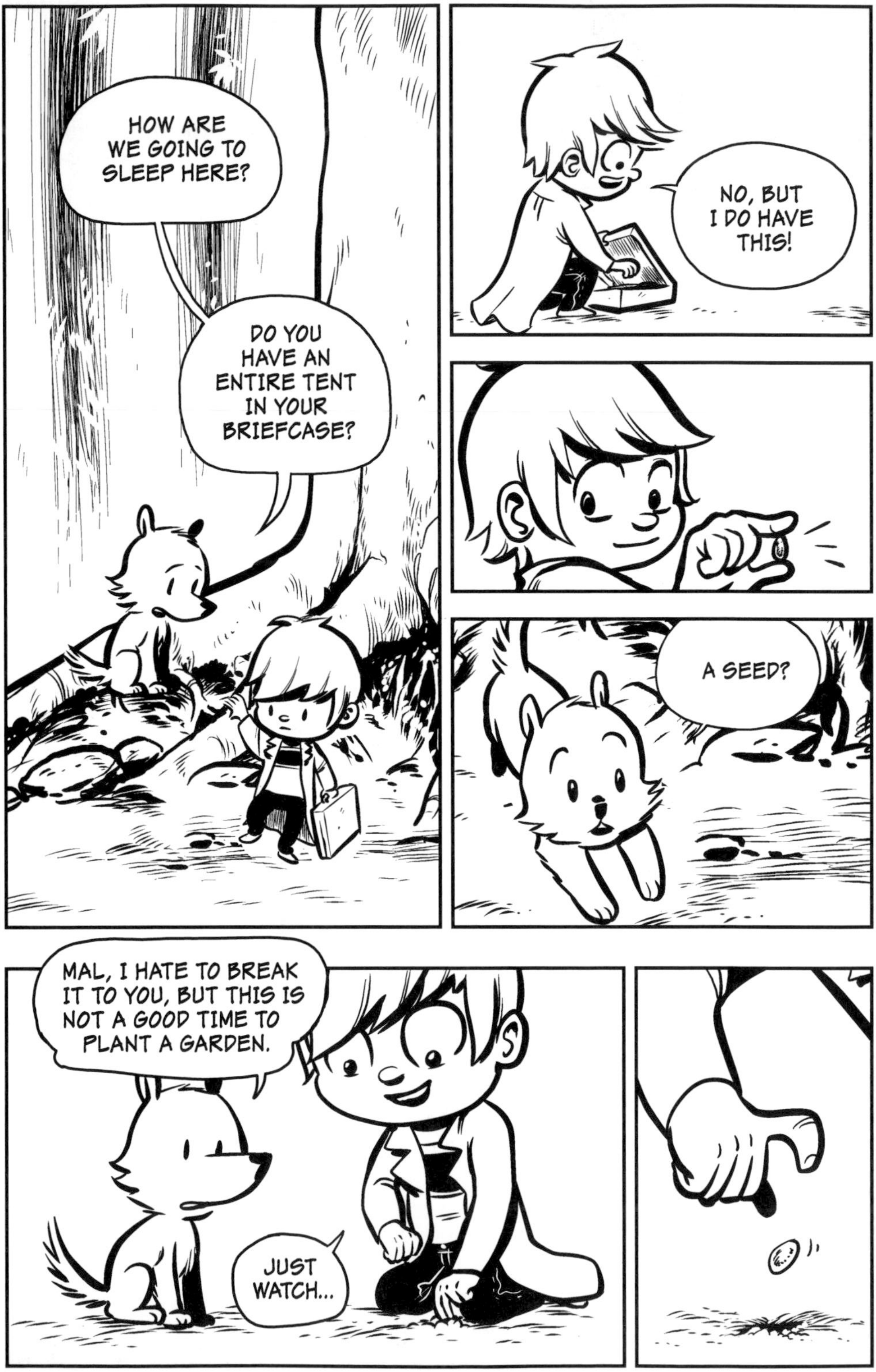
HOW ARE WE GOING TO SLEEP HERE?
DO YOU HAVE AN ENTIRE TENT IN YOUR BRIEFCASE?
NO, BUT I DO HAVE THIS!
A SEED?
MAL, I HATE TO BREAK IT TO YOU, BUT THIS IS NOT A GOOD TIME TO PLANT A GARDEN.
JUST WATCH...

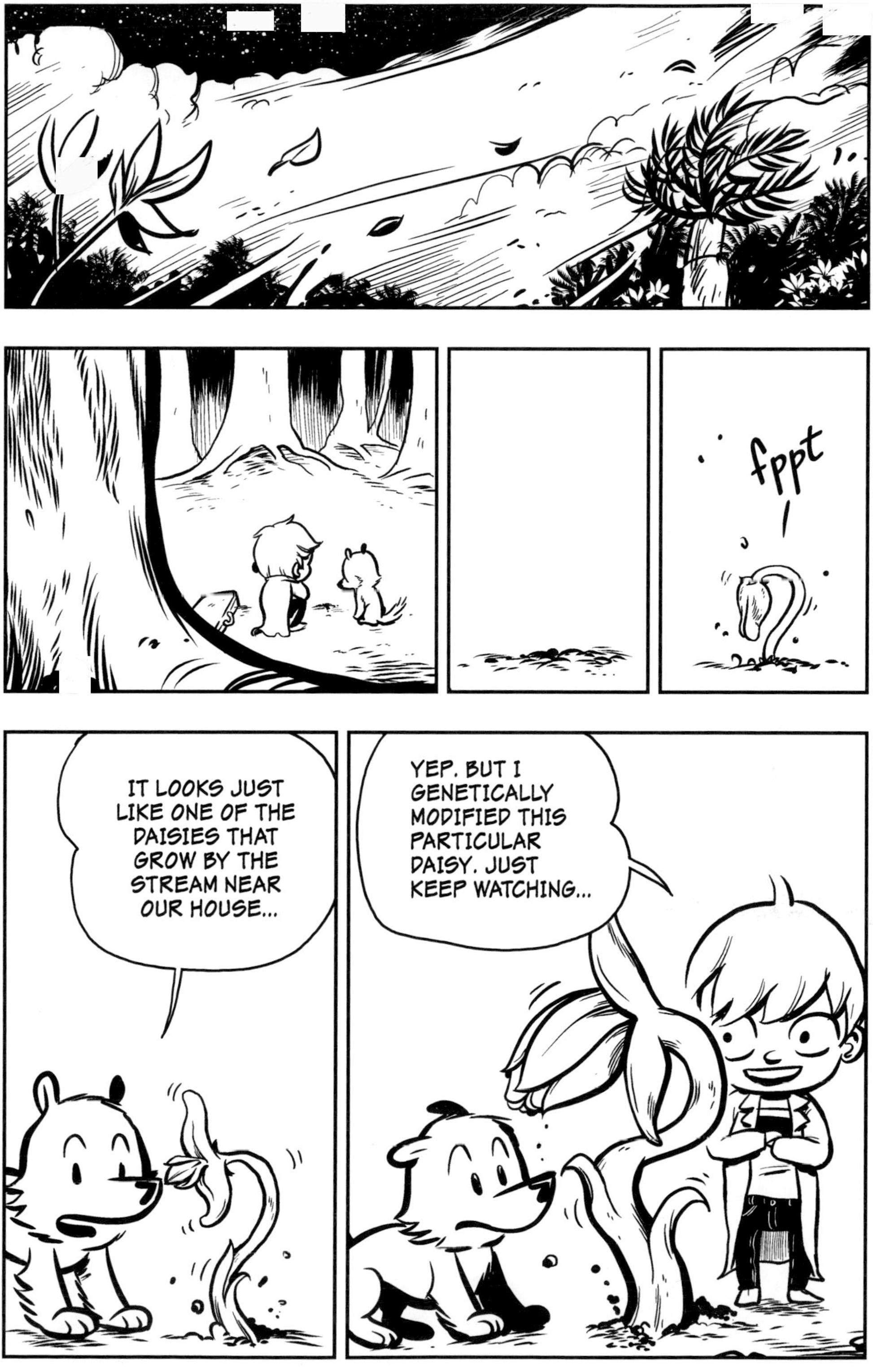
fppt
IT LOOKS JUST LIKE ONE OF THE DAISIES THAT GROW BY THE STREAM NEAR OUR HOUSE...
YEP. BUT I GENETICALLY MODIFIED THIS PARTICULAR DAISY. JUST KEEP WATCHING...

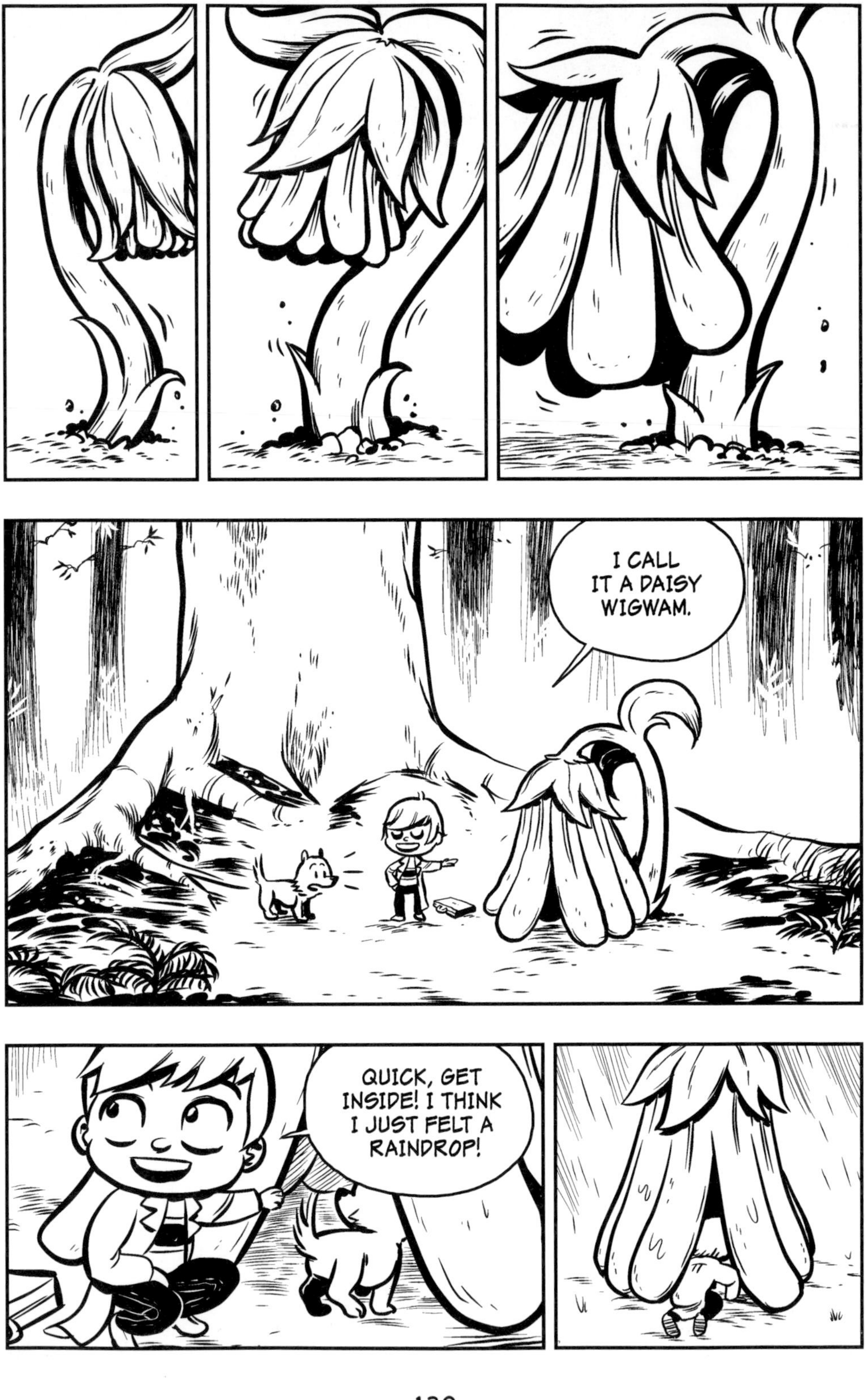
I CALL IT A DAISY WIGWAM.
QUICK, GET INSIDE! I THINK I JUST FELT A RAINDROP!

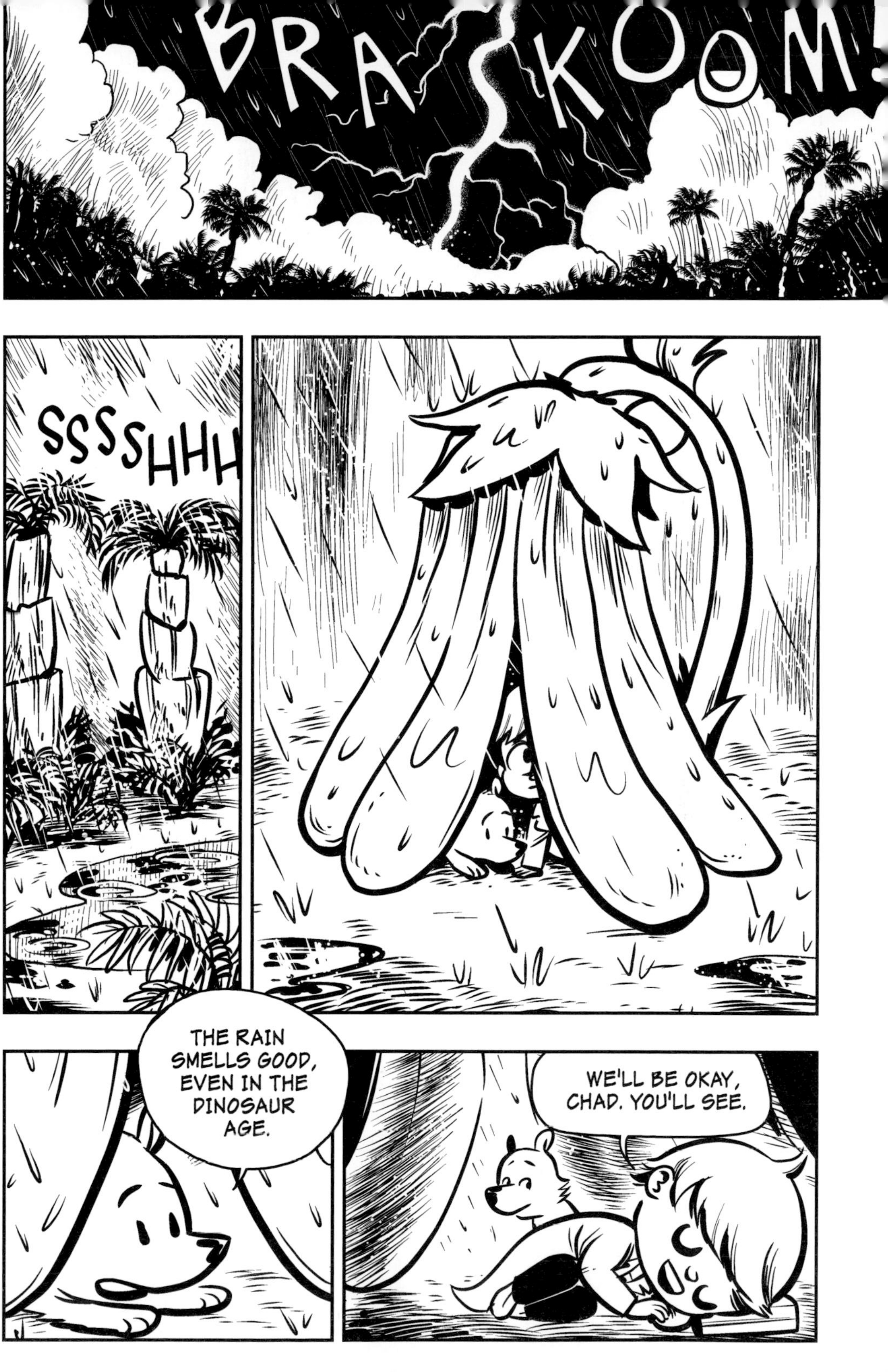
BRA-KOOM!
SSSSHHH
THE RAIN SMELLS GOOD, EVEN IN THE DINOSAUR AGE.
WE'LL BE OKAY, CHAD. YOU'LL SEE.

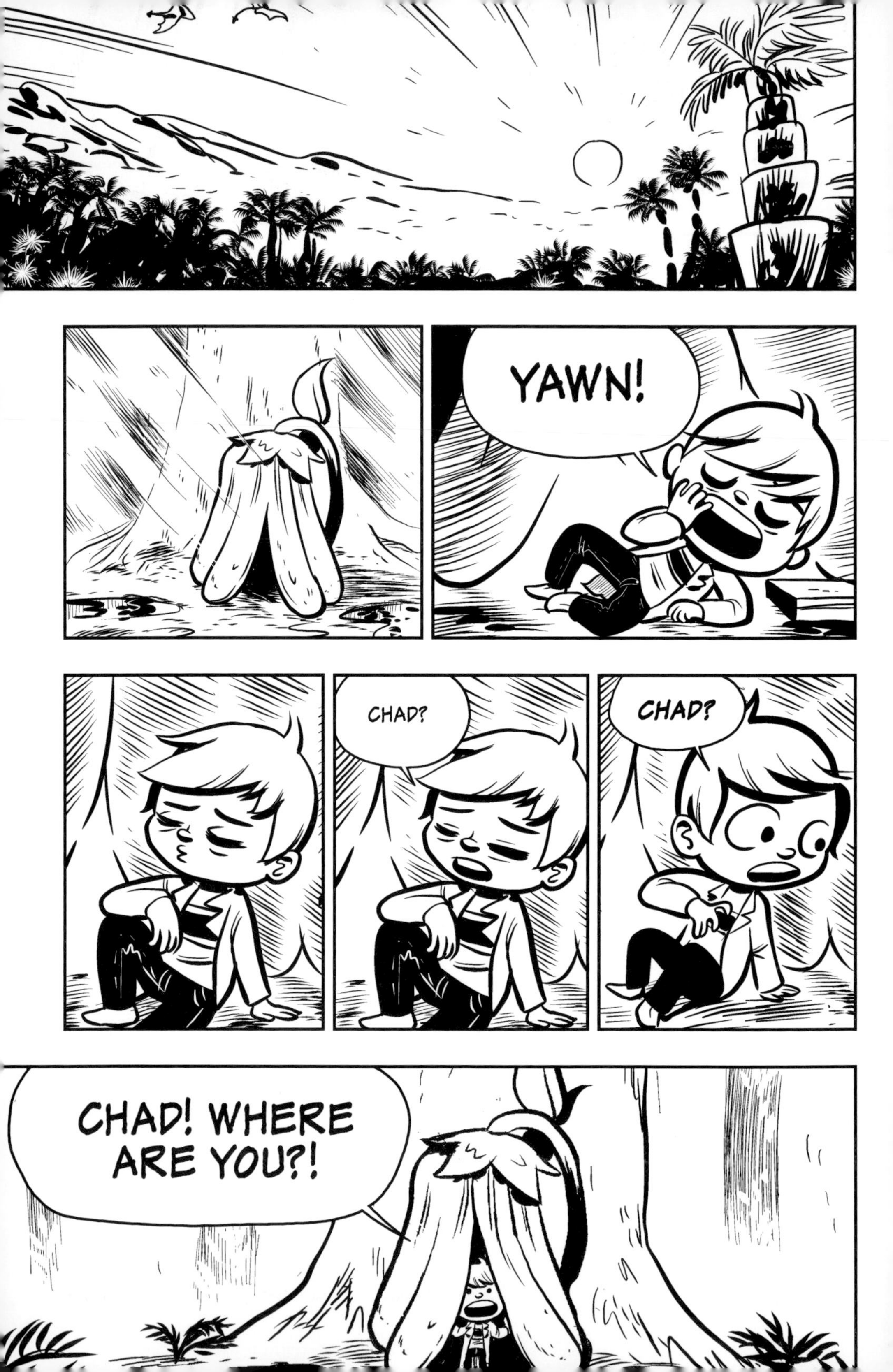
YAWN!
CHAD?
CHAD?
CHAD! WHERE ARE YOU?!

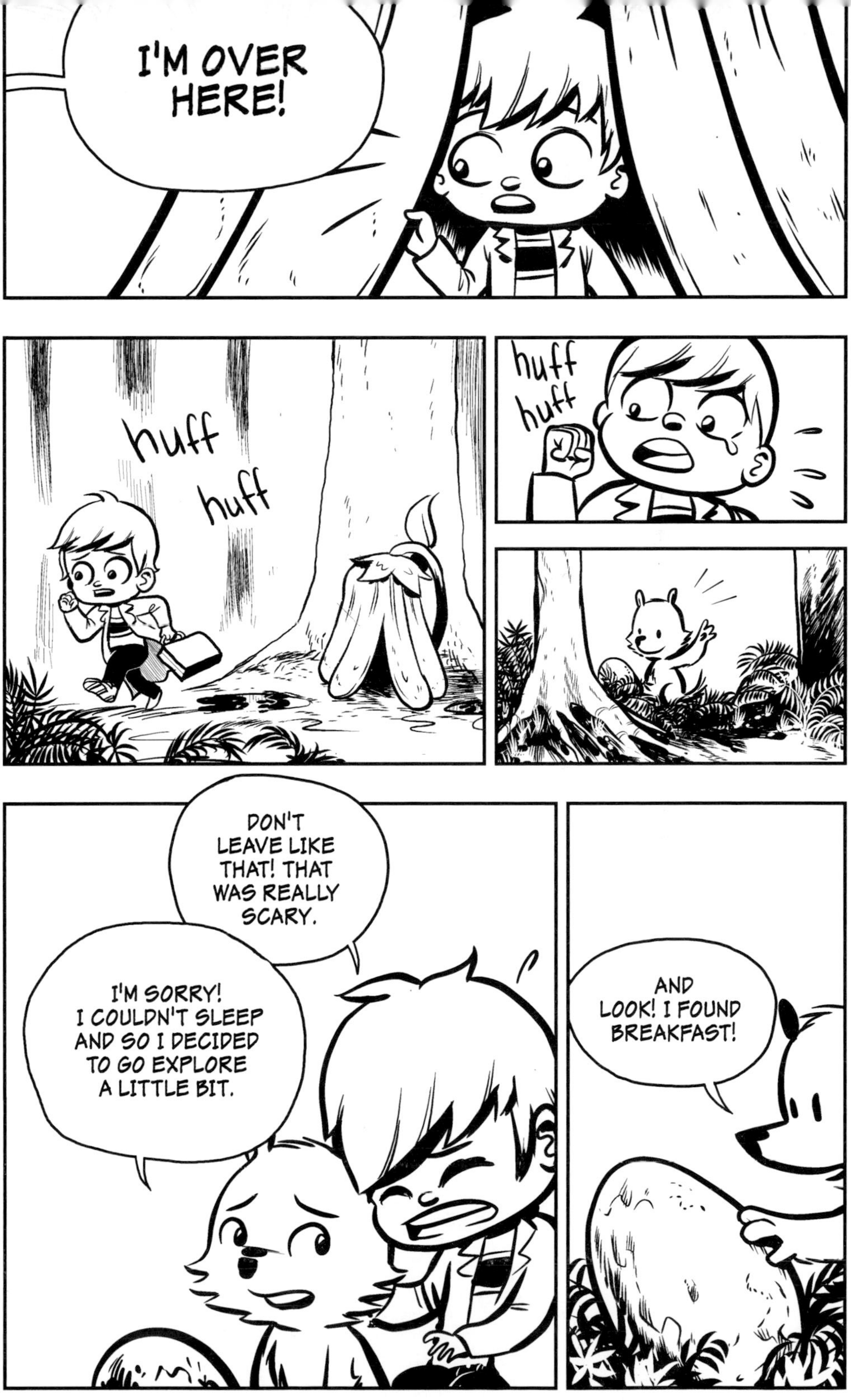
I'M OVER HERE!
huff huff
huff huff
DON'T LEAVE LIKE THAT! THAT WAS REALLY SCARY.
I'M SORRY! I COULDN'T SLEEP AND SO I DECIDED TO GO EXPLORE A LITTLE BIT.
AND LOOK! I FOUND BREAKFAST!

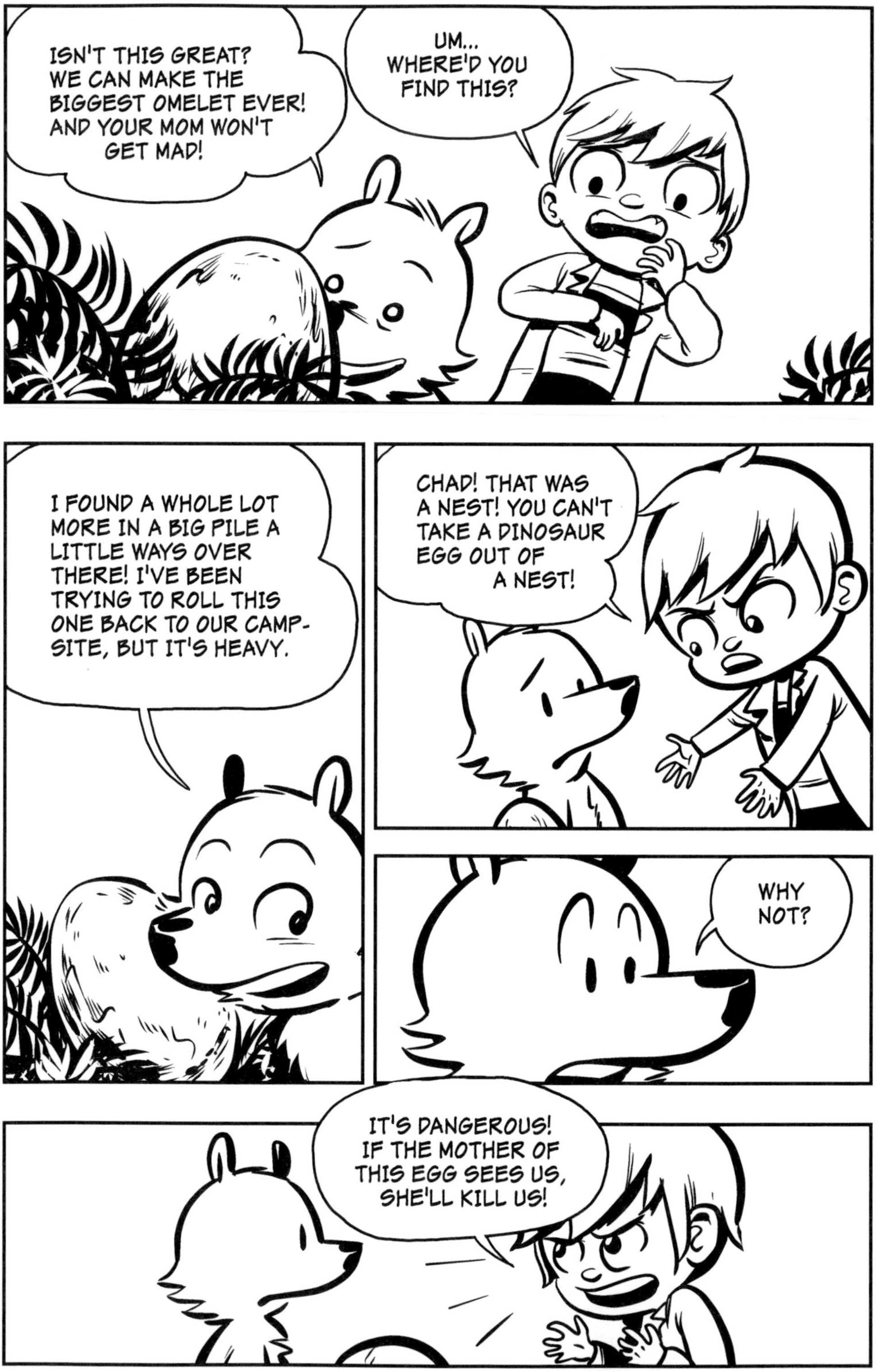
ISN'T THIS GREAT? WE CAN MAKE THE BIGGEST OMELET EVER! AND YOUR MOM WON'T GET MAD!
UM... WHERE'D YOU FIND THIS?
I FOUND A WHOLE LOT MORE IN A BIG PILE A LITTLE WAYS OVER THERE! I'VE BEEN TRYING TO ROLL THIS ONE BACK TO OUR CAMP-SITE, BUT IT'S HEAVY.
CHAD! THAT WAS A NEST! YOU CAN'T TAKE A DINOSAUR EGG OUT OF A NEST!
WHY NOT?
IT'S DANGEROUS! IF THE MOTHER OF THIS EGG SEES US, SHE'LL KILL US!

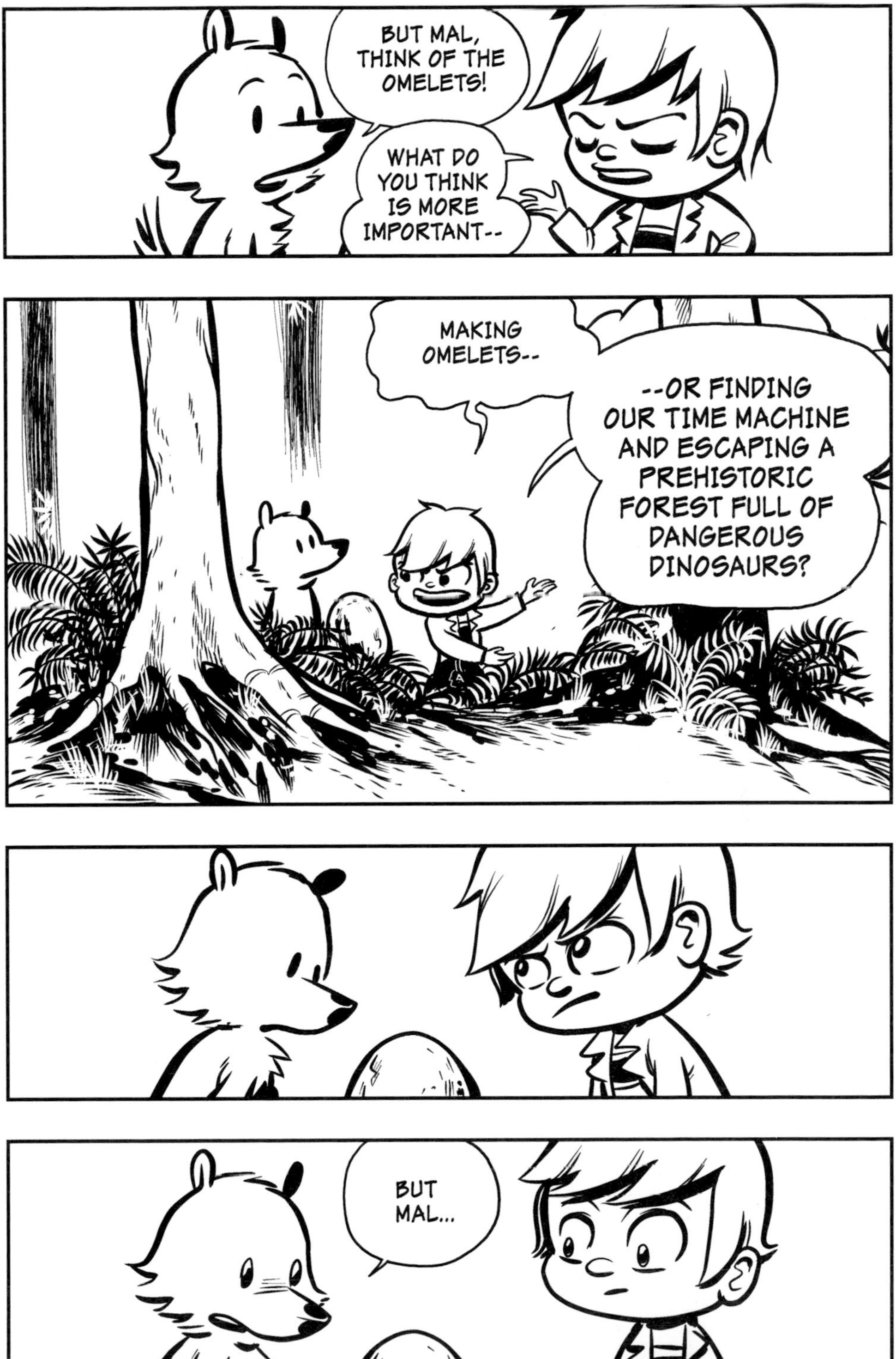
BUT MAL, THINK OF THE OMELETS!
WHAT DO YOU THINK IS MORE IMPORTANT--
MAKING OMELETS--
--OR FINDING OUR TIME MACHINE AND ESCAPING A PREHISTORIC FOREST FULL OF DANGEROUS DINOSAURS?
BUT MAL...

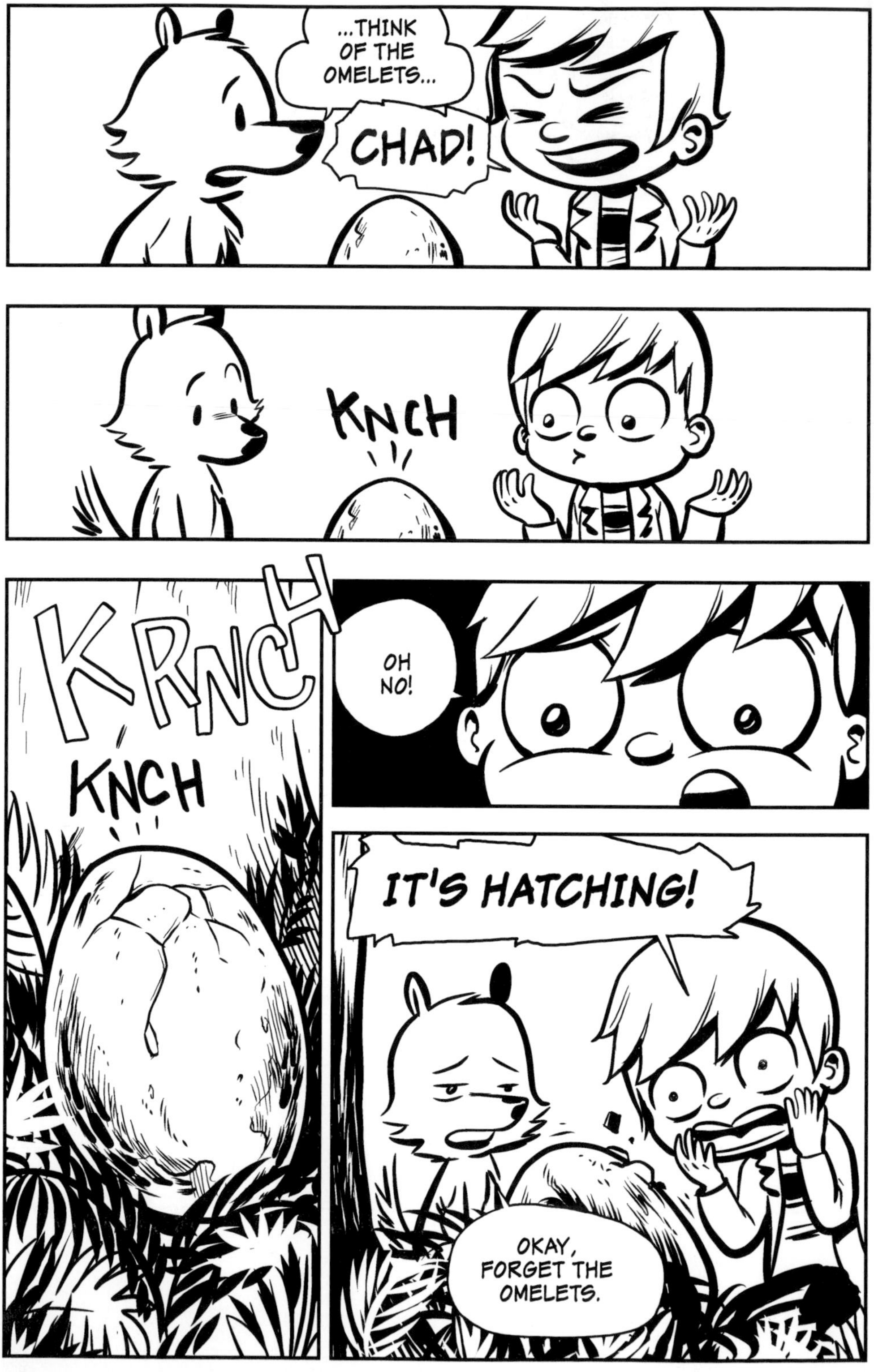
...THINK OF THE OMELETS...
CHAD!
KNCH
KRNCH
KNCH
OH NO!
IT'S HATCHING!
OKAY, FORGET THE OMELETS.

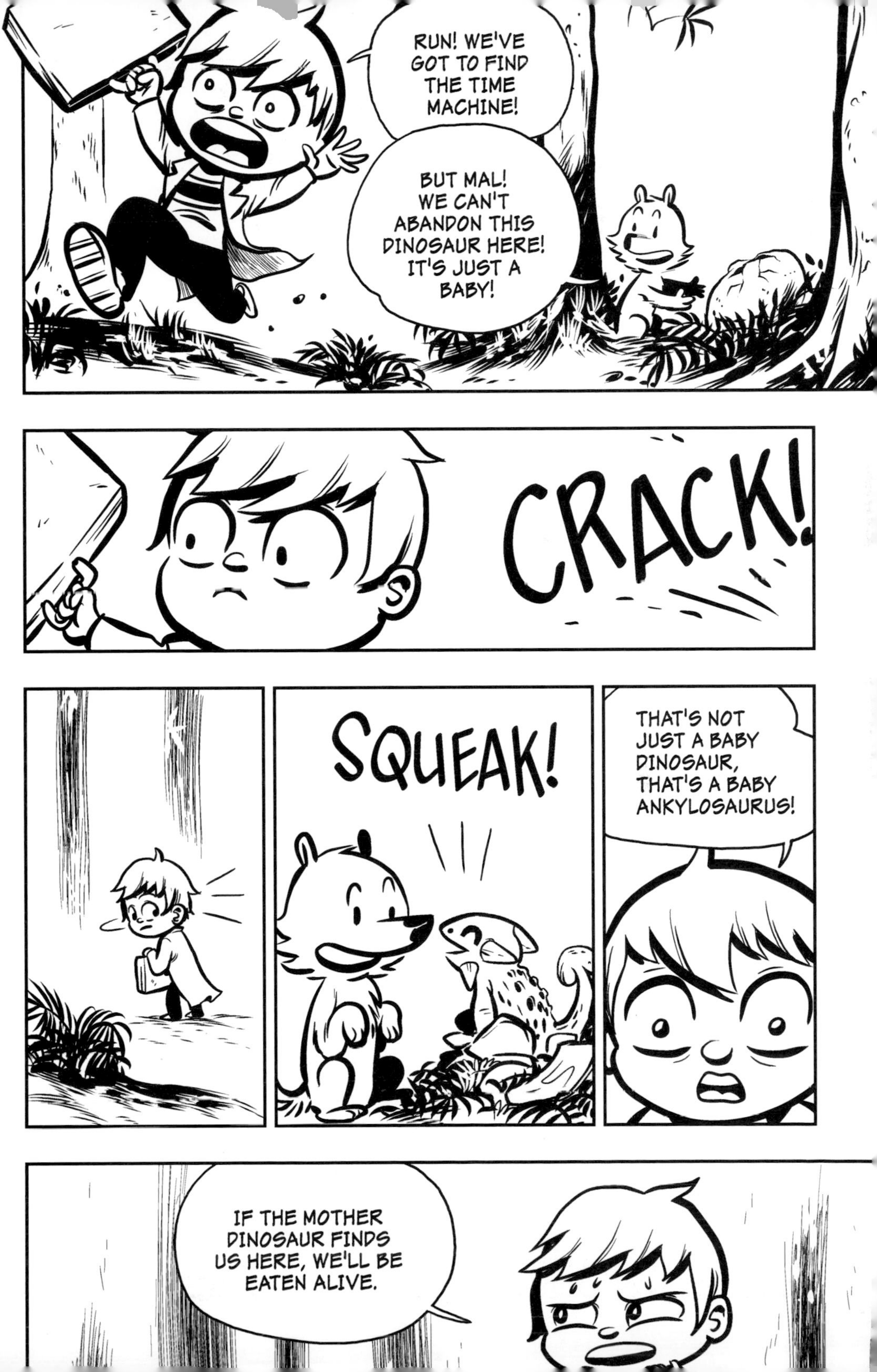
RUN! WE'VE GOT TO FIND THE TIME MACHINE!
BUT MAL! WE CAN'T ABANDON THIS DINOSAUR HERE! IT'S JUST A BABY!
CRACK!
SQUEAK!
THAT'S NOT JUST A BABY DINOSAUR, THAT'S A BABY ANKYLOSAURUS!
IF THE MOTHER DINOSAUR FINDS US HERE, WE'LL BE EATEN ALIVE.

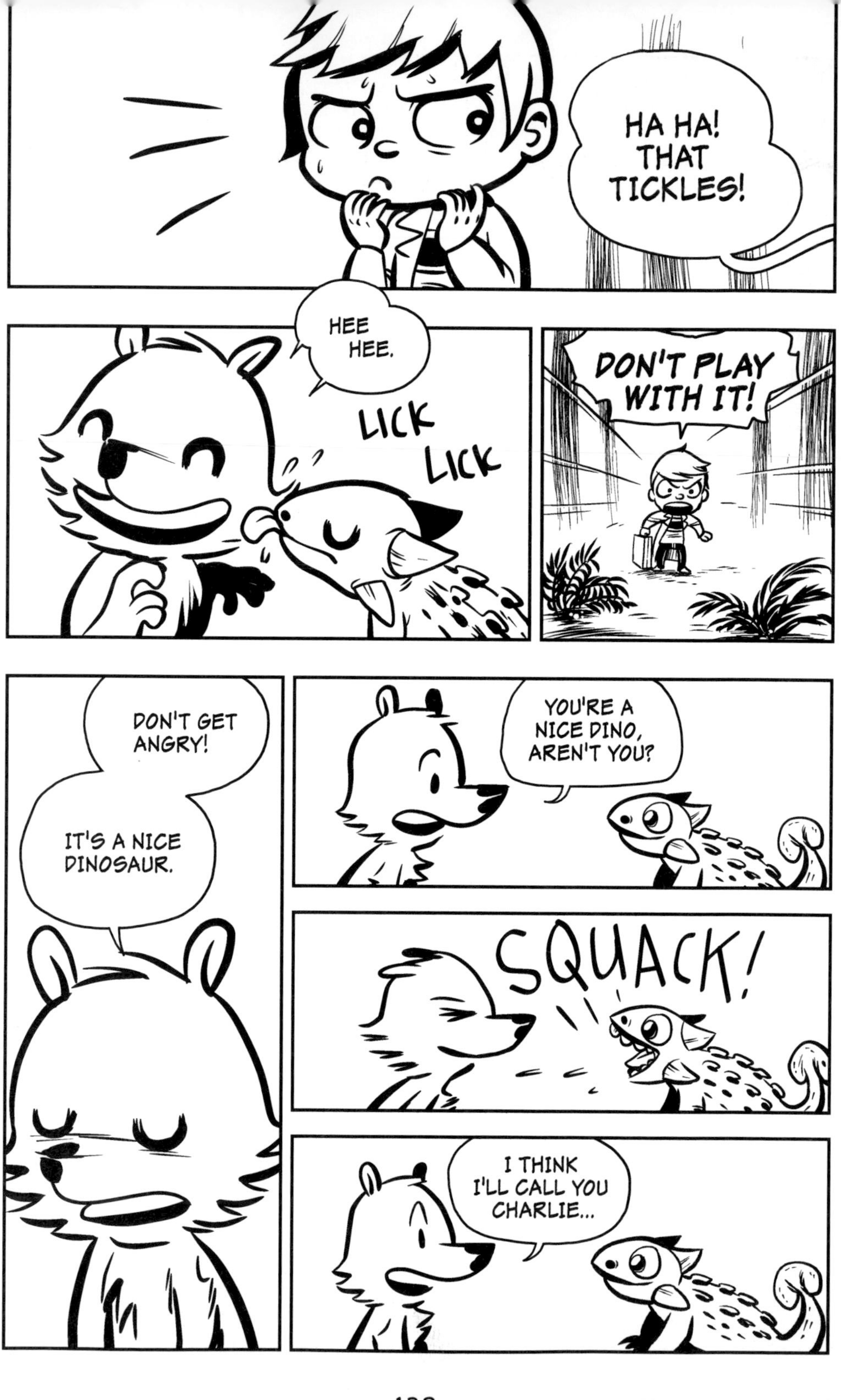
HA HA! THAT TICKLES!
HEE HEE.
LICK LICK
DON'T PLAY WITH IT!
DON'T GET ANGRY!
IT'S A NICE DINOSAUR.
YOU'RE A NICE DINO, AREN'T YOU?
SQUACK!
I THINK I'LL CALL YOU CHARLIE...

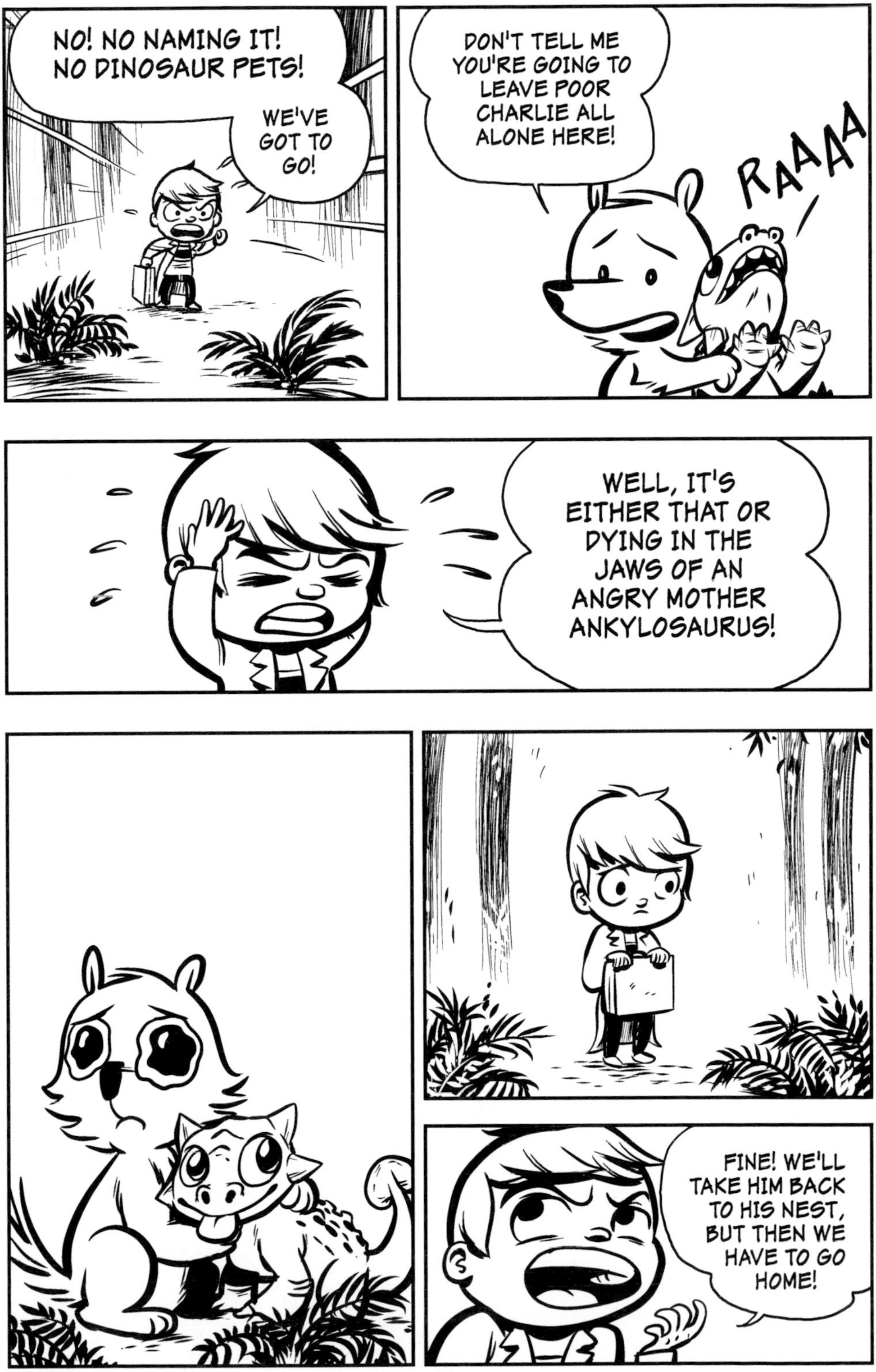
NO! NO NAMING IT! NO DINOSAUR PETS!
WE'VE GOT TO GO!
DON'T TELL ME YOU'RE GOING TO LEAVE POOR CHARLIE ALL ALONE HERE!
RAAAA
WELL, IT'S EITHER THAT OR DYING IN THE JAWS OF AN ANGRY MOTHER ANKYLOSAURUS!
FINE! WE'LL TAKE HIM BACK TO HIS NEST, BUT THEN WE HAVE TO GO HOME!

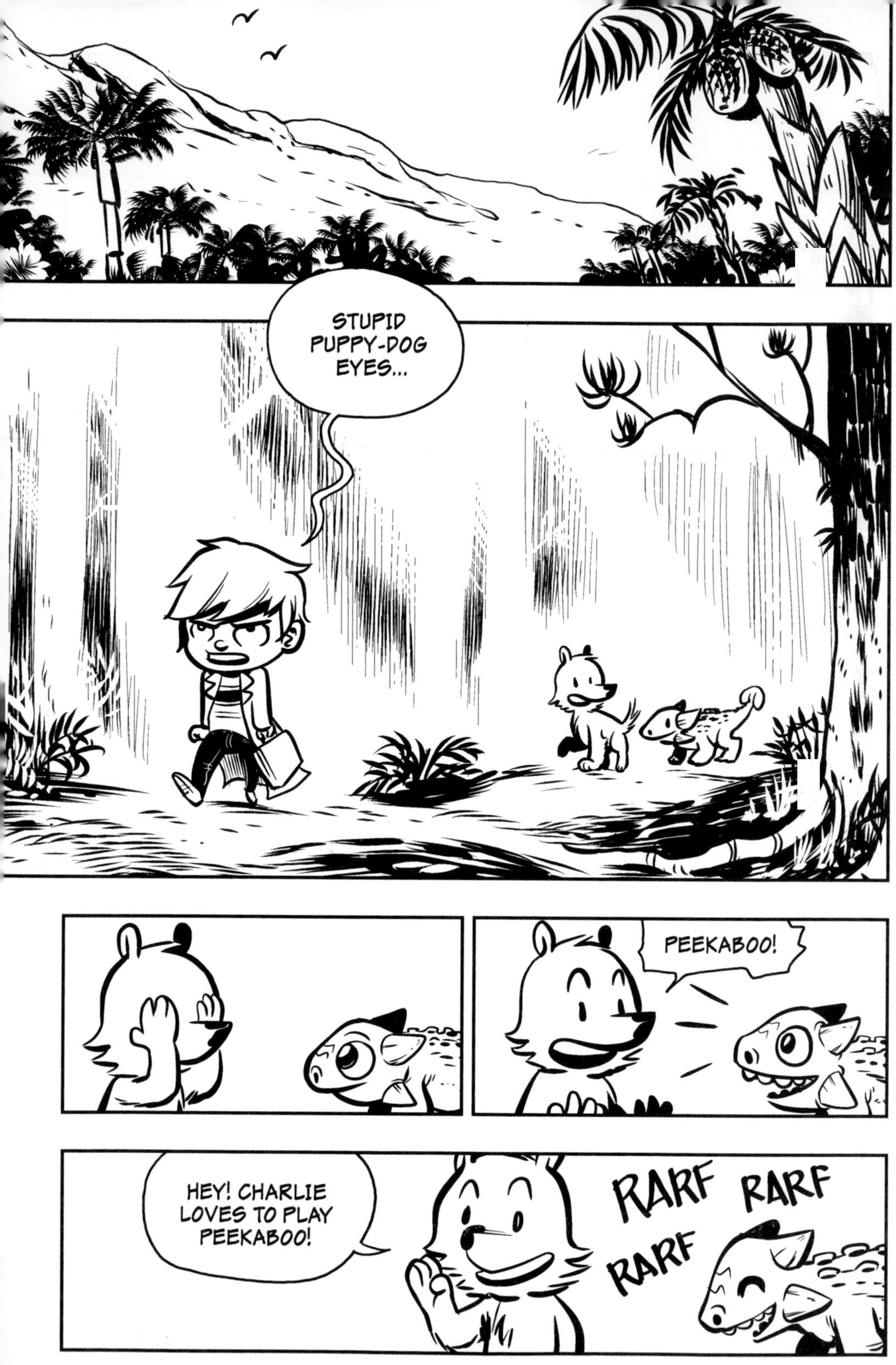
STUPID PUPPY-DOG EYES...
PEEKABOO!
HEY! CHARLIE LOVES TO PLAY PEEKABOO!
RARF RARF
RARF

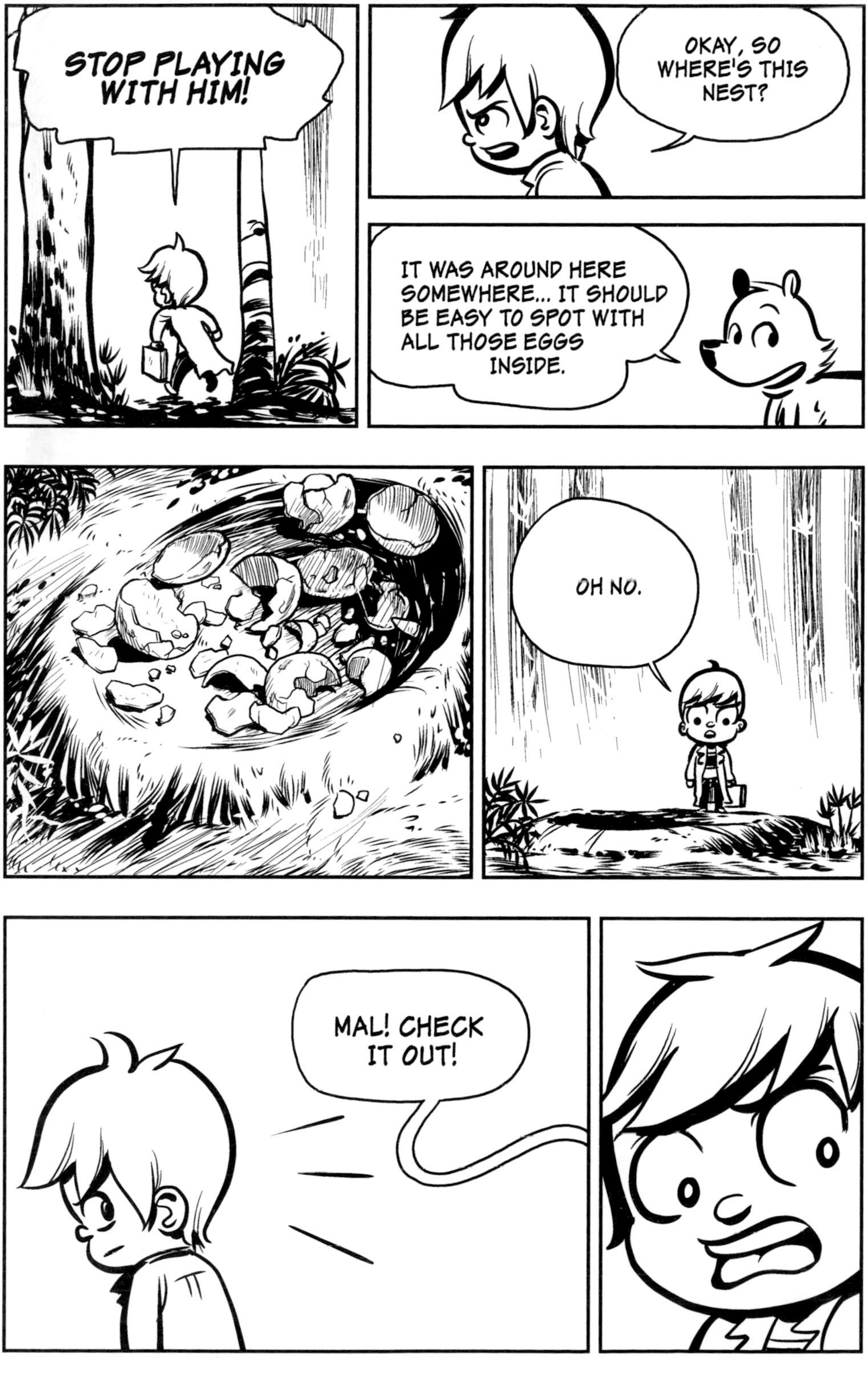
STOP PLAYING WITH HIM!
OKAY, SO WHERE'S THIS NEST?
IT WAS AROUND HERE SOMEWHERE... IT SHOULD BE EASY TO SPOT WITH ALL THOSE EGGS INSIDE.
OH NO.
MAL! CHECK IT OUT!

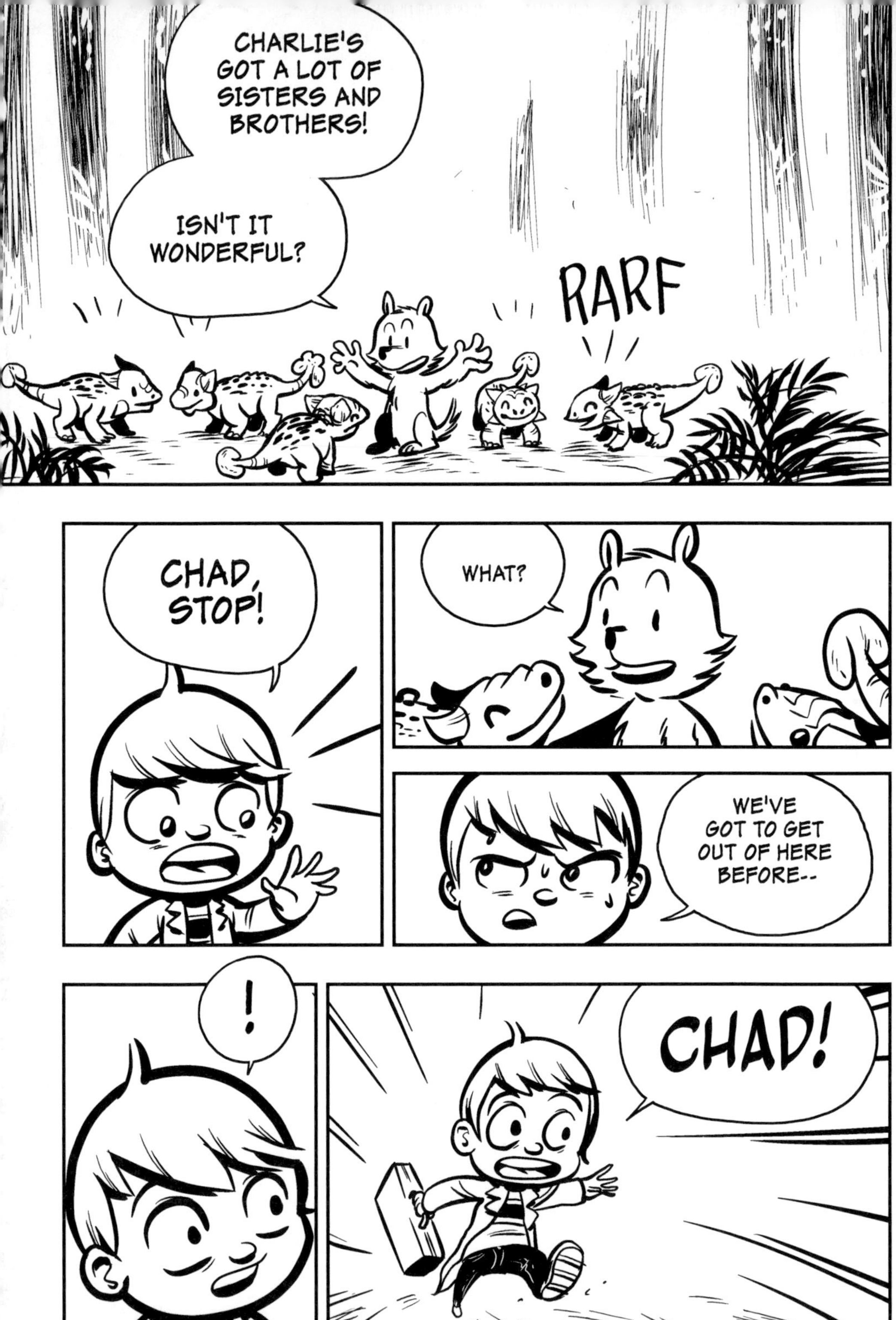

CHARLIE'S GOT A LOT OF SISTERS AND BROTHERS!
ISN'T IT WONDERFUL?
RARF
CHAD, STOP!
WHAT?
WE'VE GOT TO GET OUT OF HERE BEFORE--
!
CHAD!

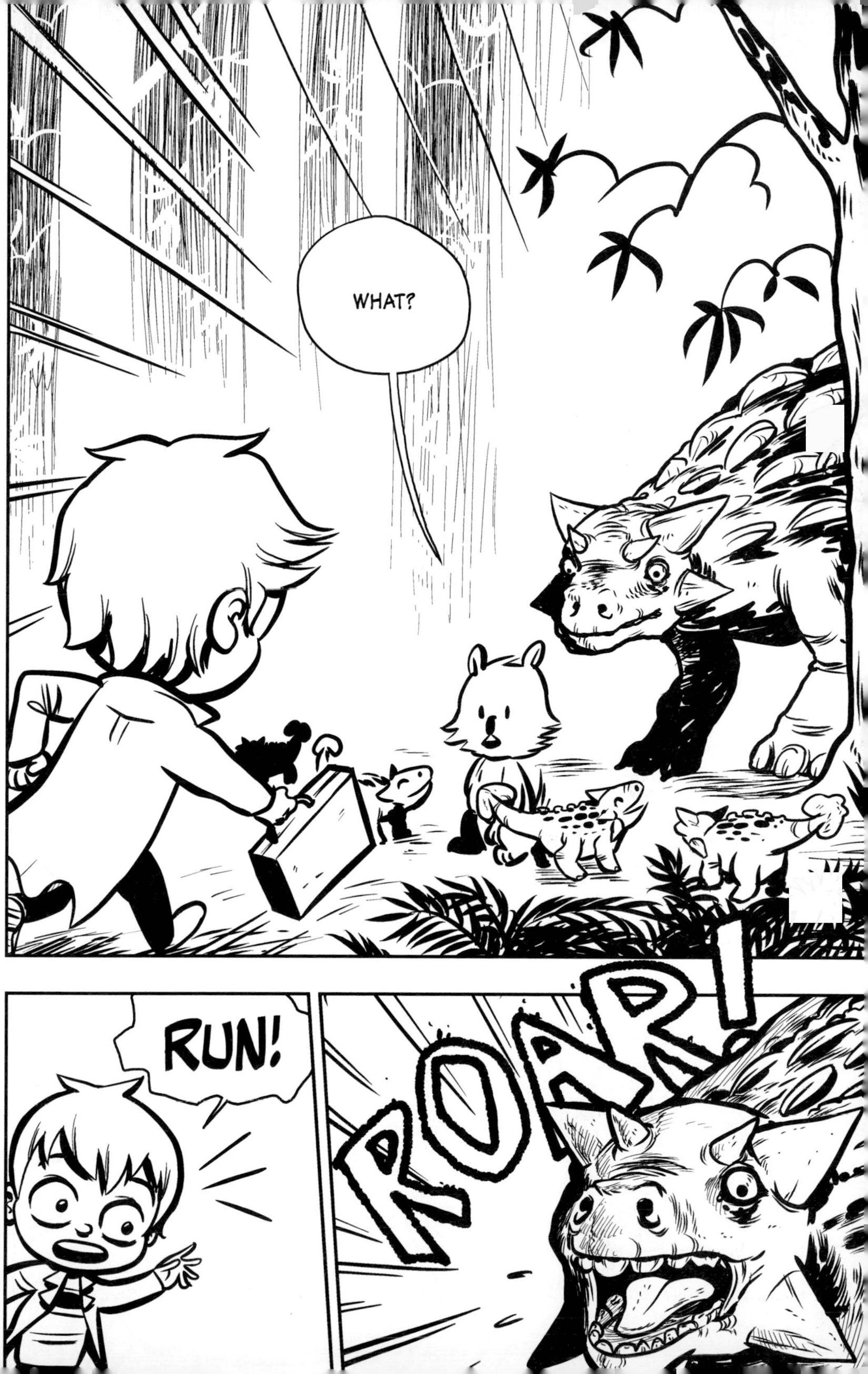
WHAT?
RUN!
ROAR!

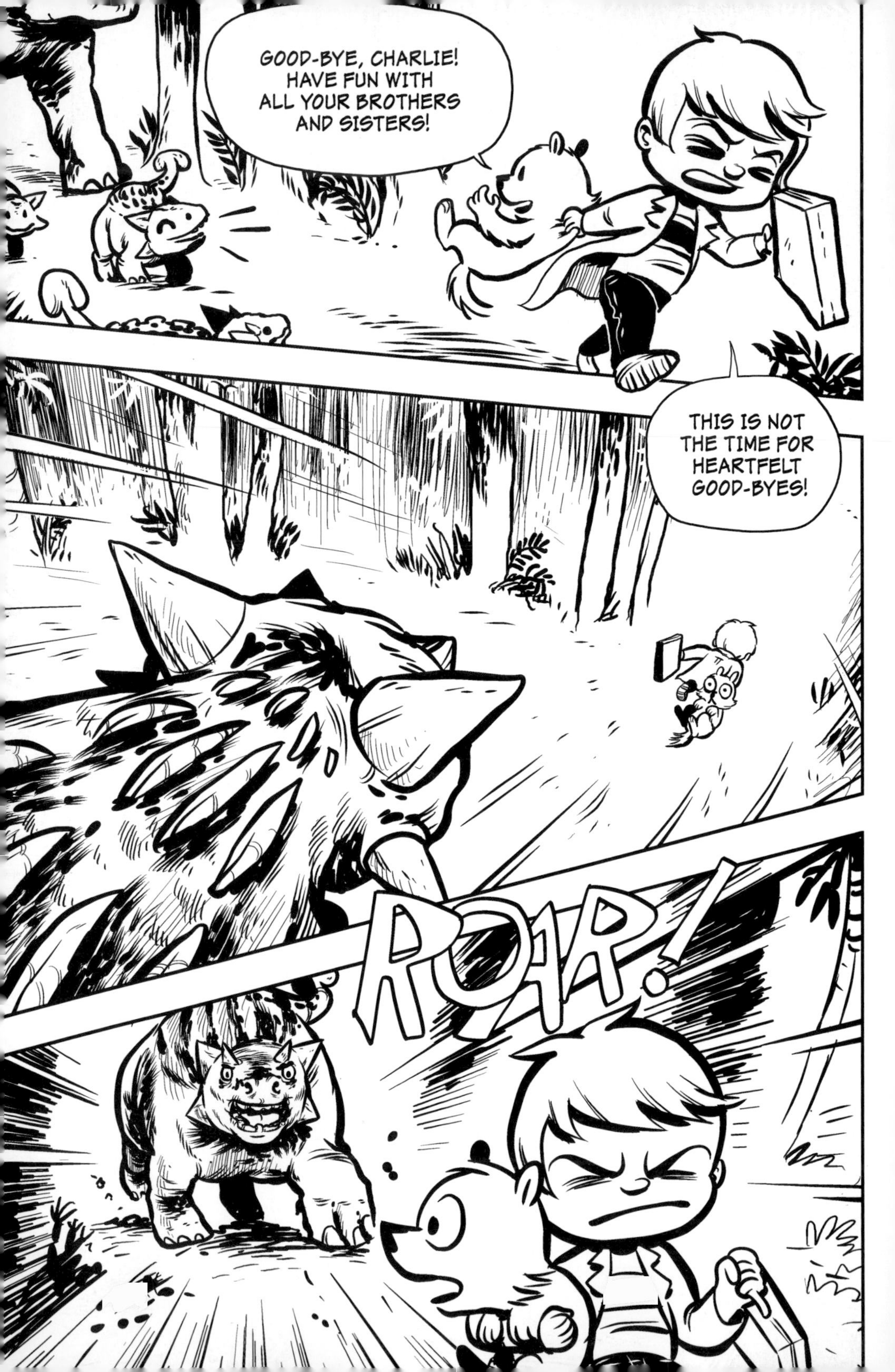
GOOD-BYE, CHARLIE! HAVE FUN WITH ALL YOUR BROTHERS AND SISTERS!
THIS IS NOT THE TIME FOR HEARTFELT GOOD-BYES!
ROAR!

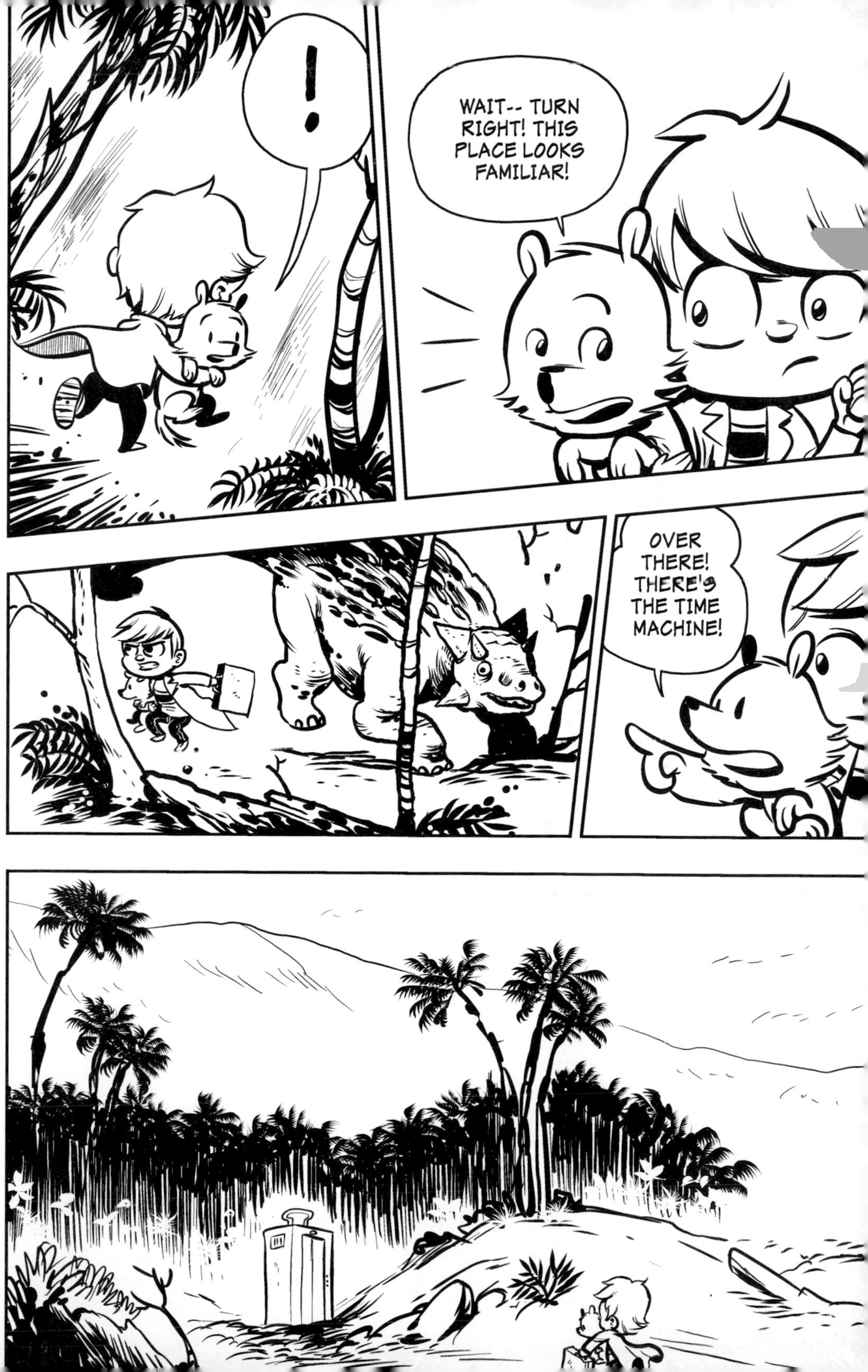
!
WAIT-- TURN RIGHT! THIS PLACE LOOKS FAMILIAR!
OVER THERE! THERE'S THE TIME MACHINE!

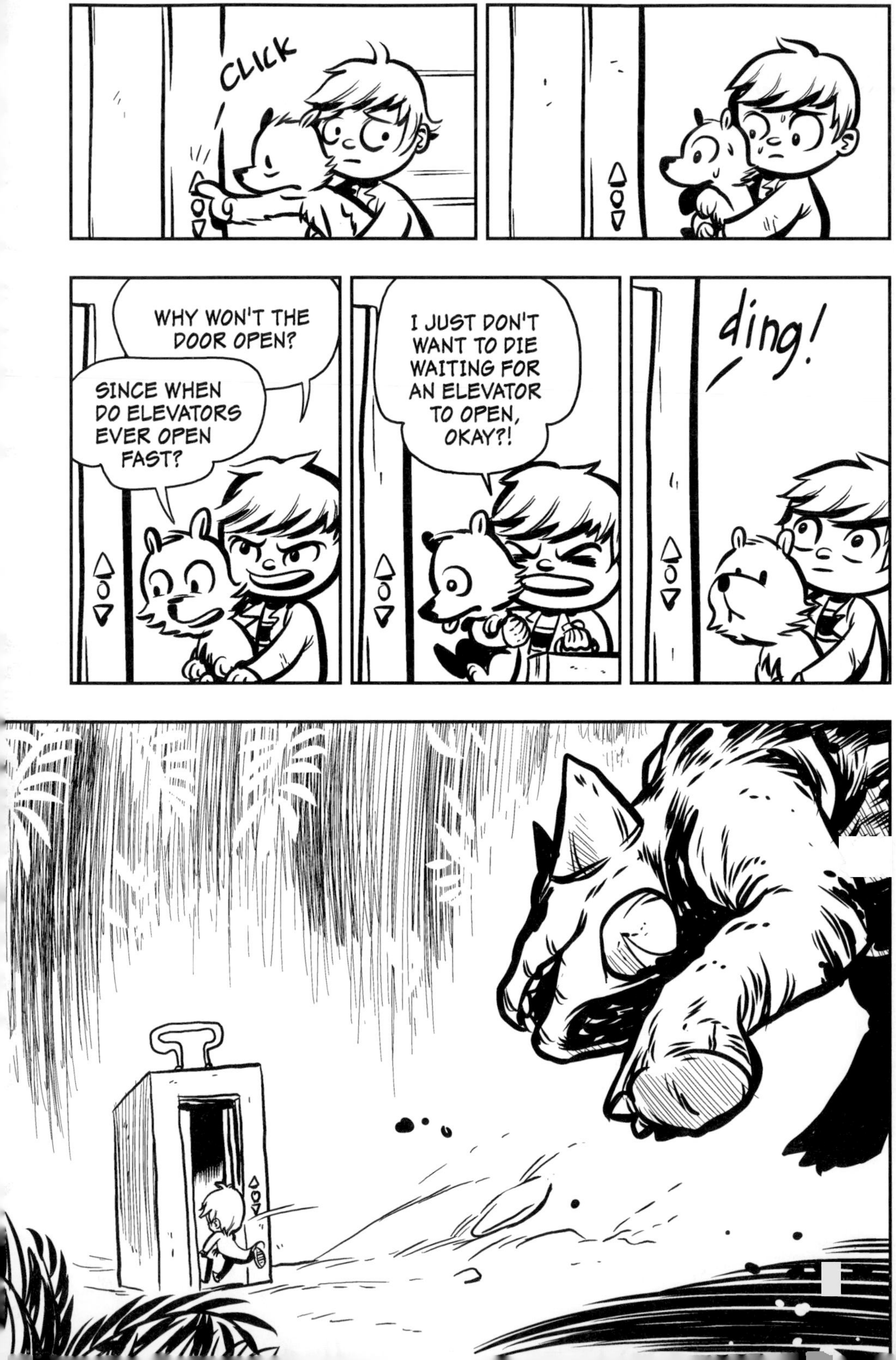
CLICK
WHY WON'T THE DOOR OPEN?
SINCE WHEN DO ELEVATORS EVER OPEN FAST?
I JUST DON'T WANT TO DIE WAITING FOR AN ELEVATOR TO OPEN, OKAY?!
ding!

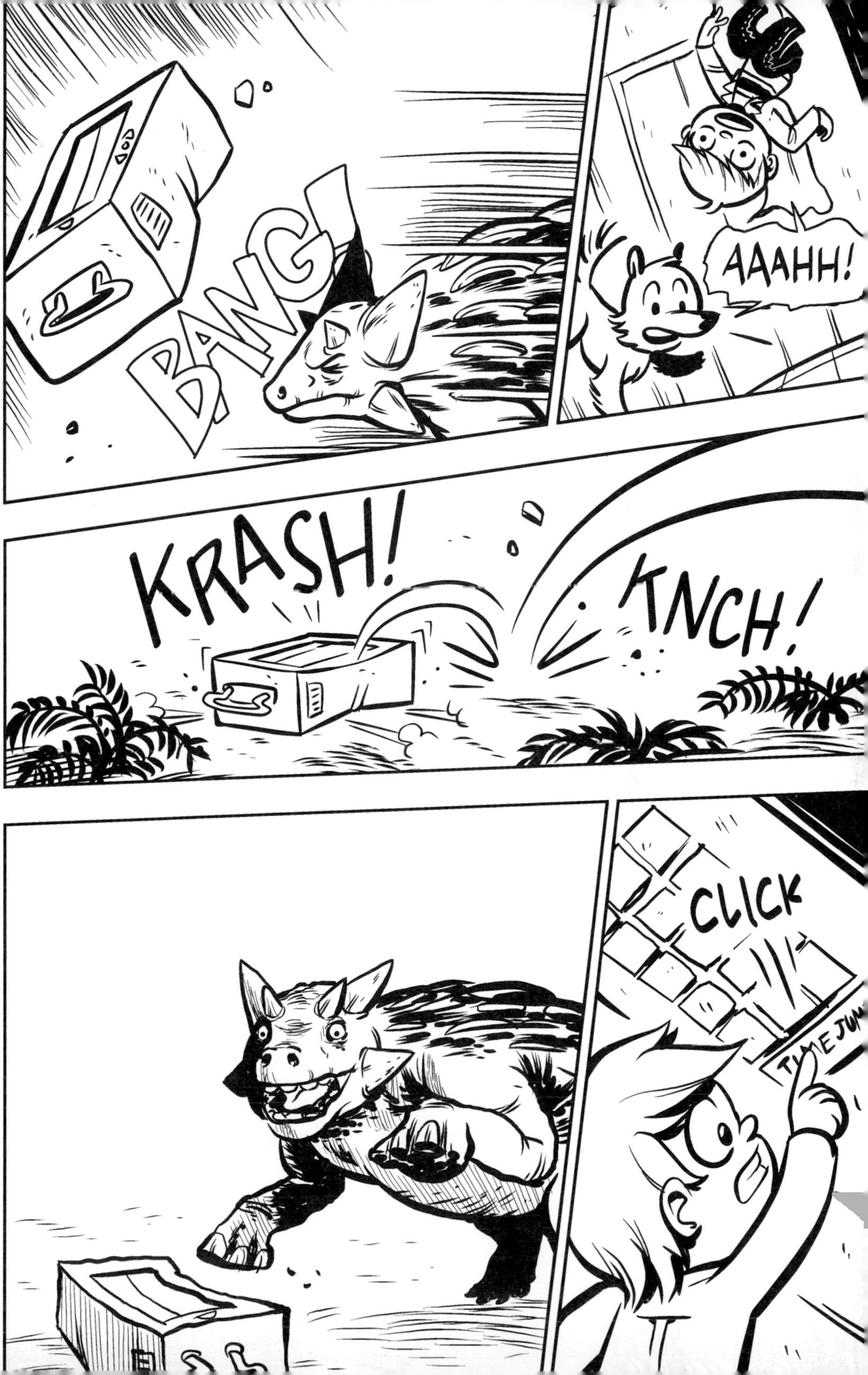
BANG!
AAAHH!
KRASH!
KNCH!
CLICK
TIME JUM

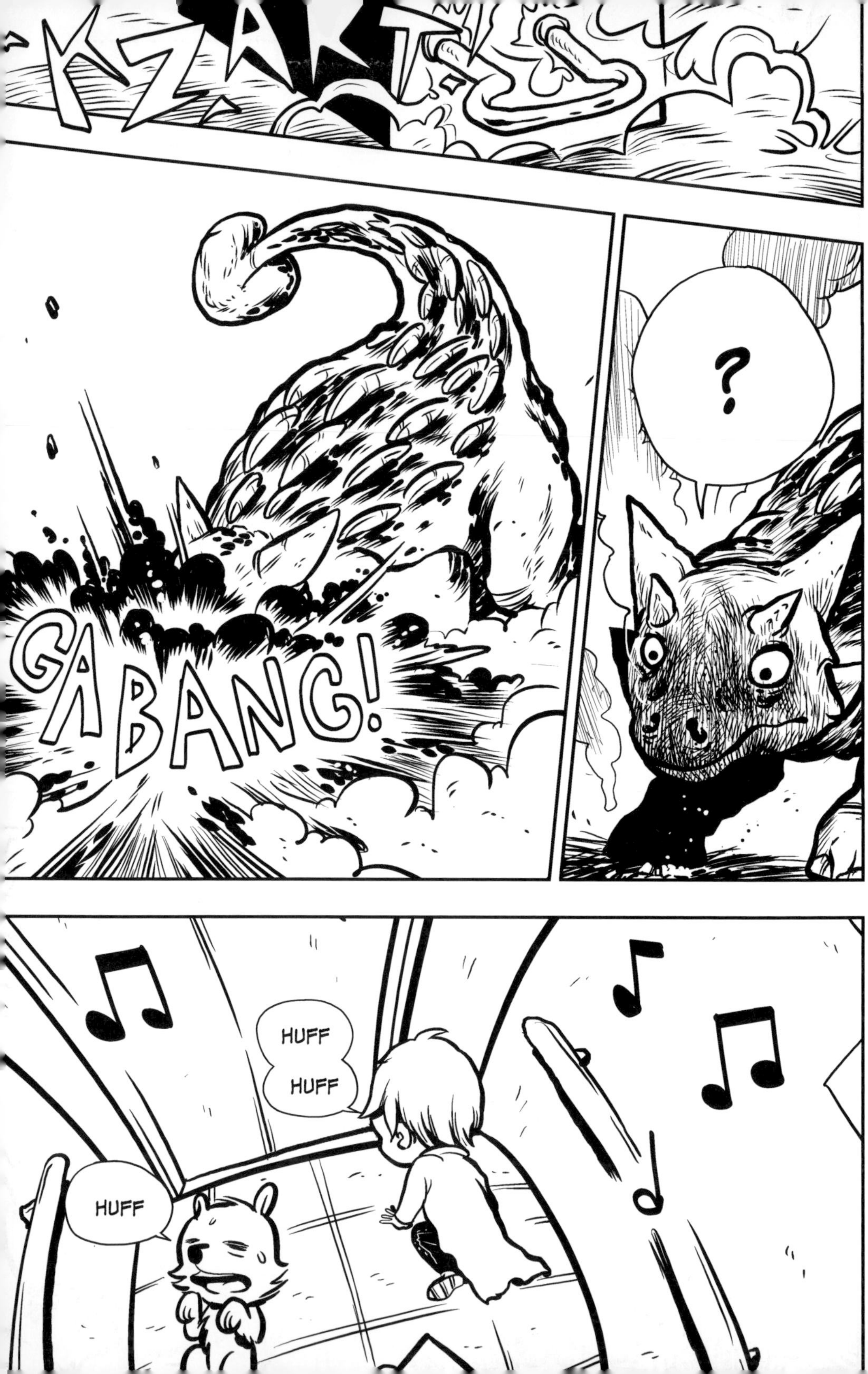
KZZAT
GABANG!
?
HUFF
HUFF
HUFF

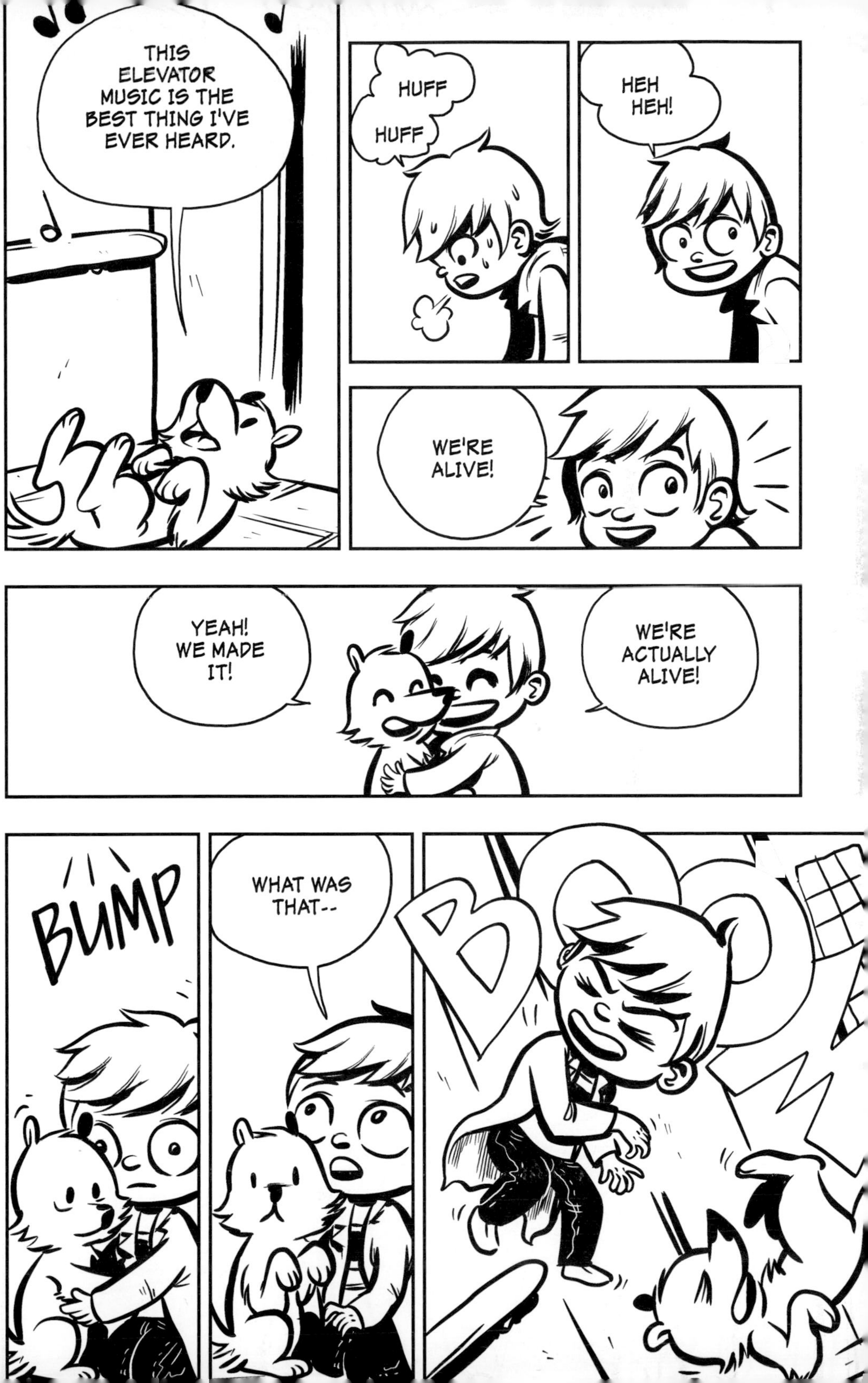
THIS ELEVATOR MUSIC IS THE BEST THING I'VE EVER HEARD.
HUFF HUFF
HEH HEH!
WE'RE ALIVE!
YEAH! WE MADE IT!
WE'RE ACTUALLY ALIVE!
BUMP
WHAT WAS THAT--

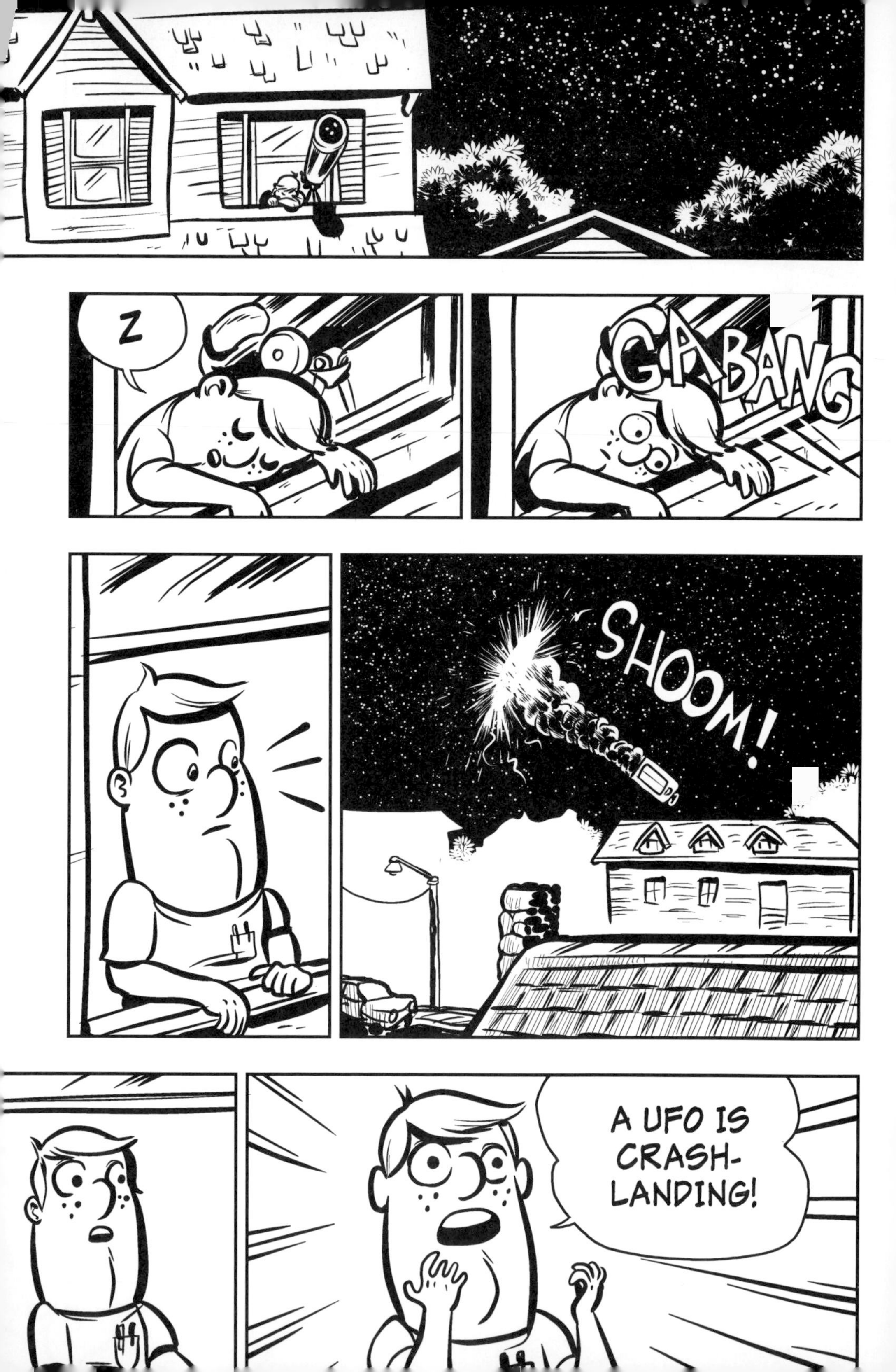
Z
GABANG
SHOOM!
A UFO IS CRASH-LANDING!

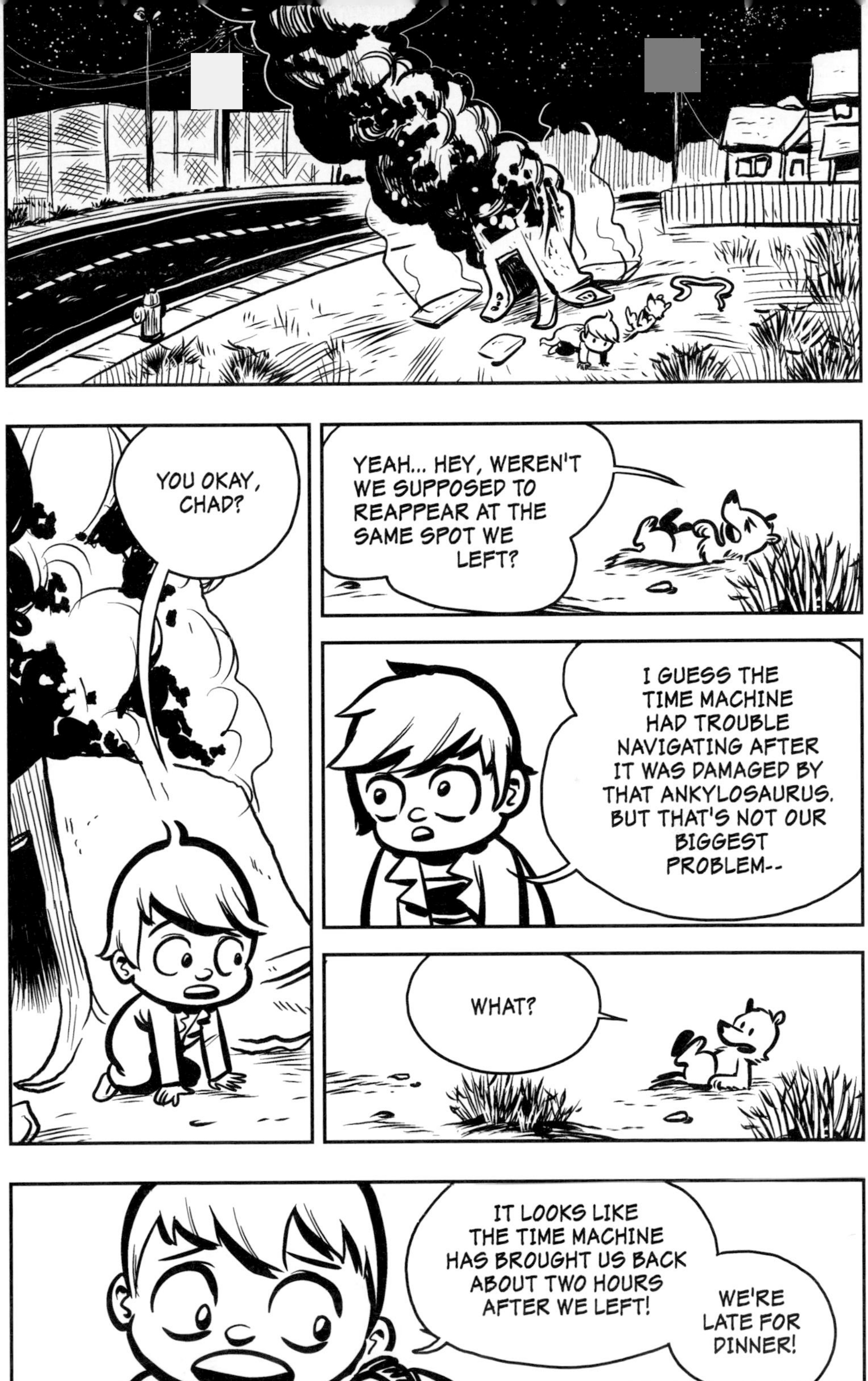
YOU OKAY, CHAD?
YEAH... HEY, WEREN'T WE SUPPOSED TO REAPPEAR AT THE SAME SPOT WE LEFT?
I GUESS THE TIME MACHINE HAD TROUBLE NAVIGATING AFTER IT WAS DAMAGED BY THAT ANKYLOSAURUS. BUT THAT'S NOT OUR BIGGEST PROBLEM--
WHAT?
IT LOOKS LIKE THE TIME MACHINE HAS BROUGHT US BACK ABOUT TWO HOURS AFTER WE LEFT!
WE'RE LATE FOR DINNER!

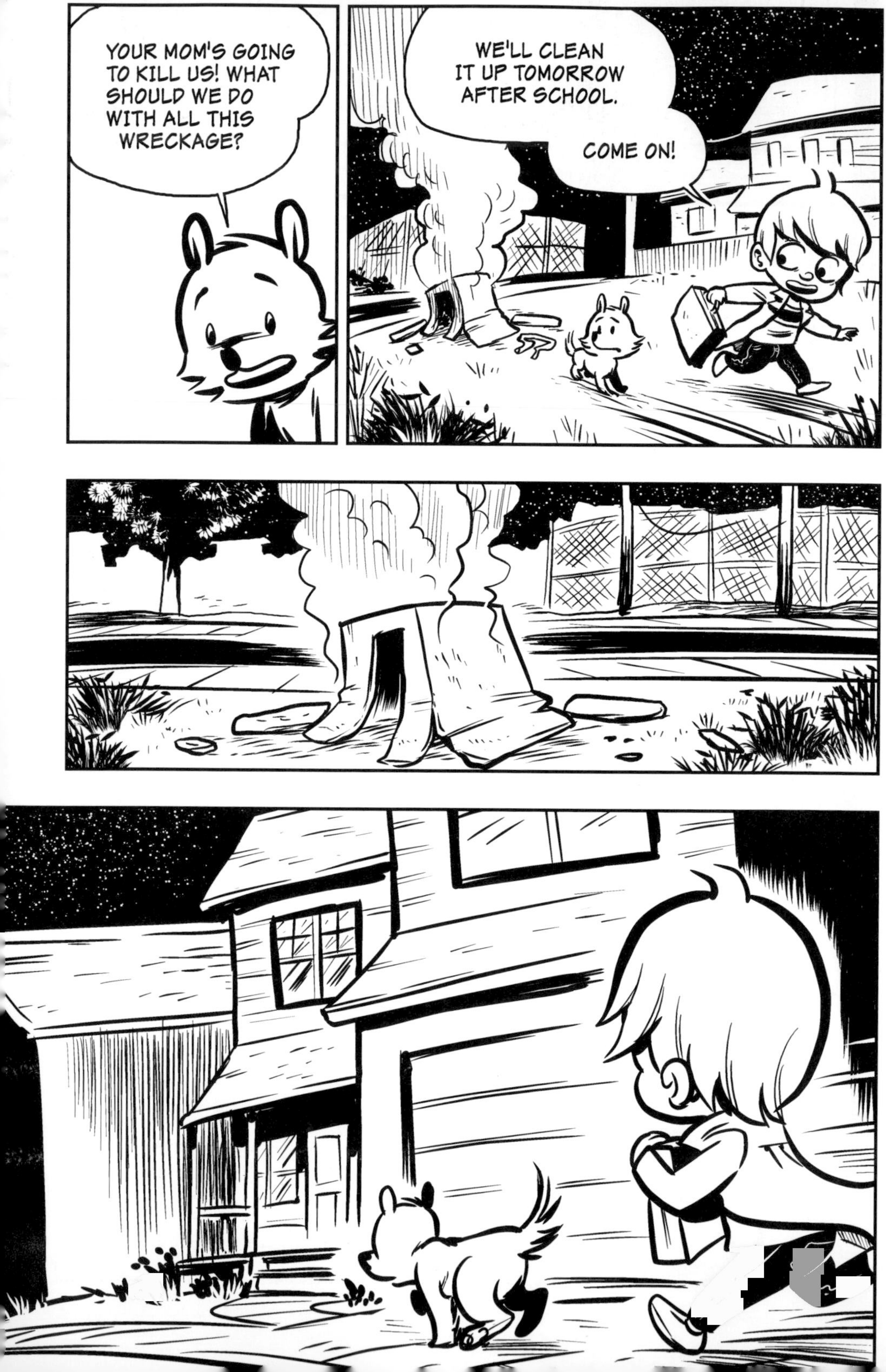
YOUR MOM'S GOING TO KILL US! WHAT SHOULD WE DO WITH ALL THIS WRECKAGE?
WE'LL CLEAN IT UP TOMORROW AFTER SCHOOL.
COME ON!

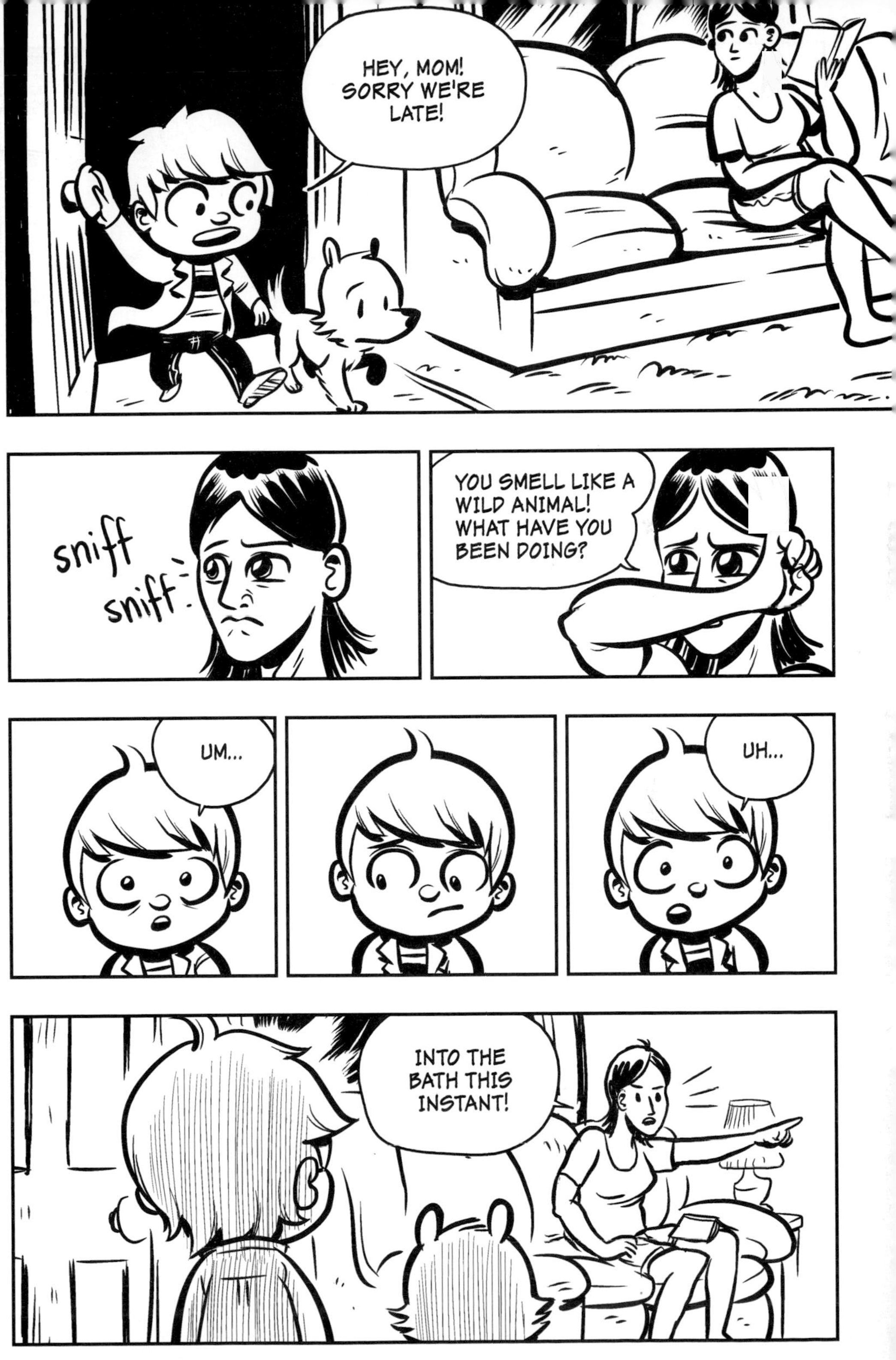
HEY, MOM! SORRY WE'RE LATE!
sniff sniff
YOU SMELL LIKE A WILD ANIMAL! WHAT HAVE YOU BEEN DOING?
UM...
UH...
INTO THE BATH THIS INSTANT!

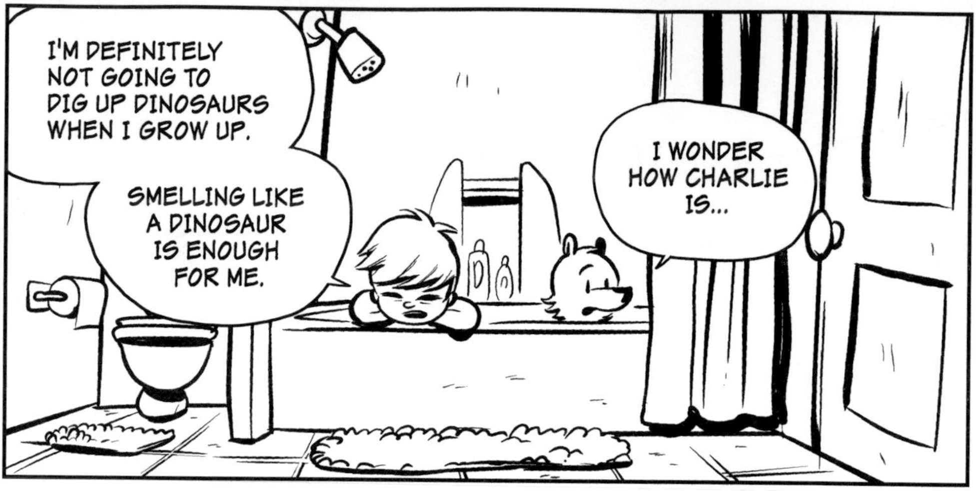
I'M DEFINITELY NOT GOING TO DIG UP DINOSAURS WHEN I GROW UP.
SMELLING LIKE A DINOSAUR IS ENOUGH FOR ME.
I WONDER HOW CHARLIE IS...

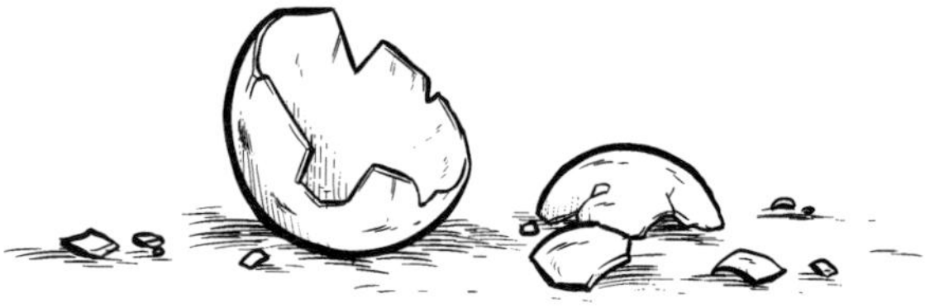

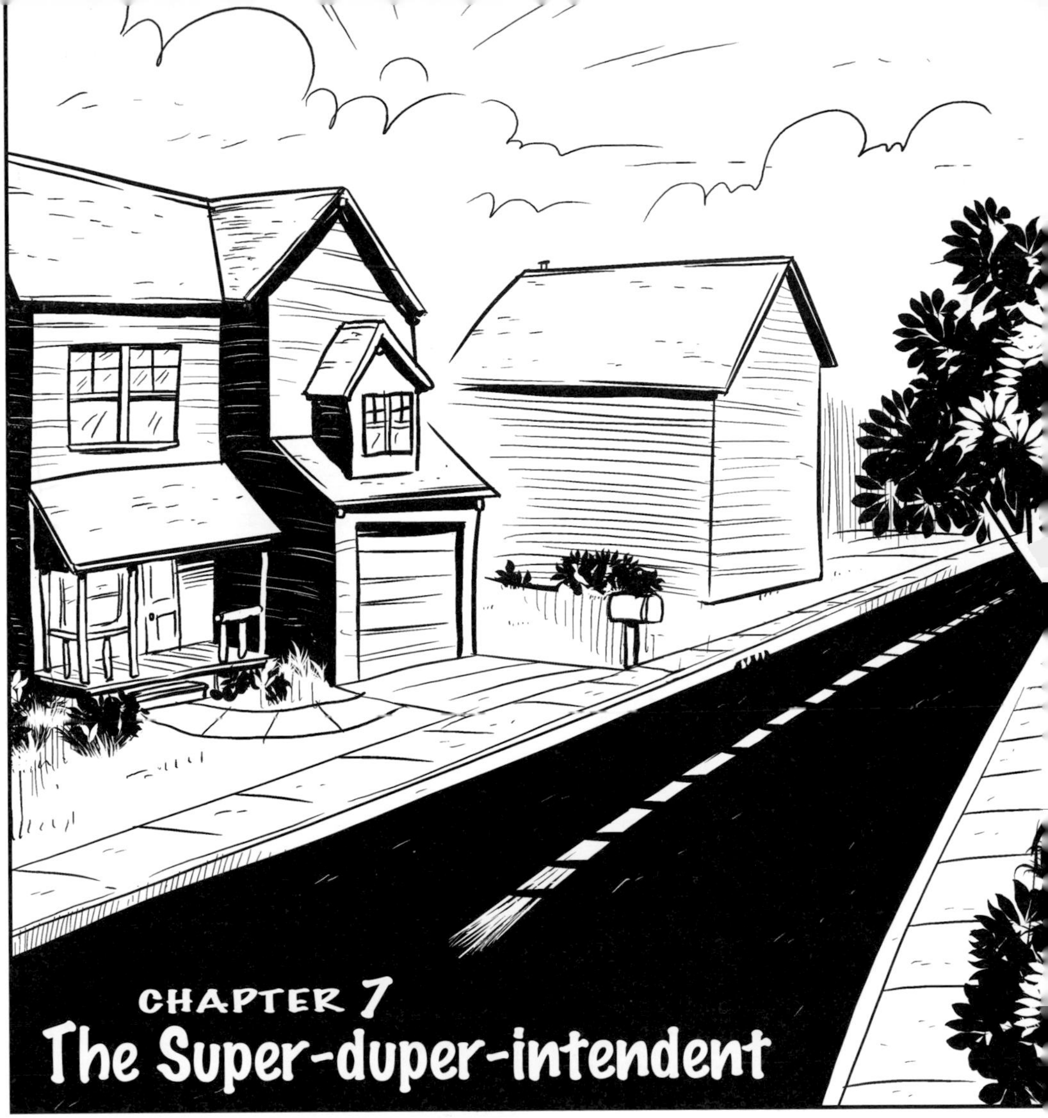
CHAPTER 7
The Super-duper-intendent

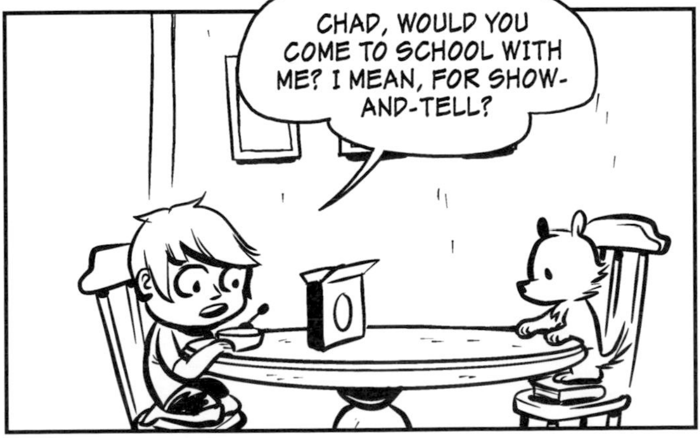
CHAD, WOULD YOU COME TO SCHOOL WITH ME? I MEAN, FOR SHOW-AND-TELL?

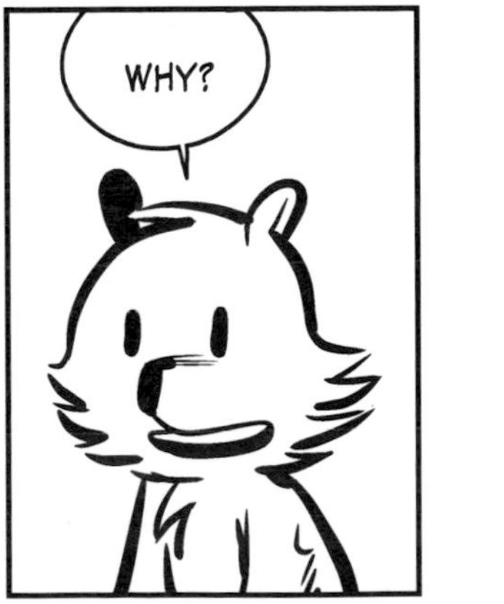
WHY?

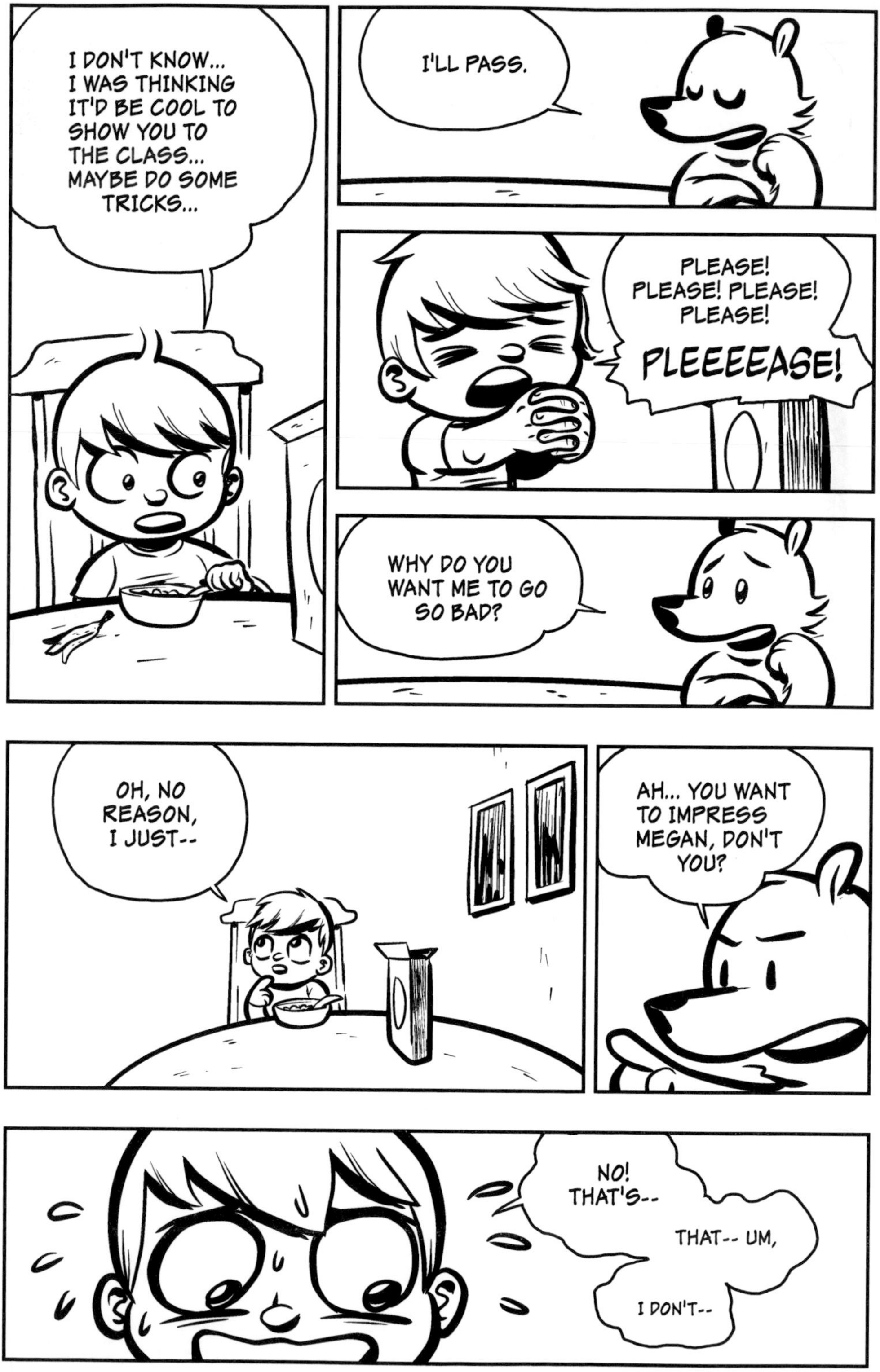
I DON'T KNOW... I WAS THINKING IT'D BE COOL TO SHOW YOU TO THE CLASS... MAYBE DO SOME TRICKS...
I'LL PASS.
PLEASE! PLEASE! PLEASE! PLEASE!
PLEEEEEASE!
WHY DO YOU WANT ME TO GO SO BAD?
OH, NO REASON, I JUST--
AH... YOU WANT TO IMPRESS MEGAN, DON'T YOU?
NO! THAT'S--
THAT-- UM,
I DON'T--

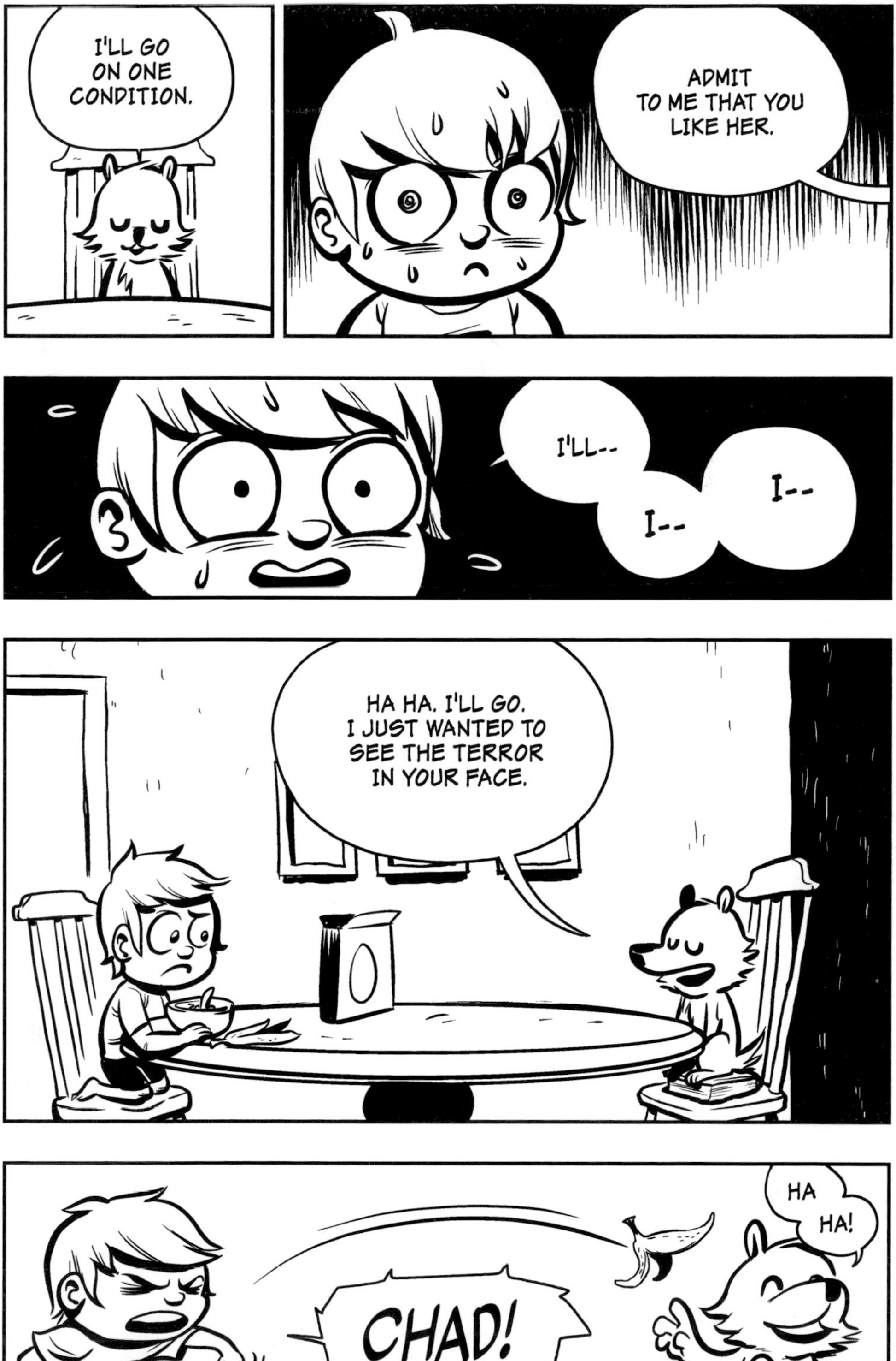
I'LL GO ON ONE CONDITION.
ADMIT TO ME THAT YOU LIKE HER.
I'LL--
I--
I--
HA HA. I'LL GO. I JUST WANTED TO SEE THE TERROR IN YOUR FACE.
CHAD!
HA HA!

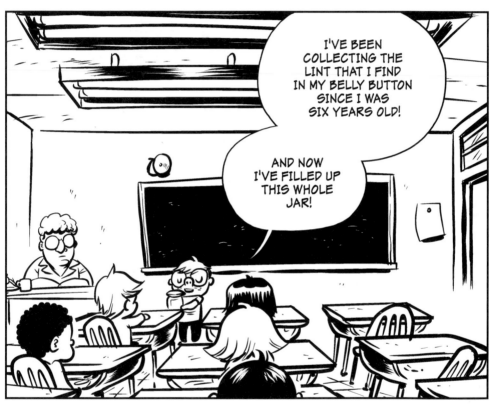

I'VE BEEN COLLECTING THE LINT THAT I FIND IN MY BELLY BUTTON SINCE I WAS SIX YEARS OLD!

AND NOW I'VE FILLED UP THIS WHOLE JAR!

SHALL I PASS IT AROUND?

AH-- NO, THAT'S QUITE ALL RIGHT. THANK YOU, ROGER.

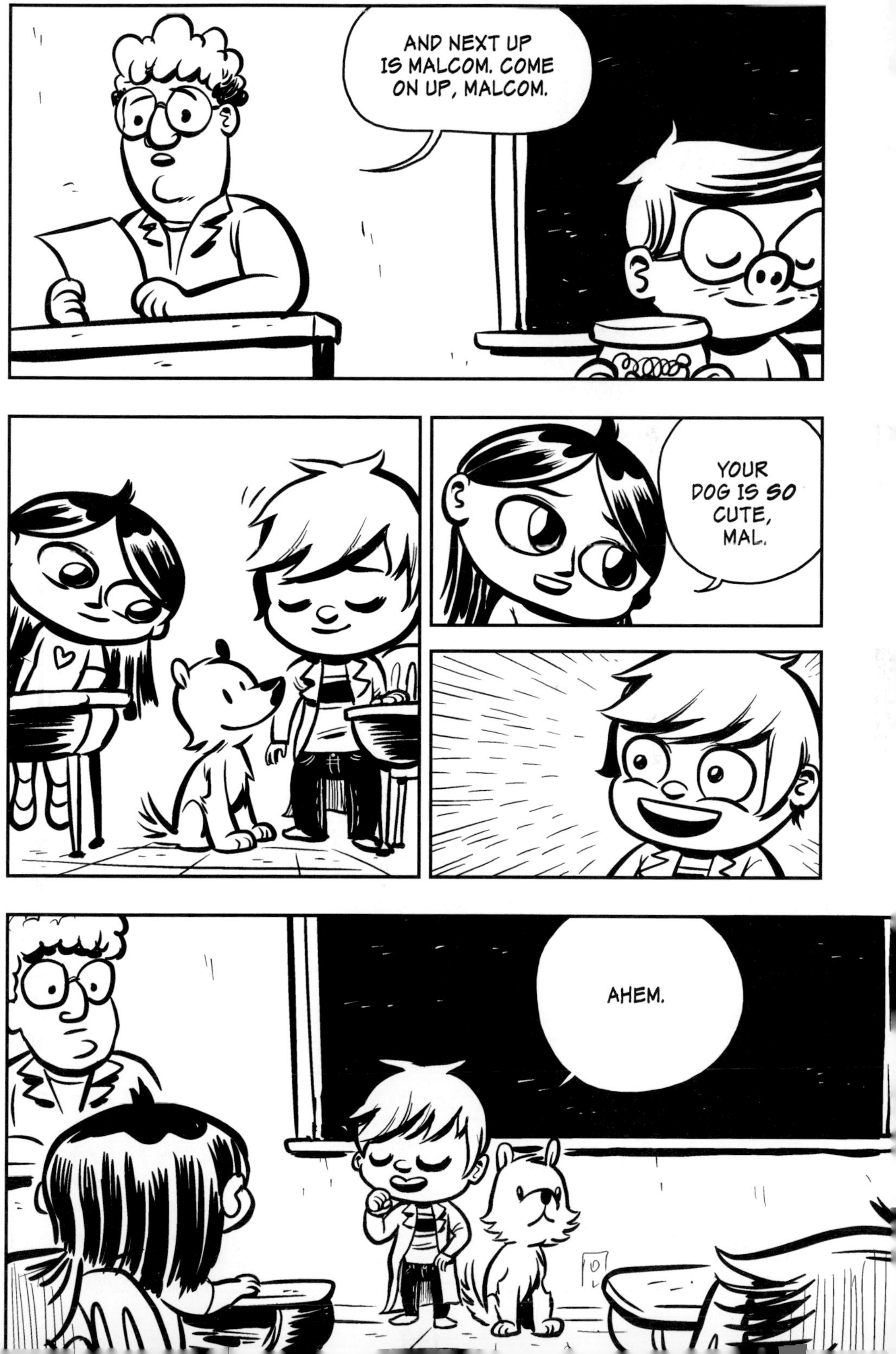
AND NEXT UP IS MALCOM. COME ON UP, MALCOM.
YOUR DOG IS SO CUTE, MAL.
AHEM.

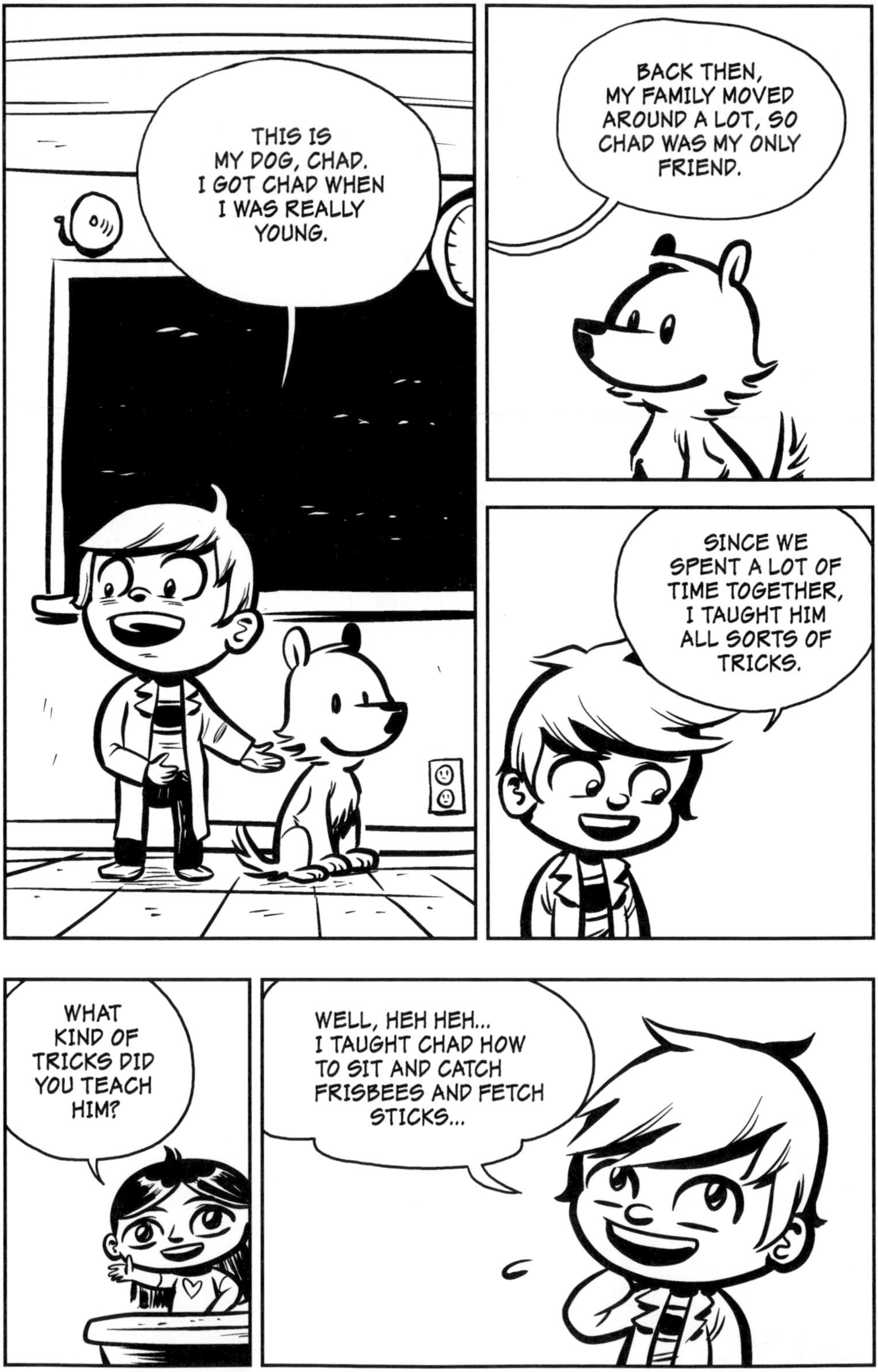
THIS IS MY DOG, CHAD. I GOT CHAD WHEN I WAS REALLY YOUNG.
BACK THEN, MY FAMILY MOVED AROUND A LOT, SO CHAD WAS MY ONLY FRIEND.
SINCE WE SPENT A LOT OF TIME TOGETHER, I TAUGHT HIM ALL SORTS OF TRICKS.
WHAT KIND OF TRICKS DID YOU TEACH HIM?
WELL, HEH HEH... I TAUGHT CHAD HOW TO SIT AND CATCH FRISBEES AND FETCH STICKS...

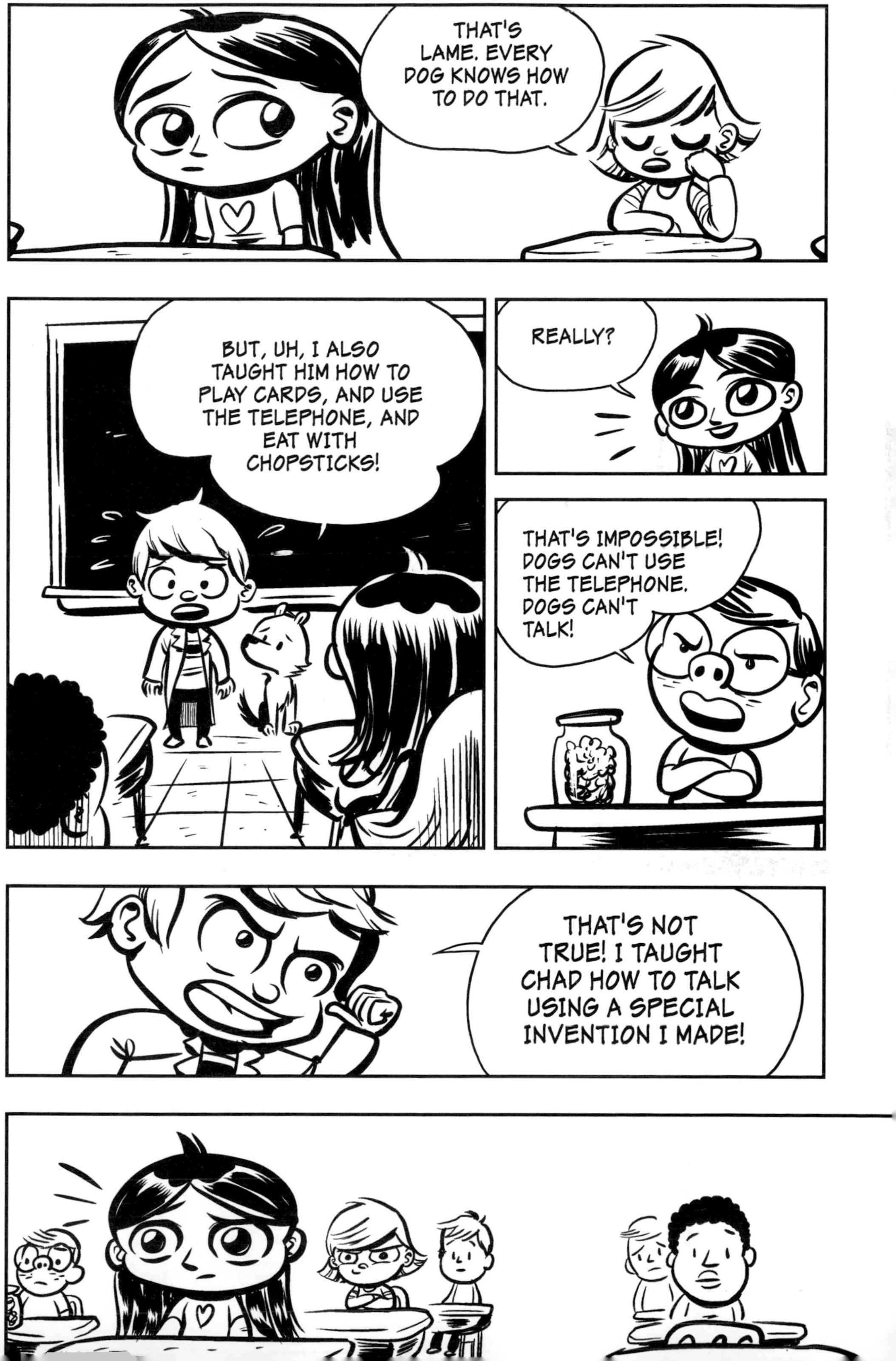
THAT'S LAME. EVERY DOG KNOWS HOW TO DO THAT.
BUT, UH, I ALSO TAUGHT HIM HOW TO PLAY CARDS, AND USE THE TELEPHONE, AND EAT WITH CHOPSTICKS!
REALLY?
THAT'S IMPOSSIBLE! DOGS CAN'T USE THE TELEPHONE. DOGS CAN'T TALK!
THAT'S NOT TRUE! I TAUGHT CHAD HOW TO TALK USING A SPECIAL INVENTION I MADE!

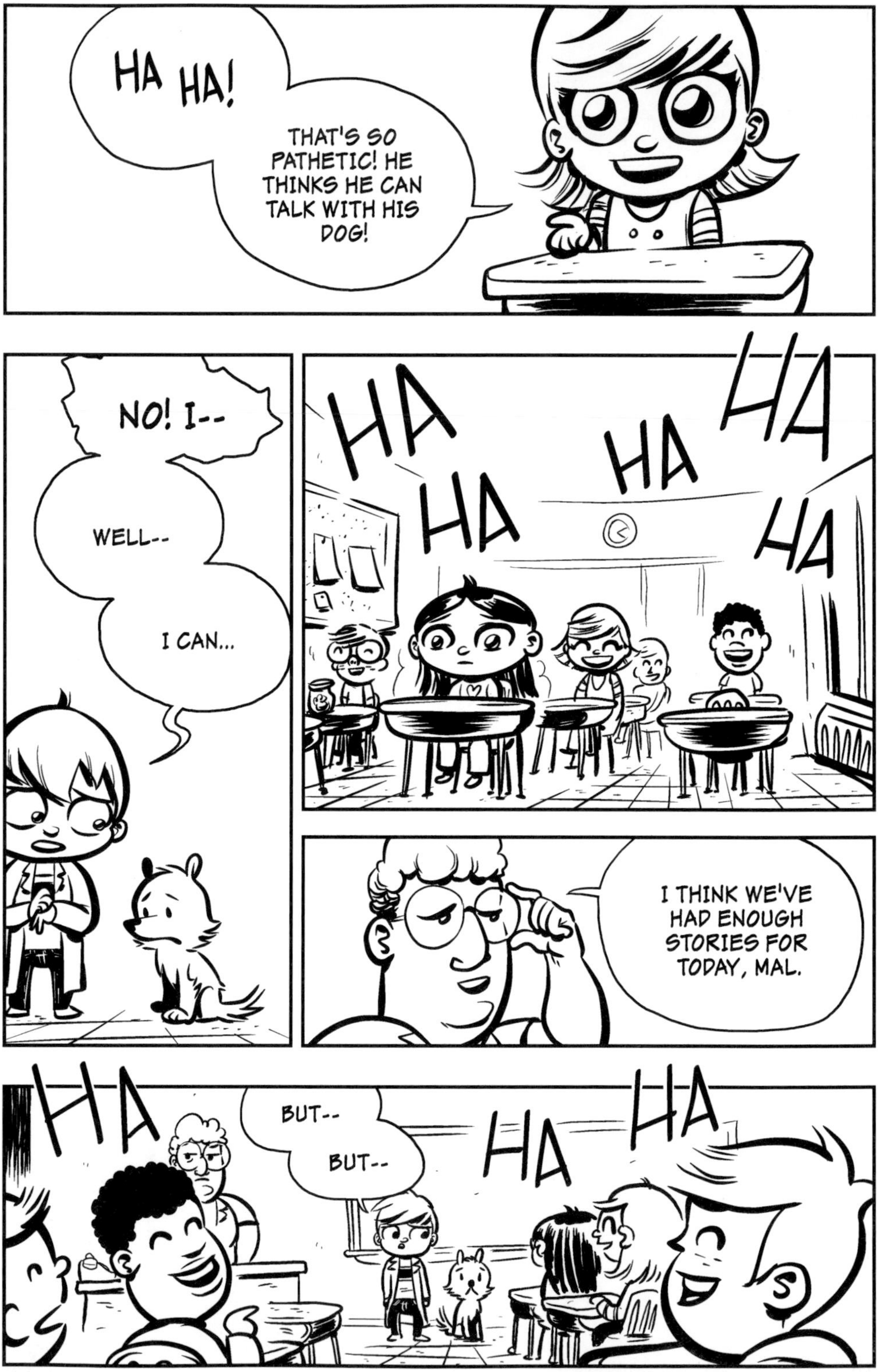
HA HA!
THAT'S SO PATHETIC! HE THINKS HE CAN TALK WITH HIS DOG!
NO! I--
WELL--
I CAN...
HA HA HA HA HA HA
I THINK WE'VE HAD ENOUGH STORIES FOR TODAY, MAL.
HA
BUT--
BUT--
HA HA

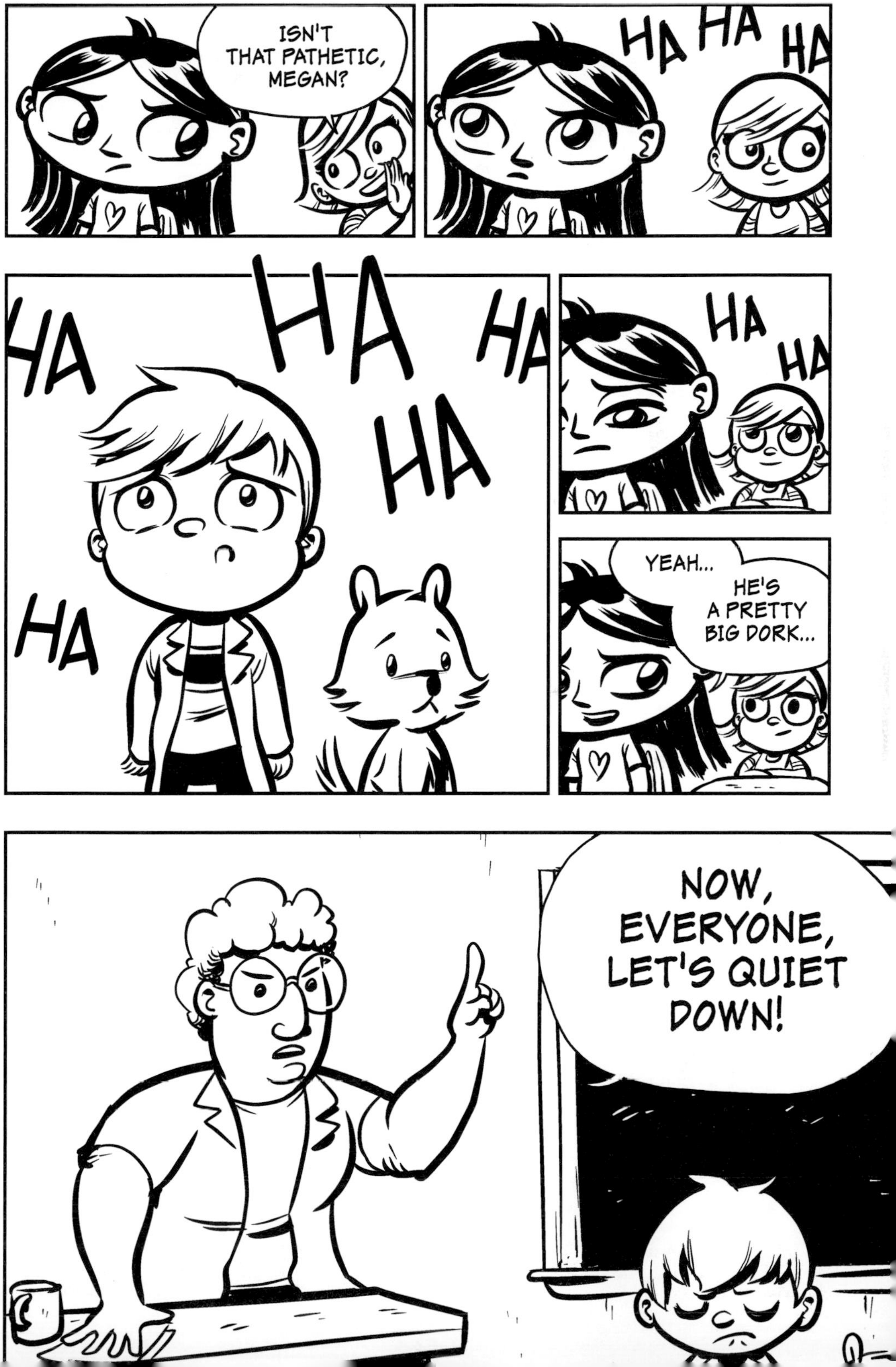
ISN'T THAT PATHETIC, MEGAN?
HA HA HA HA
HA HA HA HA HA
HA HA
YEAH...
HE'S A PRETTY BIG DORK...
NOW, EVERYONE, LET'S QUIET DOWN!

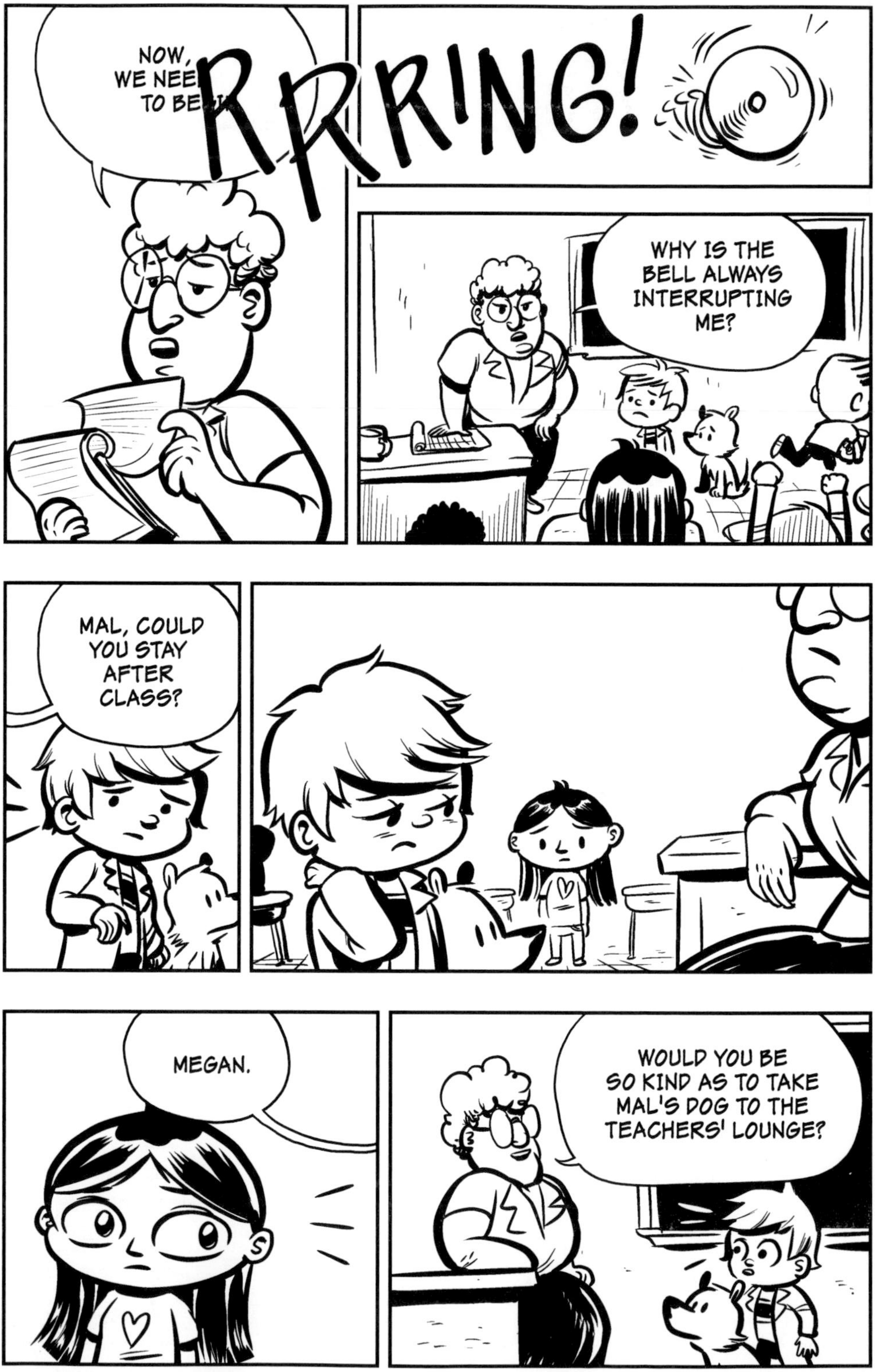

NOW, WE NEE TO BE
RRRING!
WHY IS THE BELL ALWAYS INTERRUPTING ME?
MAL, COULD YOU STAY AFTER CLASS?
MEGAN.
WOULD YOU BE SO KIND AS TO TAKE MAL'S DOG TO THE TEACHERS' LOUNGE?

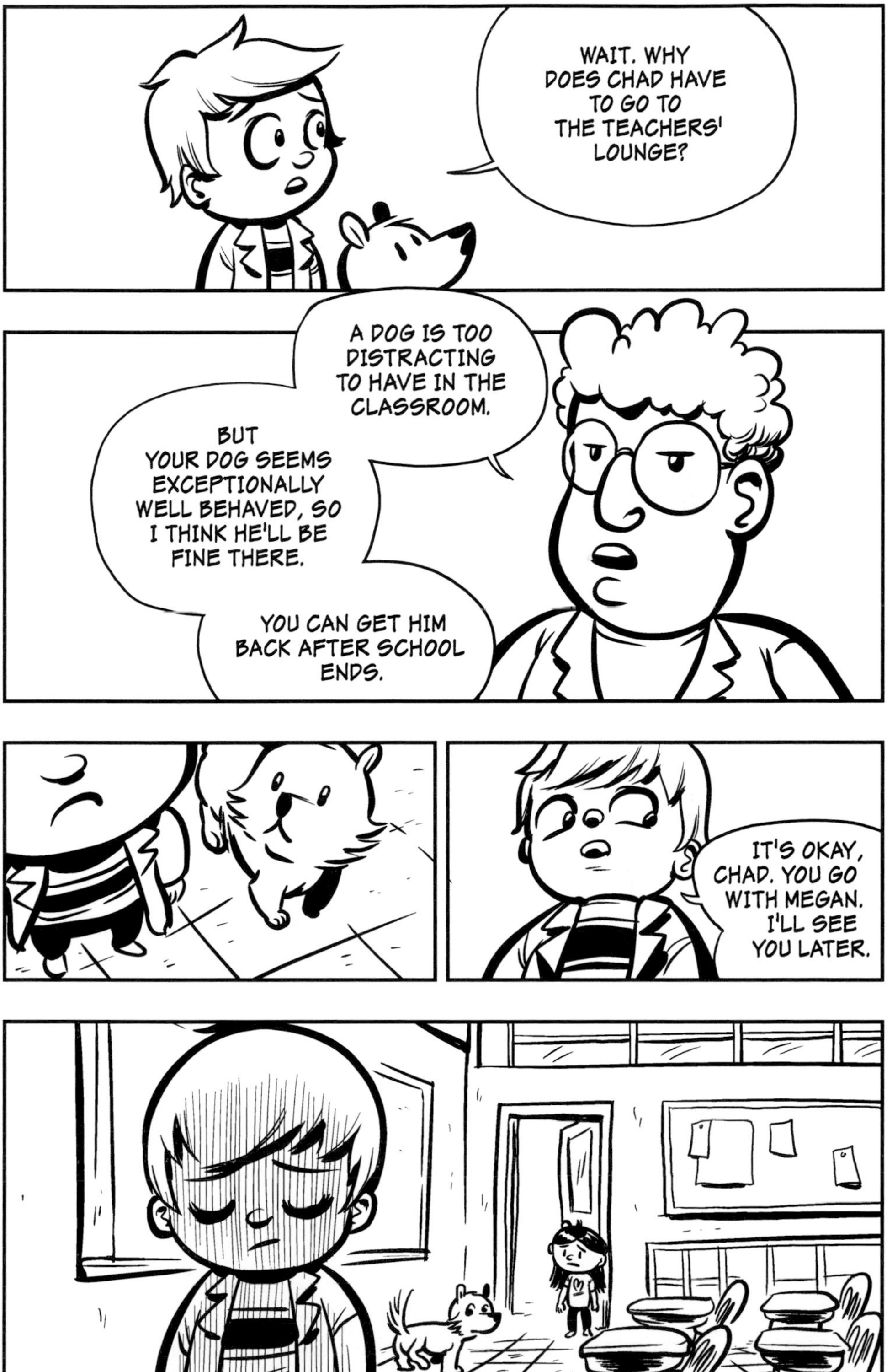
WAIT. WHY DOES CHAD HAVE TO GO TO THE TEACHERS' LOUNGE?
A DOG IS TOO DISTRACTING TO HAVE IN THE CLASSROOM.
BUT YOUR DOG SEEMS EXCEPTIONALLY WELL BEHAVED, SO I THINK HE'LL BE FINE THERE.
YOU CAN GET HIM BACK AFTER SCHOOL ENDS.
IT'S OKAY, CHAD. YOU GO WITH MEGAN. I'LL SEE YOU LATER.

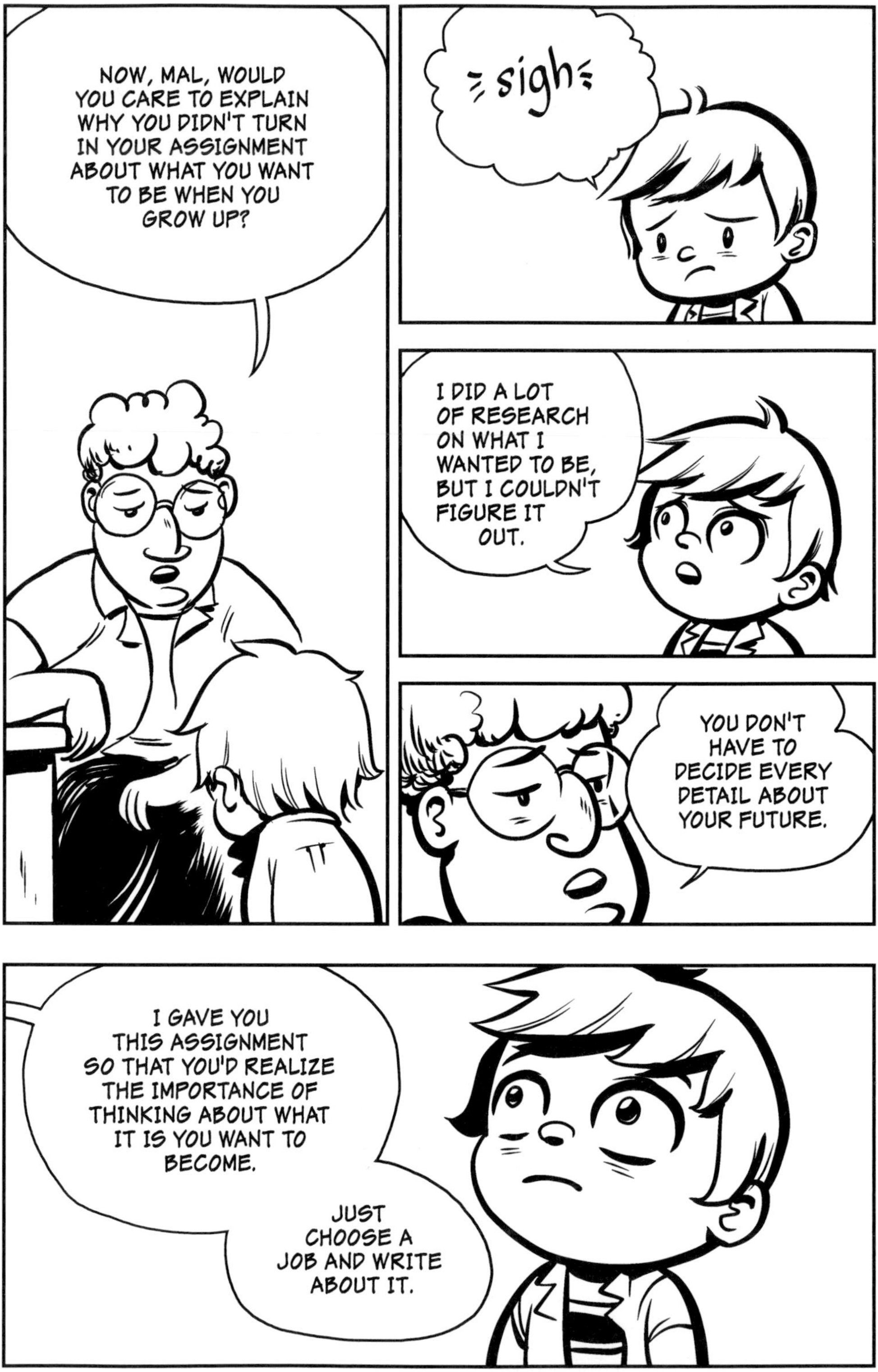
NOW, MAL, WOULD YOU CARE TO EXPLAIN WHY YOU DIDN'T TURN IN YOUR ASSIGNMENT ABOUT WHAT YOU WANT TO BE WHEN YOU GROW UP?
sigh
I DID A LOT OF RESEARCH ON WHAT I WANTED TO BE, BUT I COULDN'T FIGURE IT OUT.
YOU DON'T HAVE TO DECIDE EVERY DETAIL ABOUT YOUR FUTURE.
I GAVE YOU THIS ASSIGNMENT SO THAT YOU'D REALIZE THE IMPORTANCE OF THINKING ABOUT WHAT IT IS YOU WANT TO BECOME.
JUST CHOOSE A JOB AND WRITE ABOUT IT.

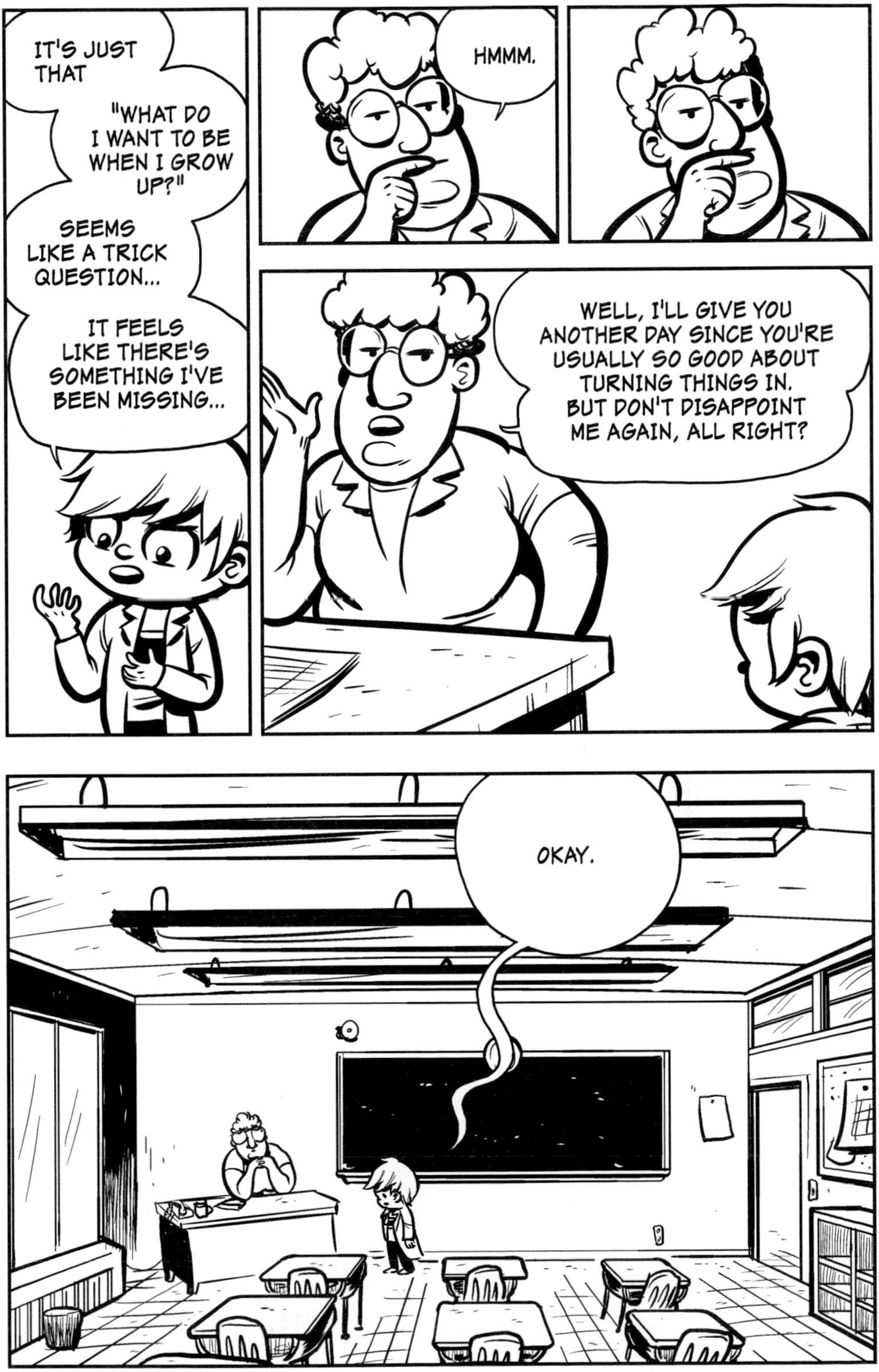
IT'S JUST THAT "WHAT DO I WANT TO BE WHEN I GROW UP?" SEEMS LIKE A TRICK QUESTION...
IT FEELS LIKE THERE'S SOMETHING I'VE BEEN MISSING...
HMMM.
WELL, I'LL GIVE YOU ANOTHER DAY SINCE YOU'RE USUALLY SO GOOD ABOUT TURNING THINGS IN. BUT DON'T DISAPPOINT ME AGAIN, ALL RIGHT?
OKAY.

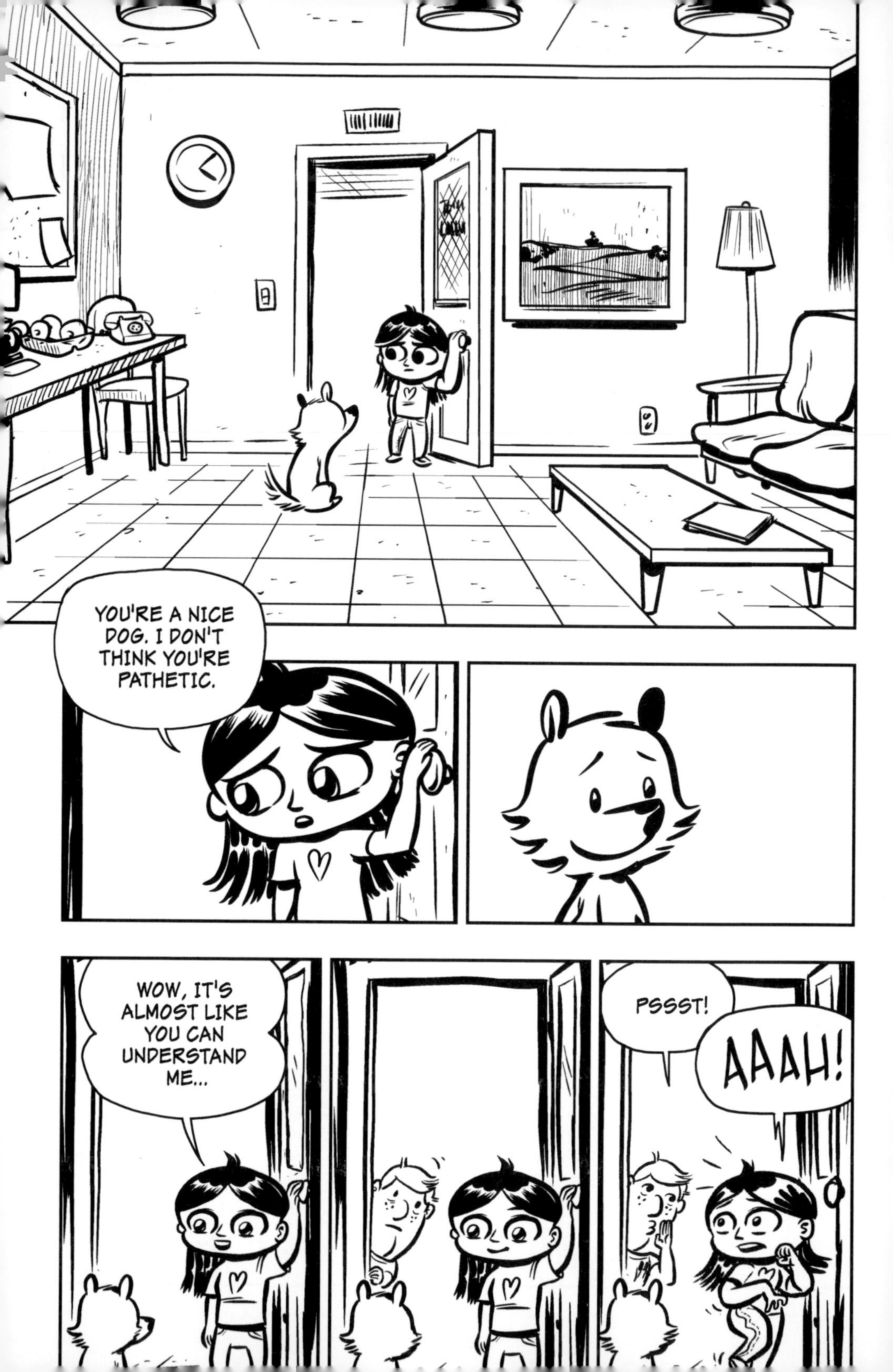

YOU'RE A NICE DOG. I DON'T THINK YOU'RE PATHETIC.
WOW, IT'S ALMOST LIKE YOU CAN UNDERSTAND ME...
PSSST!
AAAH!

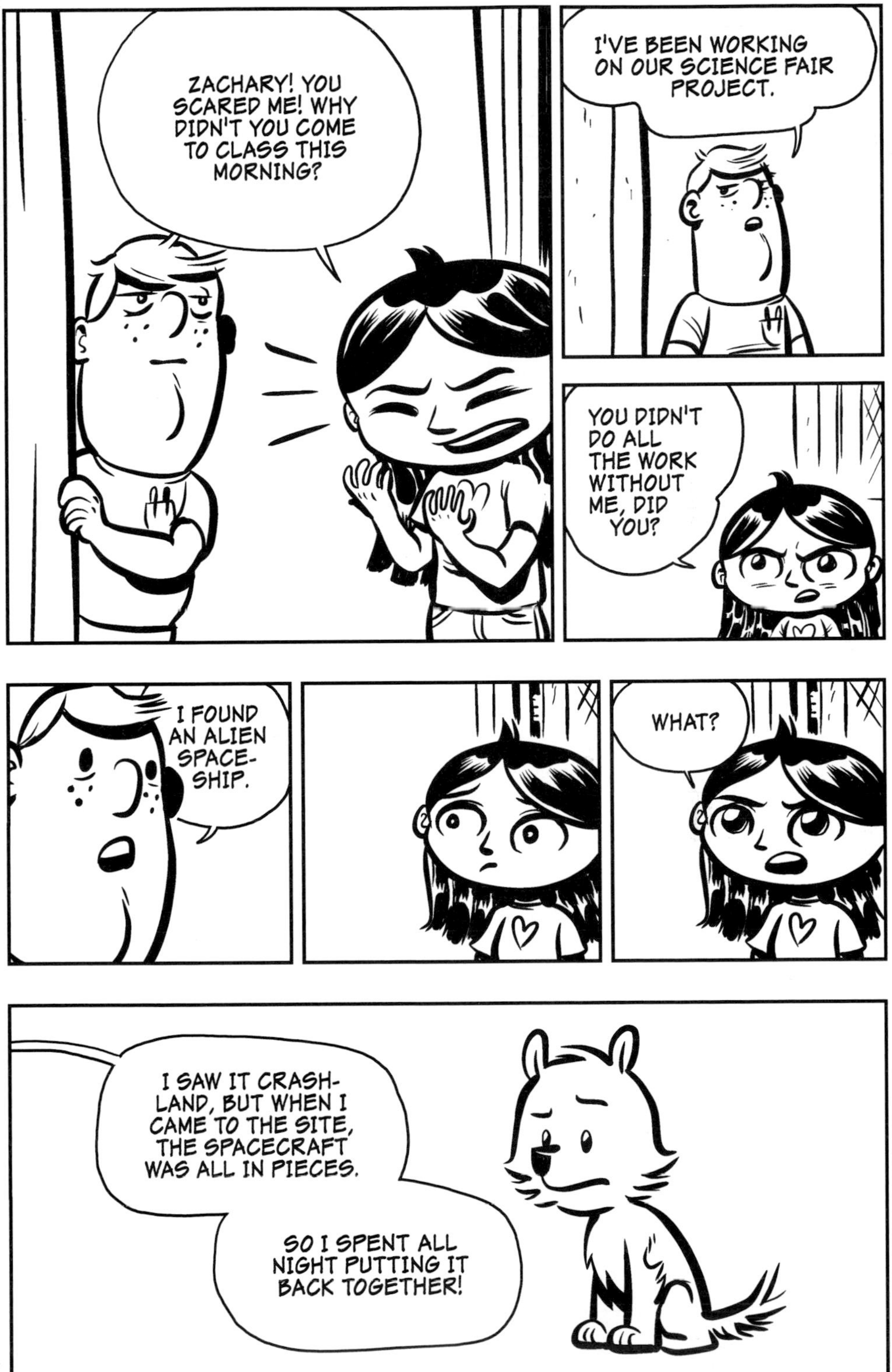
ZACHARY! YOU SCARED ME! WHY DIDN'T YOU COME TO CLASS THIS MORNING?
I'VE BEEN WORKING ON OUR SCIENCE FAIR PROJECT.
YOU DIDN'T DO ALL THE WORK WITHOUT ME, DID YOU?
I FOUND AN ALIEN SPACE-SHIP.
WHAT?
I SAW IT CRASH-LAND, BUT WHEN I CAME TO THE SITE, THE SPACECRAFT WAS ALL IN PIECES.
SO I SPENT ALL NIGHT PUTTING IT BACK TOGETHER!

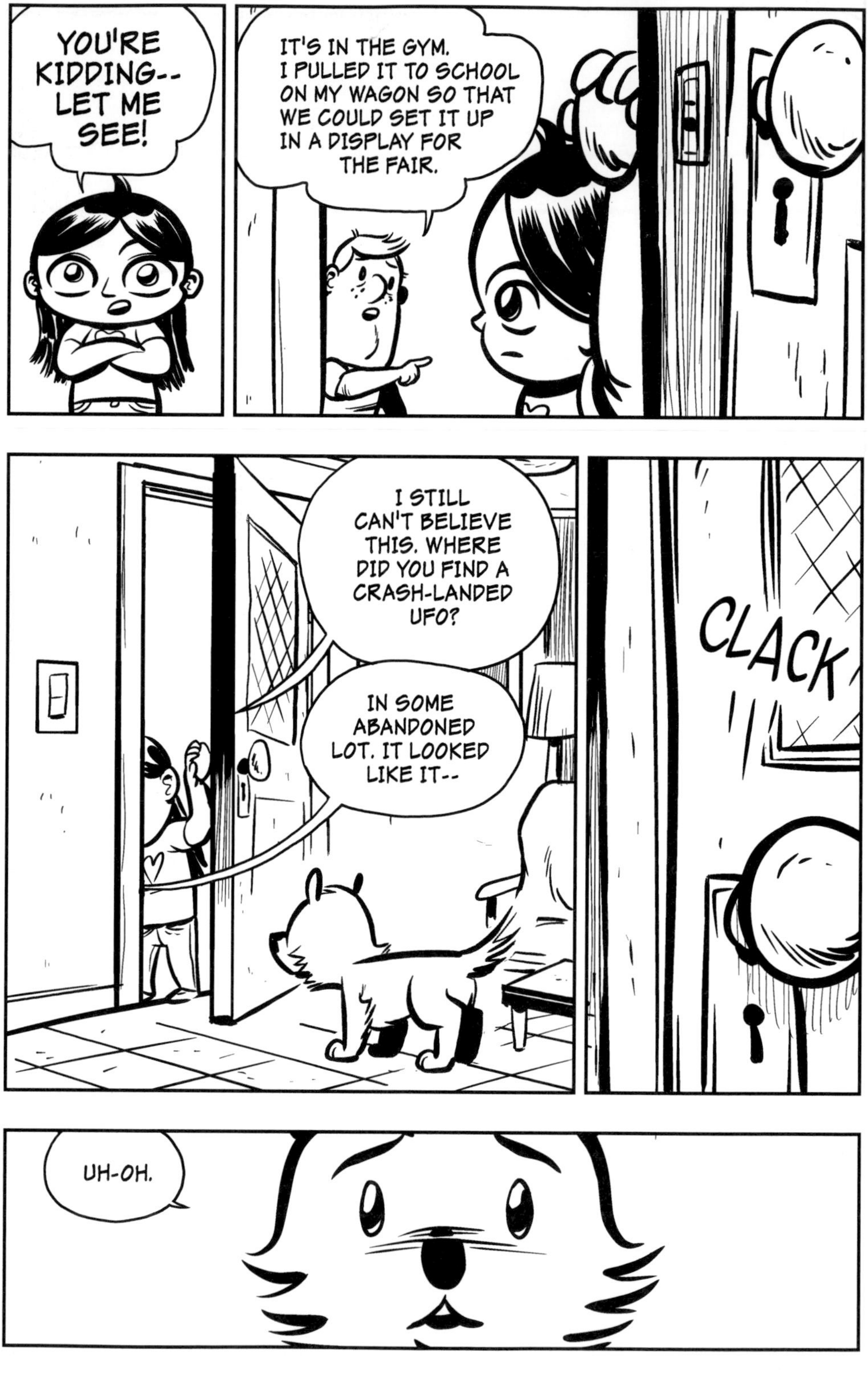
YOU'RE KIDDING-- LET ME SEE!
IT'S IN THE GYM. I PULLED IT TO SCHOOL ON MY WAGON SO THAT WE COULD SET IT UP IN A DISPLAY FOR THE FAIR.
I STILL CAN'T BELIEVE THIS. WHERE DID YOU FIND A CRASH-LANDED UFO?
IN SOME ABANDONED LOT. IT LOOKED LIKE IT--
CLACK
UH-OH.

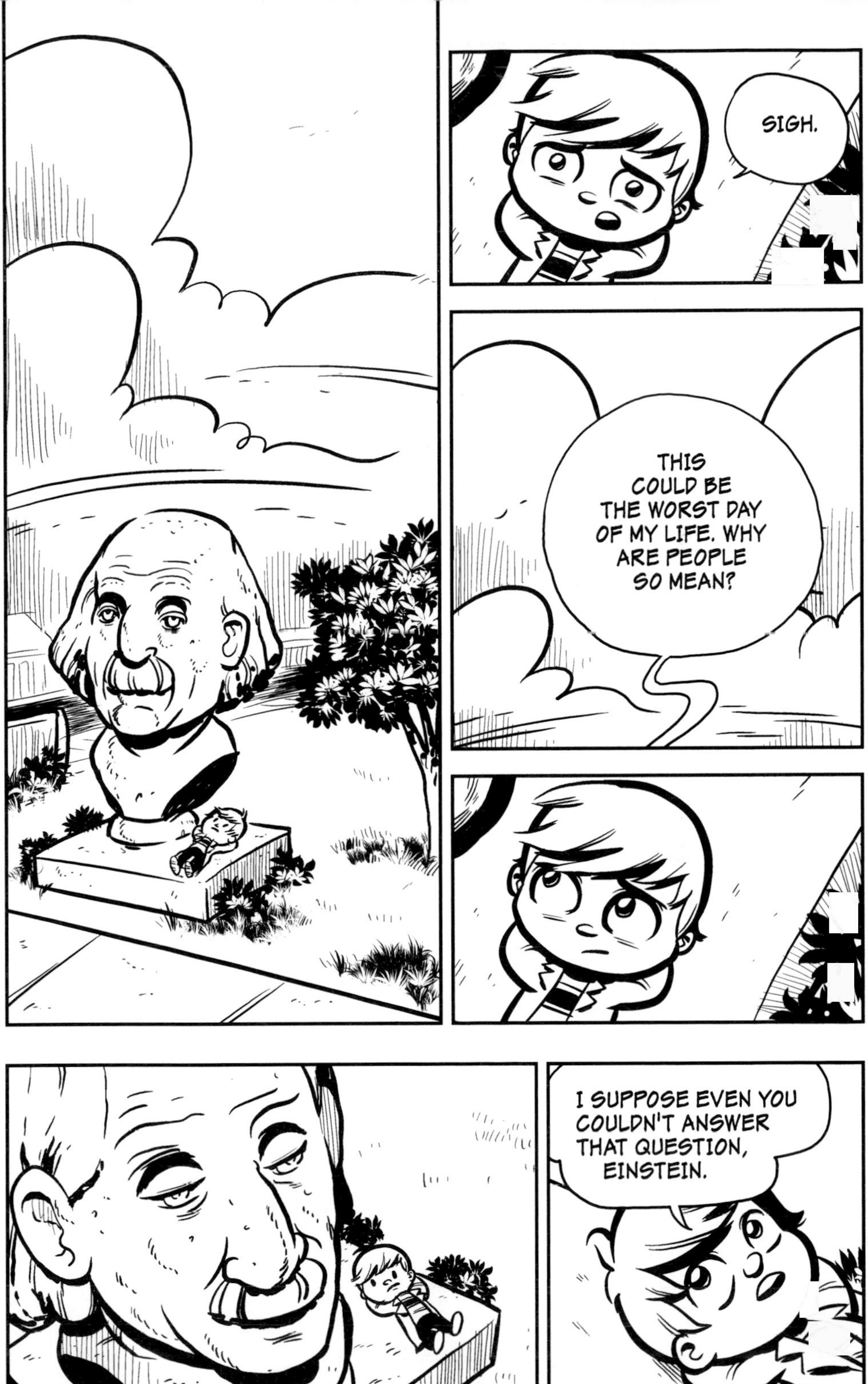
SIGH.
THIS COULD BE THE WORST DAY OF MY LIFE. WHY ARE PEOPLE SO MEAN?
I SUPPOSE EVEN YOU COULDN'T ANSWER THAT QUESTION, EINSTEIN.

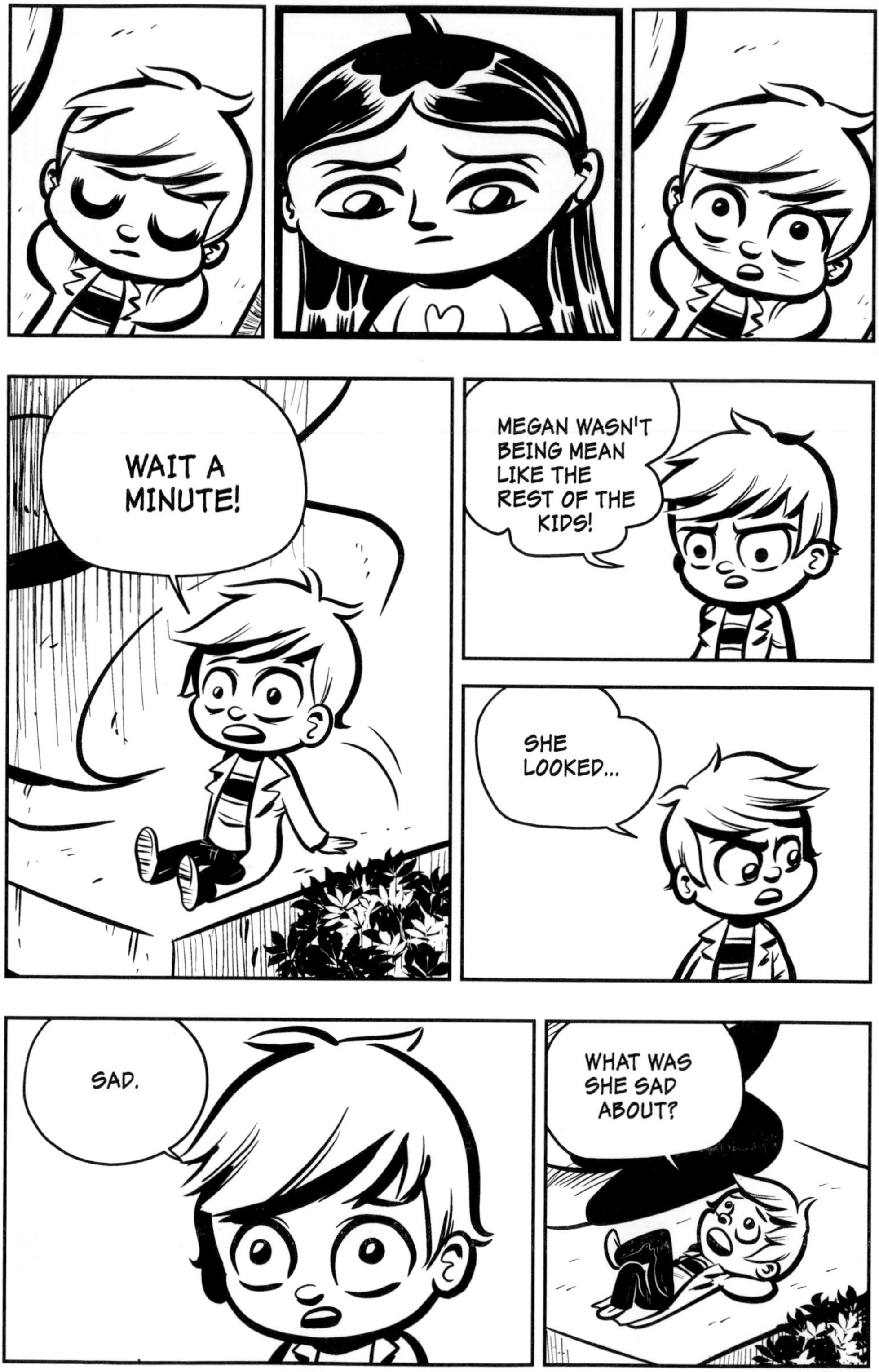
WAIT A MINUTE!
MEGAN WASN'T BEING MEAN LIKE THE REST OF THE KIDS!
SHE LOOKED...
SAD.
WHAT WAS SHE SAD ABOUT?

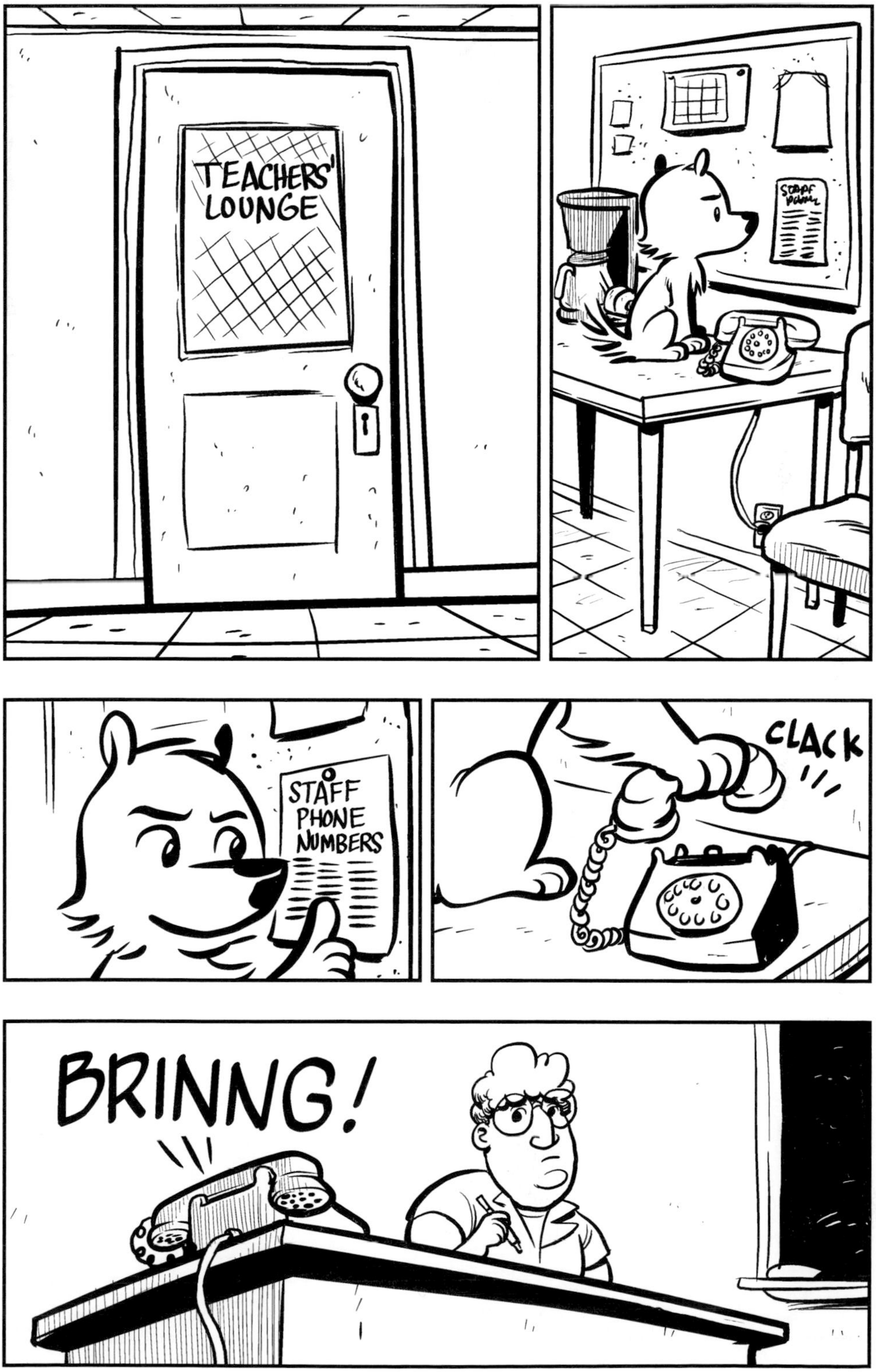
TEACHERS' LOUNGE
STAFF PHONE NUMBERS
CLACK
BRINNG!

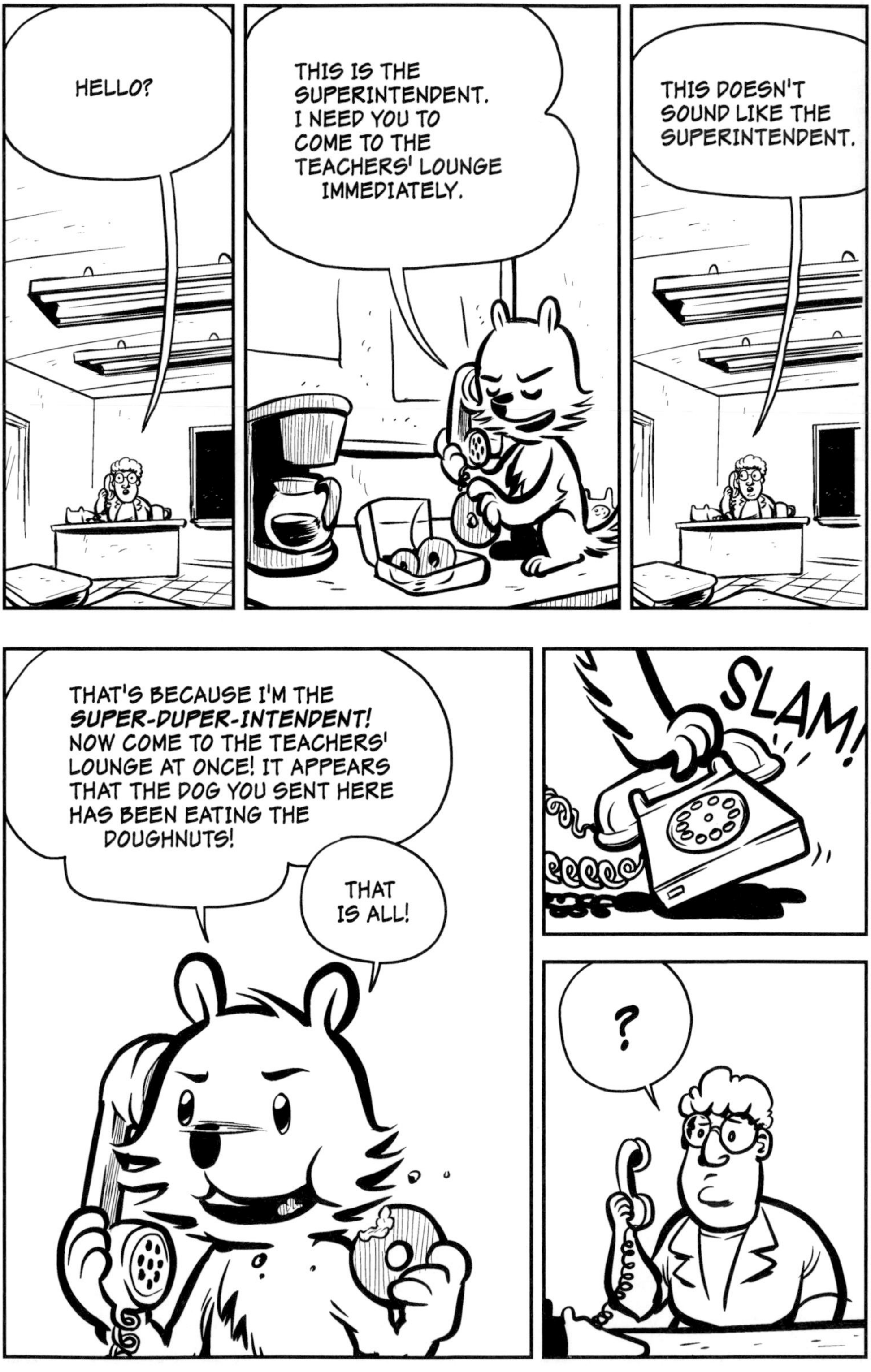
HELLO?
THIS IS THE SUPERINTENDENT. I NEED YOU TO COME TO THE TEACHERS' LOUNGE IMMEDIATELY.
THIS DOESN'T SOUND LIKE THE SUPERINTENDENT.
THAT'S BECAUSE I'M THE *SUPER-DUPER-INTENDENT!* NOW COME TO THE TEACHERS' LOUNGE AT ONCE! IT APPEARS THAT THE DOG YOU SENT HERE HAS BEEN EATING THE DOUGHNUTS!
THAT IS ALL!
SLAM!
?

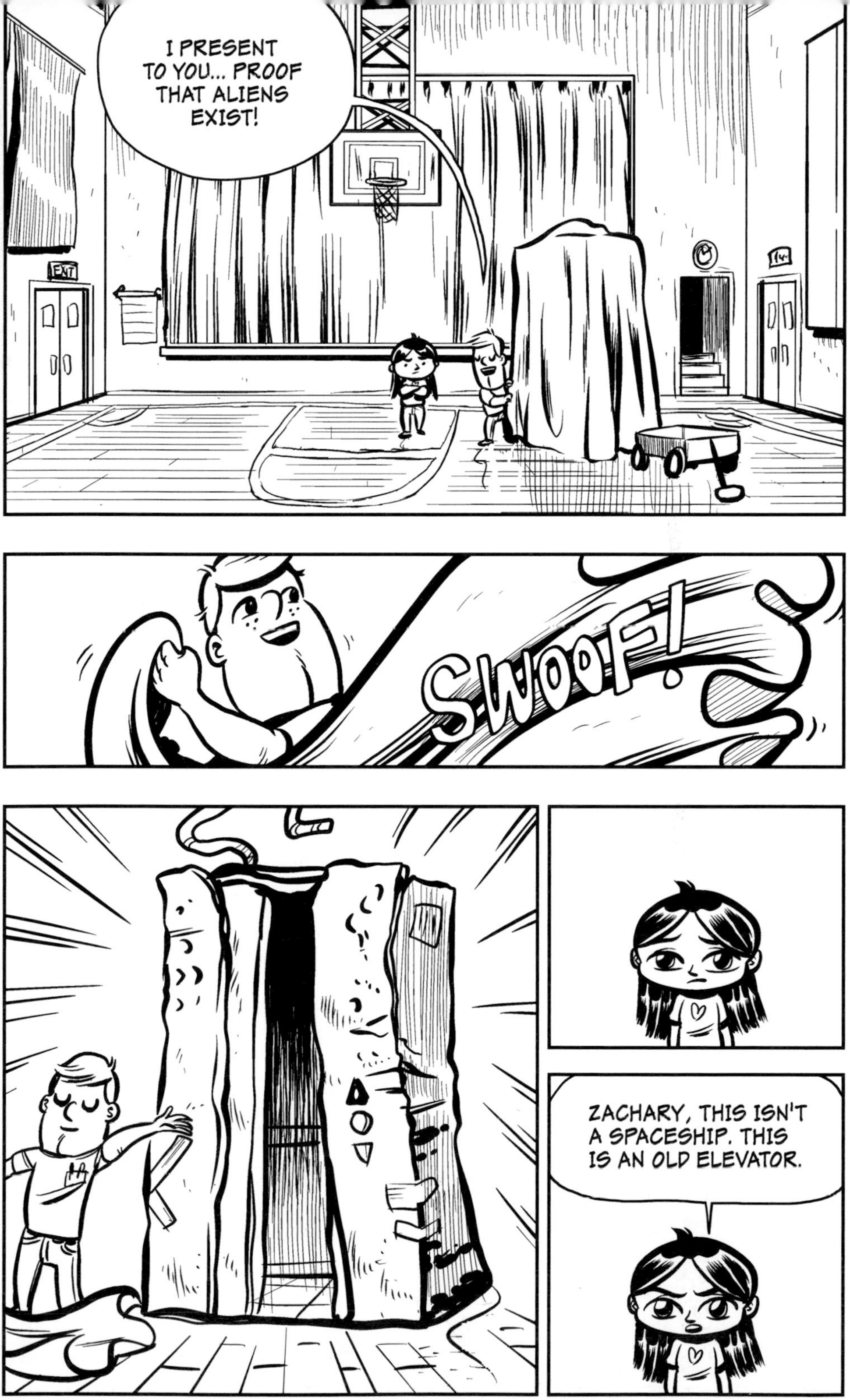
I PRESENT TO YOU... PROOF THAT ALIENS EXIST!
SWOOF!
ZACHARY, THIS ISN'T A SPACESHIP. THIS IS AN OLD ELEVATOR.

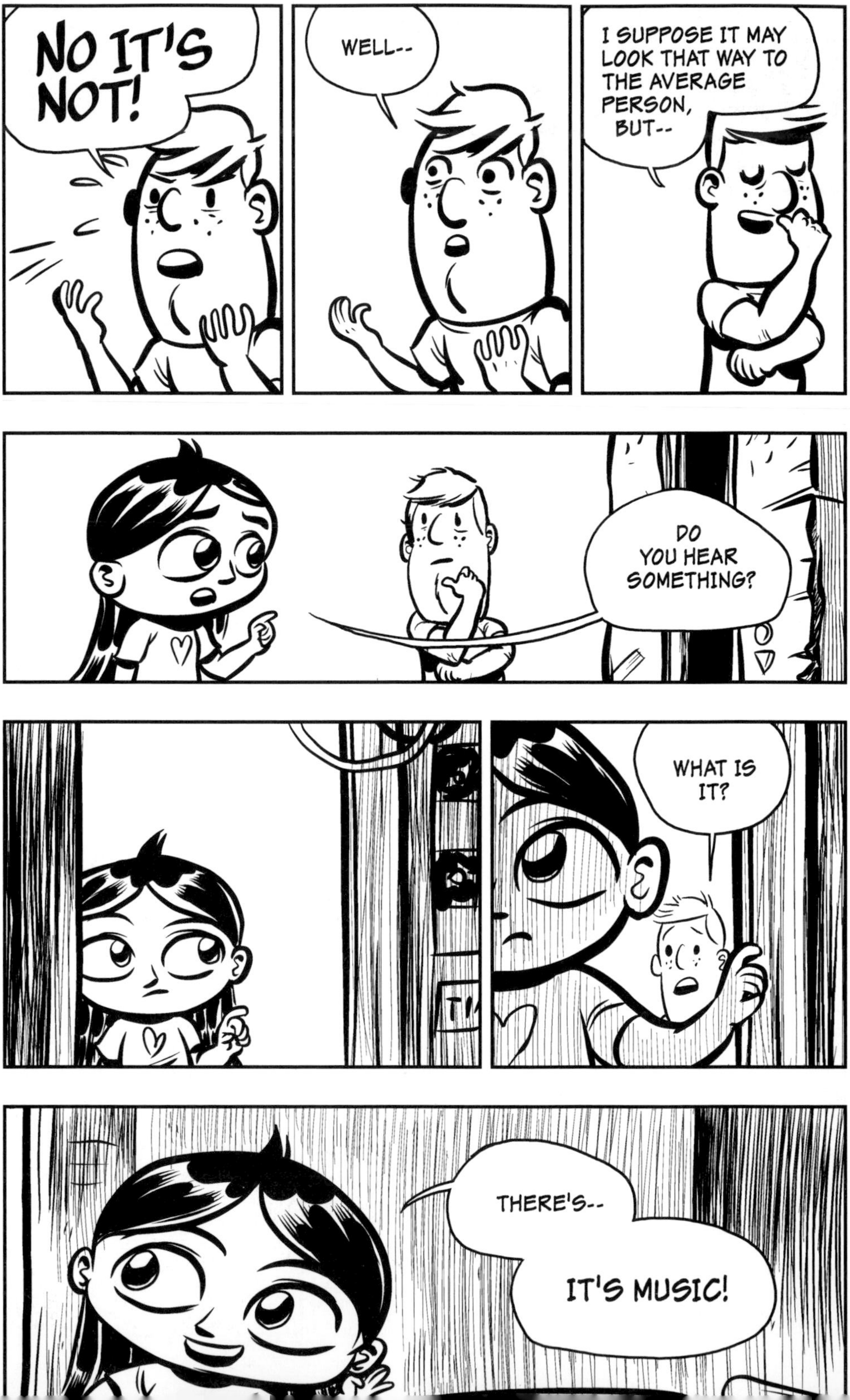
NO IT'S NOT!
WELL--
I SUPPOSE IT MAY LOOK THAT WAY TO THE AVERAGE PERSON, BUT--
DO YOU HEAR SOMETHING?
WHAT IS IT?
THERE'S--
IT'S MUSIC!

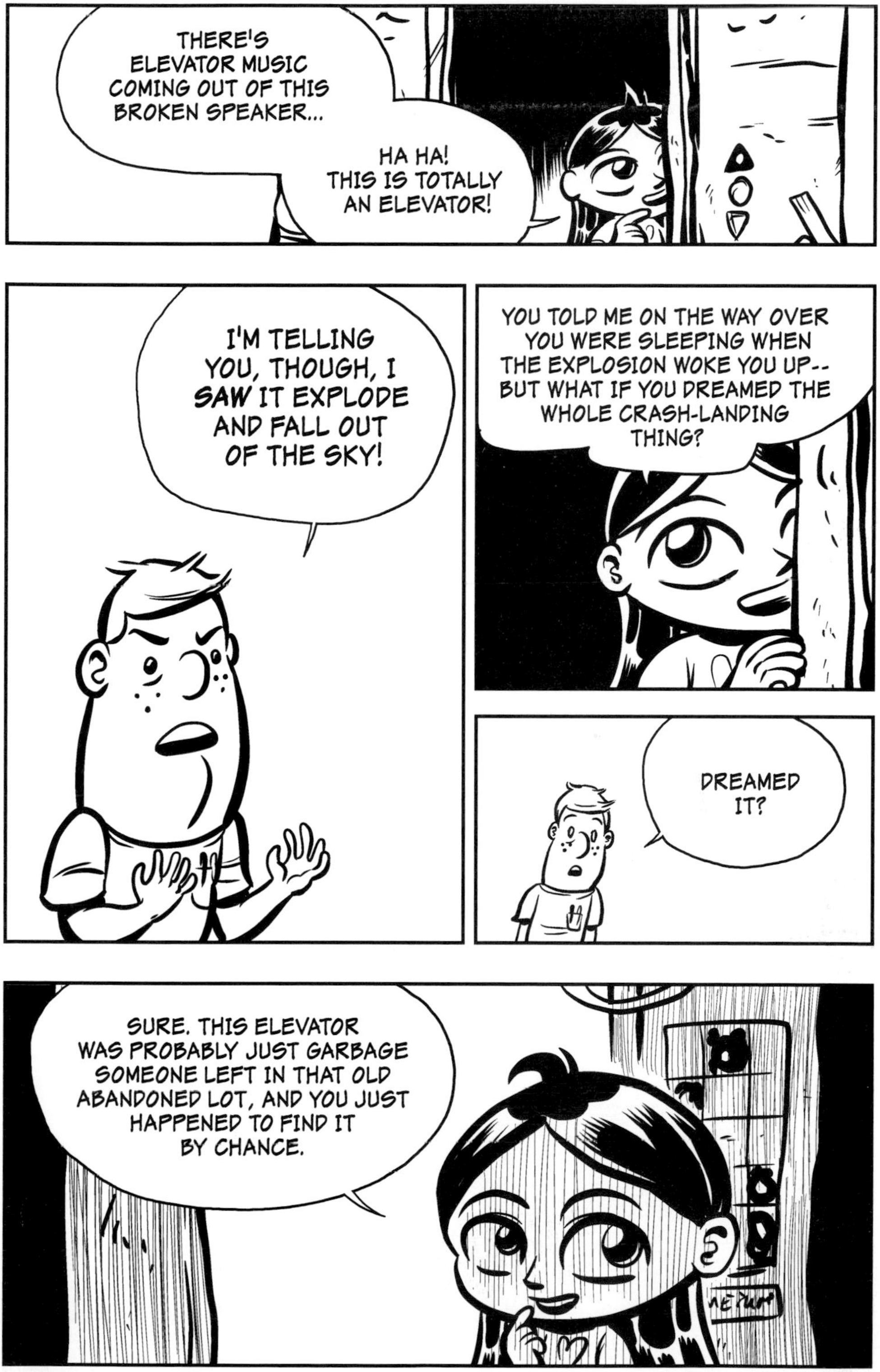
THERE'S ELEVATOR MUSIC COMING OUT OF THIS BROKEN SPEAKER...
HA HA! THIS IS TOTALLY AN ELEVATOR!
I'M TELLING YOU, THOUGH, I SAW IT EXPLODE AND FALL OUT OF THE SKY!
YOU TOLD ME ON THE WAY OVER YOU WERE SLEEPING WHEN THE EXPLOSION WOKE YOU UP-- BUT WHAT IF YOU DREAMED THE WHOLE CRASH-LANDING THING?
DREAMED IT?
SURE. THIS ELEVATOR WAS PROBABLY JUST GARBAGE SOMEONE LEFT IN THAT OLD ABANDONED LOT, AND YOU JUST HAPPENED TO FIND IT BY CHANCE.

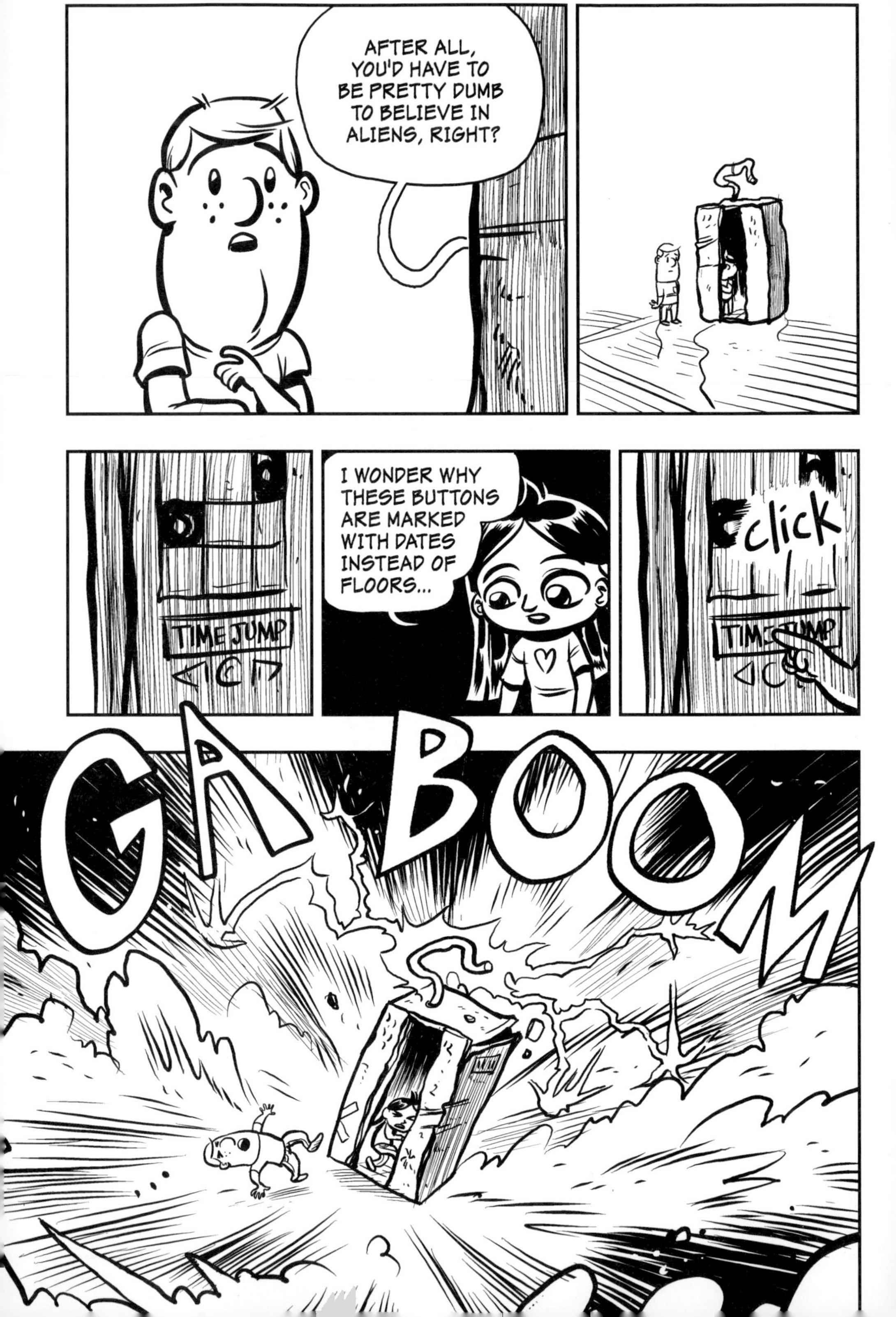
AFTER ALL, YOU'D HAVE TO BE PRETTY DUMB TO BELIEVE IN ALIENS, RIGHT?
TIME JUMP
I WONDER WHY THESE BUTTONS ARE MARKED WITH DATES INSTEAD OF FLOORS...
click
GA BOOM

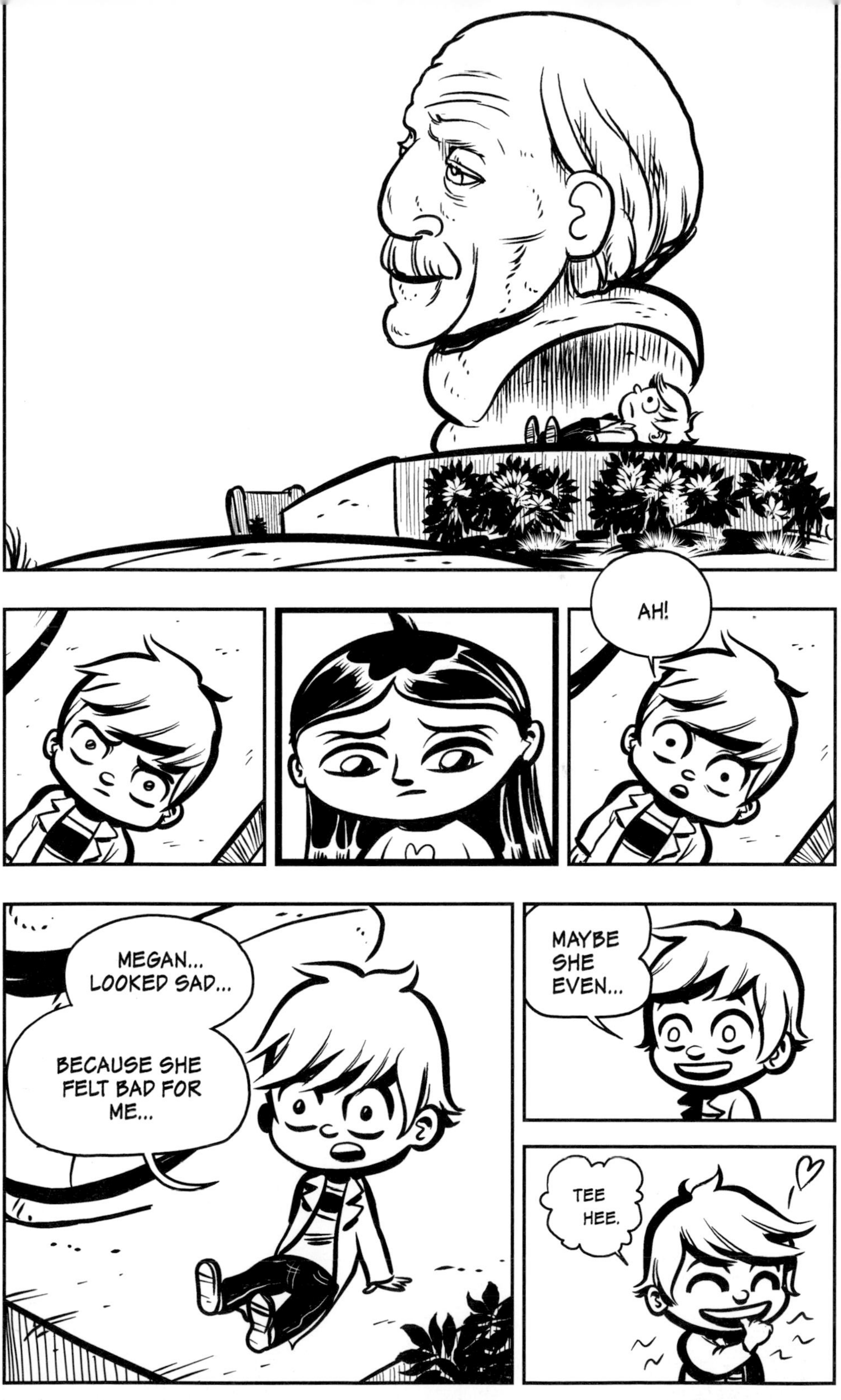
AH!
MEGAN... LOOKED SAD...
BECAUSE SHE FELT BAD FOR ME...
MAYBE SHE EVEN...
TEE HEE.

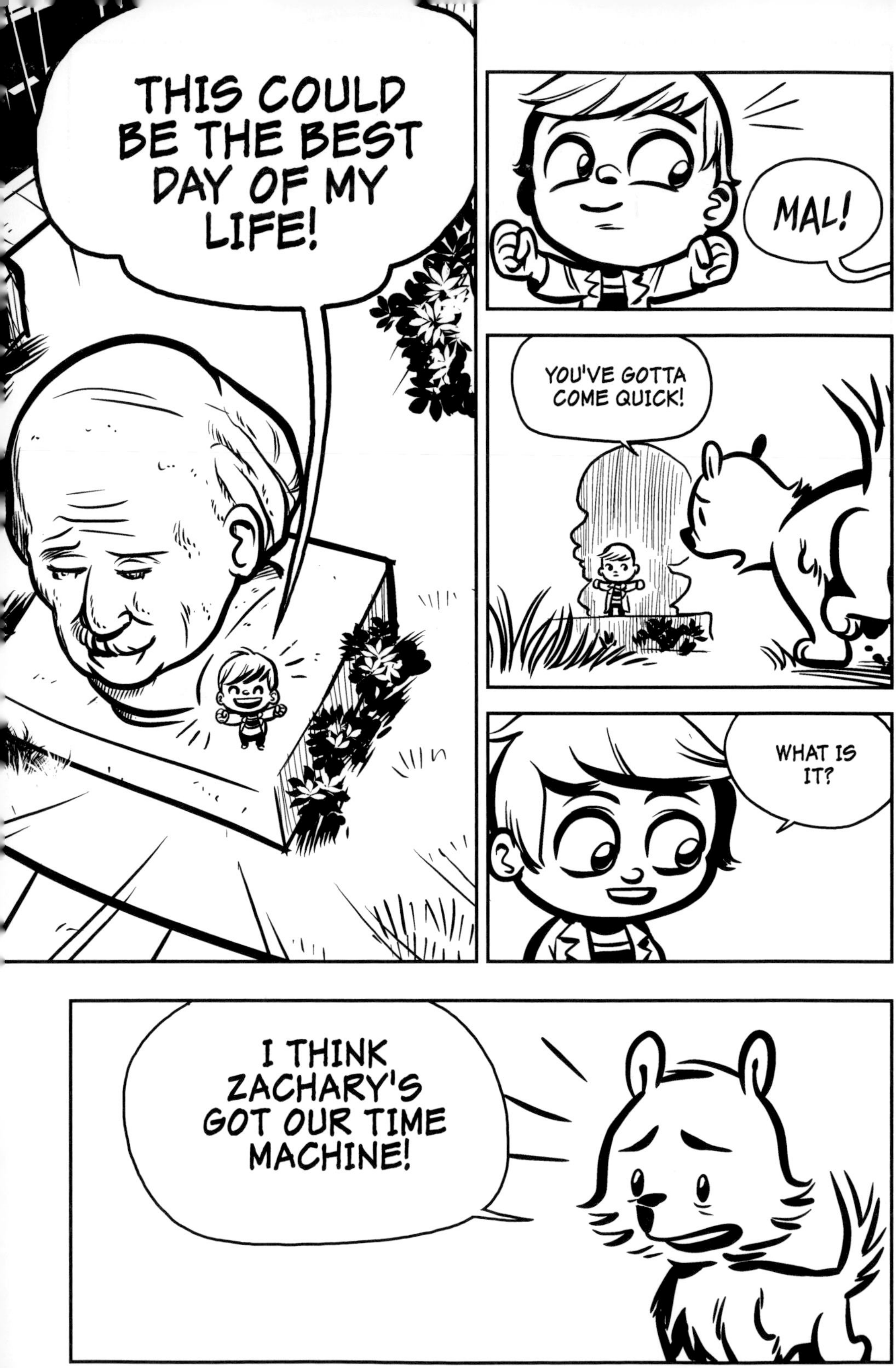
THIS COULD BE THE BEST DAY OF MY LIFE!
MAL!
YOU'VE GOTTA COME QUICK!
WHAT IS IT?
I THINK ZACHARY'S GOT OUR TIME MACHINE!

CHAPTER 8
Peekabooasaurus

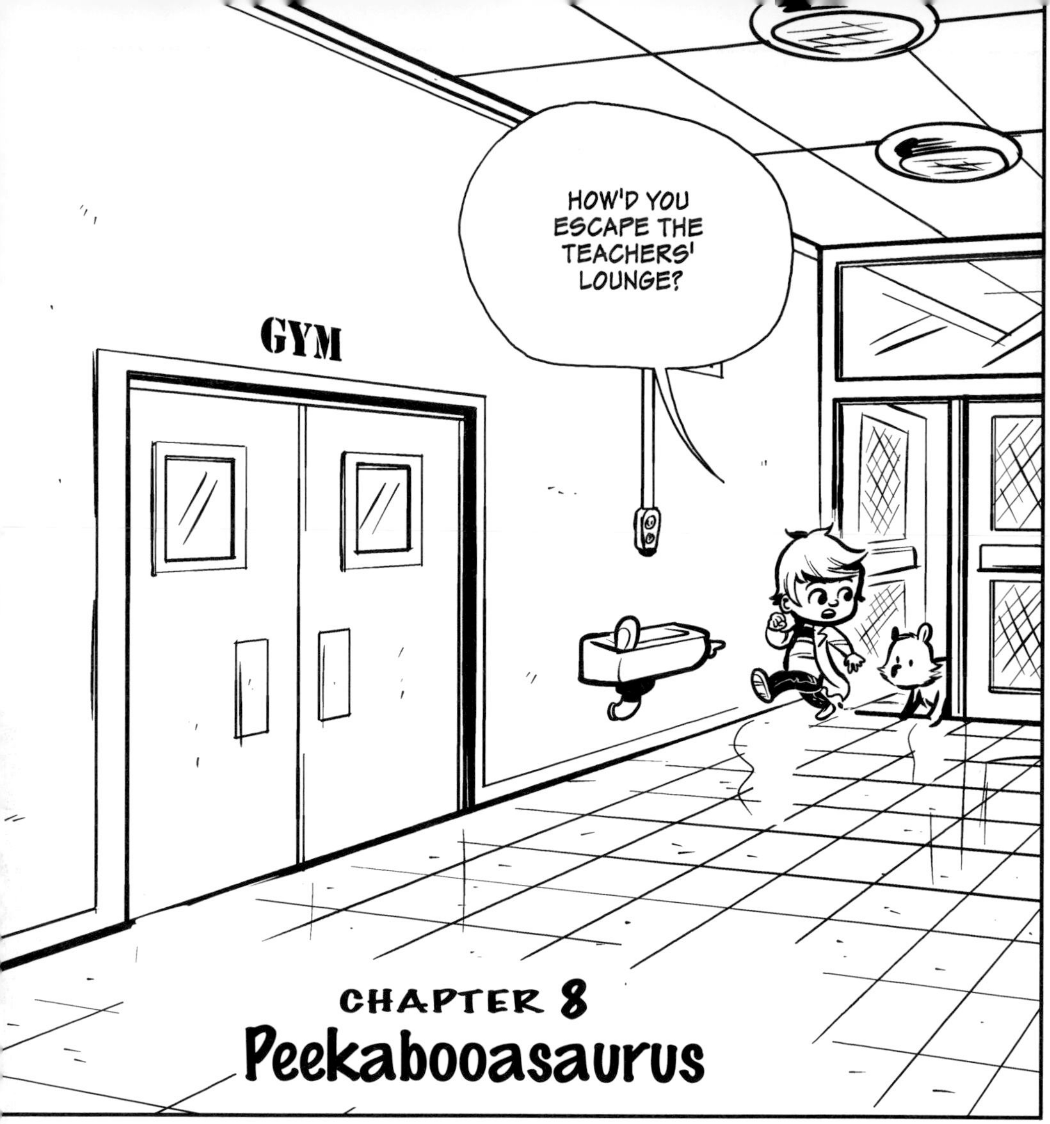

GYM
HOW'D YOU ESCAPE THE TEACHERS' LOUNGE?

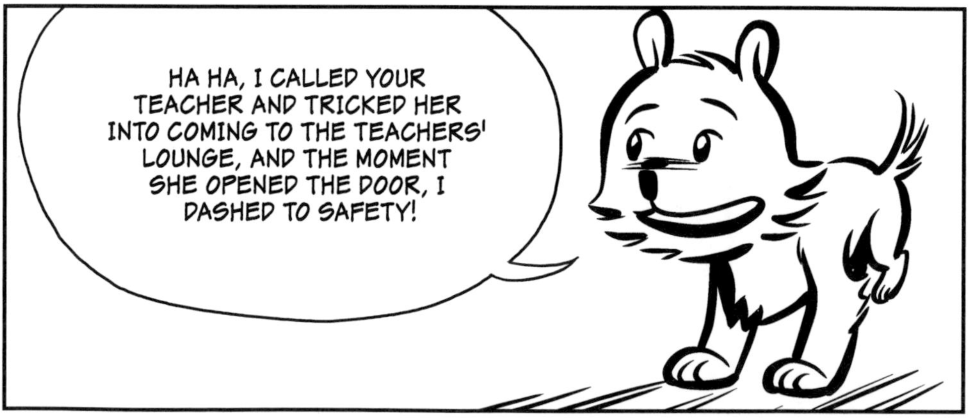

HA HA, I CALLED YOUR TEACHER AND TRICKED HER INTO COMING TO THE TEACHERS' LOUNGE, AND THE MOMENT SHE OPENED THE DOOR, I DASHED TO SAFETY!

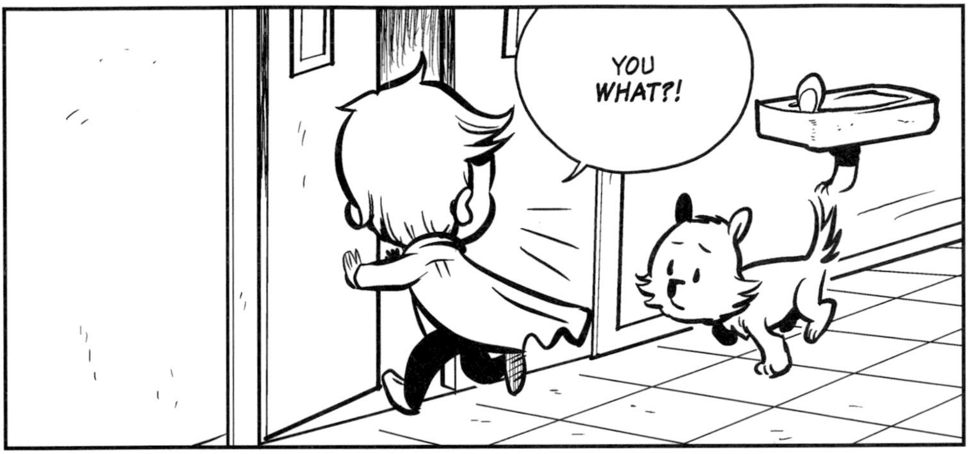
YOU
WHAT?!

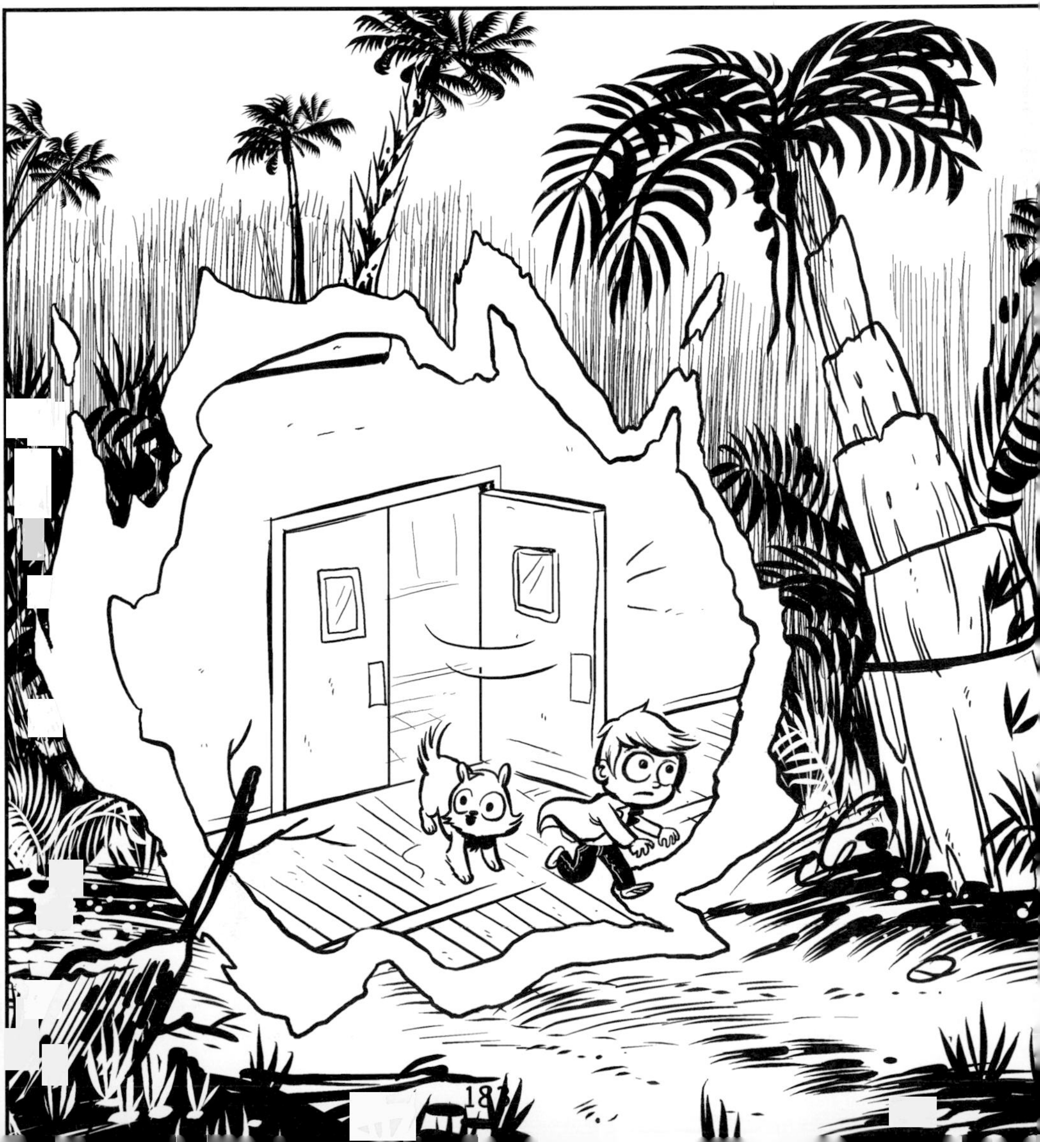

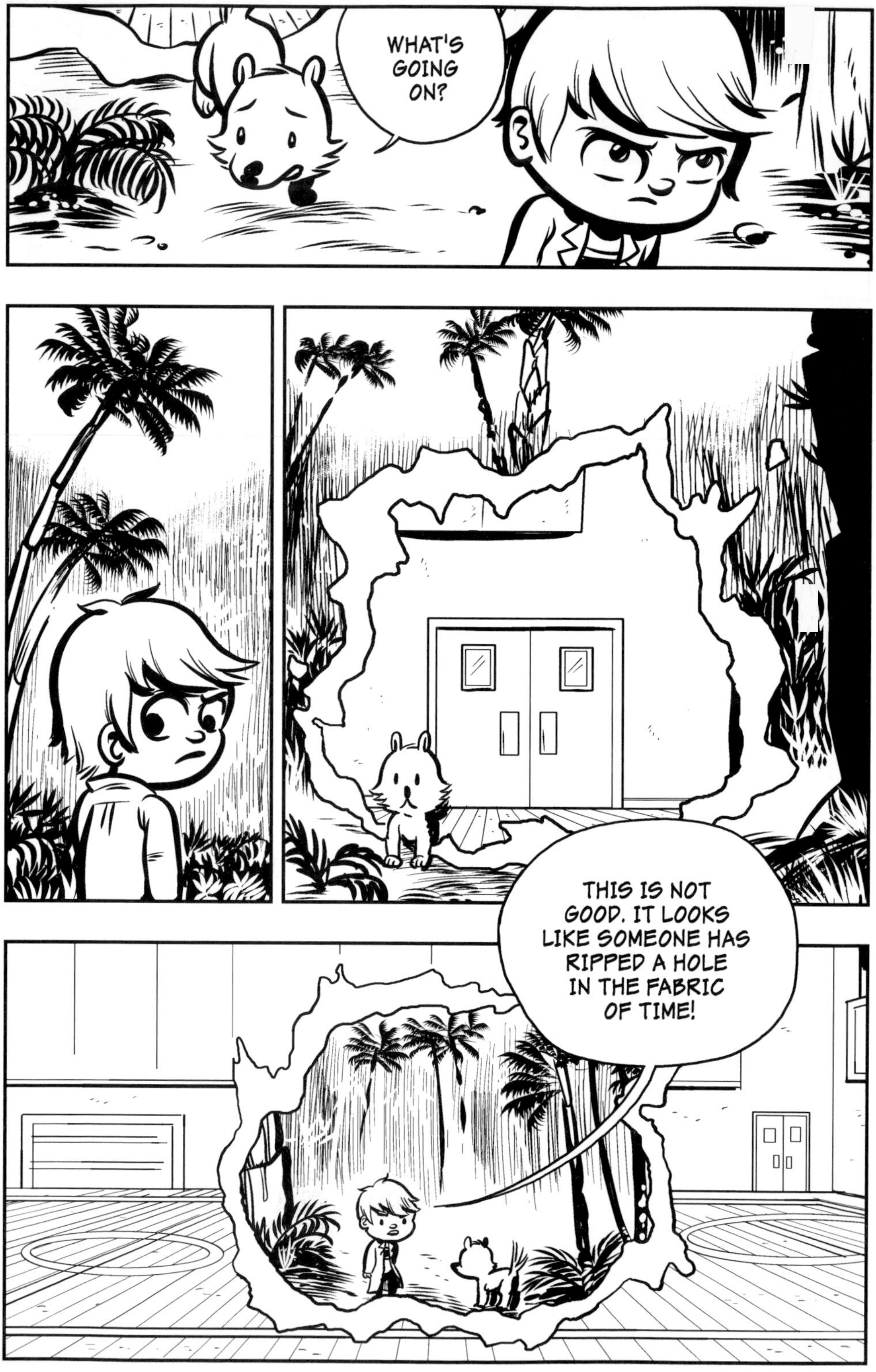
WHAT'S GOING ON?
THIS IS NOT GOOD. IT LOOKS LIKE SOMEONE HAS RIPPED A HOLE IN THE FABRIC OF TIME!

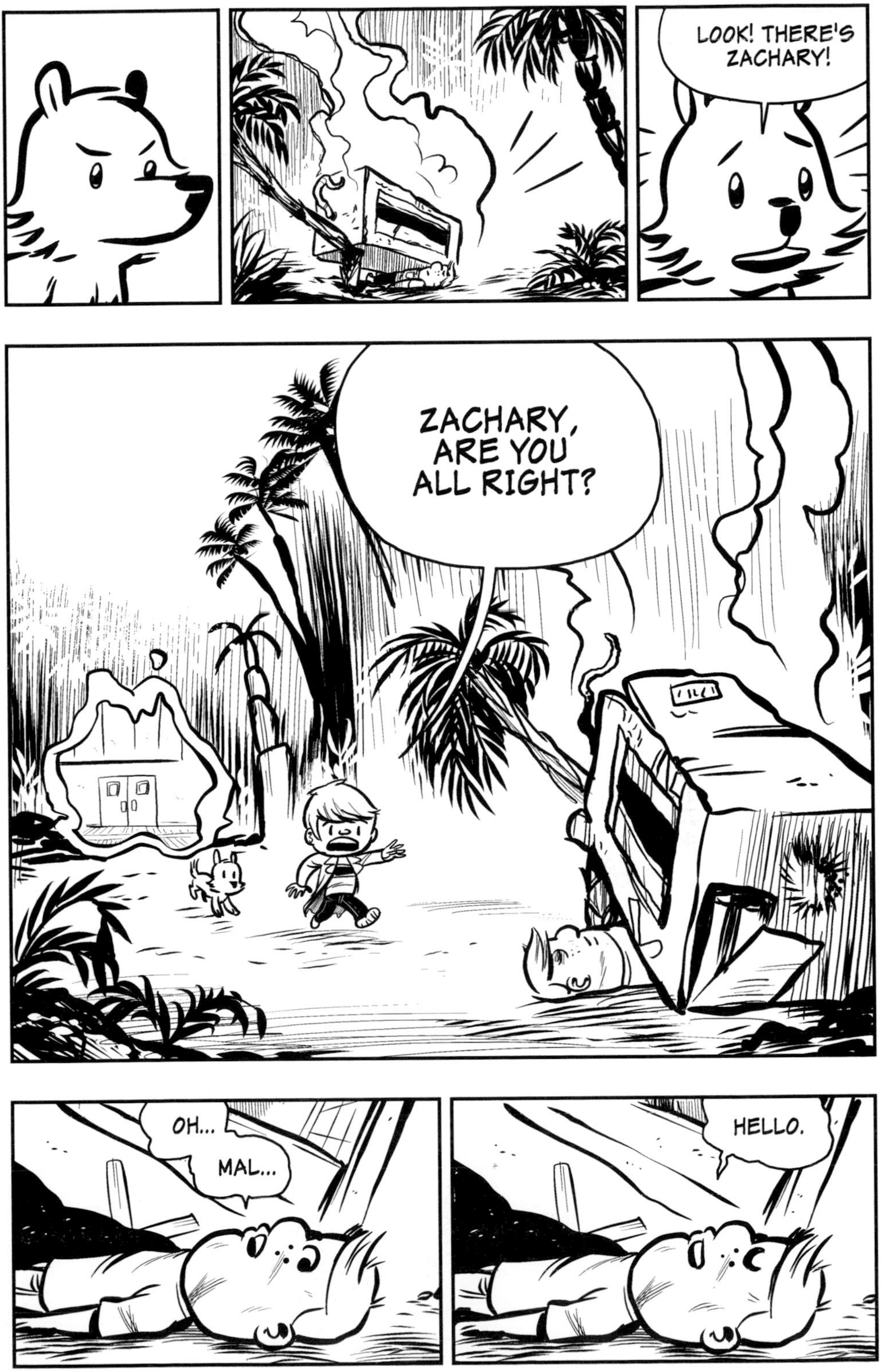
LOOK! THERE'S ZACHARY!
ZACHARY, ARE YOU ALL RIGHT?
OH...
MAL...
HELLO.

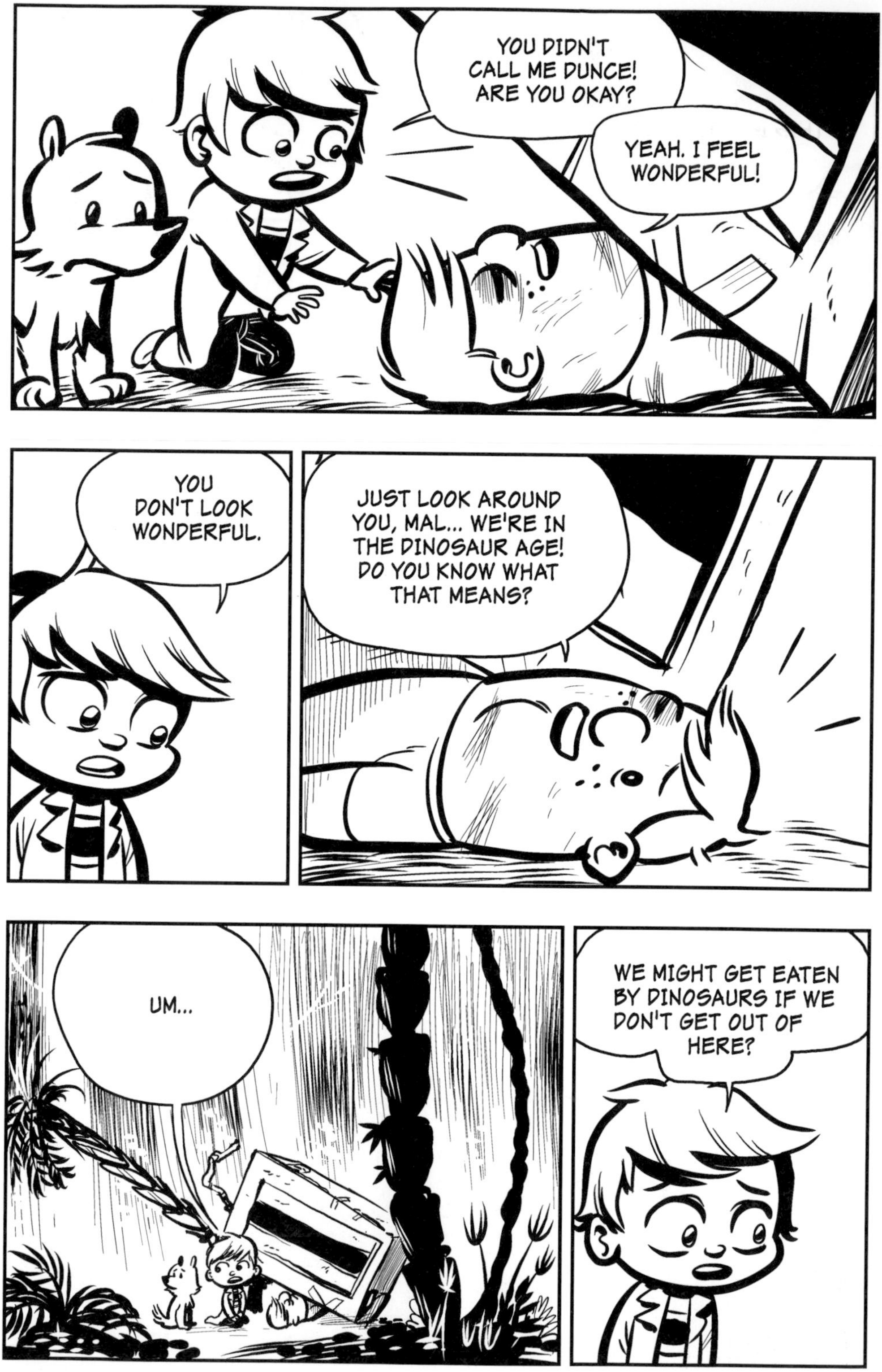
YOU DIDN'T CALL ME DUNCE! ARE YOU OKAY?
YEAH. I FEEL WONDERFUL!
YOU DON'T LOOK WONDERFUL.
JUST LOOK AROUND YOU, MAL... WE'RE IN THE DINOSAUR AGE! DO YOU KNOW WHAT THAT MEANS?
UM...
WE MIGHT GET EATEN BY DINOSAURS IF WE DON'T GET OUT OF HERE?

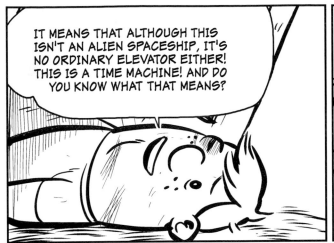

IT MEANS THAT ALTHOUGH THIS ISN'T AN ALIEN SPACESHIP, IT'S NO ORDINARY ELEVATOR EITHER! THIS IS A TIME MACHINE! AND DO YOU KNOW WHAT THAT MEANS?

UM...

WE MIGHT GET EATEN BY DINOSAURS IF WE DON'T GET OUT OF HERE?

IT MEANS THAT I'M SO SMART, I BUILT A TIME MACHINE OUT OF OLD ELEVATOR PARTS WITHOUT EVEN KNOWING IT! I MUST BE A GENIUS! AND DO YOU KNOW WHAT THAT MEANS?

WE'RE DEFINITELY GOING TO BE EATEN BY DINOSAURS.

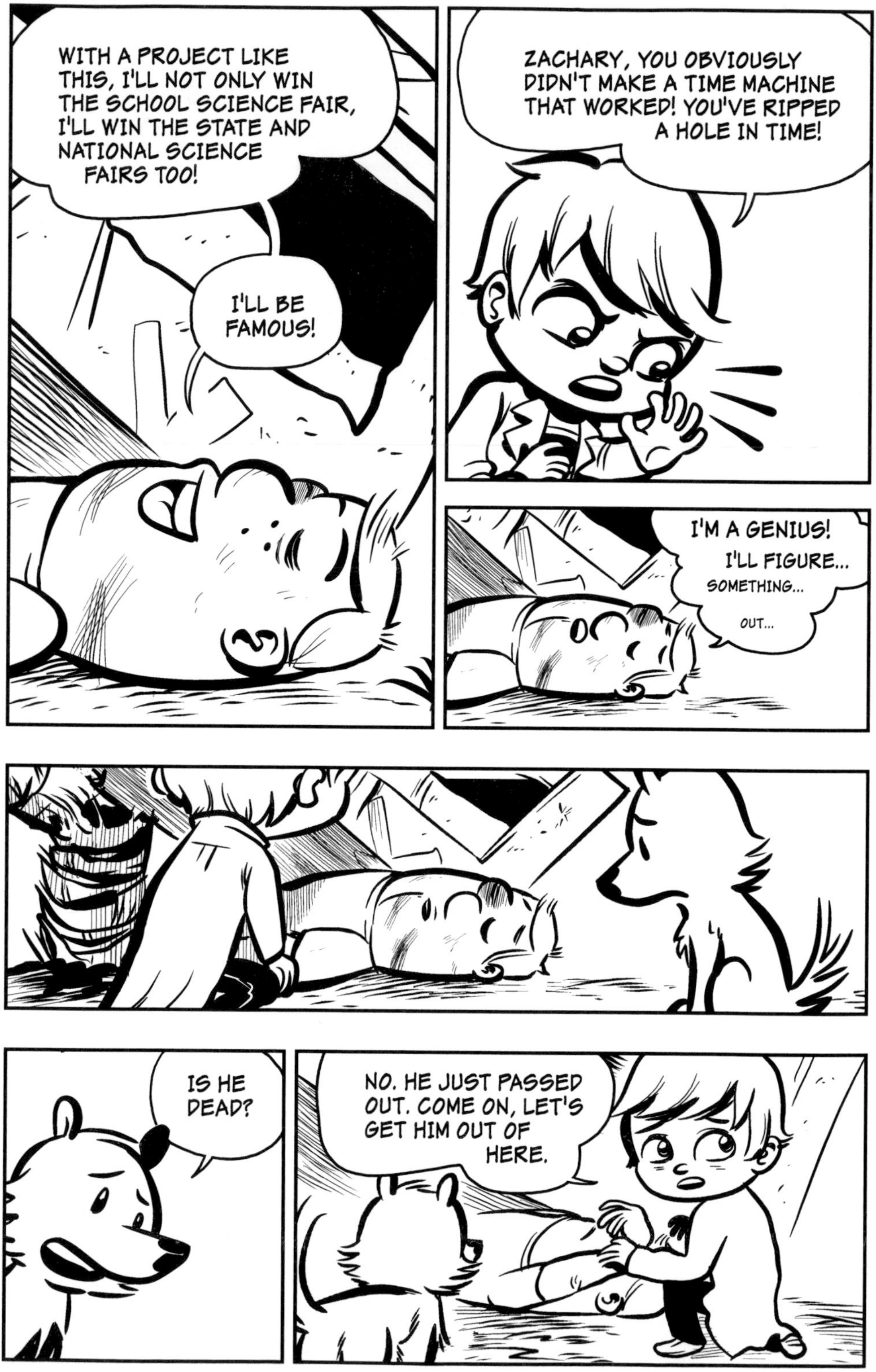
WITH A PROJECT LIKE THIS, I'LL NOT ONLY WIN THE SCHOOL SCIENCE FAIR, I'LL WIN THE STATE AND NATIONAL SCIENCE FAIRS TOO!
I'LL BE FAMOUS!
ZACHARY, YOU OBVIOUSLY DIDN'T MAKE A TIME MACHINE THAT WORKED! YOU'VE RIPPED A HOLE IN TIME!
I'M A GENIUS! I'LL FIGURE... SOMETHING... OUT...
IS HE DEAD?
NO. HE JUST PASSED OUT. COME ON, LET'S GET HIM OUT OF HERE.

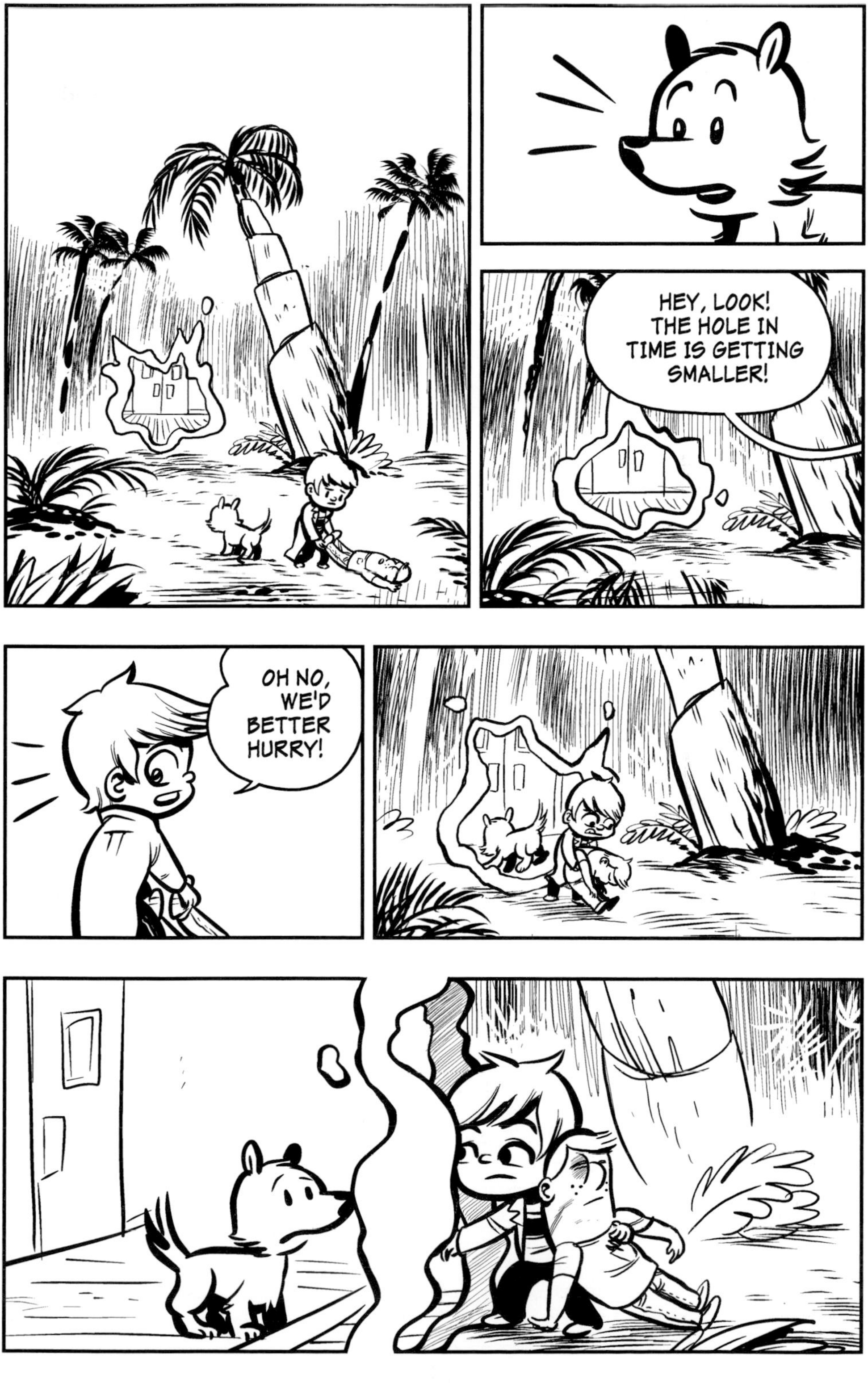
HEY, LOOK! THE HOLE IN TIME IS GETTING SMALLER!
OH NO, WE'D BETTER HURRY!

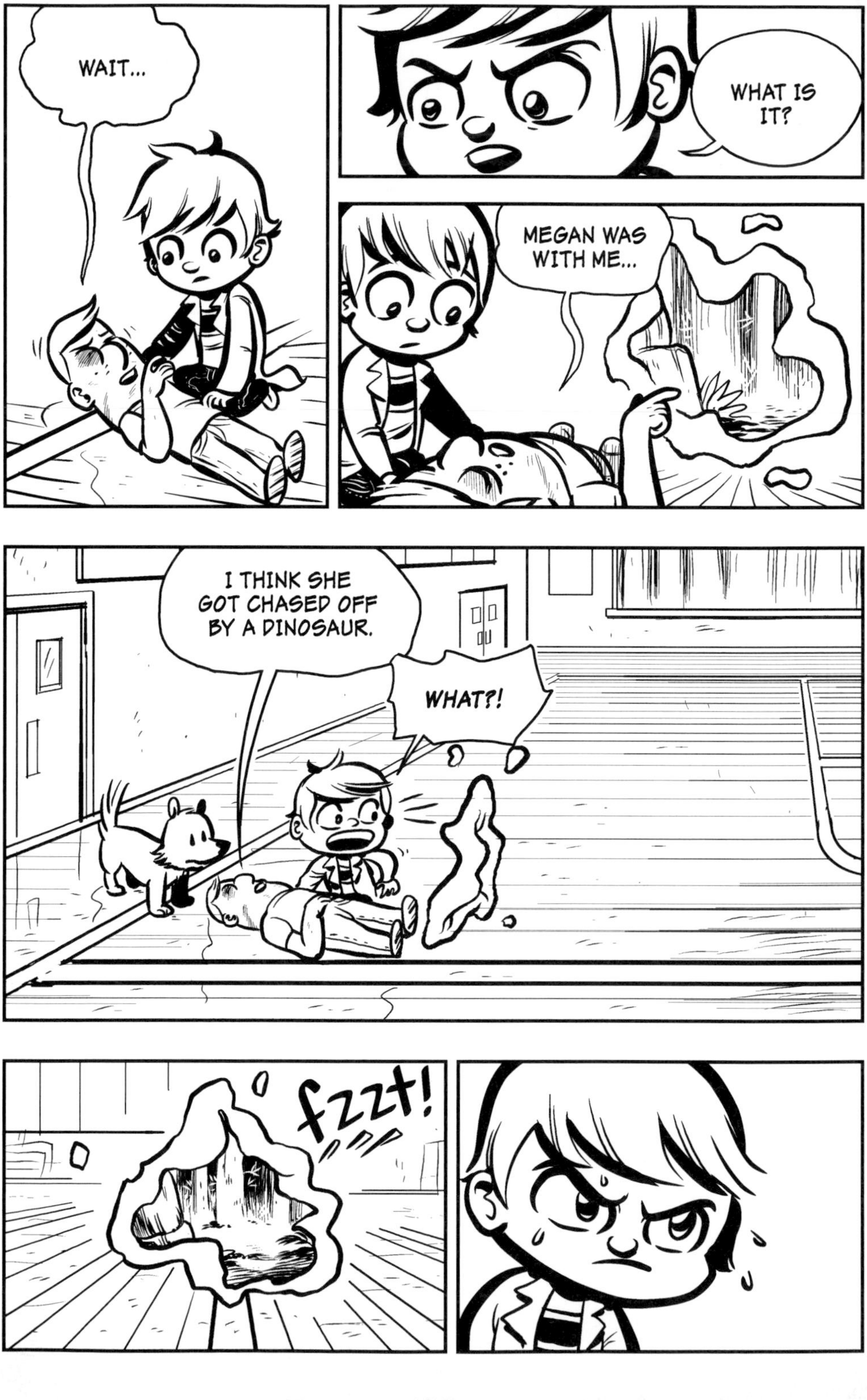
WAIT...
WHAT IS IT?
MEGAN WAS WITH ME...
I THINK SHE GOT CHASED OFF BY A DINOSAUR.
WHAT?!
fzzt!

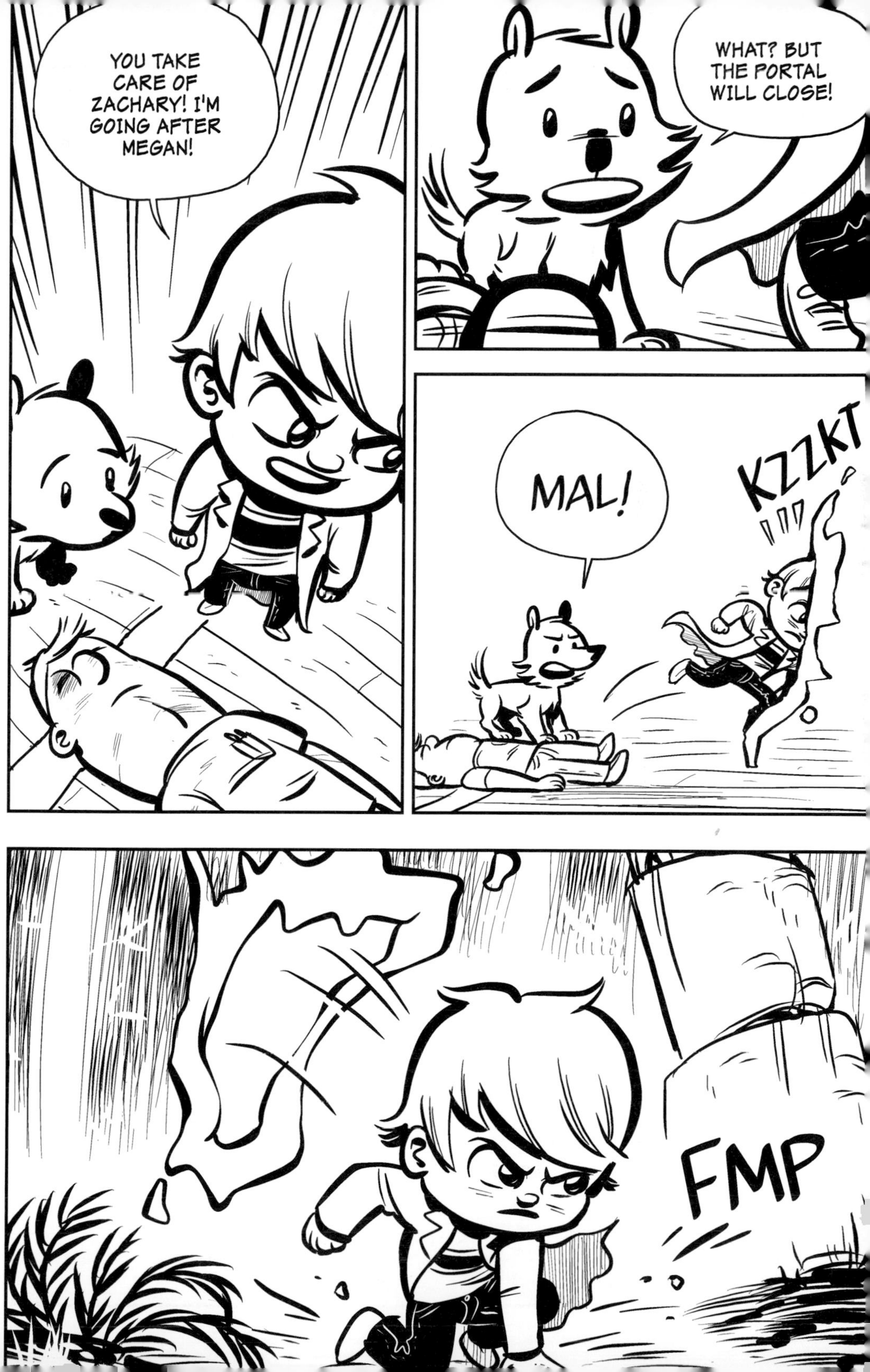
YOU TAKE CARE OF ZACHARY! I'M GOING AFTER MEGAN!
WHAT? BUT THE PORTAL WILL CLOSE!
MAL!
KZZKT
FMP

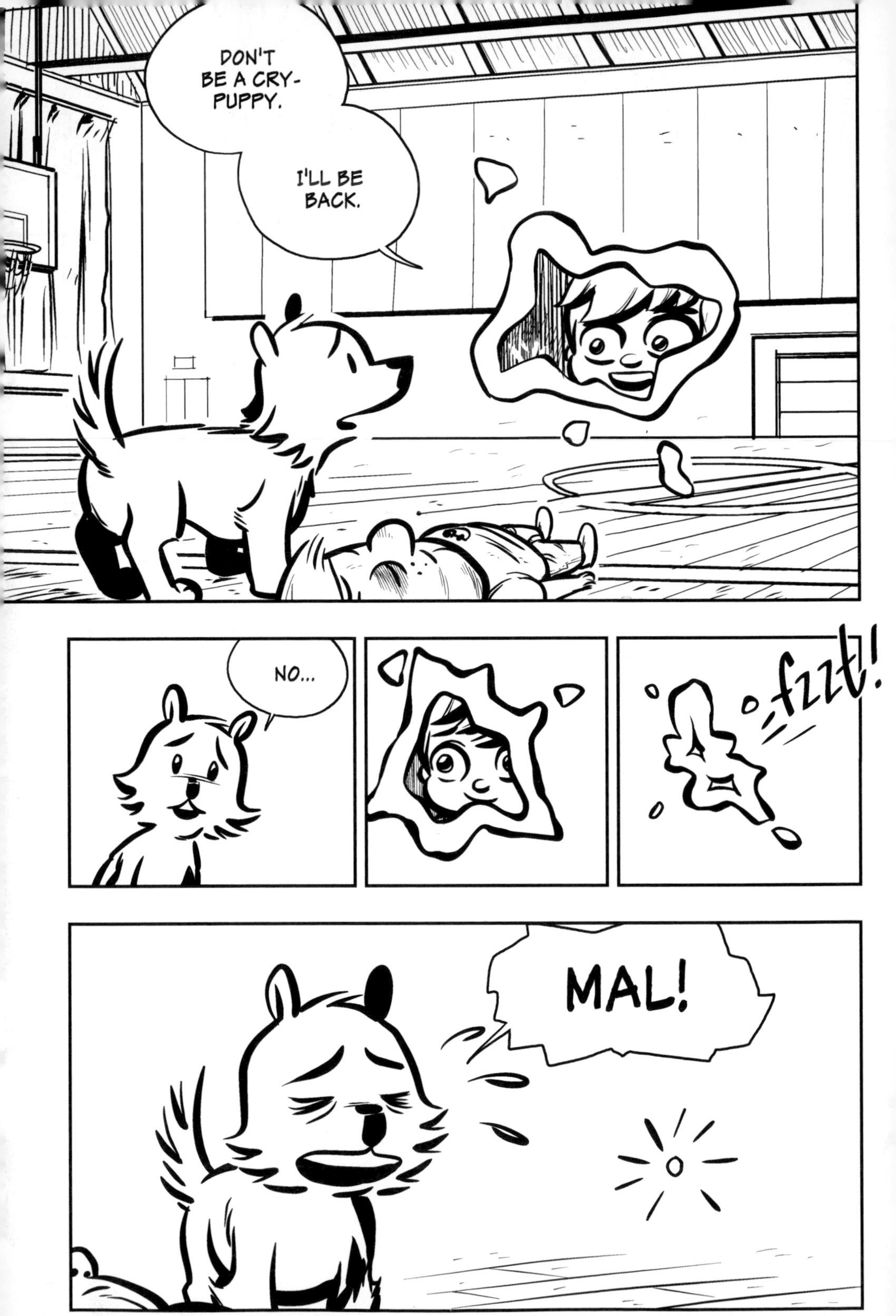
DON'T BE A CRY-PUPPY.
I'LL BE BACK.
NO...
fzzt!
MAL!

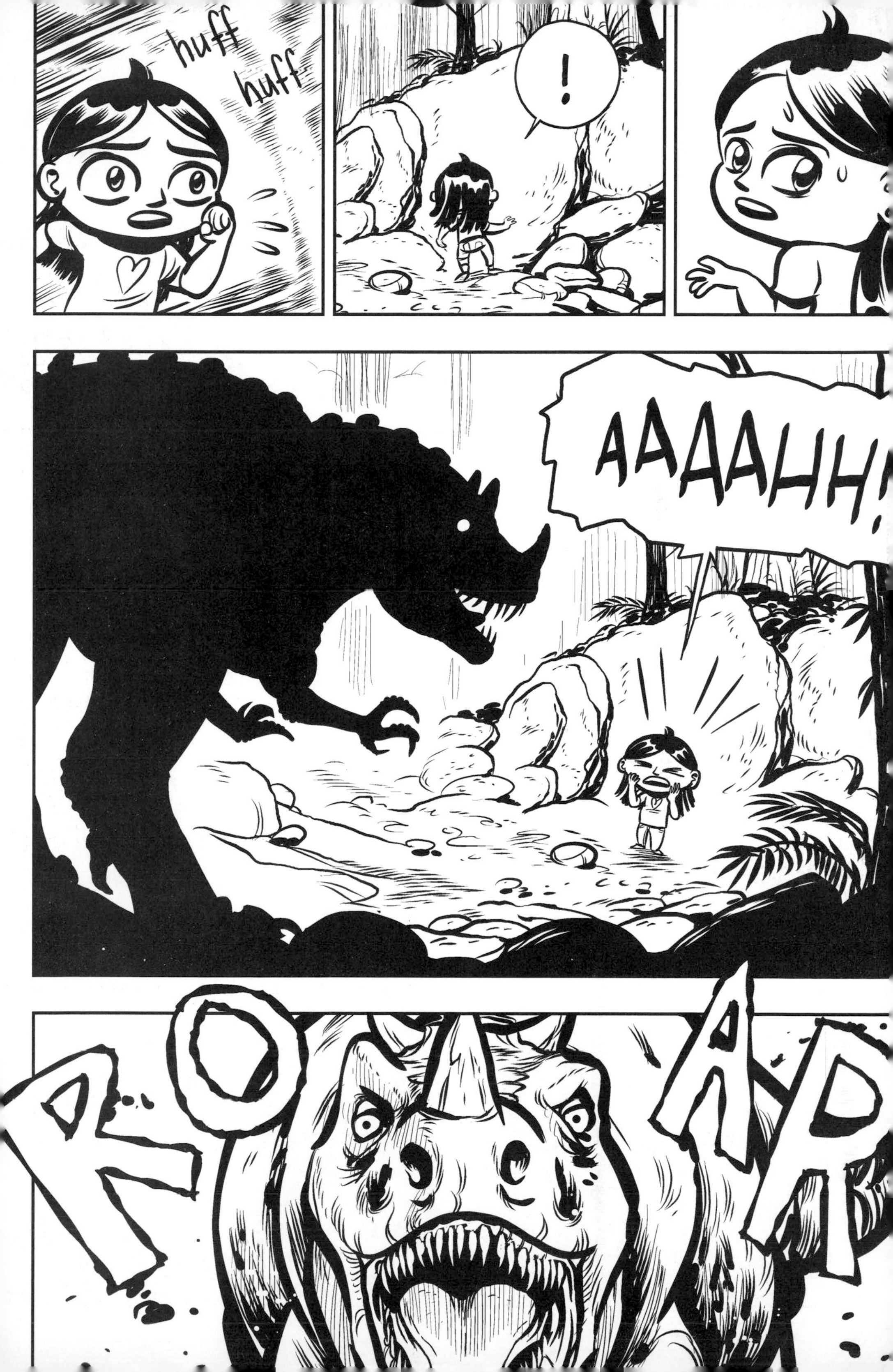
huff
huff
!
AAAAHH!
ROOAR

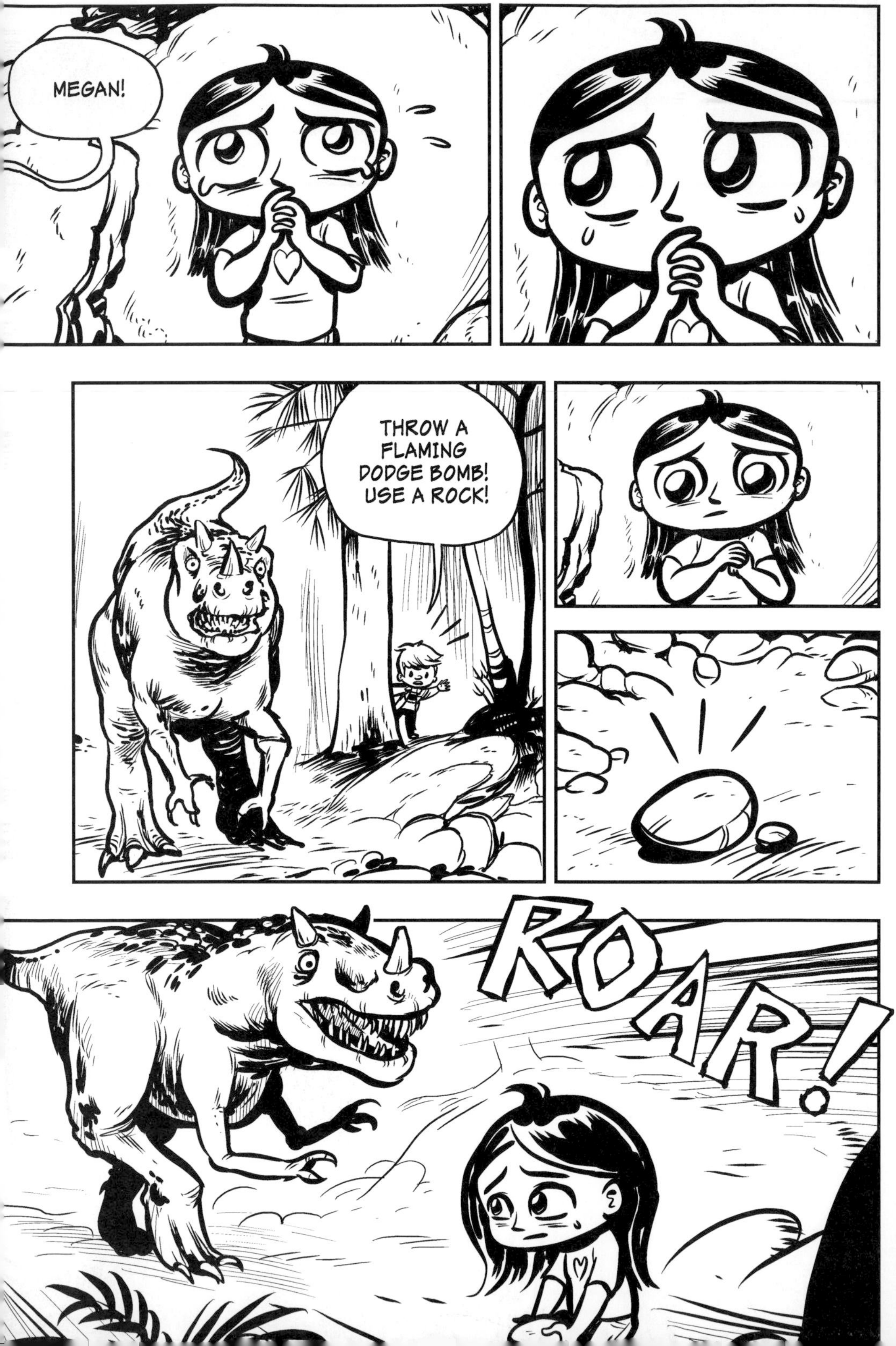
MEGAN!
THROW A FLAMING DODGE BOMB! USE A ROCK!
ROAR!

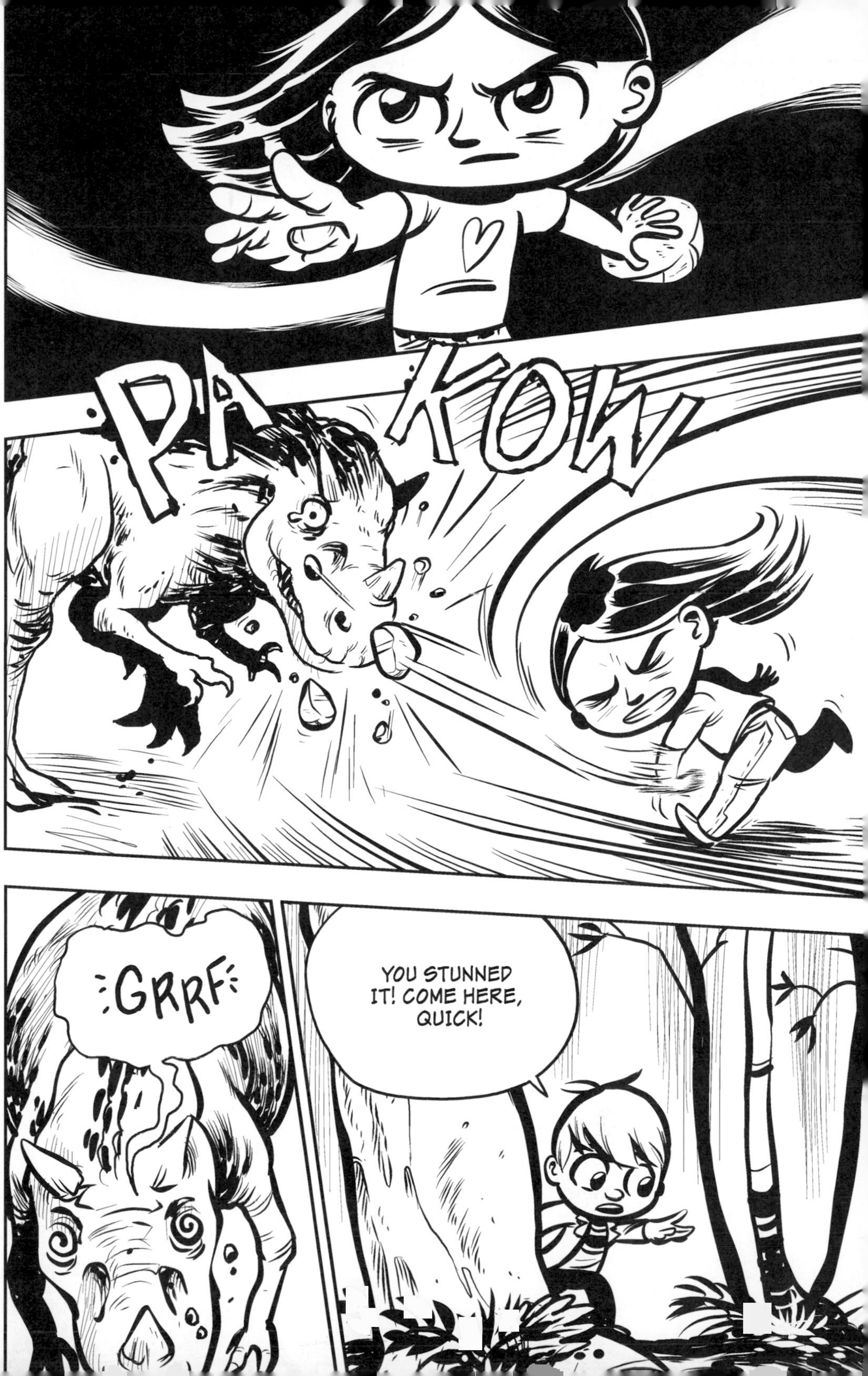
PA KOW
GRRF
YOU STUNNED IT! COME HERE, QUICK!

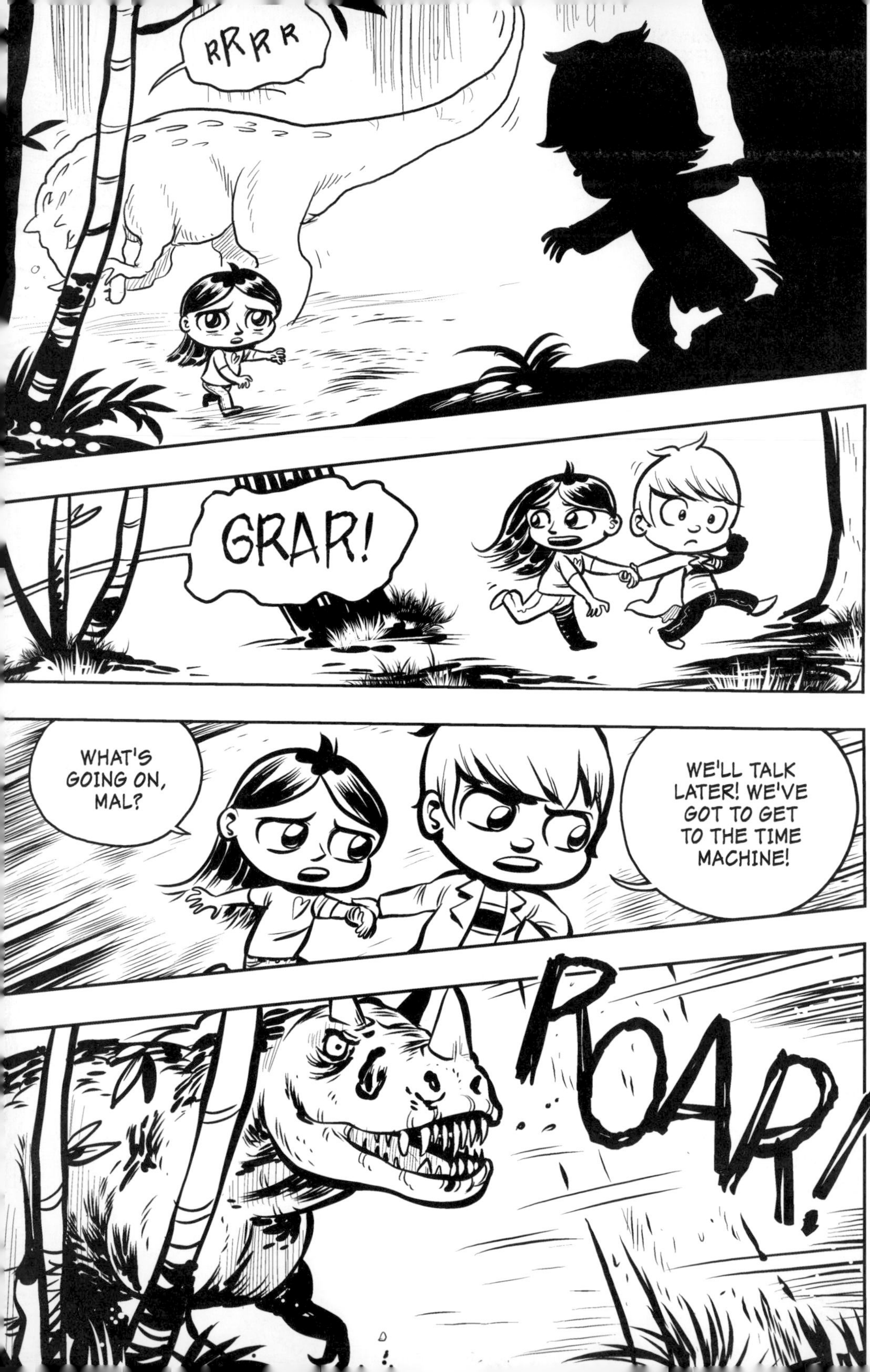
RRRR
GRAR!
WHAT'S GOING ON, MAL?
WE'LL TALK LATER! WE'VE GOT TO GET TO THE TIME MACHINE!
ROAR!

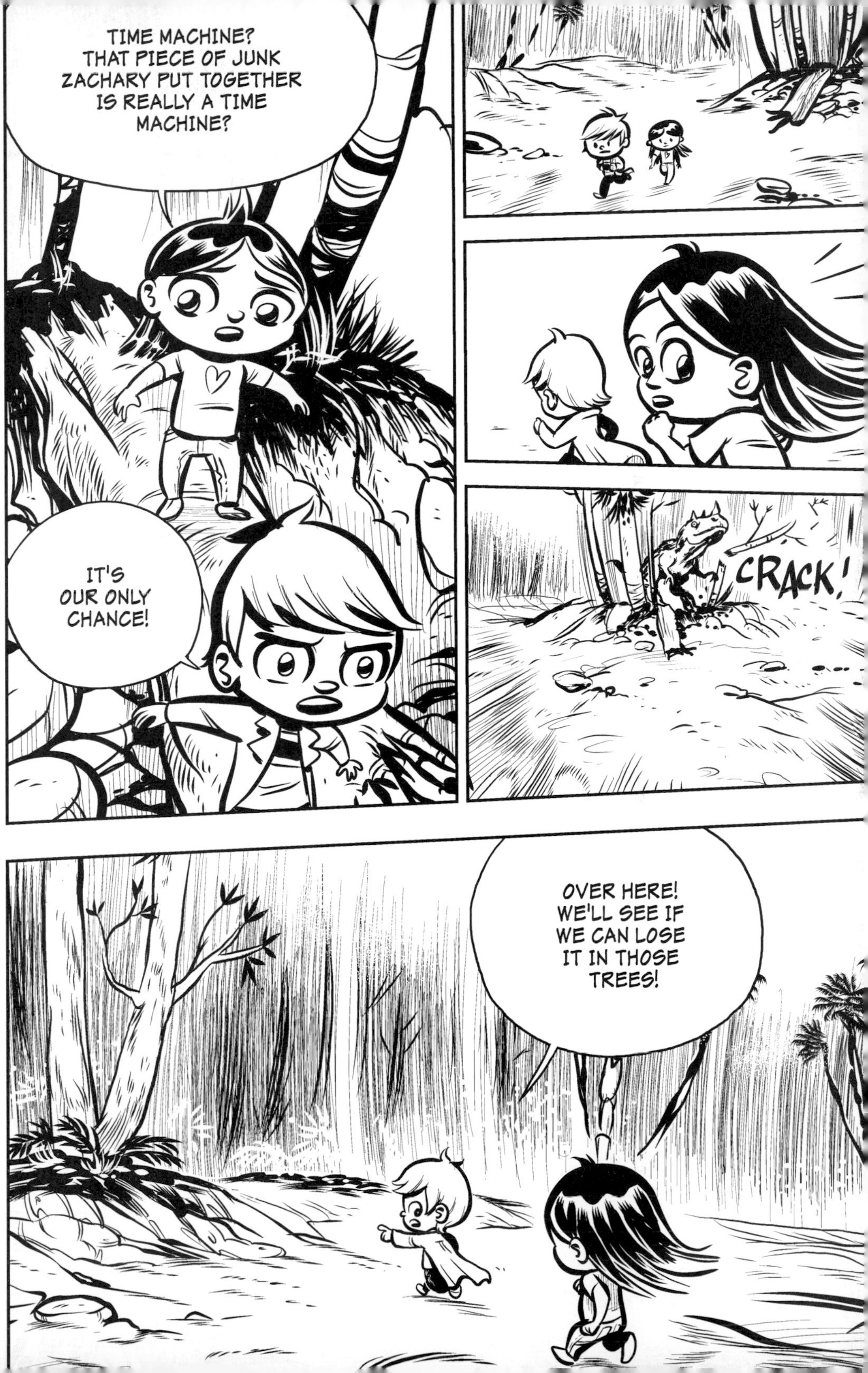
TIME MACHINE? THAT PIECE OF JUNK ZACHARY PUT TOGETHER IS REALLY A TIME MACHINE?
IT'S OUR ONLY CHANCE!
CRACK!
OVER HERE! WE'LL SEE IF WE CAN LOSE IT IN THOSE TREES!

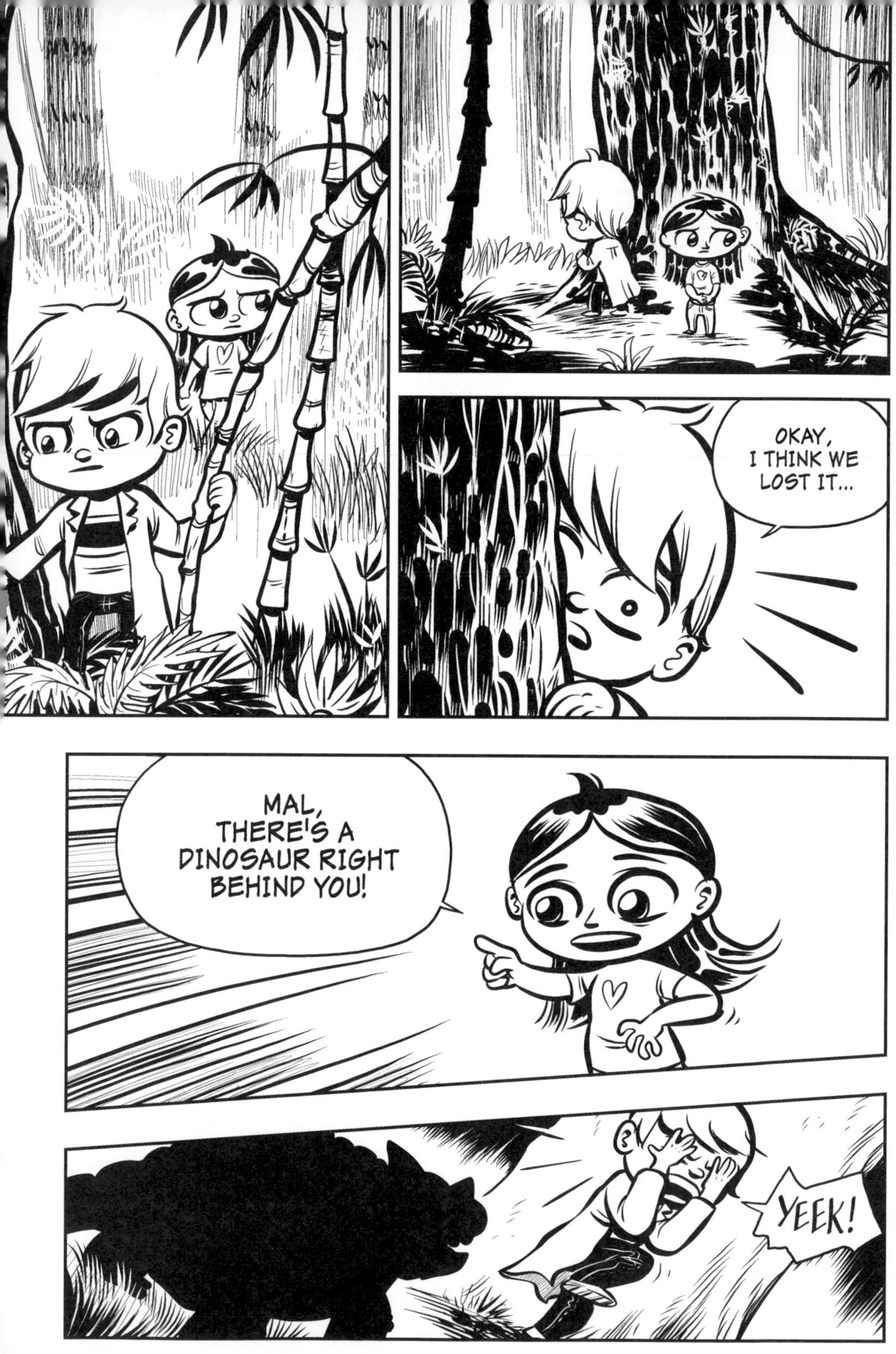
OKAY, I THINK WE LOST IT...
MAL, THERE'S A DINOSAUR RIGHT BEHIND YOU!
YEEK!

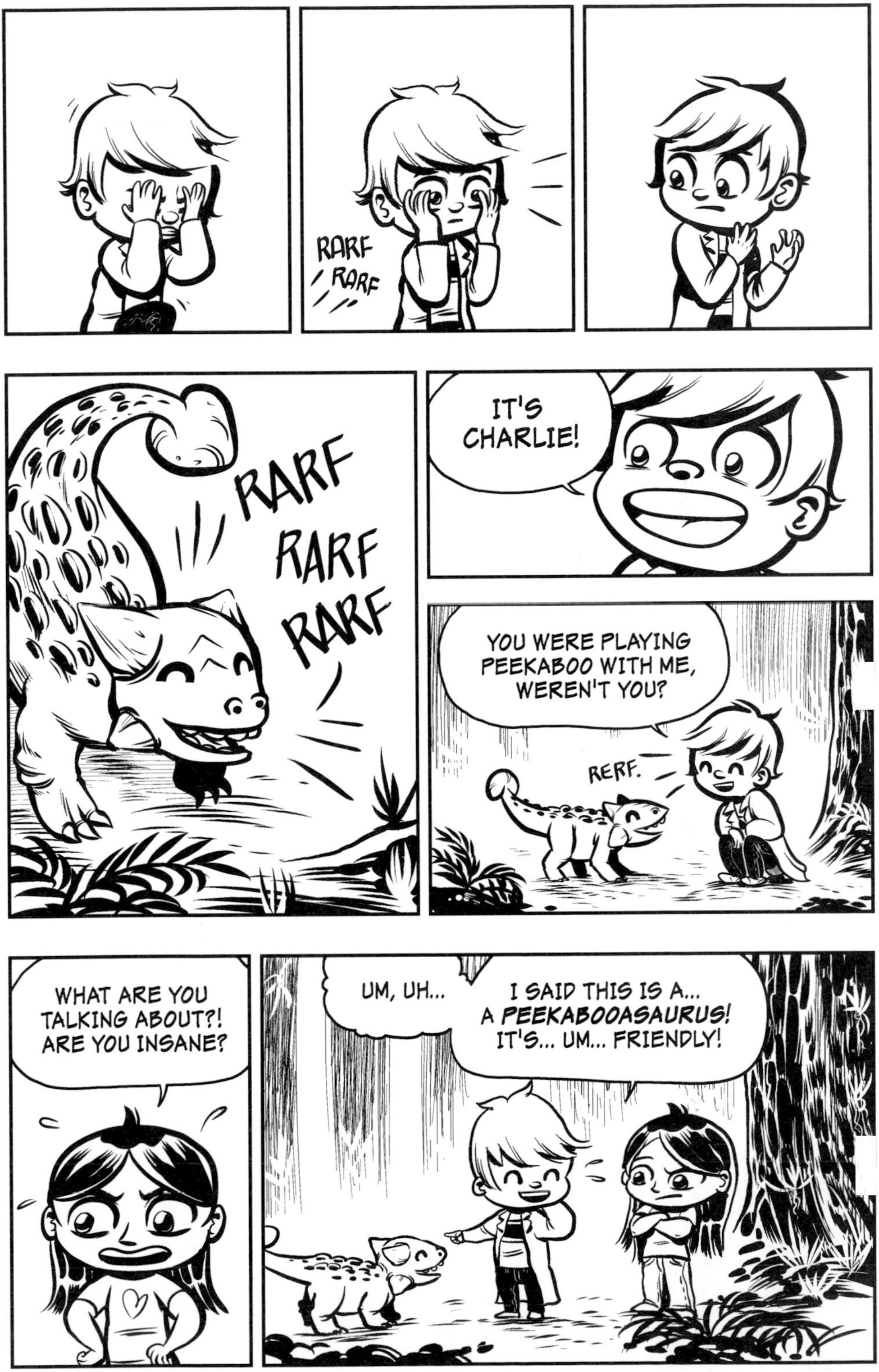
RARF
RARF
RARF
RARF
RARF
IT'S CHARLIE!
YOU WERE PLAYING PEEKABOO WITH ME, WEREN'T YOU?
RERF.
WHAT ARE YOU TALKING ABOUT?! ARE YOU INSANE?
UM, UH...
I SAID THIS IS A... A PEEKABOOASAURUS! IT'S... UM... FRIENDLY!

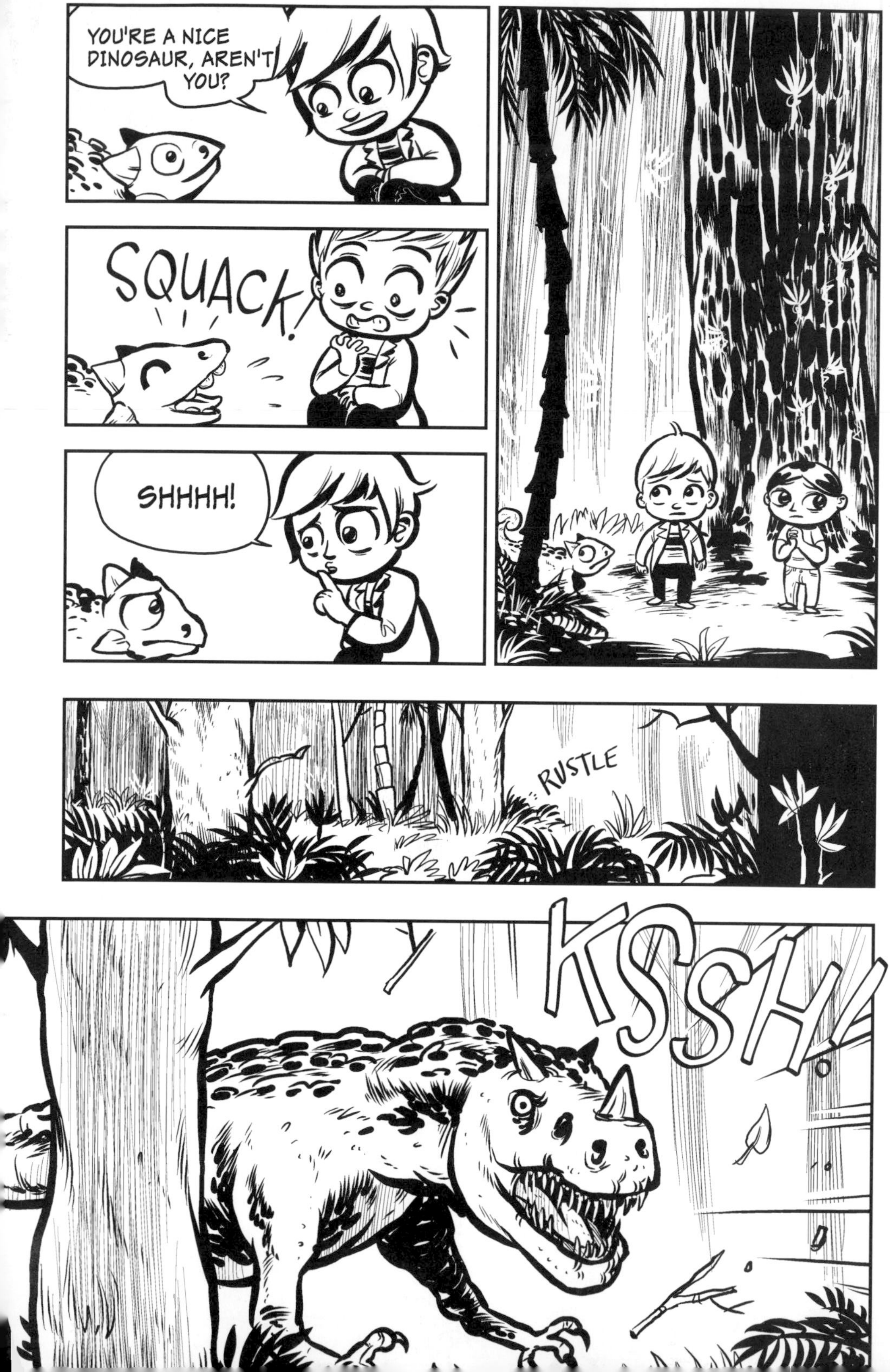
YOU'RE A NICE DINOSAUR, AREN'T YOU?
SQUACK!
SHHHH!
RUSTLE
KSSSH!

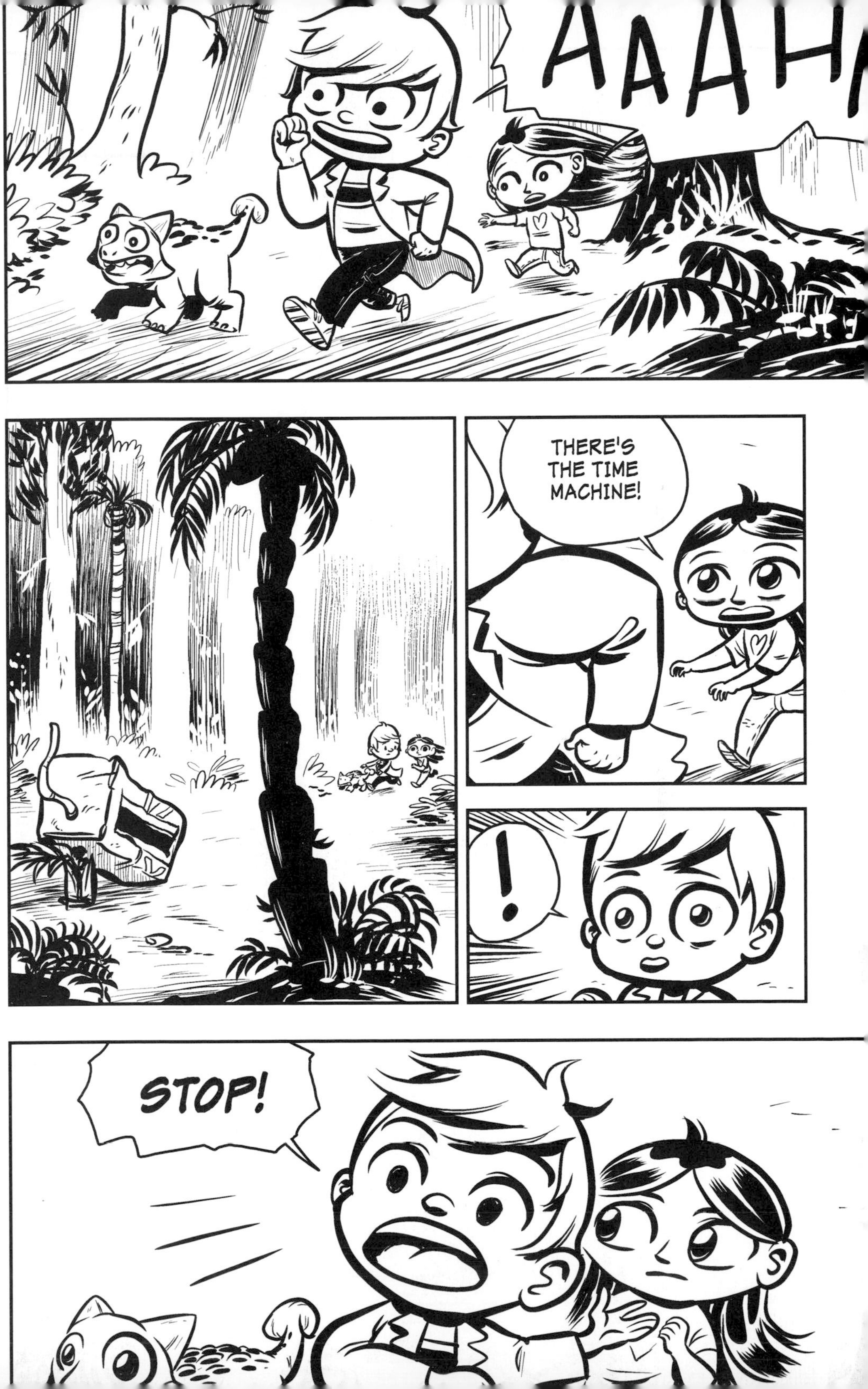
AAAH
THERE'S THE TIME MACHINE!
!
STOP!

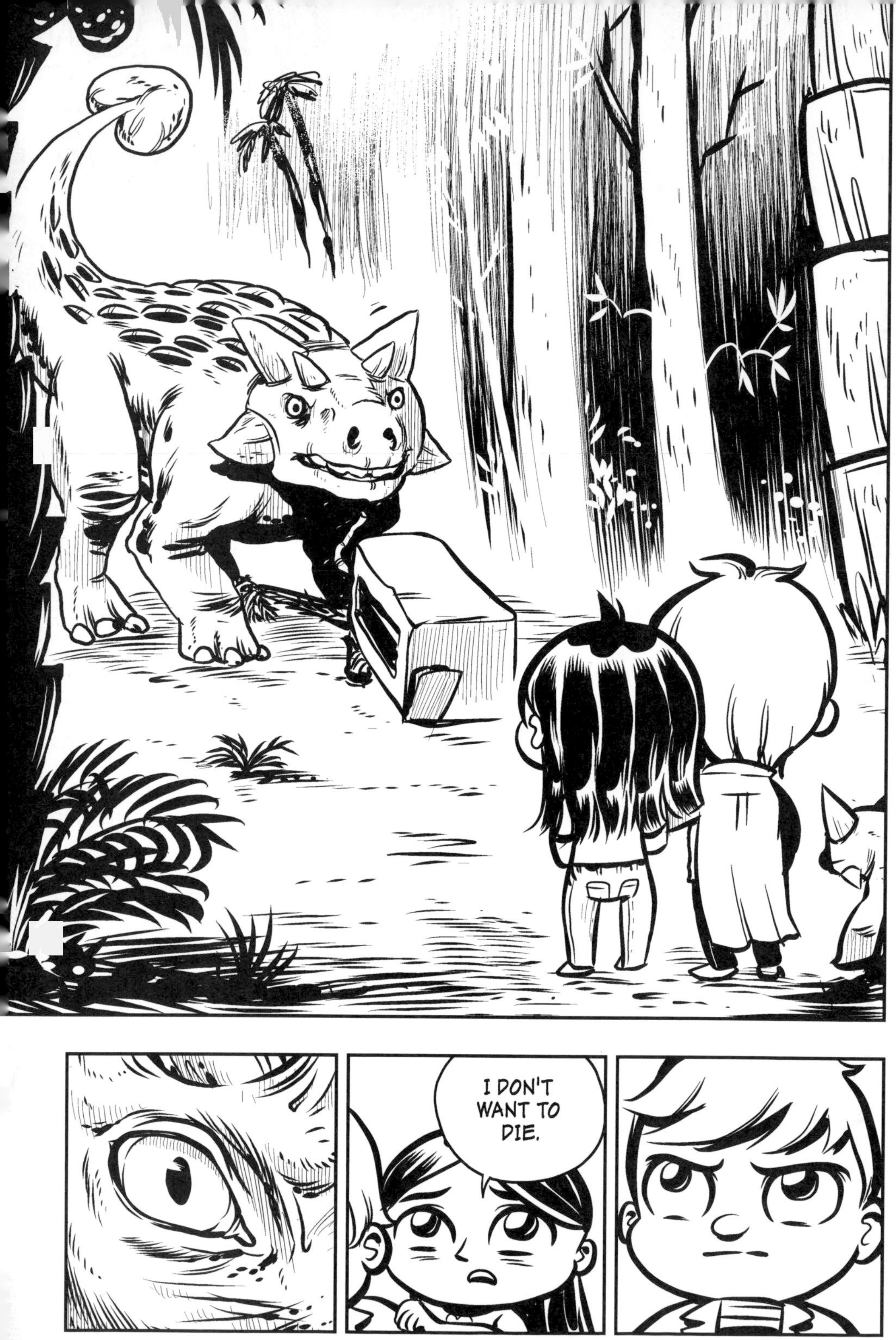
I DON'T WANT TO DIE.

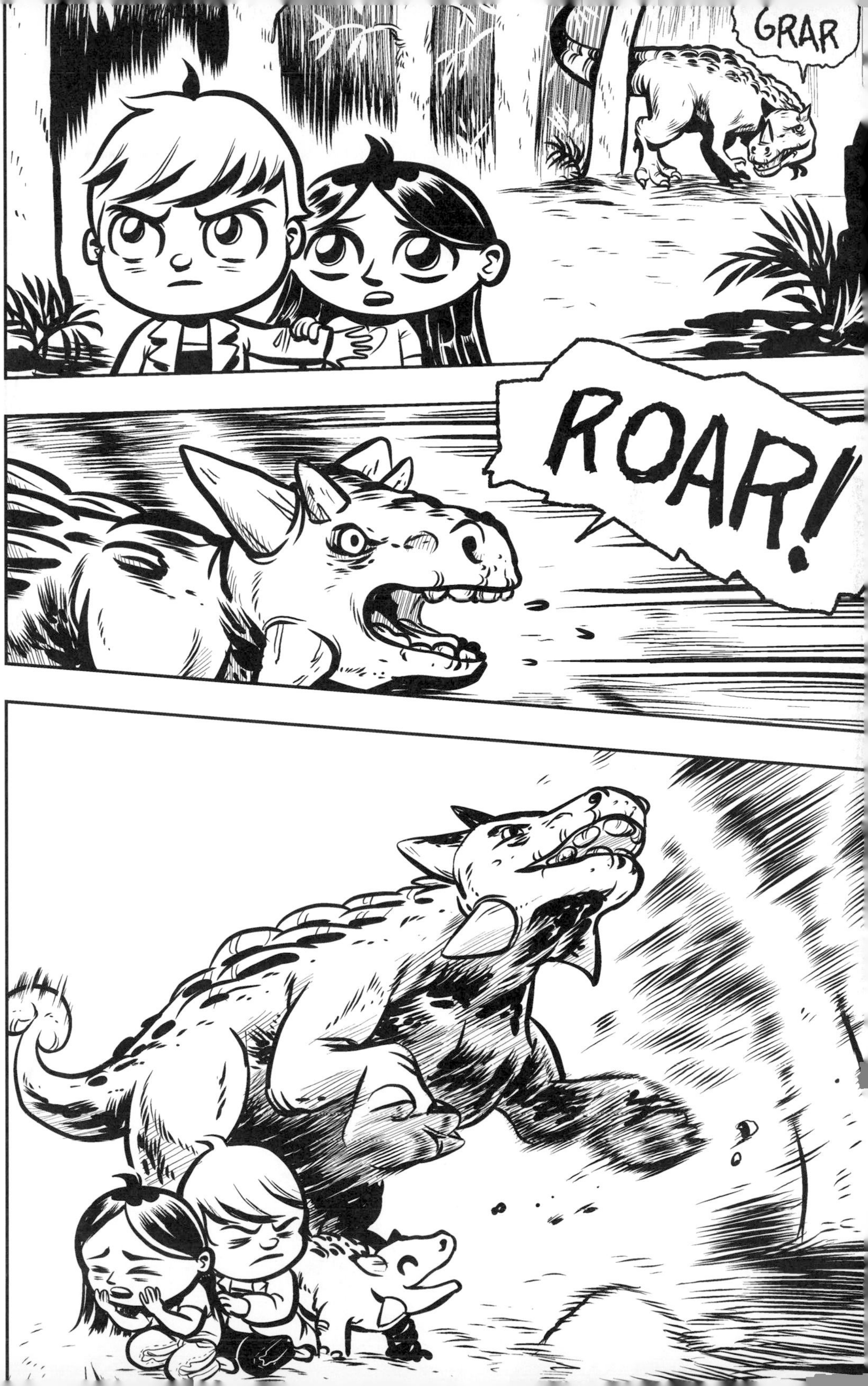
GRAR
ROAR!

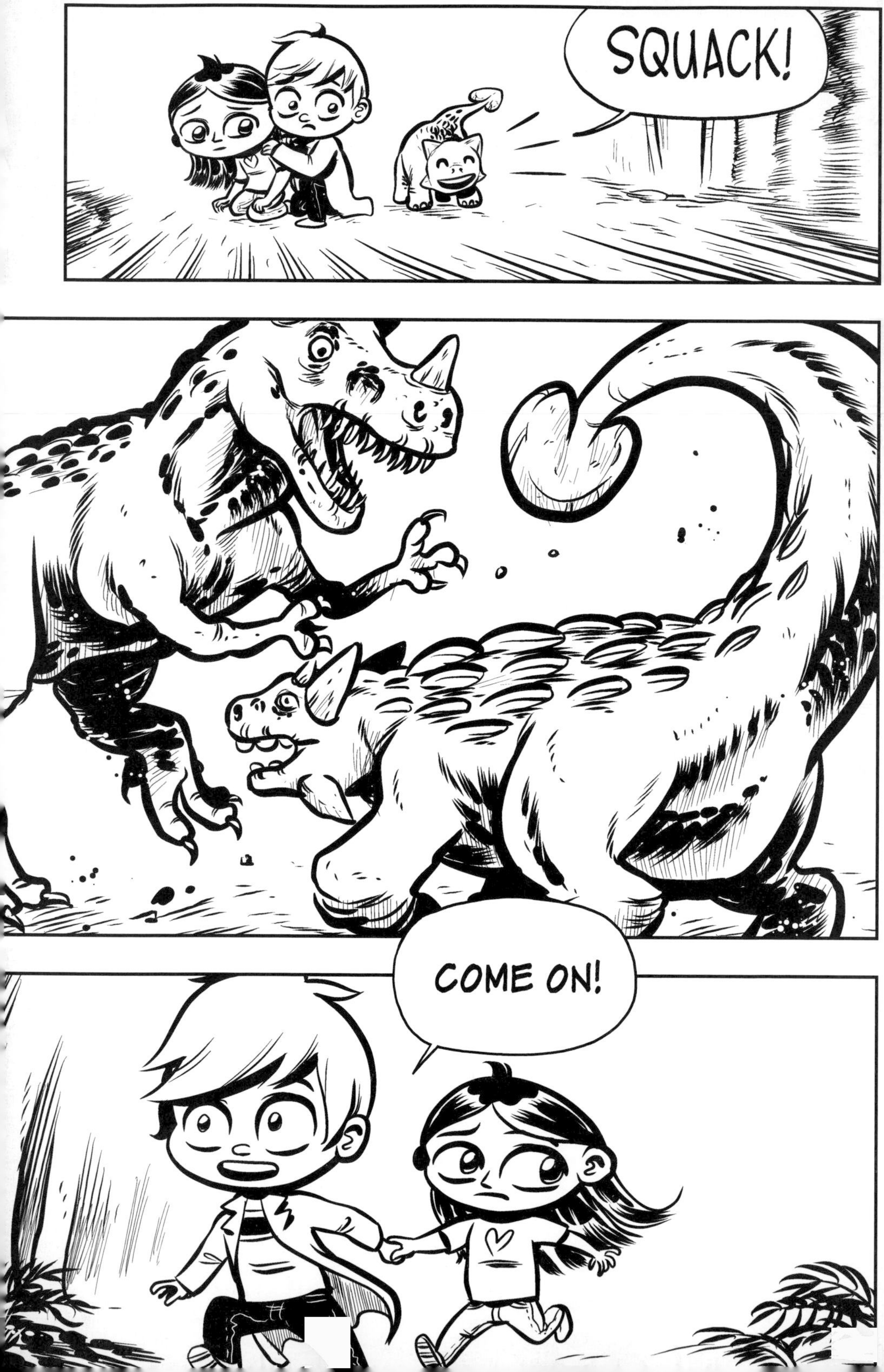
SQUACK!
COME ON!

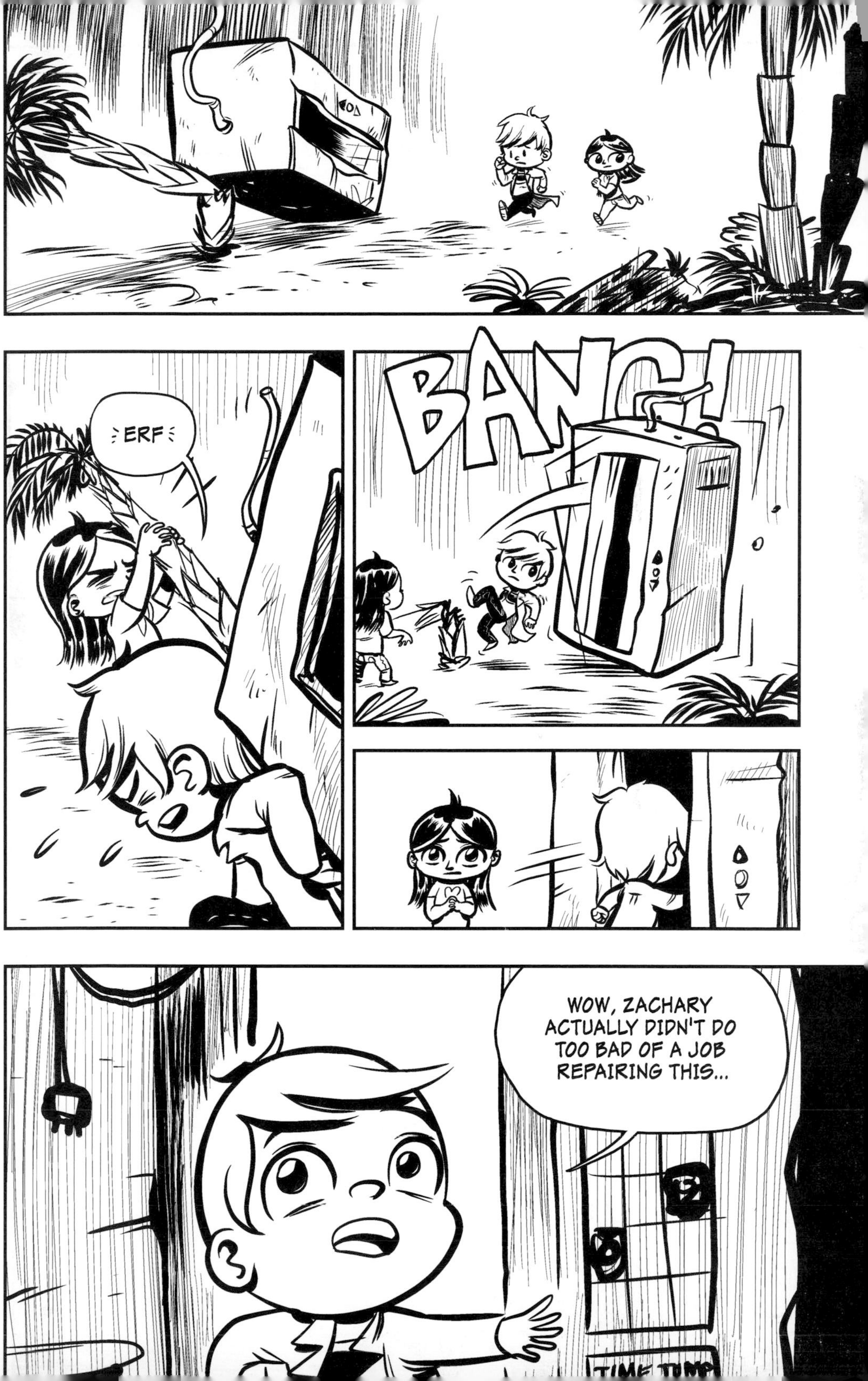
ERF
BANG!
WOW, ZACHARY ACTUALLY DIDN'T DO TOO BAD OF A JOB REPAIRING THIS...

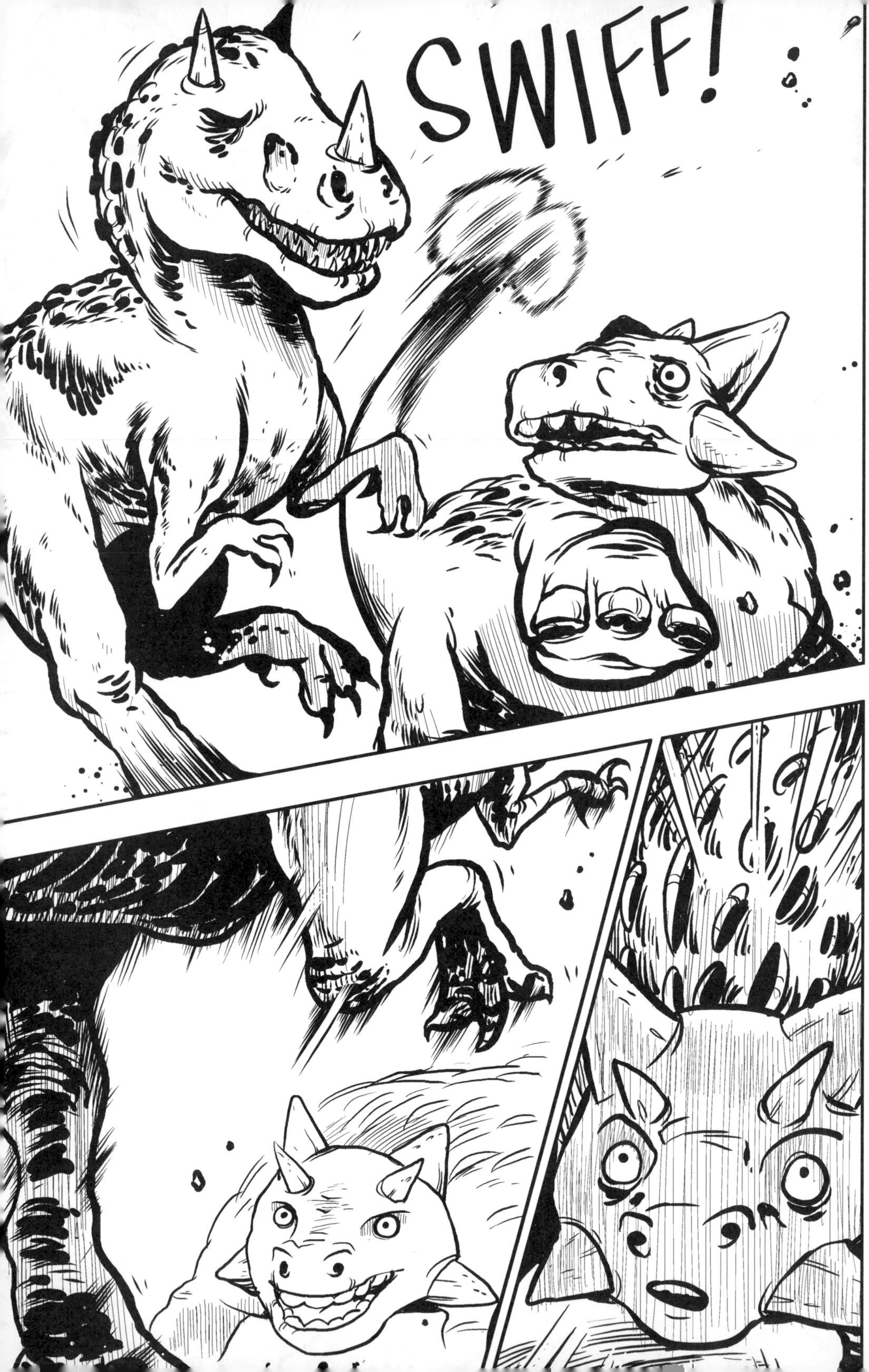
SWIFF!

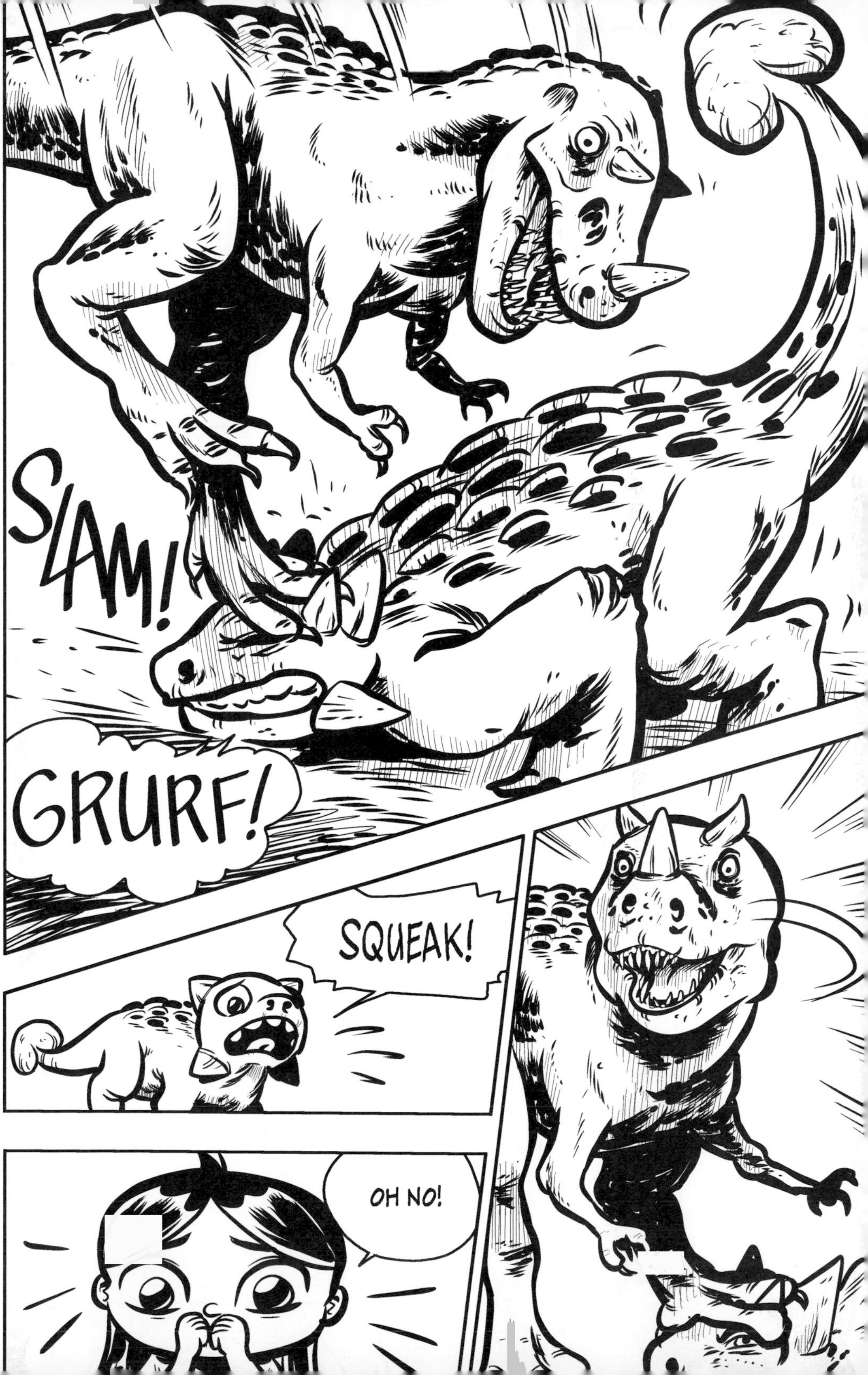
SLAM!
GRURF!
SQUEAK!
OH NO!

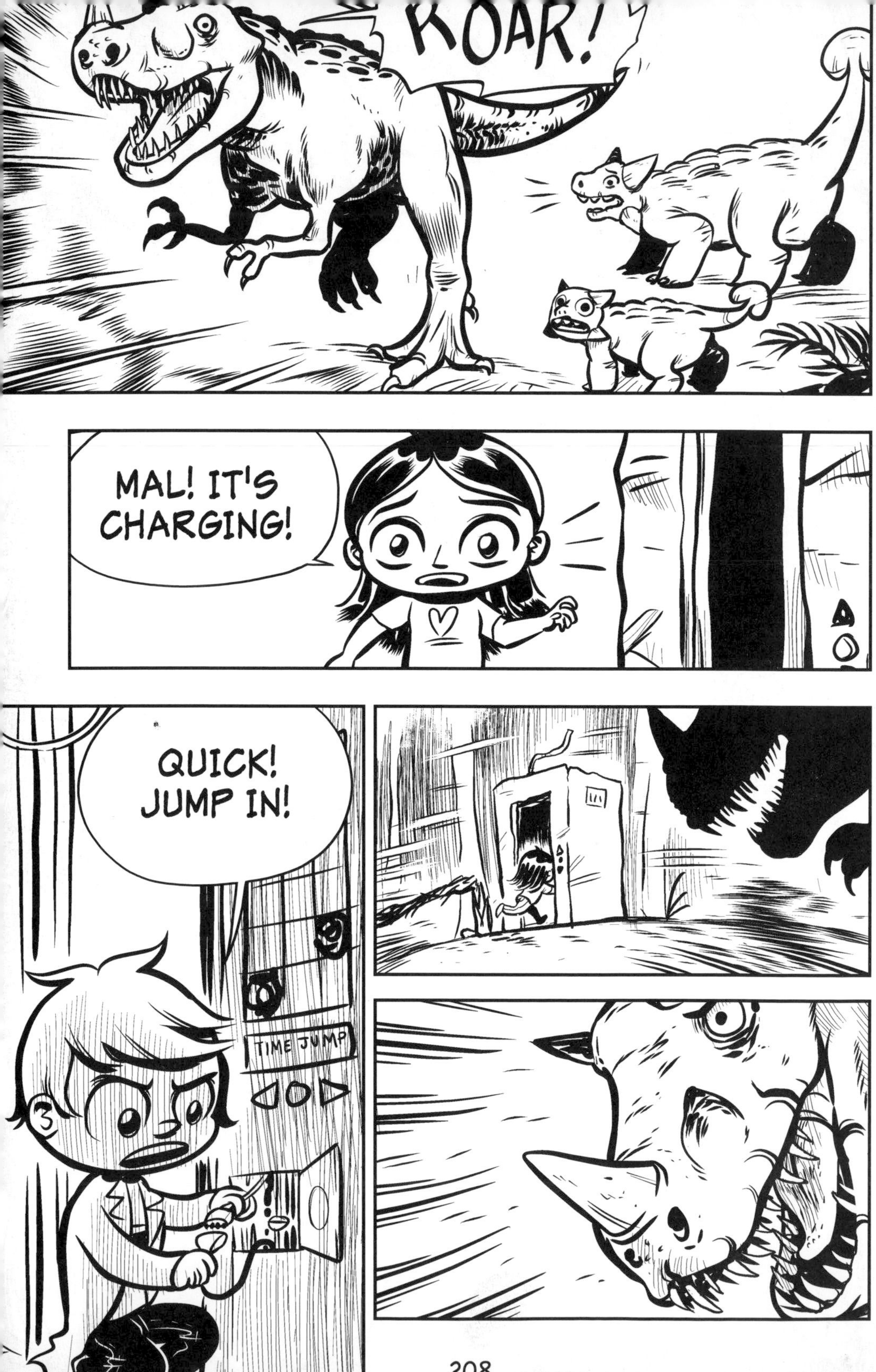
ROAR!
MAL! IT'S CHARGING!
QUICK! JUMP IN!
TIME JUMP

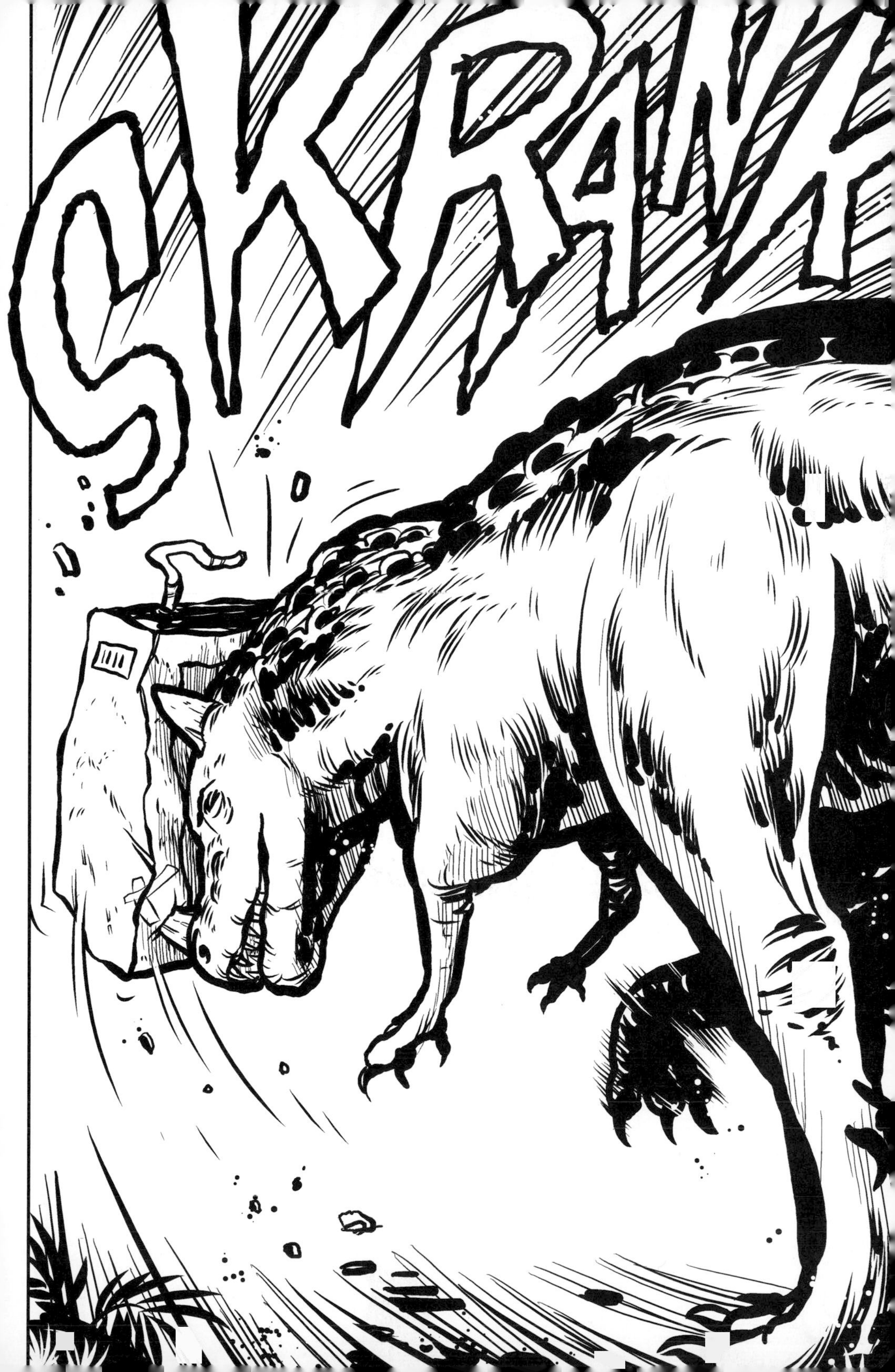
SKRAN

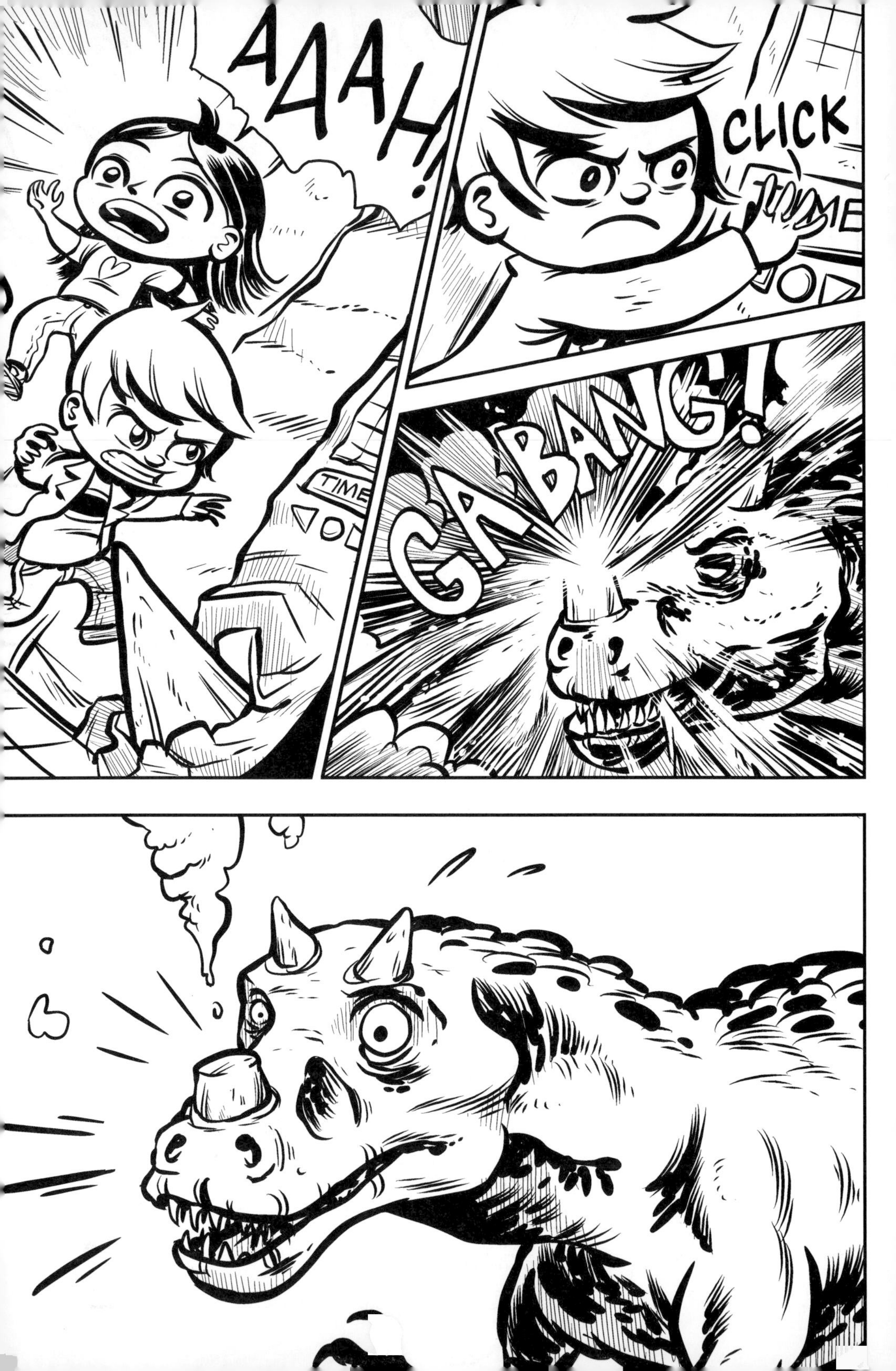

AAAH!
CLICK
TIME
GA-BANG!

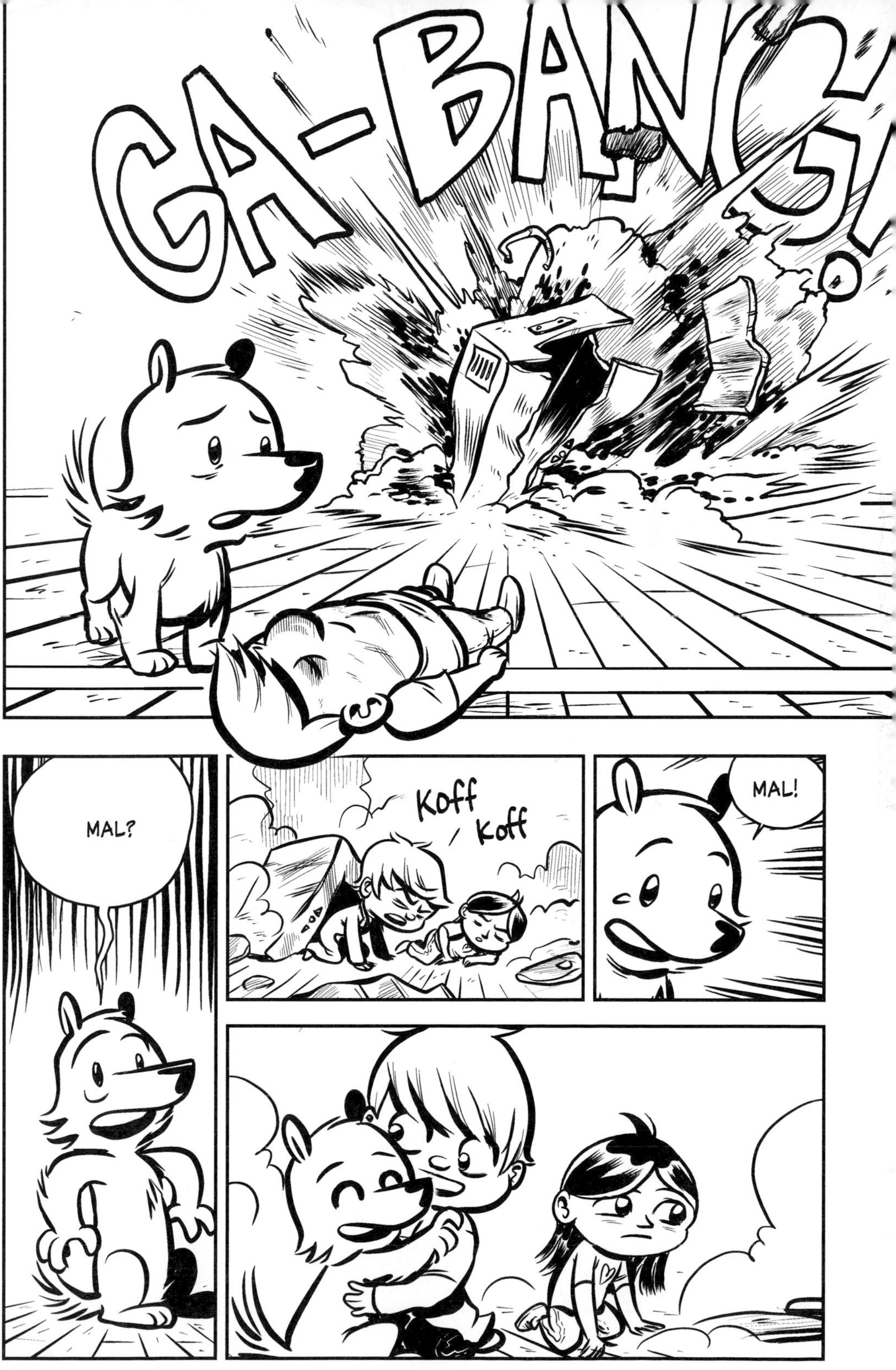
GA-BANG!
MAL?
Koff
Koff
MAL!

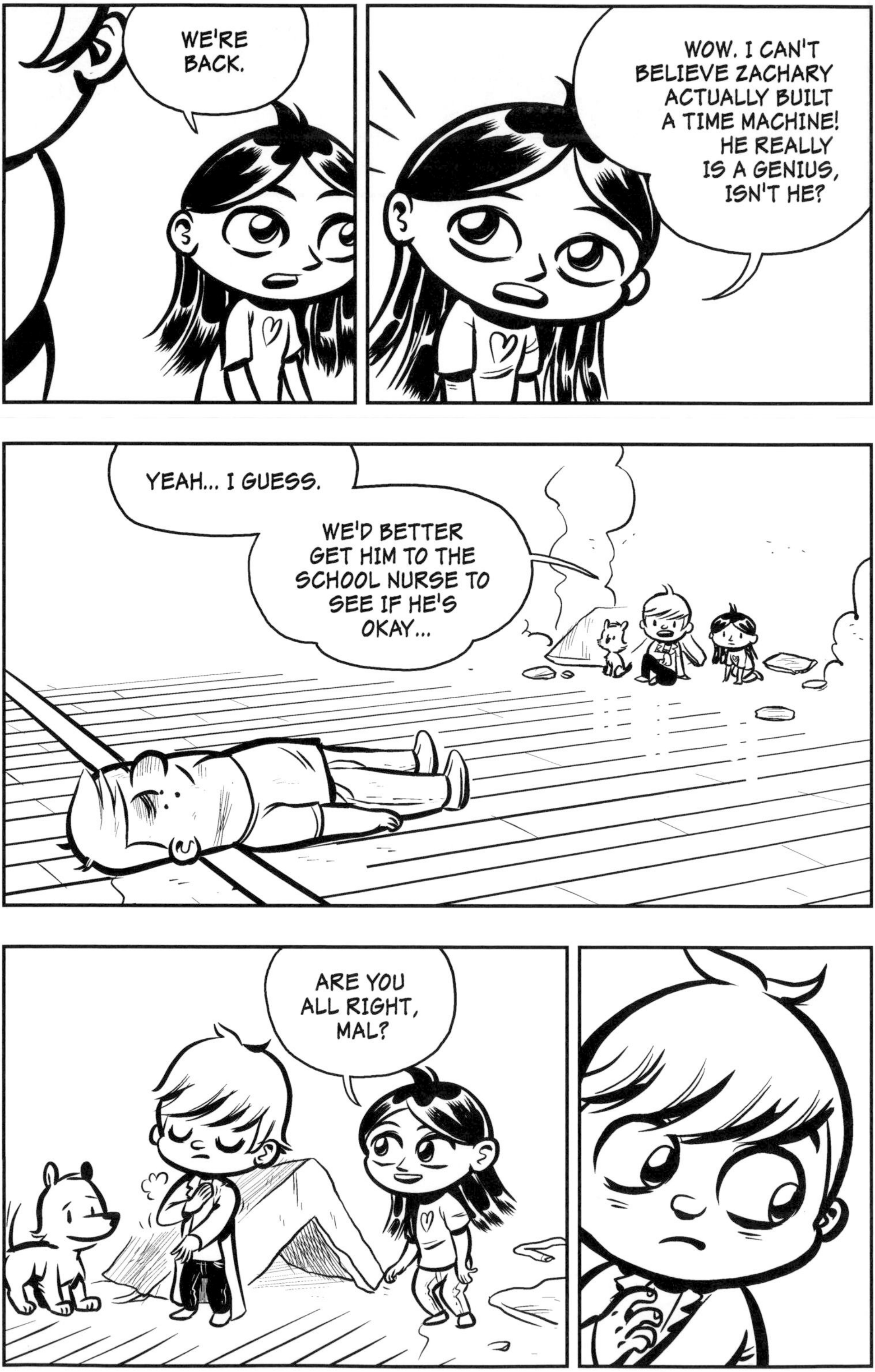
WE'RE BACK.
WOW. I CAN'T BELIEVE ZACHARY ACTUALLY BUILT A TIME MACHINE! HE REALLY IS A GENIUS, ISN'T HE?
YEAH... I GUESS.
WE'D BETTER GET HIM TO THE SCHOOL NURSE TO SEE IF HE'S OKAY...
ARE YOU ALL RIGHT, MAL?

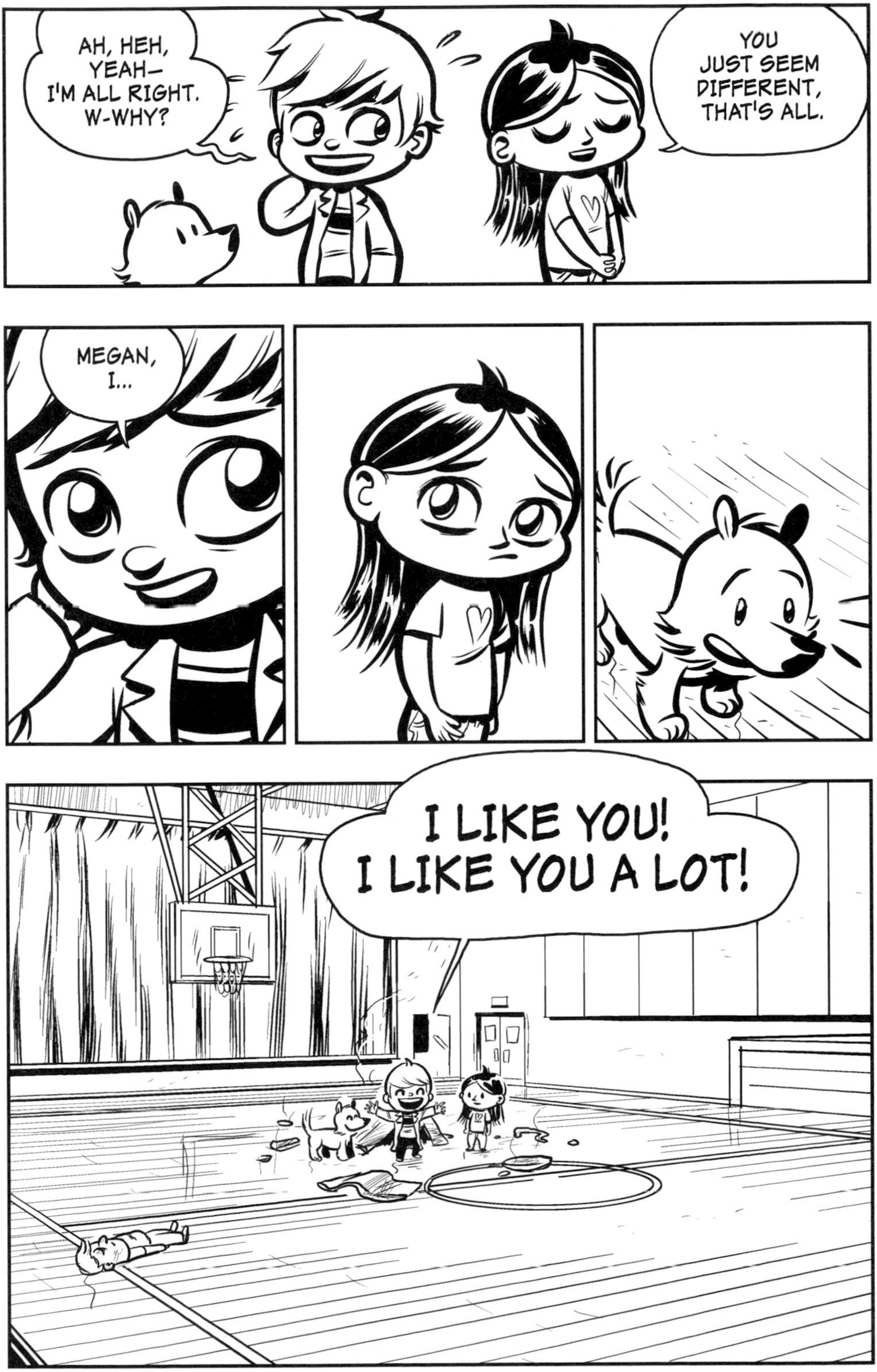
AH, HEH,
YEAH—
I'M ALL RIGHT.
W-WHY?
YOU
JUST SEEM
DIFFERENT,
THAT'S ALL.
MEGAN,
I...
I LIKE YOU!
I LIKE YOU A LOT!

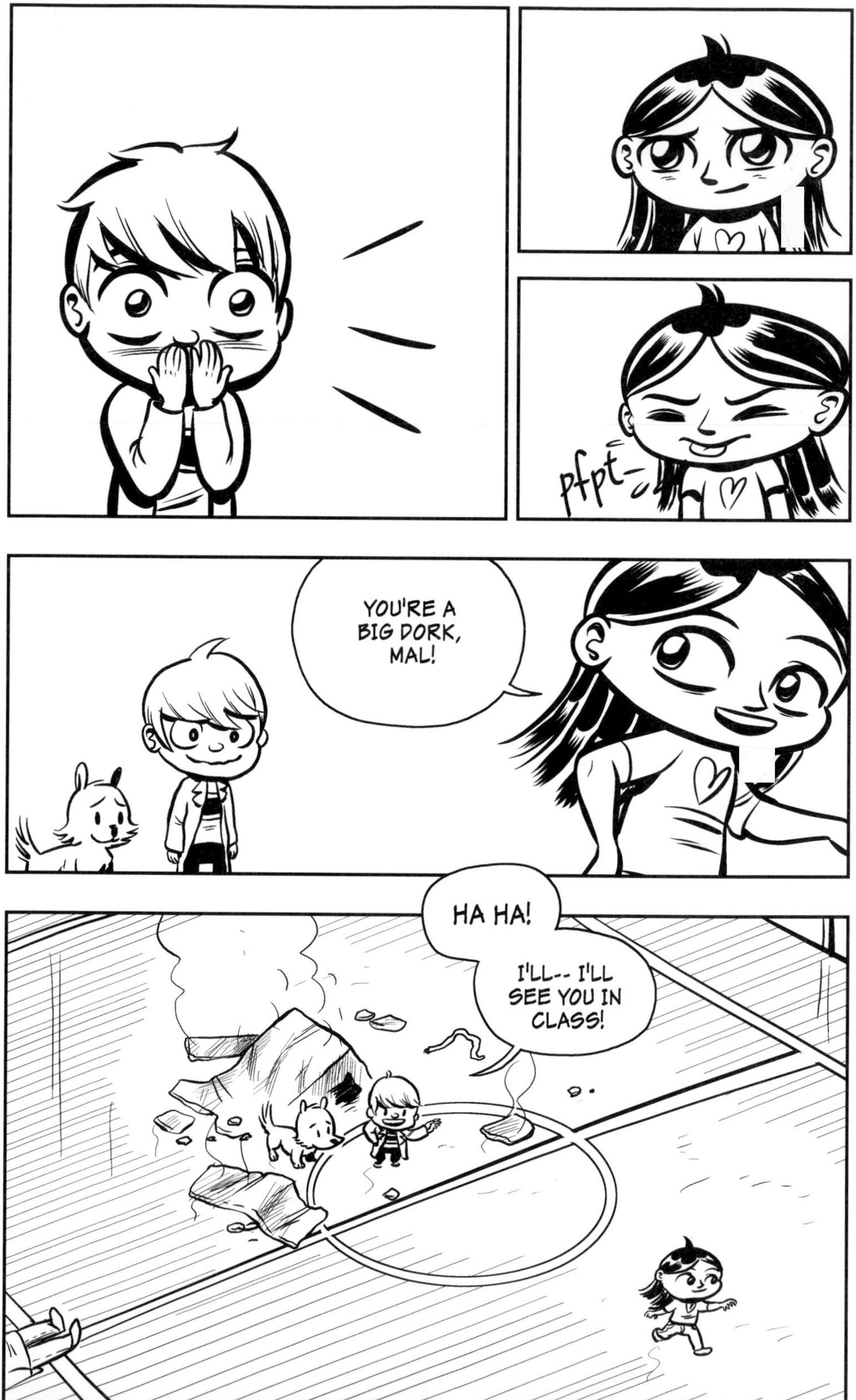
pfpt
YOU'RE A BIG DORK, MAL!
HA HA!
I'LL-- I'LL SEE YOU IN CLASS!

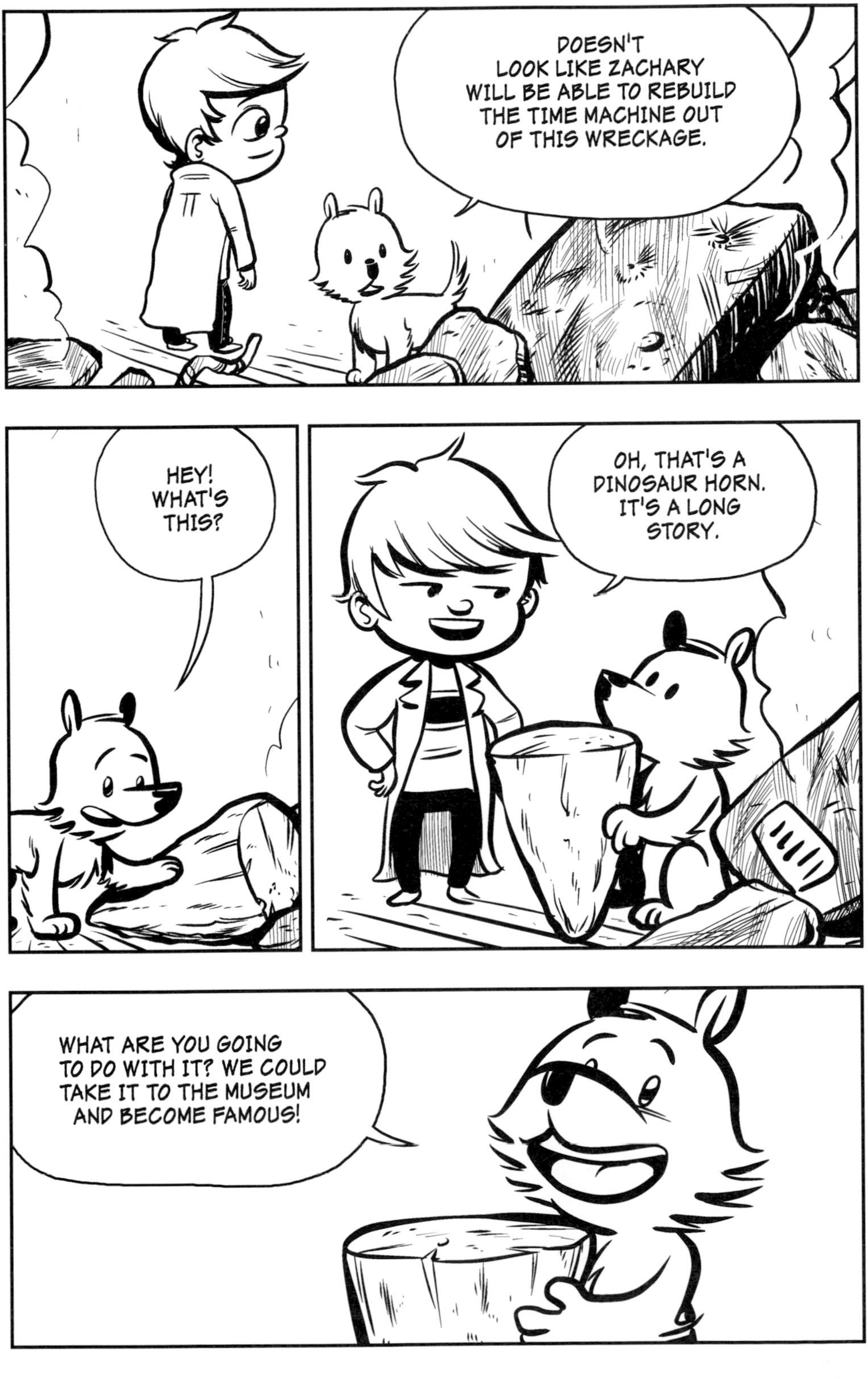
DOESN'T LOOK LIKE ZACHARY WILL BE ABLE TO REBUILD THE TIME MACHINE OUT OF THIS WRECKAGE.
HEY! WHAT'S THIS?
OH, THAT'S A DINOSAUR HORN. IT'S A LONG STORY.
WHAT ARE YOU GOING TO DO WITH IT? WE COULD TAKE IT TO THE MUSEUM AND BECOME FAMOUS!

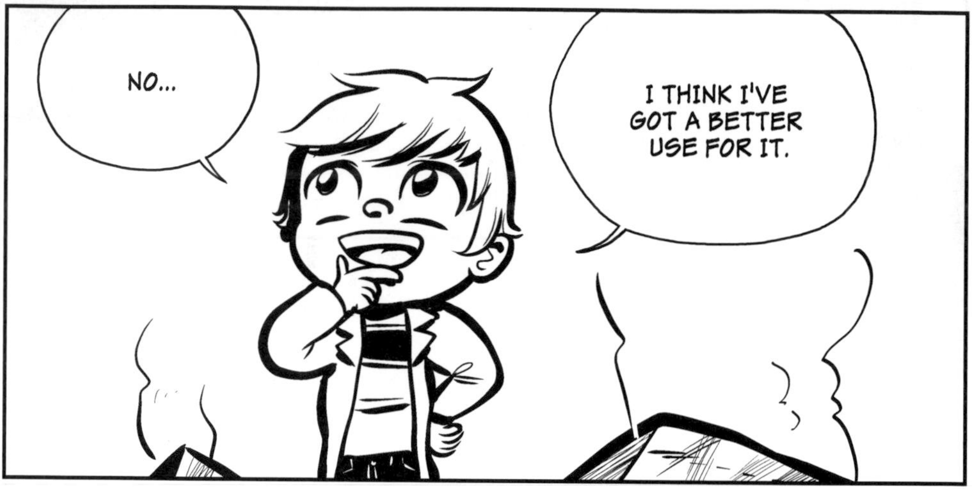
NO...
I THINK I'VE GOT A BETTER USE FOR IT.

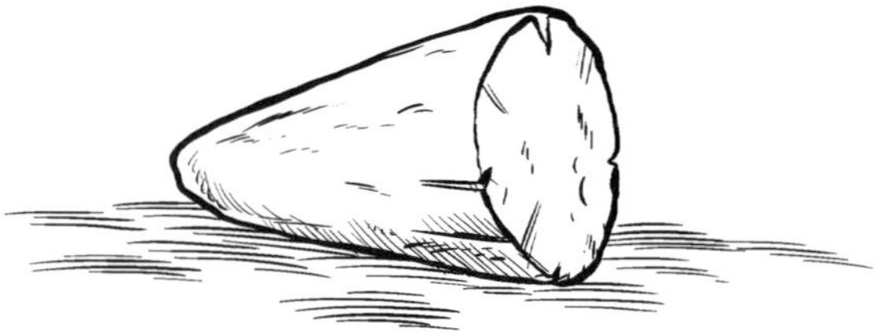

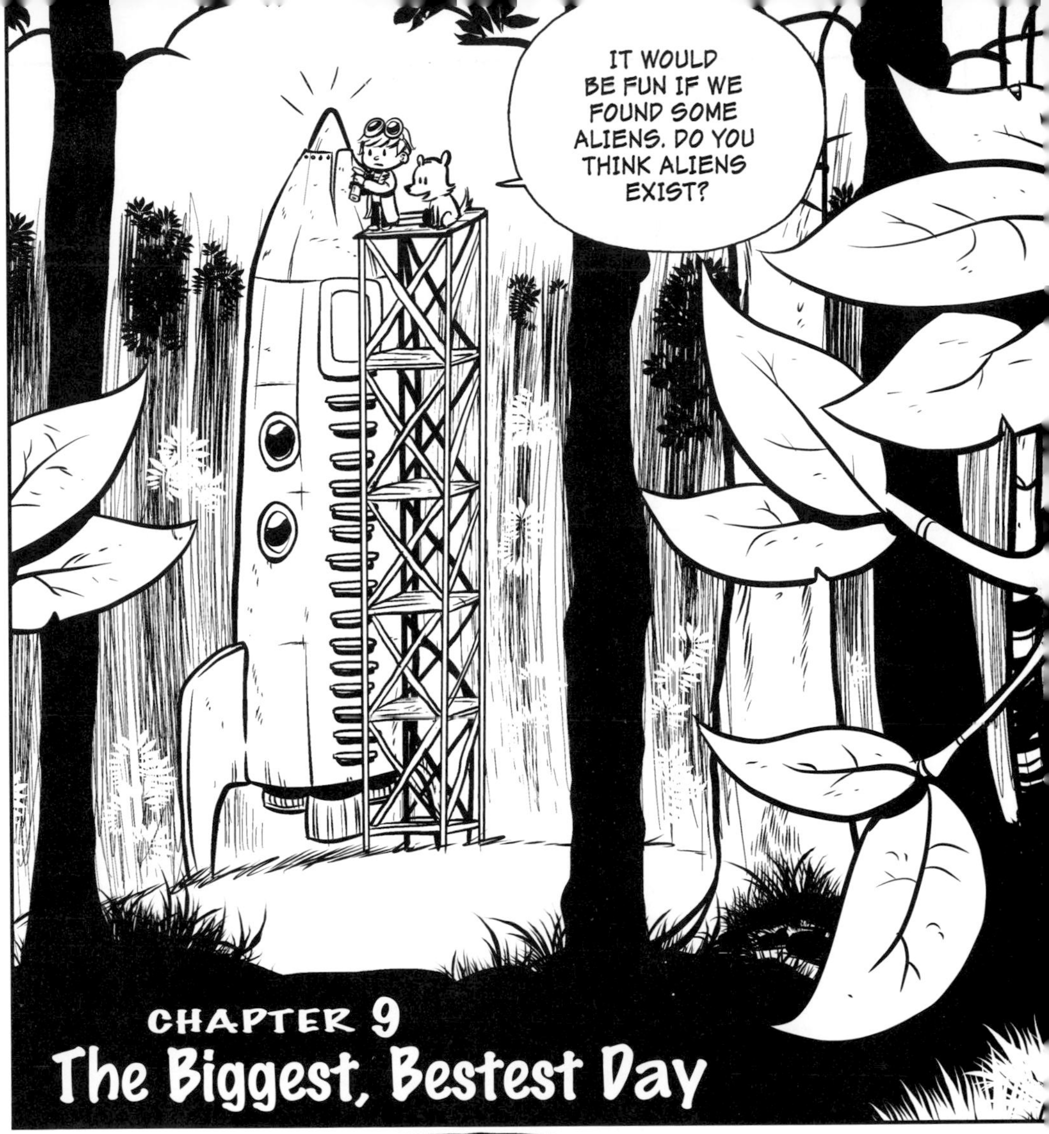
IT WOULD BE FUN IF WE FOUND SOME ALIENS. DO YOU THINK ALIENS EXIST?

CHAPTER 9
The Biggest, Bestest Day

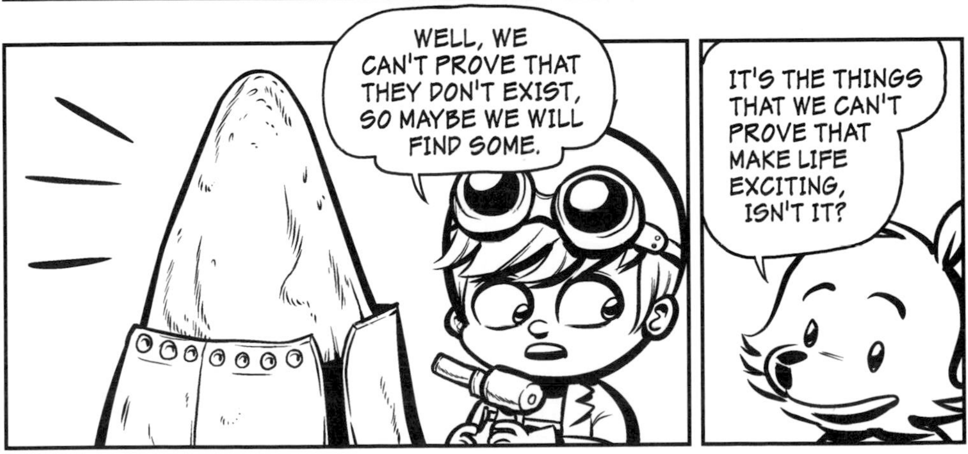
WELL, WE CAN'T PROVE THAT THEY DON'T EXIST, SO MAYBE WE WILL FIND SOME.
IT'S THE THINGS THAT WE CAN'T PROVE THAT MAKE LIFE EXCITING, ISN'T IT?

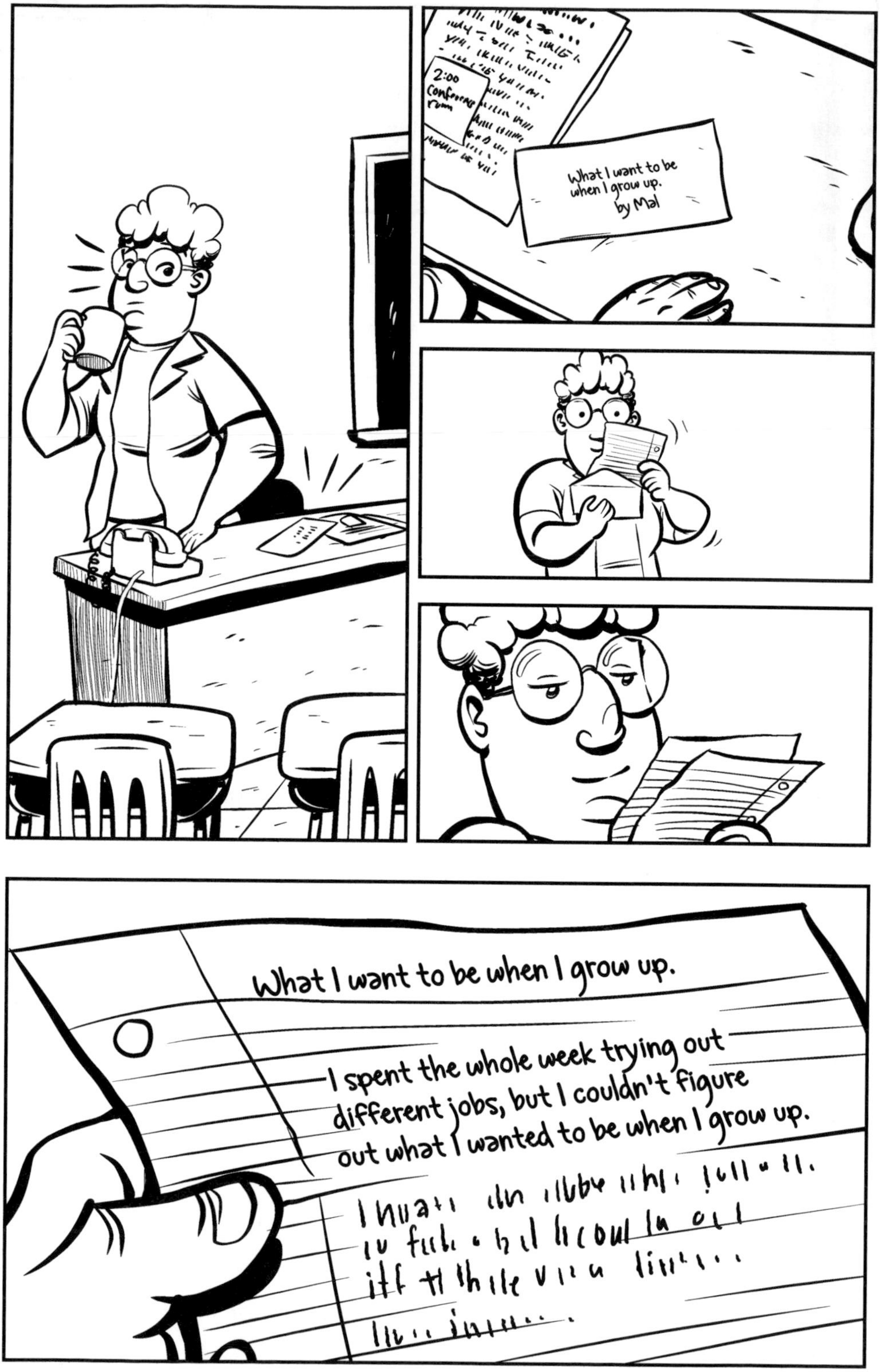
2:00
What I want to be when I grow up. by Mal
What I want to be when I grow up.
I spent the whole week trying out different jobs, but I couldn't figure out what I wanted to be when I grow up.

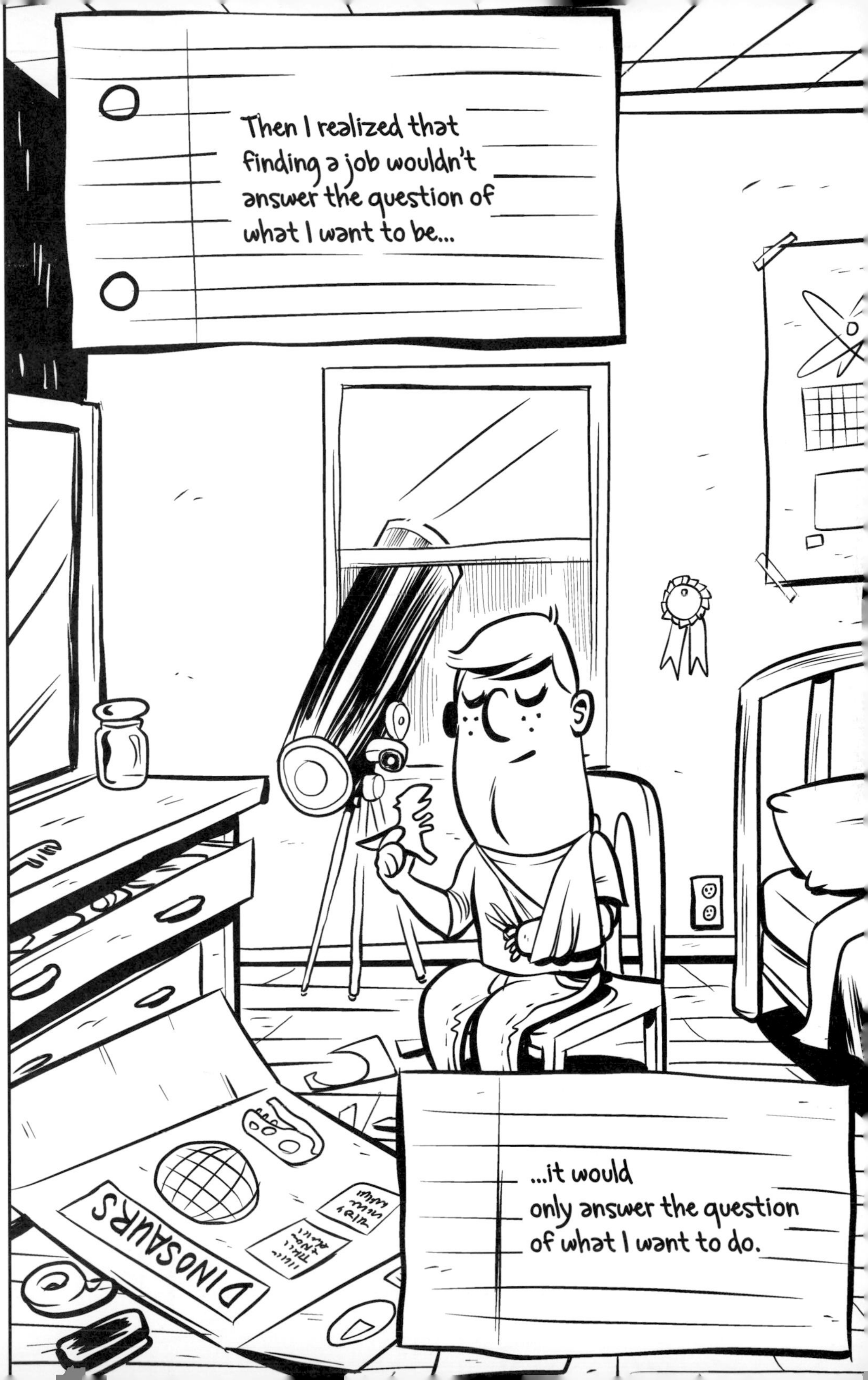
Then I realized that finding a job wouldn't answer the question of what I want to be...
DINOSAURS
...it would only answer the question of what I want to do.

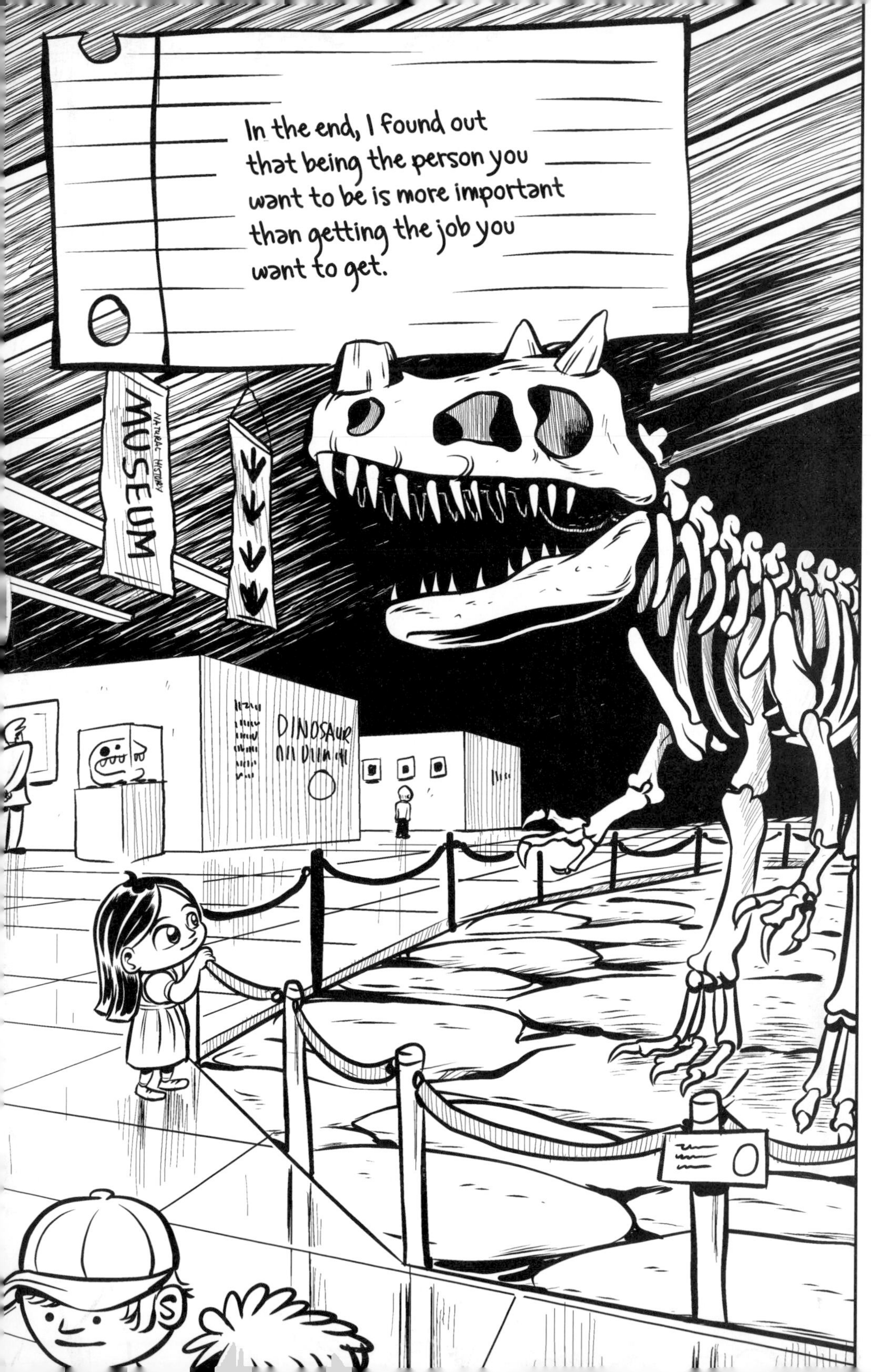
In the end, I found out that being the person you want to be is more important than getting the job you want to get.
NATURAL HISTORY
MUSEUM
DINOSAUR

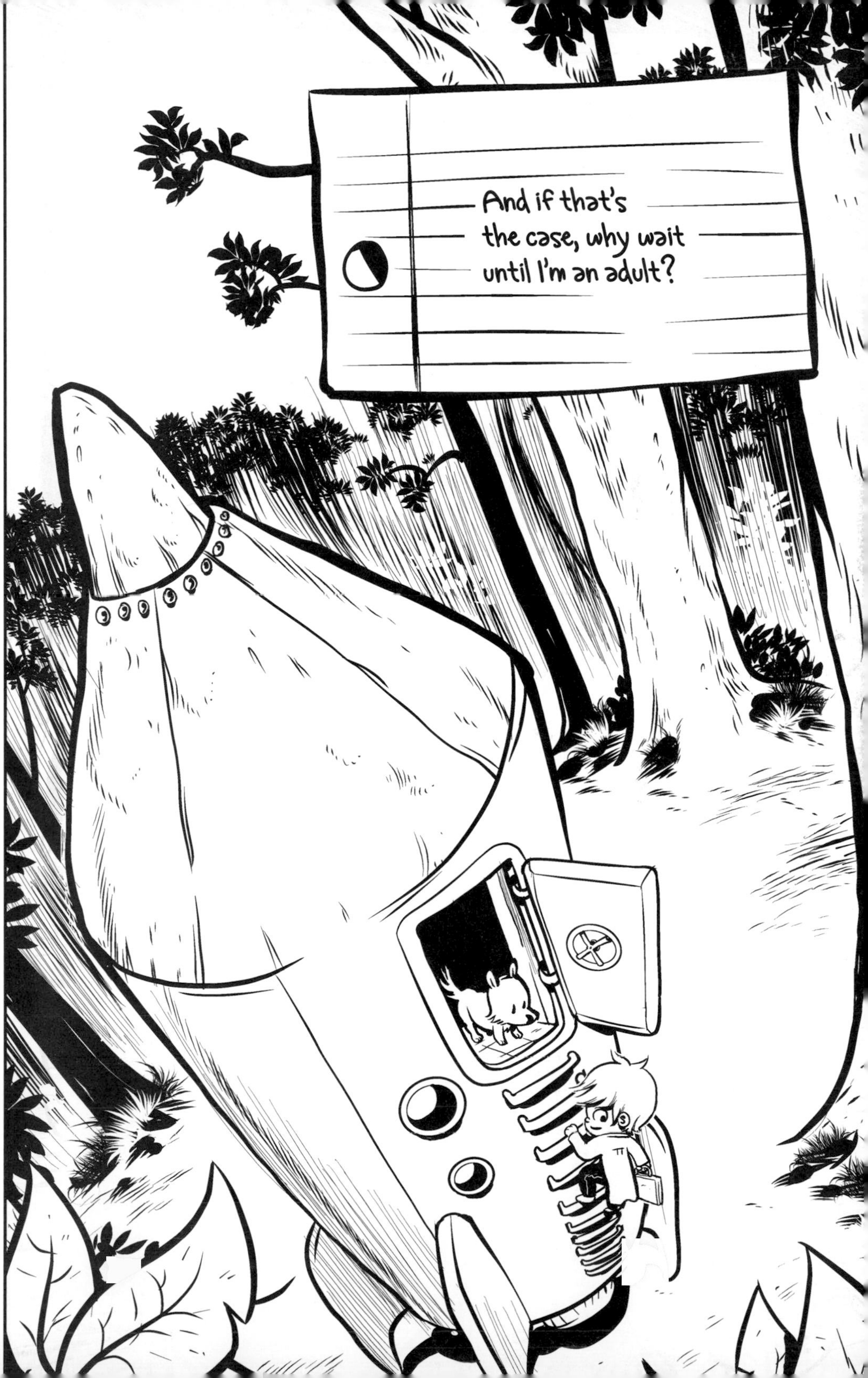
And if that's the case, why wait until I'm an adult?

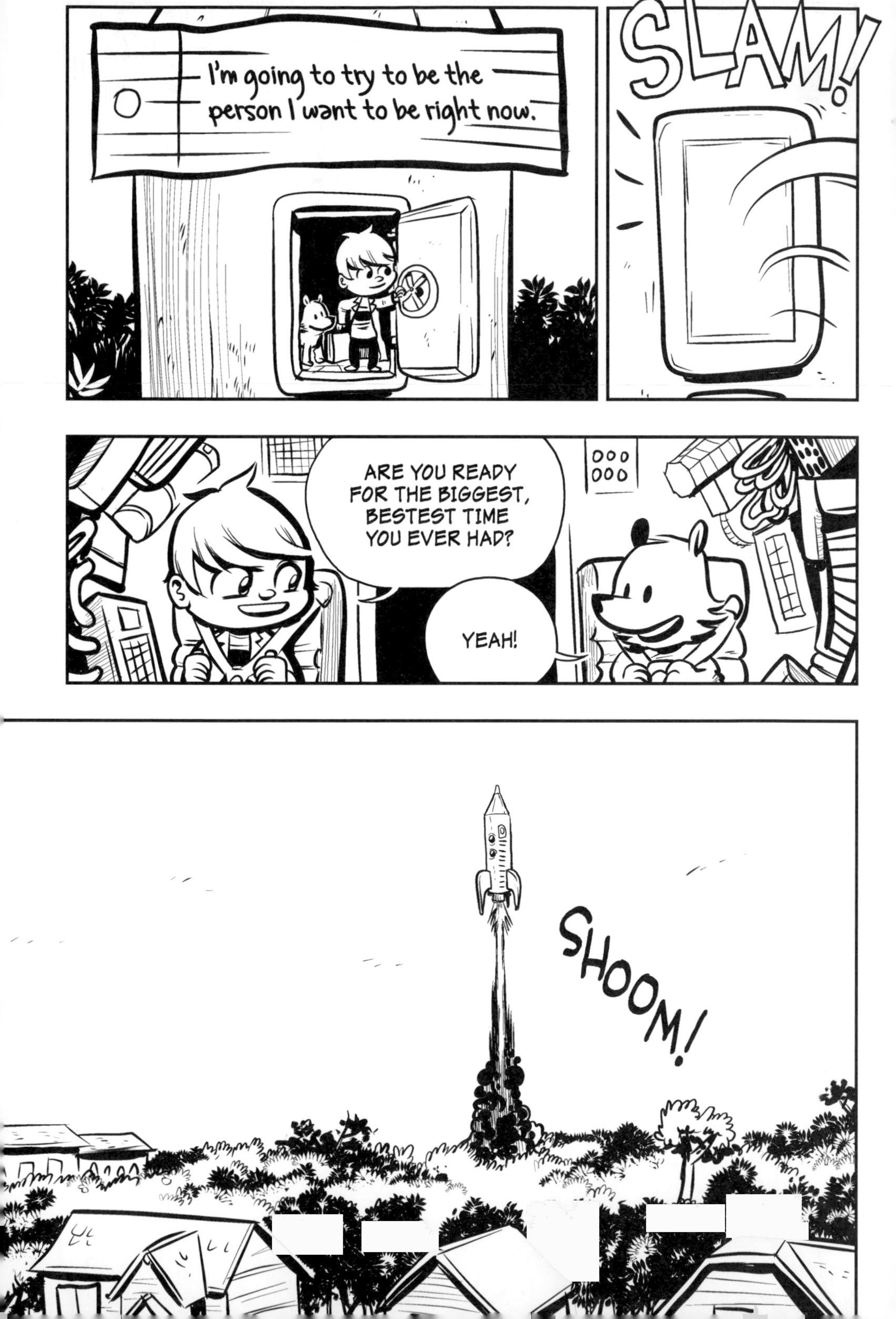
I'm going to try to be the person I want to be right now.
SLAM!
ARE YOU READY FOR THE BIGGEST, BESTEST TIME YOU EVER HAD?
YEAH!
SHOOM!

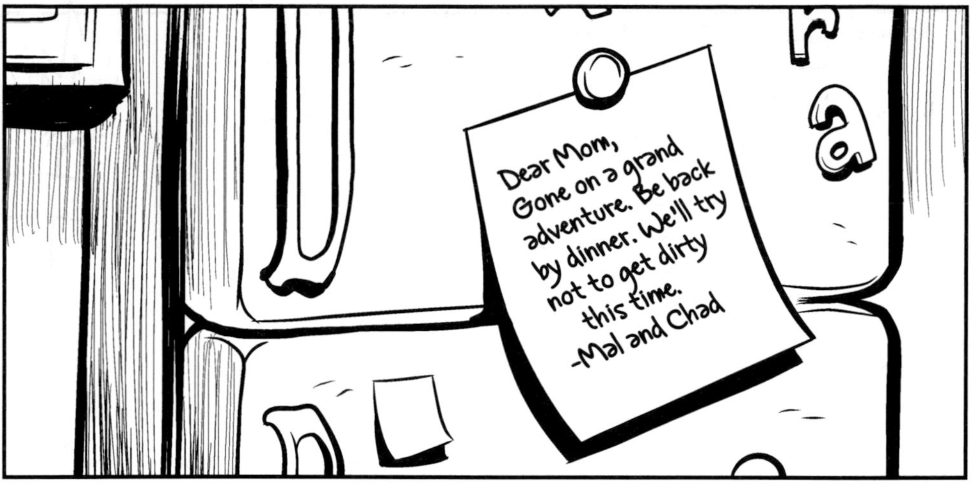
Dear Mom,
Gone on a grand adventure. Be back by dinner. We'll try not to get dirty this time.
-Mal and Chad

the end

For more fun, visit MalandChad.com,
and be on the lookout
for their next all-new book !

Stephen McCranie resides in New Mexico, working out of
his apartment bedroom. He has been drawing comics since before he
knew how to write, and the volume of Mal and Chad you are currently
holding is his first graphic novel. Stephen originally created Mal and Chad
as a comic strip for his college newspaper. You can read this strip in its
entirety, as well as find other fun stuff,
at www.malandchad.com.